RUBBERMAN'S CAGE

1st Edition

Joseph Picard

/// WARNING! \\\

This book is written using a form of English which is somewhat more *English* than *some* readers in *some* regions may be accustomed to.

As such, be advised that colour will be spelled with a 'u', as will honour, valour, neighbour, and so on.

Don't panic, it's all Queen-approved.

Also, it's "zed", not "zee".

This page was left intentionally blank.

Except now it isn't.

Okay, fine. You got me.

The truth is, every time you see something like this, it's just the publisher trying to mess with your head.

Contents

Foreword

This is the way it always was; this is normal.

You work, you eat, you sleep, you work. This is normal. You know three people and a faceless, silent leader.

This is the way it always was; this is normal.

This is all that exists. Work, eat, sleep. Or you get punished. It's not so bad.

This is the way it always was, this is normal.

Welcome to the first of what I hope will be many books in the Rubberman series. When I started this book, I assumed it was science fiction, as my previous books were, but at some point early on I realized that the story could be told with little to no need for sci-fi tropes.

That said, it still has a notable sci-fi feel. The hero explores, discovers things new to him, enters strange environments, and he meets groups that he never imagined existed.

Thanks to my usual eyes, Adam Zilliax, Dolores Picard, Meggin Dueckman, and Gilles Picard. Additional thanks to Michelle Patricia Browne, and Tabitha Ormiston-Smith, whose trained eyes whip my slop even further into a respectable shape.

Dedicated to the spirits of imagination and exploration that grow in
Caitlin and Lachlan.

Prologue

And suddenly, there was so much blood. Without knowing of death, or of vengeance, 'Six' now stood over two dead bodies, one of which was a Brother.

He turned to one of his Brothers, 'Eyes', and asked, "What…what just happened?"

"They're both sleeping. Or broken," Eyes said, with hands almost as bloody as Six's.

The mess was everywhere. The floor, the bed, the grating that had fallen. It was far more blood than Six had ever seen. It clung to him, and trying to wipe it away only made the mess worse.

The fourth Brother—unique for his smattering of freckles--sat in the corner, shocked into silence.

With a hand still trembling from combat's thrill, Six reached down to examine the target of his vengeance. "He broke, just the same. I didn't know if he would, but…I was so…"

Eyes nodded. "He deserved it; no argument here," he said.

"I didn't get shocked," Six said. "Maybe this nightmare is over."

"Fine, great," Eyes said, "but now what?"

"Yeah!" Six said, "now what? Go back to work? Back to the usual? I don't think so. We have to make use of this situation."

Chapter One

Out with the Young

Slim felt the familiar little pinch on his wrist from the bulky cuff that kept him tethered near his bed. "We're getting pricked tonight," he warned his three Brothers, who hadn't yet put on their own restraints.

The elder Brother Joints grunted as he sat on his own bed across the seven-metre wide room. "Goody." He put on his own cuff, which clicked and locked for the night. His own little jab soon followed.

Blue settled in as well, putting his cuff on and getting his jab over with.

Lenth wandered over to Slim with a gentle smile, and Slim began to return it.

Slim's eyes widened, and he groaned with pain. Collapsing back on his bed, he gripped the sides and bucked back.

"*What's wrong?*" Lenth gasped. He wanted to help his favourite Brother, but had no idea what was going on. Slim let out terrifying soft groans. His body thrashed to the side, his eyes wide in terror.

"*Lenth! What's going on with him?*" Joints yelled.

"I...I don't know!"

Slim gagged and began to slip off his bed, but Lenth helped him stay on, fighting another of Slim's convulsions.

Overhead, upon the Brothers' iron grate ceiling, the faceless Rubberman stomped, calling attention to the green light that had turned on behind the head of Lenth's bed.

"*But I have to help Slim!*" Lenth hollered up to the dark figure. The Rubberman stomped again, harder.

Lenth looked at Slim and over to his own bed. "Now? I can't leave him! *Something's really wrong!*" Lenth looked up at the Rubberman and back to the convulsing Slim.

The Rubberman stomped on the grating once more, and the room shocked all the Brothers.

Disobedience warrants punishment.

Knowing that his actions were harming his Brothers as well as himself, Lenth scurried over to bed and secured his cuff around his wrist.

Rubberman ran out of view as Slim's convulsions began to calm a little.

Slim alone was shocked again. He had a sudden, violent convulsion.

"*What are you doing to him?*" Blue yelled up to Rubberman's level. No reply, not that any was expected. Rubberman never spoke.

Again Slim was shocked.

Again.

Again.

And then it was quiet. Slim had stopped convulsing. He wasn't making any sounds at all now.

"Slim?" Lenth said. He sat up on his bed, but being tethered with his cuff, he couldn't go check on Slim. The cuff wouldn't open until Rubberman made it so. "Slim, you okay now?"

Joints leaned forward in bed to peer over at Slim. "He ain't breathing."

"What?" Blue said, puzzled. "Slim, what are you doing?"

Joints sighed. "I've seen this before, I think. Before you three came here. If it's the same thing, Slim won't be here tomorrow." Joints lowered his head.

"I...what?" Blue was alarmed. "I don't understand! Why not? If he's not breathing, why does he have to go away? He'll start again, right? Where's he going to go?"

Lenth stood up and walked as far towards Slim at the tether would let him, which was about two metres from his own bed, still about four away from Slim's. He stood silently, looking at his dead Brother, not knowing what death was.

"Slim...wake up, moron," Lenth said quietly. "I don't want you to go away, that's stupid." He turned to Joints, looking for the wisdom of his age. "Hey, away where? Where would he go? Up with Rubberman? Or the place Rubberman goes when he isn't here? What..."

Joints' face wrinkled inward with consideration. "How am I supposed to know? It's not as if I can fathom the ways of Rubberman any more than you, Brother."

None of them were actually Brothers, but they had always called each other that. There existed the Brothers, and there existed the Rubberman. And that was it.

As far as they could tell, anyway. Joints had told them before that his old Brothers had gone away, and that then, his new Brothers came. There was no explanation of '*where from*', or '*where to*'.

These were things for Rubberman to know, and Rubberman never talked.

That much was understandable, since he didn't have a mouth. Even calling him a man was a point of question. A man, or an '*it*'?

The Brothers all wore plain cloth foot coverings, slightly tougher on the bottoms, and simple cloth bodysuits, from the neck to the knees and elbows. This left a fair amount of skin showing. This was not the case with Rubberman.

Rubberman was all black rubber...even over his head. Where eyes would be, he had only a pair of large dark circles that reflected light at certain angles. Where a mouth or nose might be, there was a metal circle, about as wide as his eye. It did not seem as shiny as the eyes, and had many little holes.

But Rubberman had gone away now.

Lenth still stood there, as close to Slim as possible, pondering what had happened. What might be *about* to happen. Slim was their Brother after all, but Lenth felt the fear of losing Slim the most keenly.

The green lights behind the beds lit up again. The lights were built into the white, age-worn walls, and sealed in with a clear layer of a plastic-like material.

It was bedtime. The day was officially over.

The Brothers all tried to get as comfortable as they could on their beds. A three-centimetre thick pad was bonded to the metal bed frames, and indestructible to any force the Brothers had ever been able to summon.

"Slim doesn't look very comfortable," Blue said quietly. Indeed, Slim's position suggested that he would wake up sore in the morning if he didn't move.

Lenth stared at Slim and the lights dimmed. *Breathe, you idiot. Just breathe again.*

A soft hiss came from above.

"Sleepy-smell," Joints observed. Sometimes, sleep-smell would come when a change was going to happen.

"So...so it's true," Lenth said quietly. "G...goodbye, Slim."

Chapter Two

Spots

When morning came, they were woken by the usual tiny, room-wide morning shock. Sometimes, they were scarcely aware of the shock at all. This was one of the mercies of Rubberman.

Blue sat up and looked over to Slim's bed. But it wasn't Slim's anymore. There was someone new in it. "Brothers. We...have a new Brother," Blue said groggily. His voice carried no celebratory cheer, but no spite either. It was an observation, and nothing more.

The new one was a little smaller than any of them. Not a great deal of hair, other than eyebrows, just like the rest of them. But his eyebrows were orange. "I think we'll call him 'Orange'." Joints said.

Blue was now awake enough to put things together. "That sounds dumb. Besides, I'm already named after a colour; it would be a little redundant. Look at his face. He's got all those little dots. We should call him 'Dots'."

The new one sat up, looking bewildered. "Where am I? Who are you people?"

"*Where?*" Joints snickered. "You're *here!*" Where else would you be?"

The new one thought for a moment, but didn't have an answer. Were there other places? Not as far as he knew. "All right. So...who are you people?"

"Joints. I got the name when the Brothers were debating a name for me, and I made the mistake of complaining about stiff joints."

"Blue," Blue said, pointing at his own eyes.

Lenth looked Slim's replacement up and down. He meant no enmity, but the others could see spite on his face. Lenth sighed, and spread his arms wide. "Lenth. Like *length*, but we got lazy saying it. So, *Lenth*."

"Lenth, Blue, Joints," the new one said to himself. "So, where are my Brothers?"

"We're your Brothers now, I guess. You had other Brothers?" Blue asked.

"Yeah. I...you know, I don't remember a lot about them, but now they're gone, and you're here. My head feels kinda fuzzy."

"You got it wrong, man," Blue said. "Our old Brother is gone, and now *you're* here."

Joints huffed. "You all...it doesn't matter; here we all are. What do we call *you*, then?"

The new one searched his memory, finding only squishy fragments. "Yeah, uh, you almost got it with 'Dots'. I'm 'Spots'." He brought his hand to his face, as if he expected to be able to feel the spots. He stroked a finger along his forearm, where more of the spots could be found, but more immediately interesting was his cuff.

"What's with this?" Spots waved his arm to make the cuff's thick cable wiggle around a bit. The jostling made the now-unlocked cuff open and fall to the floor.

Blue already had his own off. "We have to put them on for the things we do, or we get shocks."

"Shocks? What do- oh...I think I remember this a bit." Spot's voice trailed off a little. He stared at his hands.

A green light turned on above one of the doors as it 'clunked' to unlock. Spots only noticed because the others turned their heads to look. Blue turned back to Spots. "Don't worry about it. If we just do the right stuff, there's no problem. Come on."

The four men went through the door to the small, subdivided shower room. The door locked behind them. There were four stalls, and each one had a cuff in it. The aged walls were the rustiest here.

The footfalls of Rubberman were heard above, but the walls being closer here made it difficult to get a good look. Most of the Brothers ignored the footsteps, but Spots peered up in fear as he cowered back.

Before Spots could ask about it, Joints offered helpful instructions. "All right, Spots. Get your clothes into the little bin there, then cuff up in a stall. After, we get fed. Easy."

As instructed, Spots got into a stall. This all became more familiar as his head gradually cleared. A cuff like the one he had on in bed hung there.

Spots heard the others already getting undressed and slapped on his own cuff. It fell off. That was wrong, he'd done things out of order. It was familiar enough, as more memory began to come back. He got his shoes and body suit off, and stuck them in the little bin, closing its hatch flush with the wall.

He put his cuff on and was pleased that the lock clicked shut. *That's how things are done; that's right.*

Naked and cuffed to the wall, Spots would have felt vulnerable if he didn't know that three other men were cuffed to walls and naked as well. *Oh wait, what about that person above the ceiling grate?*

Spots looked up. The same grating was above, but no Rubberman. There were two other things. Spots couldn't figure out what they were when one supplied the obvious answer.

Water. It was a shower room, after all. It was a perfect temperature, but that was little comfort as it spurted into his face. Spots huddled over, spitting and rubbing out his eyes. The taste was a little unpleasant, flavoured with a trace of soap.

He could hear the others moving around. He also heard sliding metal in the wall and movement of the Rubberman overhead. Spots made sure the water got him everywhere, then just stood in the downpour, trying to enjoy it. Then it stopped. Then a blast of noisy, warm air. Spots closed his eyes, and just waited for it to be over. When it ended, he found he was dry. Mostly.

"Good, I'm starved!" came a voice. It sounded like Blue. Spots looked up again, and the other object began to lower down. It came down on one solid rod of rust-caked metal in the corner of the stall farthest from the entrance. Twice the size of his fist, the roughly round object was hollow, open on the top, and full of small ochre disks about a centimetre thick and three or four centimetres wide.

Spots turned to it hesitantly, unsure of why he felt nervous. Shaking it off, he popped one in his mouth. It crumbled into tiny lumps when chewed. It was a pleasing enough taste, if bland. He realized that yes, he knew these as well. He gobbled until they were all gone.

When he was done, there was nothing to do. He was still tethered to the wall, and it didn't provide enough slack to even leave the stall. He waited for a bit, and didn't hear much. He was just about to speak up when the cuff popped open and the bin in the wall opened again, dispensing his suit. He gratefully fumbled to put it on and realized it wasn't the same suit. It was clean and unwrinkled.

He could hear the others getting dressed and the footsteps of Rubberman in the ceiling grating. When everyone was dressed, and maybe passed a silent inspection from above, the light over the door lit up green as it unlocked. He walked out and joined the others in returning to the sleeping room.

The floor was damp. Not really wet, so much as recently dried. "Did...did the room get cleaned while we were in the shower?"

"Everything got cleaned," Blue said. "I kind of wonder why we just don't get clean while in this room, but whatever."

"I don't wanna see you nekkid, and you sure don't wanna see me!" Joints said.

Traces of memories came back to Spots. Unpleasant ones, but he couldn't really identify what memories they were. "Now what?" Spots asked. Blue reached out and pointed to a door moments before it unlocked, and the green light above it illuminated. "Exercise!"

"Yup," Joints bemoaned, "my favourite part of the day." Joints stretched out a little as he headed for the door, trying to limber up. "I tried to skip out on this one day. I kind of *expected* to be shocked, but I had a little bit of hope that I could be spared."

Lenth scoffed. "Yeah, and got the whole lot of us zapped!" He turned to Spots to explain. "If you don't do what you're supposed to, you get zapped, and if you're not tethered, or on other zap-happy stuff, the zap just gets you through the floor."

"Which gets everyone. I...yes, I know," Spots said quietly, eyes scanning the rating above. "Yes. Getting zapped. I know about it." Spots nodded, following the others through the door.

"It's not like it's hard to avoid zaps," Joints called back from the front. "Once you get to know the expectations, they're pretty easy to follow. I was kind of pushing my luck."

They arrived in a room about the size of the sleeping room. The floor and walls also had the warm, damp-ish feel of being recently cleaned.

Waiting in this room were four exercise stations. Each had a bench to lie down on. They were attached by large, bare metal arms that reached down from the ceiling. Under the bench sat an idle treadmill. On the floor at roughly arm's length on either side sat a handle attached to the floor. A wide bar loomed overhead, and some kind of bulky headset dangled near it.

Spots followed the example of the others and straddled across a bench and locked a wrist into the attached tether. After that, he reached for the headset. The other Brothers all strapped them onto their heads and over their eyes.

Spots held his headset in his hands. It was rather light considering its bulk. Rubber fittings braced it around the eyes, but left a gap on the bottom edge. He pulled the straps around his head and secured it.

The inside of the headset lit up, startling Spots. He yelped and heard a chuckle from Joints. "Sorry, I guess we should have warned you!"

A simplistic illustration of a person lying down appeared. Spots heard the others lying down, so he followed suit.

The figure then reached down to the handles on either side on the floor and lifted them up, and back down. The others were already doing the exercise. Spots obeyed and pulled the handles up. He could faintly hear and feel the metal rails that dragged out of the floor as he pulled. The handles had more weight than could be seen on the surface, but they were manageable.

The image in his headset blinked a little, and a small buzz accompanied it. "Pick up the pace!" Joints warned. "Don't earn yourself a zap!"

Spots lifted the handles, trying to match the rhythm of the little illustration. It felt good for the muscles, but around the tenth repetition or so, Spots asked, "So...how long does this go on?"

"Fifty. Look in the upper part there," Lenth answered.

A series of little hollow circles filled in, each one for every repetition. Numerals counted up beside those, and in this way, all the Brothers knew how numbers looked when not spoken. By the end of fifty, everyone was about ready for that to be done.

The image in the headset changed as the overhead bar descended into place, attached in the ceiling much in the same way as the handles below. The ceiling was a grate, which would have let them see the bulky metal boxes that the overhead bar's supports slid out from—if they weren't wearing their headsets. Spots reached up and groped for the bar. A fresh set of fifty hollow circles appeared. Everyone obeyed the little figure in the displays and did fifty bench presses.

The footsteps of Rubberman were heard overhead, but no one seemed to feel the need to comment on it.

The image changed again, and showed the bench moving into an upright position. "Be ready!" Joints warned. Sure enough, spots found himself being propped up into standing position by the bench. The bench-press bar positioned itself in front to hold on to as the bench got out of the way, the arms pulling it into the ceiling.

The treadmill started slowly, and the figure in the headset's screen started running. Soon the treadmill had gained enough speed to force everyone to jog.

The circle in the top of the display were replaced with a slightly larger singular pie chart of progress. The rest of the display was filled with a flowing display of soft colours, shifting around and melting into one another.

"Ooh, pretty," Spots said.

"Enjoy it while you...while you're not sick of it. Now and then, it shows other things," Blue said.

Yes, it did look familiar. He remembered once: he'd hurt his ankle, and a visor showed him that he could rest it. Bits of memory were always coming back. These Brothers were new to him, but he knew of Brothers. He definitely remembered other Brothers...but...still so foggy. There was something else that felt different. "So," Spots finally asked, "Tell me about that guy in the ceiling?"

Blue gave a short laugh. "You don't know?"

"I...can you just refresh my memory?" Spots asked.

After brief moment while the other three imagined the possibility of anyone not knowing Rubberman, Joints nodded with a short grunt. "That's Rubberman! He...he watches us."

"All right," Spots said with an uncertain tone, "Why?"

"Ha!" Blue said, "To zap us when we don't do what we're supposed to!"

"Oh, don't be like that," came Joints' wizened voice. "It keeps us motivated, that's for sure, but it seems to me we only do the things we need. Eat, sleep, exercise, get the stink sprayed off of us, and work."

"Sleep." Lenth snorted. "Now and then, we sleep deeper than other times. Do we thank Rubberman when that happens?"

A strange quiet ended all conversation as they continued jogging. Spots didn't understand about the 'deeper sleep', but he could tell it was a touchy subject for some reason.

Eventually, Spots brought up another question. "He doesn't talk?" Spots asked. "It seems to me that he...he talks sometimes."

"Nope!" Joints said with a chuckle. "Never has, probably never will. I don't think he can!"

Spots could remember Rubberman talking. Yelling. Making unsettling sounds when...when something bad happened. It was all so muddy in his head. Things weren't all matching up. It must be his head.

"Joints, you mentioned 'work'? That's the only one I haven't done yet. What is it?"

"Work," Lenth said gruffly. Almost a snap.

"Yes, what kind of work?"

"Tedious work." Blue added, "It's been known to change, but for a long time now, it's been our usual—we open up a thing, take out a piece, take out a dirty piece, clean it, and put it all back together."

"What is it for?"

"For Rubberman!" Blue said. "We don't know what it is, and it doesn't matter."

When the progress meter was full, the treadmill slowed down to a standstill, and the tether cuff dropped off the Brothers' wrists. A short walk to another room revealed four alcoves.

Each alcove sported a seat, a small workbench attached to the back and side of the alcove, and a tether cuff.

Lenth wordlessly sat down at one and put on his cuff.

"Is something wrong?" Spots asked Blue and Joints quietly.

Joints sighed and rested a hand on Spots' shoulder. "You see, it seems you're only here because one of our Brothers, Slim, is gone. Lenth is worrying about him the most. Lenth and Slim were close." Joints shrugged. "Not to say that I don't worry, but there's nothing any of us can do about it. Slim had some kind of problem, stopped breathing, and the next morning, he was gone, and you were here."

Spots looked over at Lenth and gave a small nod "I...I see. Lenth? Lenth, I..."

Lenth held his untethered hand back towards Spots. "Forget it. Can we just all shut up and get to work? I can't get started until everyone's tethered in."

Once seated and tethered in, Spots found that he could not see the others in their alcoves. Directly in front of him was a clear plastic wall, with gloves attached so one could reach inside without actually touching anything inside with his skin.

"What do I...?" Before he could finish the question, the alcove answered.

A section of the back wall lit up, revealing itself to be a display of sorts. At the same time, the work bench slid open, revealing a large, bulky cylinder, about forty or more centimetres wide and sixty tall. Not far from its top, there was a seam all the way around it. Beside it was a brush with hard bristles.

The display showed the top half of the cylinder turning around and coming off. A few round pieces came out, the last of which was thick and dark. The brush scrubbed it with the help of some water. Spots only now noticed that there was a nozzle and a button in the alcove, to the side. The round piece in the display was now white, and it all went back together.

Spots copied the looping display. Unscrew the top part, take out two pieces, pull out the thick black one, and scrub. Bits of black flaked off onto the bottom of the alcove. He pressed the button over on the side and some water came out. He got the brush and the black disk wet, and found it softened up a little. Scrubbing seemed slightly more productive now.

"Am I doing something wrong?" Spots called out.

"Why? Are you cleaning the black piece?" came Blue's voice.

"Yeah, but it's not cleaning as fast as the pictures show."

"Nope, I wish. Just keep at it. You're using some water, right? It'll get white eventually."

"Oh...Okay, yeah, I'm using the water. But what is all this work for? What's the point?"

"Work! And you're doing it," Blue said with a small degree of pride.

Spots tried to rationalize the results, but deeper contemplation was interrupted by a little electric jolt from the cuff.

"Ow!" The pain was gone as quickly as it came. It wasn't so bad, but it was unsettling. And familiar.

Joints chuckled softly. "That means you gotta stop dawdling! Go, go, go! I'm working on the same one as yesterday; they can take a while!"

Spots resumed scrubbing. Yeah, okay, there was a little patch that looked a bit lighter.

"When are we done?"

Lenth answered. "See numbers in the top corner? When it says eight, dotty-thing, oh, oh, dotty thing, oh, oh."

Spots watched the numbers on the left count up, one, by one..."That's going to be quite a while..."

"Yes," Lenth said dryly.

Spots wasn't winning any points with Lenth today. Spots had 'replaced' his best friend, which made for a really bad starting point. Spots got back to work as hard as he could, give or take the occasional fumble.

Eventually, the timer hit eight oh oh, oh oh, and everyone's cuffs fell off. The four Brothers got up from the work benches. Lenth was first to the door, which for whatever reason, had not yet been unlocked by the Rubberman. Blue and Joints turned to Spots, taking advantage of the delay to chat.

"You got the hang of it?" Joints asked Spots.

"Yeah, yeah. I found a rhythm to it. I got going kinda fast."

Lenth huffed, still facing the closed door, leaning his forehead on it. "Slim was fast," he mumbled.

Everyone was quiet for a while, staring at Lenth. The habitat's silence took the kind of control that only true silence can.

"Lenth..." Joints said, "You better not be blaming Spots for Slim going away, it wasn't his idea to—"

"*Who do I blame then?*" Lenth seethed.

As if on cue, the footsteps of Rubberman along the overhead grating got closer. Lenth kept his head down and thought of the wordless spectre above. "Blame...even if blame was justified, what would the blame matter?"

The Rubberman pulled something up from the top of the door, unlocking it, and the Brothers were soon again in the main room where the beds were.

Lenth shuffled to the middle of the room and looked up through the grate to the Rubberman. "Rubberman?"

"What are you doing, Lenth?" Blue asked. "It's not like he'll answer you." Lenth ignored Blue, and continued to query Rubberman.

"Rubberman, did you create us? We all talked about it, and none of *us* created us, so I figure it had to be *you*."

No one was really expecting an answer, but all the Brothers looked up at Rubberman nonetheless.

"You're just going to get us all zapped," Joints moaned.

Rubberman looked down to them, and placed his hand at the side of his head. A few moments later, he took his hand down, and did something unimaginable. He took his rubber hand off, and a man-like hand rose from the stump, all in one smooth motion. Rubberman placed this fleshy hand by his head, and held it there for a while.

The Brothers all held their breath and stared. What did it mean? Did he pull the flesh of the men from his mind? Oh, why wouldn't he simply speak?

Rubberman reluctantly put his rubber hand back on and walked away.

Chapter Three

A Hole

Spots got used to the routine fairly quickly. In a dozen sleeps or so, it would be tough to tell that he hadn't been at it as long as the others. Not that life was complex.

Things were always the same. Once the others had told Spots all the stories they had to tell, such as the time Blue held a mouthful of food in his mouth until Lenth tickled him, resulting in a mess that lingered in the exercise room, on Blue, and on Lenth until the next morning's shower.

Or the time Slim spent days imitating Joints (by doing things like walking a little slower, rubbing his elbow, stretching his leg) before Joints noticed anything was going on.

But the supply of amusing memories was drying up, and standard issue monotony was taking firm grip again.

And that was okay. That was normal.

Lenth had warmed up to Spots, more or less, but there were times that Spots noticed Lenth looking at him oddly, or looking into nowhere with troubled eyes. The loss of Slim was still very strong for Spots' Brothers, but for Lenth, it stung the most.

Sleep, wake, wash, eat, exercise, work, repeat. That was okay. That was the depth and breadth of reality.

--Until there opened a hole. While the Brothers were idly chatting in the near-dark, waiting for sleep to come, a soft but gritty scraping came from above. At first, they assumed it was Rubberman, but no. There were no footsteps, and even in this darkness, incomplete darkness, Rubberman would have been visible, if one looked carefully.

The scraping sound came again, and the attention of all four Brothers locked on to a spot *above* where Rubberman walked. Rubberman's ceiling.

One more scrape, shorter and more decisive. That spot in the ceiling moved up and aside, revealing a darker darkness. Reality was broken. A void on the upper crust of the known universe.

The Brothers dared not speak. Dared not move, aside from nervous glances at each other.

A shuffling sound came from this darker darkness. Then, a voice.

"Oh. Hmm." A man that looked a lot like the Brothers poked his head down from the darkness and looked around.

Lenth was the one to find his courage first. "Who are you? Are you a Brother?"

"What?" The stranger peered down to the Brothers, leaning his head back and forth, as if it would make it easier to see through the grating that Rubberman walks on. "A Brother?"

"Are you where Slim is?" Lenth asked. "Maybe you're where Spots came from?"

The stranger furrowed his brow. "I don't know what you're talking about. I'm just looking for the 'females'. Are there females in there?"

The dumbfounded looks on the Brothers' faces told the stranger all he needed to know. "Oh, forget you guys. Bye." The stranger disappeared into the darkness again, then one more scrape closed the hole, as if nothing ever happened.

Spots turned to Joints, looking for the wisdom of age. "What's a female?"

Joints only shrugged.

Lenth jumped off his bed and forcefully pointed to where the world had opened, yanking on his tether. *"What was all that about? What was that? SOMEONE—"*

"Hush, idiot!" Joints said. As if on cue, a footstep was heard. Lenth was back in bed before the next footstep was heard. The Brothers were all silent, all eyes shut except for Lenth's, who glared up as Rubberman came and paced about a little.

Rubberman didn't look up to where the hole had opened. Rubberman had no idea; he had only come because of Lenth yelling.

There had been a hole in the world, and Rubberman had no idea. It didn't seem like something that should be possible.

Rubberman looked down at Lenth. At least, it seemed like it. It was always hard to tell where Rubberman's eyes were aimed. Lenth pinched his brow and shook his head.

"I had a nightmare, I think."

Blue played along. "Well, shut up about it. Some of us are trying to sleep."

Lenth grunted at Blue and settled in again. After a few moments of silence, Rubberman seemed content with the situation and went back to wherever he came from, with a quiet 'clunk' to mark his exit.

The morning came like it always did. The spot on Rubberman's ceiling looked just as it always did.
"Seriously, guys...did I dream that?" Lenth asked, pointing a thumb upwards at the ex-hole. Answers came to him as heads discreetly shook no. What would Rubberman do if he knew?
How does he *not* know? The Brothers assumed that Rubberman was the one responsible for their food, their work, their showers, their lives.
Everything.
Now that was cast into doubt. They'd never actually seen Rubberman dispensing the food, or much of anything else other than functions that helped herd them around.
"I wonder if the stranger is Rubberman's...'Rubberman'," Spots quietly said as they left the shower area.
"Why would he have to peek in like that? And why does he look like us?" Blue asked.
"If you ask me, he didn't want to be seen by Rubberman either," Joints said. "He was sneaking. He wasn't where he was supposed to be. But then ya gotta ask, where in blazes *was* he supposed to be?"
In the exercise room, some of the Brothers expected that the images in the visors might reflect the stranger's appearance, but it showed only the usual shifting colours. The stranger had no impact. He was there, then he wasn't. Despite his origins beyond known reality, puncturing into the common world, the status quo survived.
The status quo thrived, in fact, ignorant of the short yet fantastical event that the Brothers could not help but think about.

Snippets of theories passed about when Rubberman wasn't around.
"Think he made Rubberman?" one Brother might say.
"Does he have his own Rubberman?" another would later muse.
"Does he have Brothers?"
"Are *we* his Brothers?"
Finally it was Lenth who made the more assertive stance. "I'm going up there," he said one evening. He pointed to the spot that the stranger peeked from as his cuff dangled from his wrist.
"Yeah, good luck with that." Blue said.
Lenth threw Blue a sullen glare. "Well, not right *this second*, obviously."
Joints chuckled softly to himself. "All right, I'll bite; what's your plan?"

The next waking passed, and the exercise, and the work. Quietly, Lenth managed to convince Spots to help. When it was time to sleep again and the lights were low, both Lenth and Spots closed their cuffs, but not around their wrists. Instead, they simply laid down on top of their cuffs and wrists. This way, Rubberman above could not see that they were not tied down.
When Rubberman walked away, his footsteps could still be heard. Lenth and Spots sat up and looked at each other, listening to the footsteps fade.

Then they heard the 'clunk' sound that marked the end of footsteps.

Lenth nodded. He and Spots sprang into action while Blue and Joints watched.

Spots knelt at the head of his bed and awaited Lenth. After some fumbling due to inexperience, a foot found a knee, clasped hands, and a shoulder. Lenth climbed him.

Lenth touched the bottom of the grate. It didn't even shock him. It was so easy; why had this never been done before? He stuck his fingers up through the grate and wiggled it this direction and that. And then...up?

"This kind of hurts," Spots said, Lenth's feet digging into his shoulders.

If Rubberman's ceiling could be pushed aside, why not the grating? Lenth pushed up and found that the section of grate came loose. Possessed by a sense of urgency, Lenth sent the metre-square chunk of grating sliding across the top.

Lenth grabbed the edge of the hole he had made and pulled himself upwards. Unable to pull himself all the way up, he looked down at Spots. "Push! I'll pull you up after!"

"Crazy. You're crazy!" But Spots obeyed. At least the first part. When Lenth was up top, he stood, and looked around, jaw agape.

The Brothers looked up at him.

"Well? What's up there?" Joints asked.

Lenth looked back and forth. "It...it's big. I mean, we kind of knew. Down there is almost as big, but we have walls in between it all. Up here, there's less walls, and they're further off. I don't see Rubberman anywhere. I see the top parts of the thing we get food from, the exercise stuff...that kind of thing. But...it's big up here."

"And the stranger's spot?" Spots asked.

Lenth looked up. "It doesn't look any more special from here. I bet I can open it as easy as the grating." He turned back to the hole to reach down for Spots. "Come on up, give me another boost!"

Spots sighed and began to reach up when the clunk sound came again. "Rubberman!" Spots whispered urgently. His eyes welled up in terror. "Come back down! We can just—"

"Too late," Lenth said. "He sees me."

Spots waved at Lenth all the more frantically, but Lenth wasn't paying attention. Lenth stared at Rubberman, and Rubberman stared back.

Behind Rubberman was a light. A doorway! That's what had been making the clunking sound. Lenth wanted Rubberman to approach him more; to get farther from the door. But Rubberman instead took a step back and reached for a counter that sat just inside the door.

Lenth charged at the doorway and Rubberman. Rubberman looked back and forth between Lenth and the counter and the buttons on it. He hit buttons repeatedly in panic.

A trace of sleepy-gas got to Lenth as his Brothers were dosed directly. In a reduced density above the grating, it was not strong enough and not fast enough to put Lenth to sleep. He tackled Rubberman, and they fell together into the room through the doorway.

Chapter Four

Fill

Large rubber fingers wrapped around Lenth's neck and threw him aside. With no idea what to do next, both of them stumbled to their feet as quickly as they could and backed away from each other defensively.

Lenth nervously looked around, never letting Rubberman out of his sight. The room was small, less than half the size of the sleeping room. The vaulted walls and low ceiling were dingy white, and behind Rubberman was a counter with a clutter of buttons and a small screen. The floor was a dimmer shade than the walls, but solid; not a grate.

Rubberman relaxed his stance, arms dropping to his sides. Lenth cautiously lowered his arms. A bit. No longer rushed, Rubberman found a specific button on the counter and pressed it, causing the doorway to close shut with the familiar 'clunk'. Seeing what it looked like closed, Lenth could now see that the opposite wall was very likely also a door.

But for the moment, he was simply trapped in a small room with Rubberman.

"Crap," came a muffled voice from inside Rubberman's head.

"What? You...you *can* talk?" Lenth asked, jaw agape.

"You've violated your quarantine level. I guess I'm going to have to sterilize you now." Rubberman turned his back and knelt down by the side of his buttons, reaching for something.

Lenth considered attacking. But to what ends, exactly? He considered messing with the buttons. But which ones, and again, to what ends? Escape to where he came from? Or open the other door to end up in…in who knows where?

This moment of hesitation didn't last very long as Rubberman was turned around again, now with a muted yellow scrap of cloth. He came at Lenth with it, pushing away Lenth's resistant hands with one big rubber hand, and used the other to superficially clean Lenth's face with the rag. Rubberman then took the rag to Lenth's hands, then feet. All the while, Lenth made attempts to evade this ceremony; attempts that became less and less concerted as it all became plain that it was harmless.

With all exposed skin 'cleaned' with token 'scrubbing', Rubberman stood back. "There," he said. "You're sterilized."

"I'm *what?*" Lenth held out his hands to look at. They looked the same as always.

Then, Rubberman began sterilizing himself all over with superficial scrubbing. He leaned forward and stuck his big rubber hands around his face, which was obscured by the floppiness of the rest of his head. After a little wiggling, the rubber face fell to the floor, big glassy eyes and all.

In horror, Lenth yelped and pressed back against the wall.

"What?" Rubberman picked up his face and stood up again. Under his face was a *face!* A person's face! "Oh, I get it. Calm down, calm down."

"A person!" Lenth said. "You're a real person in a bunch of rubber… clothes?"

Rubberman pulled back his large hood. A person, a human, plain as day. About as old as Joints, maybe. The sides of his head, his jaw, and the area around his mouth were matted with grey hair, as if fluffy eyebrows had sprouted out all over spots of his head. Lenth had never seen hair on top of a head more than a few millimetres long before it disappeared again overnight.

Lenth looked at him and stroked his own chin and jawline questioningly. Where Rubberman had bunches of hair, Lenth had only ever felt rough stubble, or nothing at all.

Rubberman sighed. "Hair. I haven't shaved in a while, all right? I didn't expect company. "You don't have much because I shave you every other week or so."

Lenth's eyes widened. He pulled the neckline of his suit out a little and peeked down at his body.

"No," Rubberman said, "just your face and head. That hair doesn't get messy. They just told me to shave your beard and head. Well, not the eyebrows."

"*They? Who are they?*"

"You may as well know now: they're going to come down or call or something when they see your cuff isn't reporting your pulse."

"*Who?*"

"The Providers. They supply our food and stuff. They want to keep you and your Brothers safe and happy."

"That…that's good. Safe and happy are good." Lenth looked around skittishly and slid down to sit on the floor. "I…how many more rooms are there?" he squeaked, still in disbelief of his current situation, let alone *more* undiscovered places.

Rubberman looked towards the door that Lenth hadn't seen open yet. "At least a few. The Providers don't tell me a lot. Just what I need to know, I guess."

Lenth looked back and forth at the two doors. "One in there, and one up? I think I saw one of the Providers from the higher place."

Rubberman frowned and squinted. "What do you mean, what 'higher place'?"

Further conversation was cut short by some beeping from the panel of buttons. Rubberman turned to face it. "Yup, there they are." He pressed a blinking green button and spoke. "I'm here, Providers."

A canned-sounding voice came from the panel. "We read an unscheduled gas deployment, and two pulses unaccounted for."

Rubberman gave Lenth a serious stare, making sure Lenth wasn't feeling chatty. Rubberman then replied to the voice. "Yeah, two of them were feeling overly energetic and didn't go to bed in a timely manner. I decided gassing them was the better option than shocking them all."

A bit of silence passed before the voice replied. "Next time, stick to routine, all right? Have the 'strays' had a pattern of disobedience?"

"No, not really."

"Then tuck them in before they wake up, and adjust the timetables accordingly."

"Got it."

The light on the button went out, and the two men were left staring at each other. "Two," Rubberman said. "Oh, of course, the Brother that helped you up wasn't in his cuff either. Lenth, are you going to go to bed nicely? And not talk about what you've seen? It's that, or the Providers might replace you." Rubberman's tone was reasonable, almost kindly despite the underlying threat.

"Replace me?" Lenth looked to the door and glanced upwards. "Is...is that what happened to Slim? He was replaced?"

Rubberman lowered his head and shook it slowly. "Not by his fault or anything. I'm not sure yet what happened. He was only replaced because he...well, because he died."

"Died?" Lenth looked around again looking for explanations. "Died? What is that?"

Getting up, Rubberman sighed in the face of Lenth's innocence. "People can't keep living forever. I'm old; I have less time than you, I know this. But Slim's death...when you stop living, and can't even be awake again...Slim's death was a terrible accident."

"*Can't ever be awake again?* Why not? Where is he? I can wake him up, just let me try!"

Rubberman opened the door back to the grating above the sleeping area. "When you die, your body begins to decay, it won't work anymore. It's just the way it is."

"What's *decay?!* You're not making any sense! *I want to go find him!* Help me go up!"

Lenth ran over under the stranger's spot and pointed up. "Come on, boost me up!"

"Presumptuous thing, aren't you?" Rubberman followed behind slowly, his gaze sliding between Lenth, the spot he was pointing at, the beds below, and the second door in the back of his own room. "I told them I'd toss you back into bed."

Only a little deflated for a moment, Lenth shrugged. "Don't! Just don't! I have questions for ceiling guy!" He couldn't reach the ceiling here by himself any more than he could reach the grating alone. "The ceiling opened right here! Boost me up!"

"If it will shut you up, and you'll get back in bed after. We have a minute. Just don't be upset when you can't open anything, and you realize it was a dream or something." Helping Lenth up, he nearly dropped him when he saw Lenth pop up a section of the ceiling and slide it to the side. Before Rubberman could collect himself enough to object, Lenth grabbed onto the edge and clumsily clambered up with feet flailing about until he managed to pull them up.

"Get down here!" Rubberman hollered.

Lenth laid flat on top and peeked down. He looked into the darkness around him, then back to Rubberman and down to his Brothers. He wanted his Brothers with him, but the need for answers about Slim outweighed his fears.

"Rubberman...please tell them where I've gone. Tell them I'm okay, and that I'm going to find Slim." Lenth waited as Rubberman stared up at him with a furrowed brow. Rubberman looked down, then looked up again. "I don't speak, remember? Get down here now!"

"Nope. No going back now. I'm going. Just point up when they ask about me! Can you do that much?"

Rubberman huffed and lowered his head in resignation. "I can try. What do I tell the Providers? And why am I asking *you* that?" Rubberman held his head in his gloved hands and moaned. "You're putting me in a really bad situation, I think."

Lenth frowned. "I'll wish you luck if you wish me luck."

"Child," Rubberman said softly, "the things you don't know. Stay right there; I'll be back in a second."

"I'm not changing my mind!" Lenth suspected that Rubberman would try to trick him, or do something to force him down. It would be easy to slide back into safely, though. So he waited, and it wasn't long before Rubberman was back.

"Catch." Rubberman tossed up a small tied bundle. Lenth caught it with one hand and looked at it questioningly.

"You'll probably need that stuff," Rubberman explained. "I ripped off half of my sterilization cloth. If you get into any situations where you think you might get infected by something, give yourself a bit of a scrub with it, right? And inside I bundled some food. If you only eat one when you're really hungry, they should keep you going for some time. Don't be a pig like you boys usually are. And you won't have your medication, so if your body does anything you don't expect...well, just don't freak out about it."

"Medication? What's that? And what kind of funny things might happen?"

"Don't worry about it. And if you see any Providers, avoid messing with them."

Lenth looked at his gift from Rubberman. "Why are you helping me now?"

Rubberman looked away. "I just am. Besides, I couldn't expect you to wake up with those guys down there and keep your mouth shut. It would mess things up more than they already are. I hope the Providers see it that way, too."

Lenth stuffed the little care package up his sleeve. "Thanks, Rubberman."

Rubberman smiled. "Phil."

"Fill what?"

"My name. It's Phil."

That made sense to Lenth. *Fill fills the food dispensing machine, and maybe the water for the showers, and the supplies for the work. So someone named him 'Fill'.*

"Thanks, Fill."

Lenth disappeared into the darkness, and the panel slid back into place, leaving Rubberman standing above the three remaining, sleeping Brothers. He shook his head in disbelief.

"There's more 'up'."

Chapter Five

Six & Eyes

Once the ceiling panel was back in place, it was very dark. A kind of dark that Lenth had never known. Even when it was time to sleep, there was enough light to see by. This was different. Maybe 'up' didn't have light. Maybe he would simply have to adjust.

He reached up and found the ceiling very close. There was enough space to crawl, but only with a lowered head.

Which way to go? In the absence of light, it all looked the same. He went in the general direction of Rubberman's room. If there were some structure above it, it could at least serve as a landmark. As he went, he found the occasional hard ridge that needed to be crawled over, being mindful of his shins especially.

He bonked his head on something hard enough to hurt a bit. He snatched at it, and found it was a cylindrical piece of metal that his hand wouldn't close around. It was very warm, and he couldn't find an end to it to the left or right. Not from where he was, anyway. This seemed more interesting than getting above Rubberman's room.

Left? Right? He turned to his right, and followed the pipe by touch. After some time, he wondered what he was over now. Feeling around, he didn't find anything below him that felt like he could lift it up and peek through. Onward along the pipe.

It went on for a long time before he felt it divide into two. One branch went down into the floor. The downward pipe was sealed tightly against the floor, which also wouldn't open, so he continued on with the branch that kept going forward. It led on and on. He must have already crawled several times the distance of…of what he used to think was the whole world.

More 'up' was a staggering concept. But he hadn't expected to also be amazed by the amount of 'sideways' there was. How much sideways could there be? Any fear he had was dwarfed by wonderment.

Lenth was unsure when it happened exactly, since it was so gradual and subtle, but he realized he could now see a little. A glint of light along the pipe, mainly. Then he spotted a little bit of sheen reflecting off his thumbnail. It was still so dark. But there was hope.

The further he went, the more he could see the pipe, and himself. At last, he saw something different. The pipe ran alongside others nearby, all going together to several other pipes from many directions. Where they all met, they bent together upwards. Where they all led up to was a sizable rectangular hole.

As Lenth got closer to the hole, he could feel the combined heat from all the pipes radiating out to him. Light was coming down from the hole, and when he got close enough, there was enough room to stand comfortably next to the bundle of pipes. Some of the pipes made sounds as water rushed through them.

Together, the pipe bundle was wider than a person, and metal fittings on them seemed to be situated randomly. Many of them had numbers and other symbols on them. Lenth knew about numbers from the exercise and work displays, but these other symbols were unknown to him. They looked like forgotten numbers or something.

One was like a zero, but with a piece missing from the right side. Another looked like a backwards three, but boxy, instead of rounded. Another looked kind of like a backwards seven, with an extra stick sticking out from the middle. Many didn't look familiar at all, but they all seemed to belong with each other.

Up the hole, the pipe bundle fed into a large object that was attached to a higher portion of the wall. Above it was another ceiling, but across from it was an opening where the light was coming from.

Planning for a climb, Lenth put his hand on a pipe. *Hot!* It was one making sounds steadily. He touched one that was silent. It was merely 'very warm'. Touching and listening to all of the pipes, Lenth found the ones that were coolest, and provided for good handholds.

Careful not to accidentally touch a hot pipe, especially with any bare skin, he made his way up high enough that he could get his hands on the ledge of the opening. He abandoned the pipes, and pulled his torso up onto the ledge, so he could rest a little, and still be able to drop quickly if something unpleasant came.

Looking forward, there stood a set of metal doors within arm's reach. The upper parts of the doors had a series of wide slats that were letting light in from the other side. Lenth pulled himself up, and looked through the slats. He paused for a bit to let his eyes adjust to the brightness.

There was a room much like the one he and his Brothers slept in, but different somehow. Not as bright? Well, the light was bright enough. The walls and floor were discoloured. Dirty?

He gently opened the metal doors and walked into the room.

Against opposite walls sat two beds with large, soft looking lumps on them. Two more beds stood upright against a wall, by an open doorway. Lenth had never considered the notion of a bed that wasn't attached to the floor. But he'd also never seen beds like the other ones with big lumps...*that...move*?

The lumps were breathing! They were alive!

Lenth panicked, and staggered back, hitting the metal door to the piping with a clatter.

Suddenly the lumps on the beds were moving even more! One of them sat up, groaning. There was a head on top of the lump now! And on top of the head was...something? Black, like its eyebrows; it was hairy like Fill!

Lenth squealed. "Ahh! Are you Providers?"

The other lump sat up, and it had a head now too. He had something on top of his head too, matching his light brown eyebrows. Hair! They had long hair! Not as Long as Phil's; maybe two centimetres long. "Are we what?"

"I know you!" Lenth said. "You're ceiling guy!"

Ceiling Guy's head wiggled, and an arm came out of the lump. "I...oh, you're one of those guys from that Unit. Uh...what are you doing here? I never found any females or anything. Which is a shame."

The other head wriggled more, and an entire human came out of the lumps. He stood beside his bed, looking a little threatened. "Wait a second, who is this guy? You know him?"

Lenth pointed at the discarded lump pile on the bed and laughed nervously. "It's just like big clothes you were sleeping in! I...why?"

Ceiling Guy got his other arm loose and patted his lap through the lumpy pile. "It's called a sleeping bag. We found them a couple days ago. They're comfortable, but ya get too hot. And yes, Eyes, I know this guy. Well, I've seen him anyway."

'Eyes' looked back and forth between Lenth and ceiling guy, pointing. Lenth understood how he got his name. 'Eyes' had very different eyes than himself or ceiling guy. Narrower. They sort of looked half-closed. His skin was a little bit darker as well.

"Well what do you want?" Eyes asked with frustration.

"I'm looking for my Brother, Slim. I have to wake him up."

Eyes and Ceiling guy exchanged grim glances. Ceiling Guy spoke in a cautious tone. "Pal, when you say you need to wake him up...are you sure he's not dead?"

"Yes! Dead! Rubberman used that word. I have to wake Slim up from dead."

"You can't do that, moron," said Eyes bluntly. "Dead is dead. It's the last thing you do. I doubt you could even find the body anyway. Just go back where you came from before you get us all caught by a Provider or something."

"What's a Provider?"

Eyes sighed with more than a little exasperation. "They get supplies to this area. Yellow suits, not very social."

"Oh, oh! Yeah, Rubberman mentioned the Providers."

"You were taking with a Rubberman? We're thinking about the same thing, right? Guys in the black rubber suit? And the mask?"

"Yeah? But I found out his name is Fill."

"Ooh right, I'll be right back!" Eyes jogged to the next room, and shortly came back wearing a Rubberman's mask. "Ooga booga! I'm a Rubberman! Zap! Zap!"

"Moron," Ceiling Guy said.

Lenth backed away from Eyes, as stupid as he looked without the rest of the Rubberman suit. "What are you doing with Fill's mask?"

Eyes slid the mask up and perched it on top of his head. "Relax. It's not as if there's only one of these. And it's not like there's only one 'Rubberman'. Me and Six used to be Rubbermen."

"We were not," Ceiling Guy said sternly.

"You're no fun."

Lenth was still disconcerted by the mask, but was gradually starting to overcome it. "So...Ceiling Guy's name is Six? Why? And where did you actually get the mask?"

'Six' finished getting out of his sleeping bag and yanked off a shoe to raise a foot and wiggle six toes. "Six. And the mask, we...found in one of the rooms back there. There's a whole suit back there, and a bunch of other junk."

Lenth wandered slowly towards the doorway out of curiosity. Eyes made a motion to intercept, but Six waved him off silently before Lenth even noticed. "Hey, let me show you around," Six said.

Lenth smiled in gratitude, then looked at the door frame itself. He ran a finger along its side and peered at the top edge. "Is it always open?"

Six made his way past Lenth, and pointed at a darkened control panel in the second room. "Yeah. I think that used to open and close it, but if it did, it doesn't work now."

This second room looked a lot like the room Lenth had confronted Rubberman Phil in. It even had another door on the other side, but it was closed. "No way to open that, then, I suppose."

Eyes gave a mirthless little chuckle. "I think that's where the Providers come from. If that ever opens, I'm jumping back down into the dark where you sprouted up from. There's other places to hide. This spot just has the most room."

Lenth stared at the closed door. "You guys seem to fear the Providers. Fill seemed to not be super comfortable with them either. What do you know about them? Could they have Slim?"

"If your Rubberman doesn't have him, it's a safe bet. There's no one else to have him," Eyes said.

"That's pretty short sighted," Lenth said. "The last time I woke from sleep, I didn't know you or the Providers existed. I'm betting there's more. I get the idea that you haven't been in this room forever. Where did you come from?"

Six bellowed, *"Yes, yes we do fear the Providers, all right?"* Six paused to regain a little composure, and no one spoke until Six continued. "That's enough, isn't it? They didn't take too kindly to Eyes or me, so now we're here, and your Slim isn't the first person to have died. If your Rubberman is still in a good mood, you might be better off to just go home and hope for forgiveness."

Silence. Lenth shook his head a little.

"Yeah," Six said, "I didn't think so."

"So now what?" Eyes asked, leading the way back to the first room again. "We have enough room here, and access to enough food," Eyes' hospitality was reluctant, but in earnest, "but I'm getting the idea you didn't leave your place to just go live in another hole."

Lenth just pointed up.

"What do you hope to find?" Six mumbled. "Your buddy is dead, and dead is dead."

"Answers, I guess. Why he's dead. Well, Fill told me how, sort of. He didn't know the details. I need more answers."

"What you *need* are the right questions," Eyes said.

"*Why* seems like a good question," Lenth said softly.

"Why *what?*" Six asked, still a little snippy.

Lenth nodded slowly, staring into nothingness. "Yup. Why what."

"You wanna know why we're here?" Eyes asked with a thin smile.

Six gave an exasperated grunt. "Oh, here we go!"

Lenth looked at Six with a curious expression. Six just threw his hands up in the air. "You may as well let Eyes spill his theory!"

"Hey, it's the real deal!" Eyes hunkered down, his hands wiggling for emphasis. "We're all the same things! You and I, and the Rubbermen, and the Providers? We're the young ones! Every now and then, one of our kind just disappear, right? When we get old enough, we become Rubbermen! Or Providers; I'm not sure how it works, but it's something like that. When the Rubbermen and Providers get older, I don't know. Maybe they die when they're too old."

"Really?" Lenth asked.

"Doubt it!" Six chirped in with sarcastic enthusiasm.

Lenth tilted his head. "One of my Brothers, Joints, he's pretty old, about the same as my Rubberman Fill..."

"Well, it's obvious!" Eyes said. "Your Rubberman must be a pretty new one, and your Brother *must* be just about to become a Rubberman! One day your other Brothers will wake up, and he'll be gone, and some new guy is there!"

Lenth tried to rationalize that and compare it to Slim's death. But Slim was young. "Any chance younger people turn into Rubbermen?"

Eyes knew what he was talking about and slouched down. "If he's dead, no. I don't think so. Dead is dead."

"Are you sure? How much do you know about being dead, really?"

"No, no, no..." Eyes looked a little confused, and the two of them took a moment to ponder. Neither of them took particular note that Six had slipped away into the other room, but now he was back.

Walking in a floppy, exaggerated manner, Six marched into the room wearing the full Rubberman outfit. "Graaaahhhh! I just became a Rubberman! I knew I was feeling old! I'm gonna shock you both if you don't go to bed right now!"

"Moron!" Eyes snapped at him.

Six tossed back the hood and threw the mask onto the floor. "I've told you before, it's just clothes!" He ripped off a glove so he could pinch the end of Eyes' sleeve. "Clothes! Rubbermen just have different clothes! They're just like us!"

Eyes pulled away from Six. "What do you know? Then what's a female, huh? Is *that* just clothes?"

"*I don't know!*" Six yelled. "If I ever find a female, I'll ask him to take his clothes off, and we'll see what happens! I wish I had more time on that learning thing I found before Providers showed up."

"All right, settle down!" Lenth pleaded, picking up the mask. He looked at it and fiddled with the fittings a little. "So where can I go up more?"

Six paced a little, calming down. "The noise box is probably the best bet."

Eyes nodded.

"Great; where's that? How do I get there?" Lenth asked.

Six pointed back to the closet Lenth had come from. "You head down there, go left and follow the thickest pipe until it divides into two. Don't follow either one, but just keep going forward until you hit your head on a wall, and feel around for a cable, and—"

"Six, just shut up and take him there already."

Six shot Eyes a nasty glance, then looked at the exit, then at Lenth, then at Eyes once more. "Yeah. Okay." He shed the rest of the Rubberman suit and dumped it all on the floor. "Come on then, Lenth. Put on the suit. You might be able to blend in if you get spotted by Rubbermen or Providers."

Six led the way to the hole down, carefully finding the cooler pipes to slide on. Before following Six, Lenth turned to Eyes. "You not coming?" Lenth asked as he hurriedly put the suit on. Putting the mask on for a moment, he found the view very dark, so he just let the mask hang off his neck.

Eyes shook his head with a smile. "I'll go back to that whole 'sleep' thing, thank you."

Soon, Lenth was in the darkness again, following the sounds of Six leading the way.

"Okay, follow the sound of my voice."

"Right. And thank you, by the way."

"No problem. I didn't have anything else to do."

"But should we be talking so much? I mean, what if someone hears us that we don't *want* noticing us? And what if we don't notice them noticing us?"

"I've never heard anyone else when in these dark places, I don't think anyone out there can hear in here, either. But yeah, I'll warn you when we get closer to where strangers might be. In short, if you see light, that light is probably there for someone else."

"And that could mean people like my Brothers, Rubbermen, or Providers."

Six stopped crawling for a moment to think. "I...I don't know."

"What happened with your Rubberman?" Lenth asked quietly.

Six huffed a little. "His floor, our ceiling, just sort of snapped one day. I woke up and one of my Brothers was screaming like crazy." Six paused, and Lenth could only imagine the look on his face while his voice drifted away. "The edge of the grating...and what could any of us do?" Six said, pausing again. "There was our Rubberman, lying on top, as stunned as the rest of us. He panicked and struggled to get up, but that just pushed the grating down harder. My Brother...he was almost two pieces. Eyes went crazy, it was ...it was crazy. Eyes came just short of killing the Rubberman, but he wasn't looking good when we got out. One Brother dead, another scared out of his mind, curled up in the corner...Eyes and I got out. We found out we could go above...well, like where I peeked on your and your Brothers."

"Yeah," Lenth said, a bit stunned, "in two pieces...my...when I left, it was a lot less violent. He let me go."

"...just let you?"

"Well, once I was up on his floor, we fought a little, but in the end, yeah. He was as surprised as I was that his ceiling had more 'up' in it."

"Huh." Six could be heard to turn and continue forward. "Kinda sad that he couldn't imagine there was more to life."

Lenth followed without comment. Until he spotted Six that first time, he hadn't thought about it either. But now the borders were...well, the borders were still there, but he now saw them for what they were. "How far does it all go? How many Rubbermen and groups of Brothers are there?"

"That I know of? Four Rubbermen, each looking after four 'Brothers'."

"Does that count *your* Rubberman, Six?"

"Ha. Yeah, I don't know if mine got better, or died and was replaced, but there's a Rubberman where I lived until me and Eyes got out. And four new Brothers. All strangers to me."

"We're...we're all replaceable...even the Rubbermen...?" Lenth asked. He fidgeted with the Rubberman mask hanging from his neck. Had this suit belonged to Six's Rubberman? It felt like Six was holding back details, but Lenth didn't feel like prodding.

"Replaceable?" Six mused. "Maybe. All thanks to our generous Providers, I guess. And just because I only know of four Rubbermen and Brother sets doesn't mean anything. I haven't been as eager as you to explore. I have a cozy corner, access to the things I need, and I have no plans on messing that up."

Lenth nodded. "I guess I can understand that."

It wasn't long before they crept into the first signs of light. Lenth was able to make out Six's face as Six turned back to cover his mouth. Lenth nodded and covered his mouth to signal understanding. It was quiet time.

They came to a grouping of pipes that were much larger than those that Lenth had been seeing so far. Each as wide as his thigh, and none of them were warm in the slightest.

There was sound, though. A soft, yet somehow large hiss, which grew louder the closer they got to the nexus of them. The low ceiling opened up a little, enough that they could sit up on their knees.

All the pipes led up to a huge, three-metre wide metal box looming overhead...It was the source of the sound. Six got closer to Lenth so he could communicate without yelling.

"If you climb up to the height of the box, you're gonna see a floor to one side, a bit of a room, and a door. Skip all of that. Providers come out of there sometimes. I almost got caught here. Wearing that Rubberman suit might help you out if you meet a Provider, but don't count on it. Keep going up. I don't know if further up is any safer, or free of Providers, but..."

Lenth thought maybe that talking to the Providers was exactly what he should be doing, but between Six and Phil's uneasiness about the Providers, it was reasonable not to go running to the first Provider he saw.

"Hey Six. If Eyes is right, do you think there's something else above the Providers? Something they become when they get old?"

Six smirked and shrugged. "If you find out, you come back and let us know, huh?" He patted Lenth's shoulder and headed back down into the darkness, leaving Lenth to tackle the noisy box.

Chapter Six

Beyond the Noisy Box

Trying to keep out of view from the door as much as possible, Lenth climbed to the back of the box. All the pipes attached to it made for excellent handholds.

The walls around him and over by the door were strange. They were just flat light grey. They didn't look rusty...maybe not even metal at all.

With his body against the back of the box, he could feel the small but fervent vibrations from machinery inside. Getting to the top, he rested his torso across the top, between a few of the larger pipes, his legs dangling off the back.

He rested his head on the box and nearly didn't hear the door open. He slid back a little so that his head was less visible from the door and watched. A man in a yellow suit, presumably a Provider, came in. His clothes were baggier and covered him head to toe, but it was still a lot more like Lenth's outfit than the bulky Rubberman outfit.

He had a lot of hair on his head, too. It was the same colour as Six's hair, he had but more of it. Where Six's stood tall, sticking out of his head a centimetre or two, this man's hair was at least five centimetres long, and had fallen to the side a little.

He came in and closed the door. It was thinner than the kinds of doors that Lenth was used to, and the handle was more compact, but it looked like it operated in much the same way.

Lenth assumed that the Providers would look at least as intimidating as a Rubberman. Phil was afraid of these guys? *Then again, just because Phil wears a big suit, that didn't make him any stronger.*

The Provider carried a box of ..."*Wait a second,*" Lenth thought, *"those are the things I worked on! This is where they get used?"*

Many of the pipes going into the box were about the same width. The Provider walked right up to the front of the big box.

The sound of the big box started to get quieter. Then he heard a sudden, hard screeching sound that seemed like it would never end. It left silence in its wake.

A moment later, he heard a much lighter metal sound. Then, *scrape, plunk. Scrape, plunk.* Four times, which was as many cylinder things that the Provider brought with him.

Then *tap, scrape, click! Tap, scrape, click! Tap, scrape, click! Tap, scrape, click!* When all that was done, the smaller metal sound happened again, and the box's big sounds started up again.

Peeking over the edge again, Lenth saw the Provider leaving with the box again. Eventually would these things be sent back to Phil to get them cleaned inside? Lenth felt a sense of understanding despite still not knowing what the objects were actually accomplishing.

Lenth stared down at the big, noisy, metal box he was sitting on. So this is why he did the work he did? To 'feed' the box? He leaned forward more to look at the front. There was an array of letters, but to Lenth, they were just meaningless scribbles.

This was too interesting to ignore. He slid forward more and reached to open the metal door that the Provider had opened. As he'd figured, the things were in there, snuggled tightly, plugged in and held down with little straps of metal. He could see they connected to pipes on both ends, on one side also attached to some other big chunks of machinery—*those* were the noisy chunks.

The box was pumping in...air? Doing something to it with the cylinders, then passing it back out. Why? What were the Providers doing with the air?

Putting more weight forward over the edge of the box than was comfortable, Lenth got a grip on one of the cylinders and pulled on it. Trying to wrangle it out caused the seal to open just a little, causing a furious hiss to escape, blowing a small but mighty stream of air against Lenth's hand. Startled, he jammed the cylinder back into place. Hopefully the noise wouldn't bring that Provider back.

Lenth looked to the door and looked up. Taking Six's advice, he started heading up.

When he had climbed far enough up the pipes, he found himself in a very similar space, with an identical door in the same direction. The pipes split into several directions, all of them going through walls or ceiling. This appeared to be the end of the line, as none of the pipes had any further space to crawl alongside.

Did Six know that this was all that was above the big noisy box? It didn't matter, the choice was now between doors. *One definitely has a Provider behind it, but the other? Who knows.* Lenth was starting to see Six's lack of enthusiasm for going up more. *Up to what?*

Focus. Have a snack. He moved from the pipes, and sat on the floor in front of the door. He pulled Phil's care package out from his sleeve and took a single food disk from it. He chewed idly while staring at the door.

He stared for quite a while, imagining opening it, rallying the courage. Realising he had already eaten three disks when he had only meant to eat one, he hurriedly put the rest away.

He stood and made two bold steps to the door. And stopped. The metal piece to operate the door was some kind of handle, but it was different than what he was used to. Trying to remain quiet, he grabbed it and pulled.

Nothing, it wouldn't open. Maybe it was broken, or maybe a Provider needed to press a button somewhere else.

It sounded kind of broken. He wiggled it a little, and it made rattly sounds. He moved to the opposite edge of the door and grabbed the handle, ready to yank it. When he did, the handle gave way, turning enough that Lenth lost his grip and fell backwards, landing in the corner.

The handle...could turn! He got back up, and stood in front of it, turning it carefully. It clicked, and the door became loose.

Lenth took half a step back and took a deep breath. His hands felt unsteady. *Breathe.* He put the ominous mask on, and fitted the hood around it. Well, he should look the part now. He let his eyes adjust. On top of being dark, his field of vision was restricted notably.

He opened the door slowly, just enough to get himself through, and closed it behind him.

He found himself in a hallway made of the light grey, non-rusty, non-metal material. He could go left or right. Both directions looked like they ended up splitting in two directions again. There was also another door right in front of him. With the threat of being caught increasing, the thrill of having choices was becoming less and less... comfortable.

He couldn't hear anything from the door, so he quietly went in, feeling proud to operate another of those turning door handle things quite deftly.

This room was vast, many times the size of the room he and his Brothers slept in, and twice as high. The amount of emptiness was a presence in and of itself. He found it even more unsettling than the long hallway.

Shelf after shelf of boxes sat with various numbers, and those strange numbers, which aren't numbers. A group of symbols he didn't understand, and the number 1000. That was the biggest number he had ever seen, but he had seen '100' often enough while exercising, and more or less understood what an extra '0' must mean.

He walked over to a box far from the large aisle down the middle of the room. He pulled one of the boxes a little closer and fidgeted with the lid until it popped off. Inside were more food disks than he had ever seen before. 1000, apparently. A box like this probably could feed him and his Brothers for more than ...well, it was too hard to guess! Dozens of meals! This was never anything he had needed to worry about. It was always there, thanks to Phil and the Providers.

The realization gave Lenth pause, a moment of genuine gratitude before he remembered his mission—finding Slim.

Lenth popped another food disk from his sleeve-stash into his mouth.

He looked around for anyone else, then restocked his care package before closing the box again and putting it back in place. He looked at the symbols on the side of the bin. This combination of symbols would seem to mean 'food disks'. That was a lot of scribbles to represent something so basic. Numbers were easy; these new symbols were crazy. There were ten types of symbols for numbers. These others? Seemed to have no rules. *There's got to be at least twenty of these things!*

Feeling safe for the moment, Lenth wandered down the aisle in the middle of the room. There were so many boxes of food. And they were all labelled. *Wait...that one has a different bunch of symbols on it.* He pulled the lid off and found large cylindrical containers with more symbols on them, the number "1", and a single symbol after. A *singular* symbol seemed important, so he made special note of it. "*L*". *Something something, "1L".*

If the food box had a number for how many were in it, but no "L". *This container has one of something. And a bent line.* The top of the container had some kind of latch on it, but fiddle as he may, he couldn't get anything to open. Maybe it was better to not open. For all he knew, it was full of sleepy-gas. Then again, he was wearing a Rubberman mask. *Hmm.*

It didn't seem important to mess with, so he put the container away and continued down the aisle. He got to the far end and was ready to inspect another door when it opened from the other side.

Two surprised, yellow-suited Providers stared at Lenth, aghast.

Chapter Seven

Fair

"What are you doing here?" the first Provider asked with a bewildered look on his face.

"What Unit are you from? Why aren't you there?" The other demanded.

"Uh...Unit...four?" Lenth said. It didn't seem to offend the Providers.

"Unit four? What's wrong in Unit four?"

What *is* wrong in Unit four? Why wouldn't he have just used the talking machine to call the Provi...*ah. Yes.* "I can't seem to talk to anyone up here. I think something's broken in the...machine."

The second Provider relaxed and rolled his eyes, turning to the other Provider. "Great. Ugh. If we're lucky, it won't be a short in the wiring. Last time that happened, there were half a dozen of us crawling around in the dark, testing things for days. Are things otherwise okay in Unit four? Why did you need to call us?"

Why? Why? "The food supply was less than usual, I wanted to find out if you knew, and, uh... why. It's not an urgent thing right now, but..."

The second Provider turned to the other. "I'm going to see Rick in a little bit. I'll get him on this if you deal with the electrical."

The first Provider sighed. "Yep, I guess I'll get at that after I check off today's outgoing."

"I guess you can go," The second Provider told Lenth.

"Uh, I don't know where..."

"Heh, yeah, I forget how this floor can be for those who don't come here regularly." The Provider pointed down the hall behind him. "Just head that way, make the left at the second last intersection. Just forward from there, and the elevators will be on your right. Can't miss 'em."

Lenth nodded. "Thanks." *Now what the heck is an elevator?* Lenth went in the direction he was pointed.

Behind him, he heard one of them comment, "—must be ex-Subject. Cute how they usually don't take their masks off except in their own spaces. It's like they're hardwired from Unit protocol or something. I saw a Subject-turned-Unit Manager take his mask off once. It was awkward for everyone."

Providers called a Rubberman a 'Unit Manager'? Okay.

He wasn't familiar with the word 'intersection' either, but he made a good guess. He found where he thought he needed to go and turned back to the two Providers, who were still chatting. Lenth pointed down the hall.

One of the Providers waved his hand. "Yeah! Down there!"

Lenth waved back in thanks and headed down the hall. He passed a few Providers as he went. None of them took a whole lot of notice of him, other than an odd glance. Walking at a normal pace seemed to give him a look of confidence. A look of knowing what the heck he was doing, and that he had the right to be here.

He almost passed by the flat metal doors of the elevators when a helpful Provider reached over and hit the 'down' button for him. "There ya go. Down, I assume? I know those gloves can be a pain." The Provider didn't question as to why, if they were such a pain, he didn't simply take them off to press buttons. It was assumed to be normal that a 'Unit Manager' just kept them on. That was handy.

The Providers seemed all right with talking to a Rubberman, but they didn't seem eager to see one out of his suit. There were lines drawn. Social norms.

The metal door slid open on its *own*. Insanity. Come to think of it, the door to Fill's room could do the same thing. Stepping in, he found a rather small room. It had railings around the walls and a panel of buttons near the door. Before he knew it, the doors closed behind him.

All right, now what?

He took a closer look at the panel of buttons. One was lit up, and had the number '2' on it after a letter that looked like a circle with a broken top. There was also a '1' and a '3' button with the same symbol attached. Most of the buttons had a number and a symbol to go with them.

He pressed the one that was lit up.

He waited.

Nothing happened.

He pressed a random one, and it lit up! It was a "1" with a symbol that looked like a stick with a couple of smaller sticks attached to one side, sticking out.

He was about to press another, when he felt the room do something. The world seemed to be invisibly pushing down on him. Terrified, he staggered back from the buttons and leaned against the rear wall, gripping the railing.

Okay. It didn't feel quite so strange now, but the room was making a noise. It was a smooth noise, but Lenth still found it unsettling. He was considering pressing more buttons, but what would that do? Make it shake more? Stop?

It was then that he noticed the trail of lights above the door. The looked a lot like the buttons. Only one was lit up, and every few moments, the next one in the row would light up.

Okay, what did it all mean? He figured that something would happen when the light above the door was lit on the number he had pressed, something would happen.

The upper light of "1", with "*stick with two sticks sticking out of it*" lit up. The same unsettling feeling washed over him, but this time the force was pushing him up a little.

The sound ended at the same time as the feeling dissipated. A short moment passed and the door slid open again.

The outside has changed since I got into the little room! Lenth was amazed for a moment before he realized that the little room had moved him to another place.

Which was also pretty amazing. *Rooms that move. Crazy.*

This new room had vaulted, dingy walls. A lot like Phil's room, but much larger. Near the middle sat some kind of thin but wide platform. It had thick round disks attached with little metal arms under each corner, holding the platform up off the floor. The disks were a bit bigger than a fist, and black, except in their centres where they attached to the little arms.

A handle stuck up from one side of the platform. The handle had a rounded triangular piece of metal pipe at the top to grab, with a smaller red piece where one's fingers might rest.

A small, random scattering of black...something...powder? Sat beside it. Lenth was eager for a closer look, but carefully glanced around.

The room had a closed doorway ahead that was held shut with some kind of large latch. Not far from this door stood a ladder. Lenth had never seen one before, but its purpose was obvious enough.

Well, he had been aiming for 'up', so the ladder won out. At the top, through a wide opening, sat a small room with vaulted walls. It was bare, other than a door with a heavy lever for a handle.

Lenth yanked on it and the door gave way reluctantly. He stepped through and the heavy door eased itself back into place.

He found himself in a bedroom: a bed, a small door, and a big door. The small door went nowhere. It was storage for clothes.

In the bottom of the little storage space sat several items that had unusual images and some symbols on the front. Most were only a little bigger than his hand. He picked one up and found that it opened easily. One side remained stuck together, but the rest of it split into hundreds of super-thin pieces of something like cloth, but thinner. The pieces were an off-white colour and had hundreds and hundreds of symbols on them.

He stared at the groupings of symbols on a random page for a while. Looking at how they were arranged in rows, the rows stacked one on top of another, sometimes with a gap here or there.

It started to seem that these symbols were more important than just labelling things such as food bins. For now, this wad of symbols would have to remain a mystery. He put it all back the way he found it and turned his attention to the other door. It opened to a room almost exactly like the room he had his chat with Phil in. Yup, he was in a Rubberman's domain.

Thankfully, the resident Rubberman wasn't at home, but the open door on the other side of the little room suggested pretty plainly that he wasn't far. What now? The curiosity drove him to the doorway to have a listen. Footsteps, far off. And talking. Strange voices, higher pitched than any he'd heard before.

Lenth looked across the iron grating floor and looked for movement. It was much like above the grating of his home. Even though up here was far more open than below, there were still several walls and mechanical constructs obscuring his view.

Lenth held still so that his Rubberman suit wouldn't make any noise. Small sounds of metal on metal came from somewhere on the right. The high voices came from straight ahead. The metal was probably the Rubberman adjusting a machine, so forward he went.

As he got closer, he could make out the voices more. It sounded like they were straining, and if the layout here was anything like his home, the workout room was ahead. They were talking about the same pointless things that Lenth and his Brothers usually did.

When he got close enough to see them working out, they saw him as well. Lenth was indistinguishable from their own Rubberman, it seemed. Just like his Brothers did, these people got a little quieter when Rubberman was around. Which, for the most part, was kind of silly. It was rare that they had discussed anything worth zapping someone over.

But look at these men! They were different! They had even more hair than even Eyes and Six. As he watched them lying on the exercise benches, raising the weights from the floor, he saw how their bodies seemed to be a little smaller overall. Especially in the middle. It made their hips look a bit bigger in comparison. *And the lumpy bit that's supposed to be between a person's legs?* It was almost as if there were no bits there at all.

And their chests. Some of them had more chest than the others, but all of them had more...chest bulk than he'd ever seen.

Lenth watched them exercise. And watched. When they were done that, they shifted into a different exercise. Their bodies were so interesting! Lenth wondered what they looked like in the showers.

Lenth's breathing was becoming heavier, and only fear kept him from calling out to them.

The first clap, Lenth didn't hear. On the second, he turned around to see the local Rubberman standing between him and the door.

Whoops. He was caught.

The Rubberman waved Lenth over. At least he didn't attack. Maybe he would have if didn't mean showing the strange men below that there were more than one Rubberman.

Maybe when Lenth got over there, something bad would happen. No sense in delaying it at this point. He took one more glance down to the fascinating people below and walked to the waiting Rubberman. He silently pointed to the door.

Lenth looked at him, trying to discern intent. With only body language to go by, Lenth could impose any meaning that he wanted to see. The Rubberman wasn't jittery or moving in harsh bursts. This calm could be friendliness, or it could be anger with confidence.

Lenth walked past the Rubberman and into the door. The Rubberman followed into the small room and pushed a button to slide the door shut. He leaned over, quickly shedding his gloves and mask, rising up as he pushed back his hood.

A mane of amber hair cascaded around his gentle but terrified features. "Am I being replaced? Why? And why did they just send you, and not Providers? What's going on?" 'His' voice was like the lumpy men in the exercise room!

Lenth staggered back and fumbled with his own mask. It was being difficult, so he gave up taking it off before speaking. "*You're*...you're one of *them?*"

"Them? Providers? What do you mean?"

"No, no!" Lenth pointed at the door. "One of the lumpy-body men!"

"Women? Lumpy?"

Still entirely suited up, Lenth used his hands to outline the differences around his own body, drawing the curves that had caught his eye. He then used his arms to squeeze his middle and pushed out his chest.

The Rubberwoman tilted her head. "Are...you feeling okay?"

Frustrated, Lenth yanked back his hood, and shoved his mask off with no regard for being graceful about it. "I'm not lumpy like them!" He continued shedding the Rubberman suit and stood before the Rubberwoman, arms spread wide, wearing just his usual outfit.

The Rubberwoman took one slow step back, craning her neck forward. "I see! You...you're lumpy in the wrong places!" She pointed at Lenth's groin.

Lenth covered his clothed groin with both hands and looked at Rubberwoman defensively. "It's just fine as it is!"

"I don't think so!" She squirmed her way out of the rest of her Rubberman suit, stood with feet apart, and pointed at her own groin. "See? *That's* normal!" She pointed at Lenth's covered groin again. "And that looks swollen or something! If mine ever looked like yours does, I'd be...! I'd be darn worried!"

Lenth grimaced. "You're...you're just envious."

The Rubberwoman shook her head dismissively. "I'm just kidding with you. I know what men are, sheesh. What are you doing here, anyway? Don't you have Subjects to keep an eye on?"

The conversation was headed in directions that Lenth saw as being problematic, so he changed the topic to his central concern. "I...do you know where people go when they get dead?"

Rubberwoman tilted her head and squinted a little. "You don't know? Providers take them. Why don't you know that?"

Stupid. He did know that. *Stupid, stupid, stupid.* He was in the Providers' area, but his fear of getting caught kept him from asking directly. *Think, think,* the lumpy pretty man was staring at him. *Think.* "Yes, but then what? Where do they take them?"

"How would I know? What does it matter?" The Rubberwoman stared at Lenth with a clenched jaw. Lenth found himself mimicking her almost combative stance. They stared at each other for a while before Rubberwoman broke the silence. "Dead is dead."

Yes, yes, dead is dead, and water is water. Why did people keep telling him this? "Fine," Lenth said. "I'm leaving." He put his mask and hood back on, and went into the Rubberwoman's bedroom.

"What are you doing?" She followed behind him.

"I suppose I need to go talk to the Providers," Lenth sighed. "I'm leaving!" But the door wasn't much of a door anymore. It looked more like a bevelled wall.

"This is where I came in!" Lenth said, pawing the edges of the wall.

Rubberwoman leaned on the doorway. "And?"

Lenth waved her closer while his other hand traced along an edge. "Look here! This is where it opens! It seals nice and clean, huh? But look, you can see a little...imperfection. On the other side, the handle is right about here." He mimicked the motion of grabbing the lever.

Rubberwoman leaned in for a close look. "Huh." She backed off again. "Oh yeah, I almost forgot about that door."

"You *forgot about it?*" Lenth said. "*There's a secret door in your bedroom, and you forgot it?*"

"It's not secret, really. Well, not to me," she said. Did Phil have such a door? Maybe he never used it. Maybe he wasn't permitted? "I don't leave the Unit often, and I don't use that door. Generally I'm below, taking out product with Providers, and if I feel like it, I'll go out that way while I'm at an open door anyway. Isn't your Unit pretty much the same?"

"Product?" Lenth asked.

"Well, whatever you call the stuff your Subjects make."

"Oh...right. Those." It must be the work things. Those lumpy men probably make them too. "Out the same way? Uh...yes, now that I think of it. I just can't see the edge on the door in my room."

"Huh. Well, I'll call the Providers and get them to come open this door. We can't leave through the door below without screwing up the schedule for the Subjects, and unless it's an emergency—"

Lenth jumped a little. "Ah! No, no, don't bother them. I can get out the way I...I have another way."

Rubberwoman launched a scrutinous glare towards Lenth. "I thought so. You're really not supposed to be here, are you?"

Despite the accusation, her voice disarmed Lenth a little, and honesty began to slip out. "I've seen more today than I thought ever existed. I was just looking for my Brother and got distracted."

"Brother?" Rubberwoman stepped back slowly. "This...Brother...it's a man, right?"

Lenth looked stunned. "Until I came in here, everyone I knew was like me. Well, not exactly like me. Different faces and stuff, but same kinds of lumpies. Not like you. And not like those other lumpy men here."

"Women." Rubberwoman said. "A man that's...lumpy, as you say, is called a woman."

"What's a woman?" The puzzle pieces rattled into place in Lenth's head, then the light went on. "*Woman!*" He laughed, pointing at her groin and bust. "You're one of those females! So that would make me a feman!"

"I...don't think so. Since the word 'WO man' has the alternative of 'man', I'd guess that 'FE male' converts to 'male'."

Lenth shrugged. "Whatever." He looked back to the doorway out toward the rooms of the other lumpy m...er...WOmen. "So...can you help me get out the way I got out of my own area?"

Rubberwoman backed away a little, looking Lenth up and down. "Hey. You never told me your name."

"Lenth," he said.

Rubberwoman looked down with a resigned sigh. "Huh. Never heard of a name like that. How did you get it?"

After a silent pause, attempting to read Rubberwoman's expression, Lenth held out his arms wide. "It comes from 'length', since I..."

Rubberwoman held up her hand to stop him. "Did you have a name before you got it from your length?"

"Nope, why?"

Rubberwoman grimaced and her eyes shifted between Lenth and the panel of buttons. "You're...you're not supposed to have that suit, are you? Did you used to live under the grating?"

The cautious tone that the Rubberwoman took reminded Lenth that this suit once belonged to a real Rubberman. Maybe the one that got attacked by Eyes or Six.

"Yes," Lenth said.

"When you worked, what did you make?"

"I cleaned a part in big round containers, with different layers of stuff in them."

This answer seemed to put the Rubberwoman at ease a little. "How many toes do you have?"

"Ten."

The Rubberwoman nodded towards Lenth's feet. "Let me see."

Lenth took the boots and the usual foot coverings that he always wore, and showed off his toes. "I met someone with more. Is he—"

"Did he give you that suit? Put your shoes back on; you're not him."

"Does it matter?" Lenth asked timidly.

"The Providers want him and his Asian friend. They killed for that suit."

"They did *what?*"

The Rubberwoman shook her head. "Never mind. I guess you don't know about that kind of thing. How did you get above your grate?"

"One of my Brothers helped me. He held me on his shoulder while I lifted the grate, and from there..."

"Okay, okay. But the six-toe, where did you run into him?"

"I was in the place above my above, and I crawled around for a long time in the dark. Then I saw a light, and he was there with a guy with slightly darker skin, and eyes that always looked kind of closed. They let me have the suit when I said I wanted to go talk to Providers, and when I found some, I kind of got nervous, and ended up here."

"Okay." the Rubberwoman rubbed the bridge of her nose. "Okay, so that's useless. I don't know. You said you wanted to talk to the Providers now?"

Lenth tightened his lips and nodded. "Yeah. I think that's my next step in finding my missing Brother."

Not quite turning her back, the Rubberwoman went over to the panel of buttons. "Missing Brother? Is that why you were talking about death?"

"About dead? Yes. I miss him. So I want to see him. He became dead pretty suddenly, and it didn't seem pleasant. I hope he's doing okay."

The Rubberwoman paused and just shook her head slightly as she pressed a few buttons.

"What?" Lenth asked as a soft beeping sound came from the button panel.

"Lenth, that's sweet," the Rubberwoman said softly.

The beeping sound continued for a little longer, but eventually was replaced with a voice.

"Provider." the voice said.

"Yes, I have a stray Subject here," the Rubberwoman said.

"Are you in danger?" asked the Provider.

"I don't think so. He actually wants to talk to Providers, and he might have useful information about the killers you warned me about. He isn't one of them, but he has the suit."

For a moment there was no reply, only the smallest hiss of the speaker's noise. "We'll be there shortly."

And then complete silence.

Lenth and the Rubberwoman looked at each other expectantly. She gestured to Lenth a little. "You might make a better impression if you're not wearing the suit when they get here."

Lenth nodded silently. He found his heart to be pounding a little stronger as he shed the suit.

The Providers, the people who watched the Rubbermen. All his life they were out there, unknown to him, and now they were coming for him.

They controlled the man who controlled him and his Brothers. And they had Slim for some reason.

And now they were coming for him. They made Phil afraid, they made Six and Eyes afraid.

And now they were coming for him.

"I have to go up," Lenth said, trying not to shout. "Help me up the top, out there. Like I did above my grating. I can just go, I need to go!"

Lenth went to the door that led to the grating and pushed on it in vain. "What button opens it? Come on!"

The Rubberwoman just sighed. "No. You find a way further up? Then what? Where are you going that the Providers won't be? They're part of everything. You'll be fine. If you didn't kill anyone, you should be fine."

Lenth slumped against the door. "Should be." He slid down to sit, and the Rubberwoman want over to the pile where Lenth dropped the Rubberman suit. She began folding it. "Be polite. Be reasonable. If you run off clawing at closed doors, they're going to treat you accordingly."

He pulled his legs under himself to be more comfortable. "You know a lot about them? Fill didn't seem to know a lot. He didn't even know there was more 'up'."

"Phil?" the Rubberwoman asked as she stacked the boots and mask on top of the neat pile. "Was that your Manager?"

"Manager?"

The Rubberwoman tapped the folded suit. "Manager."

"Oh, Right. We just called him Rubberman. Yeah. Fill was nice enough once I finally met him."

"What happened to Phil?"

"When I left, he was fine."

"Did Phil help you?"

"Yeah."

The Rubberwoman nodded once slowly. "Hey. Do him a favour. If you can avoid it, don't tell the Providers that he helped you. In fact, don't tell them that you talked to him or anything. Can you tell them that he had no idea you were escaping?"

He could say that Spots helped him up where Phil had. That Spots had come up above the grating as well. Easy enough. "I think so," Lenth said, "Why? Would Fill get in trouble?"

"Almost certainly. Likely, they'd replace him."

"Replace? Like they did with my Brother Slim?"

The Rubberwoman shrugged. "While we're at it, let me get my suit on. If they ask, you just got here, you haven't been outside to my grating, and you never saw me out of my suit. We barely talked, and I called them as soon as I could." She spoke with an increasing tension that began to scare Lenth.

"What?" Lenth asked. "Why? Would *you* get in trouble?"

With only the mask left to put on, she shrugged again, but her eyes masked her trepidation badly. "Oh, you told me your name. Fair is fair. My name is Karen."

"Carin'." Lenth managed a slight smile. Obviously, her name was based on the word 'caring'. The people she grew up with must have known her to be very kind. "Good to know."

With her mask completing it all, the bulky suit made it impossible to determine that she was anything but a Rubberman.

"Good luck," She said with warmth that belied the mask's cold eyes.

They waited with nothing else to say for a few moments. Shortly, the door inside her bedroom opened. Three Providers emerged, as calmly as if they were heading to daily exercise. They each wore the same baggy yellow suits that he had seen on all Providers. Unlike the ones he had seen before, these Providers wore a helmet of sorts that concealed their heads and faces entirely.

The front was a large smooth panel that looked as dark as the eyes of a Rubberman mask, and the rest was a floppier material more like the rest of the suits.

Lenth picked up the neatly folded Rubberman suit and stepped up to the nearest Provider. "All right," Lenth said with a deep breath, "I'm ready to go." He turned to the Rubberwoman, sighed, and nodded to her once.

Chapter Eight

Eval

"So. We're not talking, then?" Lenth said to the three masked Providers. The only reply was the continued hum of the elevator. "I know you're people like me." He shifted his eyes around; at them, at the changing lights above the door, counting back down. "I mean, I assume as much. I guess you could be lumpy people. Uh...that is, females."

Lenth heard a tiny stifled laugh from one of them. Feeling a little braver since the mystery of the blackened Rubberman lenses was clarified, and having seen unmasked Providers before, he gathered the little bit of added nerve to push his luck a little. His nerves, and the silence pushed him into opening his mouth again.

He stared into the blackened window of the Provider who found his lumpy comment funny, and suggested, "I... I could just check. I could just have a grab and figure it out for myself."

His target leaned its head to the side, slowly shaking it.

"No?" Lenth said. "Maybe later?" He put his hands behind his back innocently and sighed. That was stupid. He suddenly felt lucky to have not been shocked for that.

Having seen under the masks of Rubbermen and Providers had taken away much of the mystery, and given Lenth a surge of confidence—confidence which began melting away as he realized the basic facts. *Yes, they're just people. But does that change anything for this situation?*

Eventually he felt the elevator stop, and the doors spread open into a bland concrete hall, marked with raw little imperfections, and wear of age. One Provider walked out, and the second nudged Lenth to go next. Providers number two and three followed behind.

This area was much like the place where Lenth had run into the unmasked Providers, except there seemed to be no one else around. The background sounds of activity were missing here. Lenth hadn't noticed it before, but he noticed its absence here. It made the place feel bigger. If he didn't have his escort, he would be tempted to run down a hallway to see how fast he could go.

Back home, there were no long hallways, and running was always a short trip before having to turn a corner, or jump over a bed.

After passing several doors, all identical other than a label at eye-level, the front Provider stopped at one and opened it for Lenth. Lenth looked at him, then turned to look at the two Providers behind him. Everyone stood silent for a moment. The front Provider knocked on the doorjamb to get Lenth's attention, then gestured through the doorway. The room inside was not terribly large. It had a chair welded to the floor. It was less solid than any seat he'd seen before, with four thin, separate legs instead of a solid block on one edge like at the work stations. It faced a pane of black glass, like the front of the Providers' hoods, except much, much larger.

Lenth wandered in, looking at the pane of glass, and was startled when he heard the door close behind him.

He was alone.

He went to the door, finding it locked. He knocked. No answer. Again. No answer. Maybe he'd be luckier with the pane of glass. He walked back over to it and raised his fist to give it a knock when a voice stopped him.

"Please don't." The voice that came was flat, and maybe a little irritated. And it just sounded strange, somehow.

"Ah. No need *now*, is there?" Lenth said "Um...I'm Lenth. How—"

"You can be seated," the voice interrupted.

Lenth scrunched his lips and looked at the chair. Fine. He sat. "So, where's Slim?"

"Lenth. You are here to give us information about the six-toed man, his associate, and their location."

Lenth tilted his head. "Well no, I suppose I could, but that is not why I am here. I'm here to find Slim."

There a brief moment of silence before the voice replied. "You must tell us about the six-toed man and his associate."

"If I tell you about Six and Eyes, you'll take me to Slim?"

"Tell us."

"I don't know if I trust people who hide their faces. You first."

There was another pause. "You can't be expected to know how important this is, but we...and by we, I mean you, me, and everyone, can't have a killer running around in the walls."

"What's a killer?" The Rubberwoman, Carin', had used that word. And 'kill'.

The voice sighed. "A killer is someone who kills. Who makes another person dead. And now you're going to ask me what *dead* is, aren't you?"

"Dead is dead. I keep hearing that, and I know Slim is dead now. I don't see why that's so important, or why it made him disappear."

The voice became a little softer in sympathy. "Dead people can't do anything. They don't talk, they don't move, they don't even think. They're done, they're over. It's much deeper than sleep, and they can never wake up."

Lenth stared for a while at the blank wall below the glass panel and tried to understand. "Never?"

"Never."

He let that sink in for a while. It hurt. He remembered trying to wake Slim up. He'd be like that forever? "Why?"

"People's bodies aren't perfect. They can get hurt in ways that they can't heal. A body fails sometimes, for various reasons. Eventually, they all fail."

Lenth slowly stood, still looking down, and held an arm across his chest. "And Slim?"

"We think there was a problem with his medicine. He may have had an allergic reaction to a new version of the usual kind of—"

Phil had mentioned medicine. "Medicine made Slim dead? Killed him?"

"It wasn't meant to happen. We didn't know that his..."

Walking backwards slowly, Lenth bumped into the back wall and began sliding down it. "You put the medicine in there?" he said weakly. "You killed him?" Lenth felt his shoulders cave inwards, his chest tight. "You killed my Brother...you killed Slim..."

"I'm very sorry. It wasn't meant to happen."

Lenth didn't reply, instead obeying the urge to curl up in the corner. He felt the tears building up, but they refused to give him the satisfaction of escape. He stared into nothingness, embracing slight escape through numbness.

Some time passed, and the voice remained silent for a long while. Lenth sought sleep, but sleep denied him as well.

"Are...are you hungry?" the voice asked quietly.

Lenth gave the glass pane a cold gaze. He still had food stashed in his sleeve, but it was rather squished. Not that it mattered much.

"Are you hungry, Lenth?" the voice repeated.

"Hungry?" Lenth muttered. "For medicine? Will you kill *me* too?"

"You've been having the same medicine and food since the day Slim died. It's not going to harm you."

Lenth sat up and stared at the glass panel. "No. I'm not hungry. I want to see Slim."

"I'm afraid you can't. The body is gone now, too."

Assuming that was part of death, Lenth just gave a frustrated little huff and turned his head to the door.

"Fine then. I guess I'll go home. I guess it's back to work as usual while I wait for another Brother to get dead."

"I'm afraid you can't. We'll have to find you a new home."

Lenth slammed his fist on the floor. *"Why? I live with my Brothers! They are my...my Brothers!"* He stood, defiantly staring at the glass.

Another pause from the glass pane before a reply. "Fine. Fine. But first, I answered your questions about Slim's death. Tell me about 'Six' and 'Eyes'. We believe they killed their Manager."

"Their Rubberman. If you find them, then what?"

"We won't kill them, if that's what you're worried about. We cannot afford to lose people. We will find some way to give them a home that they can fit in with, and hopefully be happy."

That sounded reasonable. He began to explain everything, starting with the escape from his home, leaving out Phil's involvement. He then described the directions he travelled as best as he could remember.

The voice asked several questions to try to get more specific. Some of the questions Lenth could answer, others he couldn't help with. Eventually, the voice seemed satisfied enough.

"That should do," it said.

"All right, then. Take me home."

"I'm afraid I can't do that. I'm truly sorry, Lenth."

Lenth strode over to confront the glass panel. *"You lied to me?"*

"I never really said that I could take you back. But yes, I guess it sounded like I was going to. I'm sorry, but finding the killer was too high of a priority, and-."

Lenth let out a roar and pounded both fists against the glass, over and over. *"I need to see my Brothers! You took Slim from me, and now you're taking them all?"*

"You know far too much for a Subject now, Lenth!"

"What does it matter? What am I going to do, knowing you're here?"

"This is the way it is. Subject level people can't know. It's forbidden. Besides, could you ever be content with your old life now?"

"Yes!" Lenth's answer resonated off the walls and he stood there, making his most determined face at the glass. He hoped he was staring directly into the face of whoever the voice belonged to, but the dark pane of glass itself was just as worthy of his contempt.

Eventually, the voice came again. "You can't." It spoke patiently, softly, but it was firm. "But there are choices to be had. More than you had before."

"But going home isn't one," Lenth said.

"Correct."

Lenth turned from the glass and walked to the back of the room. "So, what's to stop me from just going? Sneaking out when I find a way and just going home?" He knew the answer before he even finished asking.

"We'd know right away if you popped up in your old Unit."

"Right."

"And your Brothers would be compromised."

Lenth looked back to the glass. "Compromised? What do you mean?"

"Part of their value is in their ignorance. Their innocence."

Lenth glared at the glass. "Value? So am I less valuable now?"

"Arguably. But we can find you another way to contribute, as a favour. We could not accommodate more. The system has very little flexibility, especially after the trouble with 'Six', 'Eyes', and their Unit."

Lenth cooled down and looked at his feet. "Things are complicated above my old ceiling."

"You have no idea."

Chapter Nine

Gabe

Lenth was taken to another room on the same floor. The leading Provider pointed to an off-white table. This table was unlike any Lenth had ever seen. It wasn't attached to the floor, and it wasn't a big solid block. It had a matching chair, much like the one on the last room, except that it *also* wasn't attached to the floor.

Lenth picked the chair up by the back and marvelled at its freedom, turning it around at eye level.

"Hey, hey," said the Provider as he took off his concealing head-wear, "don't make things difficult. There's stuff in here that doesn't need wrecking. You're here, and not somewhere else, because...well, you seem kind of okay, so we might be able to find you a place."

Lenth put down the chair. "Oh, didn't mean anything by it. Just...loose chair! That's new!" He sat down carefully, not fully trusting furniture that was loose.

He glanced around the room. Compared to the spartan order of home, this place was a den of overbearing clutter. Several racks of shelves lined the walls. And they had random things on them, which were likely as loose as the chair. There were containers of at least three different sizes, and quite a few of those things like in Karen's closet, likely filled with those symbols.

It was only fitting that the unmasked Provider before him had hair sticking up all over his head. When the Provider put his hand through it, the hair was so long, it nearly hid his fingers.

While the Provider had his back turned, getting another of those loose chairs, Lenth copied the hand motion on his own head. At best, his own hair would have to be three times as long as it was now to even rise past the width of a finger.

The Provider sat down on the other side of the table and plunked one of those symbol-box-things down. "Call me Gabe, by the way."

"Gabe? What kind of name is that?"

Gabe smirked. "It's a name-name. It's not something that describes me, it's a regular name."

"Regular names *are* supposed to describe you," Lenth said.

"If you're a Unit Subject, sure. No one gives you names; you have to invent your own."

"Who gave you yours? And what does it mean?"

"Real names don't mean things. Mine was assigned to me, just for me, when I was little. The nursery Manager on duty when I was born picked it from the lists."

"Why didn't they give me one?"

Gabe leaned his head in sympathy. "You were going to be assigned Unit work. Intricate social interactions aren't required. In all honesty, you're lucky they teach bottom Subjects how to speak."

Lenth frowned at the tabletop. "I'm...I'm less."

Gabe shrugged. "I didn't want to put it as blunt as that..."

"How is that fair?" Lenth asked, frowning harder, not looking right at Gabe.

"It's not, in a lot of ways. But luck is luck. It could have been the other way around. It's just a matter of what jobs are predicted to be needed done when we were born. Subjects are actually the most common. Then Providers, which includes the nursery and medical, and I suppose the smallest group is the Unit Managers."

"You mean Rubbermen."

"Yeah. There's one of them to every four Subjects. It's a simple life, but a lot of them don't have nearly as much access to information as Providers. They don't need to worry about things that don't relate to working the Unit."

Lenth looked at the symbol-thing that Gabe had put on the table. Putting his hand on it, Lenth asked, "So, this thing. I've seen one before, in that...'woman' Unit. It's filled with symbols, stuck on those thin, floppy things inside?" He held a random page up.

"Yes. Those symbols are called letters, and when stuck to other letters, they make words. Want to learn how to read them? It takes quite some time."

"Is that the new purpose I'm supposed to have? Reading?"

Gabe smiled. "No, but it's a step. It makes other things easier, kind of like being able to talk does. I guess that's why they teach Unit Subjects language. Some communication is valuable for anyone."

Lenth tapped the book. "And this is *more* valuable?"

Smiling again, Gabe got up and walked over to a shelf, running his finger across the backs of a few dozen books. "It is one way that you become less 'less'."

"Then I'm in."

Gabe led Lenth to yet another room. Smaller, and more familiar. It had four seats that reminded him of the exercise stations back home, but these ones looked more comfortable, with thicker padding. Also, they had no apparent handles or bars for exercises. It did still have the headset attached by a jointed arm to the ceiling, and a cuff.

"Why the cuff?" Lenth asked as he seated himself.

"This one comes off whenever you want; don't worry."

"Then why put it on?"

"We want to get a fresh reading on your blood. You're going off the meds, uh... medicines from now on. Time to clean that stuff out of you."

Lenth looked up from the little panel of buttons on the chair he'd been toying with. "Uh...what kind of stuff is in me?"

Gabe smirked. "Well, you and your Brothers have had your sex drive suppressed since before puberty, mainly to keep life simple among your Brothers, among other things. Of course, this disqualifies you from certain other medications due to potential chemical comp—"

Gabe stopped talking, noticing the lost look on Lenth's face. "Uh...it's complicated."

"I get that. I've been noticing that a lot."

Gabe gave Lenth a sympathetic, if smarmy smile. "Baby steps, I guess." Gabe put the visor on. "Let me just start up your first reading lesson..." He reached to the little control panel on the chair and tapped various buttons for a few moments. "Right. Okay." He put the helmet onto Lenth's head. "Okay, Lenth. See the buttons I was pressing?"

"Yeah."

"You really only need to worry about these two buttons. That one will skip ahead a bit if you understand what it's telling you and are ready for the next one, and the other will go back. The one in between will stop it where it is, and can be pressed again to keep going."

Soon enough, Gabe left Lenth to his tier two education. As he sat there, the feel of the chair brought back hazy memories. Learning the sounds and meanings of words, leaning to talk, and learning numbers.

That much was all that a Unit Subject needed. But now he was being given more than even the numbers. One after another, he was shown letters and told the sound it made.

Each of the letters had two kinds for some reason, most of them with a big version and a small version which sometimes looked very different. Some of the letters made more than one sound, but this didn't seem to have anything to do with the size.

Lenth lost track of how many letters he had been Subjected to, and then something amazing happened. The letters came in quicker succession, while the names of them were spoken in unusual tones, to sound pleasing. Other sounds went with it. Sounds of...just sounds! Stimulating, beautiful sounds that seemed to carry the names of the letters along.

When it reached "zed", it ended. Lenth scrambled for the button to make it jump back, to hear it again. Half way through the second time, he started quietly humming along. Unconsciously, his head swayed to the rhythm.

Occasionally, he would fumble when the song ended, and started the next segment, but he was determined to know the song by heart. When Gabe came back and asked how it was going, Lenth put on his more noble expression, lifting the helmet towards the ceiling, and sang;

"Ay, bee, see, dee, ee, eff, jee, aych...aych... huh. Umm... Something, jay, kay, elle, en, em, oh, dee, kyu, arr, eff...no...that's not right..." He looked up at the paused screen in the helmet. "Arr, eff? Arr..."

"Ess," Gabe said. "You made some other errors too, but if you ask me, that's amazingly good for the amount of time you've had."

"I like the sounds!" Lenth said, nodding with a furrowed brow.

"Music?"

"If you say so!"

Gabe smiled and sang, "Row, row, row your boat, gently down the stream!"

Lenth laughed out loud. "There's more music? I guess that makes sense. What did that music mean?"

"I have no idea. A lot of music has totally made up words. And a lot of it has no words at all."

Lenth just smiled, shaking his head. He looked up at the helmet. "Is this my work now? How long do I have?"

"Right now? Right now I was thinking we should go eat. I know how long it's been since you've slept, so if you want to do that after, I can set you up."

Stroking a finger along the helmet, Lenth asked, "Well, after all that, can I do this more?"

Gabe nodded. "By all means."

Lenth followed Gabe back to a different elevator than before. The trip was only two lights up. The floor they came out on was very similar, except there were unmasked Providers walking the halls here and there still in the yellow outfits. They came to a very large room, with tables everywhere, and Providers seated randomly around.

"...Twenty-two, twenty-three!" Lenth whispered in awe.

"Twenty-three what?" Gabe asked.

"People! There are twenty-three people! Adding my Brothers, my Rubberman, the Rubberwoman, her four people, Six, Eyes, their surviving Brother...am I missing anyone? Oh, I...I had no idea there were this many people! And if I'm seeing right, like half of them are women! Just acting casual, as if hanging out with the men is an ordinary thing! And their skin! I mean, lots of these people have the same colour of skin as us, but some are kind of browner. That guy over there is a *lot* darker! What does *that* mean?"

Gabe snorted. "It just means he has darker skin. There's a fair amount of people here because this is a time when a lot of folks come and eat."

Lenth looked at all the empty seats. "You mean...there's even more people?"

"Oh, Lenth...you mean as in *everywhere*? All the people that there are?" Gabe shook his head slowly. "There's a lot more."

"What? Like how many?" Lenth followed Gabe to a dispenser counter, where the wall had food disks, a water outlet, and a cup, sticking up from a hole, upside down.

Gabe grabbed the cup, and the next popped up into place. "Hundreds of Providers," he said, filling his cup, "a little more than half that amount of Managers, and well over a thousand Subjects like you. Well, like you were. All in all, a couple thousand, I guess."

Staring into the wall, Lenth glazed over a little and tried to picture it. "That's got to be a lot of rooms...how far does it all go? The edge of everything?"

Gabe lazily looked back and forth as he grabbed some food, as if he could see through the walls. "Eh...quite a ways. I've walked across it all just for the sake of doing it. I haven't been all the way up and down, mind you. I don't have any business on your levels, or much farther up. Well, I've been as far up as the clinic. That's only a few floors up. No big deal, really."

As Gabe started to slowly head to a table, Lenth quickly gathered some food and water so he could catch up. "It's so *huge!*"

Gabe just tilted his head and shrugged as he chowed down. They got seated, and Lenth just looked around for a while. So many people. It was intimidating. Some of them took notice of Lenth and his blue Subject attire, but lost interest when they noticed his Provider escort.

"Are these all...are they all your Brothers?" Lenth asked in quiet awe.

"Huh?" Gabe looked around. "Oh, I get it...no. I guess they're 'friends'. Some more than others. I can't be expected to know everybody well."

Lenth continued to eat, pondering. "Hey, if I'm not a 'Unit Subject' anymore, am I a Provider now?"

"Well, no," Gabe said, "You're not a Provider. You might eventually become one. You're kind of in a grey area right now. There's some people who don't fit nicely into a category. You're...in transition, I guess."

"But I'm not a 'Manager', so that leaves 'Provider'."

Gabe smirked and shook his head. "If you really want to have a tidy little label, sure, whatever. But don't get overconfident about it. You might end up back in a Unit in the end, anyway."

Lenth was quiet after that semblance of a threat, even if Gabe delivered it in a friendly tone. "But you said I knew too much to go home."

"Your home is not the only part of the Unit level."

"But I would still know things, even if I were put in another area."

"In some places, it's okay to know things. In some, you forget."

"Forget? I don't think there's much chance of me forgetting what I've seen!"

"There's ways to help people forget. Or so I've heard."

Once the meal was finished, Lenth was eager to go back to learning, but Gabe convinced him to go with him for a change of clothes. They ended up at a clothing and laundering room.

"You're a...large/tall, it looks like?" Gabe said, eyeing Lenth up and down. "Try one on. The regular, not the containment type."

Lenth stripped down on the spot, crumbs from his old stash tumbling down from his sleeve. He put on the body suit Gabe suggested and gave it a little wiggle. It fit much looser than his old clothes, but they were very comfortable.

"Lenth, there's changing rooms right over there," Gabe murmured. A Provider tending the laundry nearby was already back to his work after witnessing Lenth changing, but his amused grin was still in place.

"Huh," Lenth said, looking over to the little door. "What do the rooms change into?"

Gabe rolled his eyes. "No, a small room you can go into so you can have a little privacy when you change clothes."

Privacy? What was that? "All right, I'm dressed like a Provider now. Can I go back to the learning chair now?"

"Yes, but there's another thing to show you." As they headed back, Gabe pointed out a room with dozens of exercise machines, much like the ones at Lenth's Unit.

When they got back to the 'learning chair room', Gabe showed Lenth that it was attached to a room with sleeping quarters for four and a shower. Just one shower, though. Learning chairs for four people, beds for four, and one shower.

This struck Lenth as quite peculiar. But he tried not to think too long on it. Sharing this single shower with his Brothers was a horrifying thought. And Joints naked! Ugh! Lenth had seen that before; it wasn't pretty.

Lenth accounted for all the things his old home had and compared them to what he now had here. The new location also supplied bed, shower, work (in the form of learning), food was in that big room, and exercise in the gym.

No Brothers though. No Slim.

Gabe went back to the doorway into the main hall and leaned on the jamb. "Okay. You'll be okay for a few hours, yeah?"

Lenth patted the learning chair with a smile. "You bet!"

"Okay then. I'll check in on you in a while, and if you have any issues, just hit the button." Indeed, there was a small, nondescript button by the door.

"Or I can just go find you," Lenth said.

"No, this door will be locked."

Lenth frowned at Gabe and at the button. "Locked? Why?"

"You're still kind of an…anomaly, you know?" Gabe scrunched his mouth and looked down the hall. "I like you just fine, but frankly, we don't know you. We know you didn't kill anyone, but other than that, you're a…you're really lucky you're being given the chances you are."

Lenth was stunned, and stepped back, stumbling against the chair. "I don't understand."

"You broke out of your place!" Gabe said with frustration. "You messed up routine, you're not doing your normal job, your Brothers are facing having to get used to another new Brother, your Manager is under investigation, you mingled with suspected killers, and you can't see why we don't want you running around loose?"

"Another new Brother? I'm…being replaced?" The thought of a new person replacing him, just like Spots replaced Slim, was a heavy blow all on its own. Replaceable, disposable, interchangeable. And to make it worse, it reminded him that he left his Brothers. That he wouldn't see them again.

Gabe left quietly while Lenth was deep in self-pity. It was the sound of the door closing and locking that snapped him back to his senses.

He hadn't escaped anything.

And now he was alone.

Chapter Ten

Eyes Witness

This new place, locked as it was, still had to have an opening. Lenth clambered up onto the back of one of the learning chairs, pulled the arm of the helmet down, and used it as leverage to reach the ceiling.

Nope, this one was much firmer than the one he'd pushed up to escape from Phil's floor. Lenth went on, inspecting every wall for signs of a movable or even breakable panel. Nothing seemed to even hint at the possibility.

Defeated, he decided to take advantage of a learning chair. Settling in, he pulled down the helmet, and started it again. It sang the letter song again, but Lenth didn't hum along, or watch, really. His confinement was distracting.

After the song, the images went on to things and the words for them, spelled out, going over each letter.

Cup.
Nose.
Foot.
Door.
Food.

On it went, with images of things he knew, as he knew them. It was difficult to pay attention. Partly because he was tired. Comfortable in the learning chair, and unmotivated to move, he let himself fall asleep.

Gabe entered quietly, but it was enough to wake Lenth. Enough that he opened his eyes. The learning chair was still prattling on. Having gone through a selection of nouns, then verbs, it was on to adjectives. Lenth slapped a sleepy hand at the buttons to pause it and shoved the helmet up.

"You're awake!" Gabe said. "You were out for quite a while. Makes sense, I guess. Hungry?"

"Hm? Uh, waking up, give me a second."

The open door was behind Gabe. It wouldn't be too hard to shove past and run for it, but the sounds of other Providers nearby discouraged such heroics.

"Sure thing."

Lenth groggily wandered over by the shower. He didn't feel like a shower, nor to keep his escort waiting too long, so he just went to the toilet and spritzed a little water in his face.

"Okay, let's go."

Breakfast was as expected, but Gabe was being a little quieter than usual until about halfway through.

"Hey, Lenth. The others found the place you described. It looks like you were telling the truth about where you met Six and Eyes."

"Yeah, so?" It hadn't occurred to Lenth that anyone could have thought that he was lying. It hadn't occurred to him to lie.

"Well, that means your trustworthiness has been improved by quite a bit."

Lenth shrugged. "Well, good, I guess. What does that mean?"

"For one thing, I'm going to be giving your learning chair a little more data access. It won't be a ton of use until you can read better. We might also start looking at long-term jobs for you."

"Like a Provider kind of job? I'd be a Provider?"

Gabe wiggled his head back and forth a little with a nod. "Yeah, pretty much, I guess. It could be learning simple repairs, running regular facility inspections, or food construction. We'll see what job's good for you and what's available."

"Neat." Not that it sounded a great deal better than his old life. Any of those jobs were sure to soon be as tedious as his old one.

Gabe gobbled down his last chunk of food. "All right. Finish up, and we can have our first department visit."

With a short elevator ride up a few floors, Gabe and Lenth walked into the clinic. Colour seemed to be forbidden here. Even signs of age and wear seemed missing from the walls. A Provider dressed in white made himself busy, going from one area to the next quietly. The people he was attending to were hidden behind curtains. More of this 'privacy' thing.

The white-clad man spotted Gabe and Lenth from across the long room and raised a hand to acknowledge them.

"He's a doctor," Gabe quietly explained. "If you get sick or hurt, it's his job to fix you up."

"Oh. I've never been that sick, or that badly hurt," Lenth said.

"You probably have been. Your Manager would have put you to sleep, you'd be treated here, and then put back before being allowed to wake up."

Lenth's eyes widened. "I've...I've been here before?"

"More than likely. If you really care, I could look up your file and see how many times."

"Then, the people here," Lenth said, pointing at the rows of curtained-off stations, "They're all Unit Subjects?"

"Probably about half."

It was then that the doctor walked up. "Hello. What seems to be the problem here?" He lowered his head a little and peered into Lenth's eyes, mistaking his stunned expression for an ailment.

"We're both fine, doc," Gabe said. "This is the Subject that was helping find that killer."

"Ah. Come this way, then." the doctor said. He led Gabe and Lenth to the end of the rows of curtains and off to the left. They went through a door with a single word on it. Lenth was proud to be able to identify several letters. M, O, R, *oops, no time to try to read* if he wanted to keep up.

This smaller room was equally colourless, but in greys instead of white. It may have just been the lighting, but Lenth felt colder here.

"He only got here a couple of hours ago, but he's been dead a bit longer than that." The doctor grabbed the handle of a metal drawer in the wall and started to pull it open. It kept coming, and coming, and coming, until the drawer was longer than a person is tall. Which worked out pretty well, as there was a person in it.

The body was covered, but Lenth could tell what it was. Gabe pinched the top end of the cover and turned to Lenth. "Okay, I want you to tell me if you recognize this person."

Lenth nodded.

Gabe pulled the cover down enough to reveal Eyes' head. The side of his head wasn't shaped right anymore. Where it was dented inward, the skin was black and blue, with red cracks in the middle.

Lenth's jaw dropped as he backed away. Eyes was as silent and still as Slim had been the last time Lenth had seen him.

"Dead?" Lenth asked in a quiet squeak.

"Yes." Gabe said softly. "I'm sorry, I guess I should have warned you."

"Massive head trauma," The doctor said. "As far as we can tell, someone just grabbed him and hit his head against the floor repeatedly. The place he was found was quite a—"

"Yes, I heard," Gabe said, interrupting.

Lenth stared at Eyes for a long while and found himself remembering being gassed to sleep the night Slim died. "So it's true. This happens to everyone."

"Do you know him?" Gabe asked.

"Yeah. Yeah, that's Eyes."

"Are you sure?" Gabe asked. "I mean, you're probably right, but there *are* other people out there with eyes kind of like his. I know you probably haven't seen many—"

"It's him."

Gabe nodded to the doctor, who covered Eyes back up and closed the drawer. He excused himself and went back to tend to patients.

"There's evidence that Six killed him," Gabe said. "It suggests that Six was also the one to kill their Manager."

Lenth looked at all the other closed drawers. "Is...is Slim here?"

Gabe sighed and shook his head. "He was, for a little while."

"Then what?"

"We all have to help society, even in death." Gabe sighed again. "It's not a pleasant thing, really. Eyes will go the same way soon enough. No one feels anything after they die, but it's still unpleasant for the rest of us."

"Where?" Lenth's distant gaze began to harden. "How? What?"

Gabe took a few steps out of the morgue, and called to the doctor. "I'm using your terminal for a second."

"Sure," came the reply.

While Lenth watched with quiet irritation, Gabe tapped at a small panel of buttons. A nearby screen belched numbers and letters too quickly for Lenth to make any sense out of, but Gabe seemed satisfied. "Good. Okay, let's go see the ladies."

Six lay in the darkness, the tight space between two floors. He was about as far from the fight as he could navigate safely.

Stupid Eyes. Stupid Eyes with his stupid eyes. Six had to kill him. Bad enough that Eyes was always messing up, risking them getting caught all the time, but when he kept bringing up his idea about going and talking to the Providers... that made Eyes too big of a risk.

He had begged. Eyes said they should split up and go their separate ways. For a moment, Six had considered it. It was still too much of a risk.

Now Eyes can't talk.

Oh, the noises he made, gasping and choking, while Six held him by the neck and hit his head against the floor. If the fool had just accepted it, he could have died quietly, but no. He had to make it a struggle.

And now he was dead. He didn't complain after that. So strange now. When his Rubberman came crashing down onto their Brother, this was a new thing. This was death. When he finished what Eyes had started on the Rubberman, this was also death.

It wasn't overly easy, but it was simple. And the Providers he had killed? All right, one wasn't too necessary. Eyes just wanted to know if they died the same way.

They did, and Eyes seemed almost as interested in it. The time after that, Eyes was grateful even. They had been caught taking food, and there was only one thing to do about it.

The next wasn't so cut and dry, but it was a matter of safety. The last one was...well, there wasn't much reason at all, but it was such a thrill! And that was around when Eyes got whiny.

Eyes didn't see the justice involved. He, nor Six, had much experience with the word, but Six felt it. Felt outrage for all the Providers, keeping all the Subjects working in ignorance. Keeping them at arm's reach with their rubber pawns, letting those rubber pawns do... what they do.

Killing them all would be ideal. But there were so many. So, so many, Six didn't even know how to start counting them.

It was a shame that Eyes couldn't see what had to be done in the face of this injustice. A partner was very useful, before it became a liability. But now he was doing the forever sleep. *Death is mercy.*

Too good for the Providers.

Too good for the Rubbermen.

If only there was a way to make them suffer. To put them to work, perhaps. But how? To give the Unit Subjects a turn on top, and the Providers a turn being trapped, worked, and regulated with shocks.

And the other thing. The other thing cannot be forgiven.

Chapter Eleven

Girl Stuff

Lenth and Gabe arrived at Karen's room. Karen had been asleep, but woke when the upper door opened.

"What's going on?" she asked.

Lenth was stunned to see her out of her Rubberman suit. Seeing the women Subjects from a distance before was intriguing, but seeing Karen in her normal clothes, close enough to touch, was nearly bewildering. He decided that lumpy was indeed very good.

"We won't be long. No problems," Gabe said. He was wearing the Provider's full contamination suit, his face concealed.

Lenth had been fully equipped as well, but lifted his mask to look Karen in the eye. "Hi. It's me." Karen's eyes lit up.

Gabe grabbed the edge of Lenth's mask and pulled it back down. "You're supposed to keep these on," he said in a grumpy voice.

"Why?" Lenth asked.

"Lenth?" Karen said with a half-smile. "New clothes?"

"Coming here was a mistake," Gabe groaned. He turned to Karen. "They're asleep?"

"Y-yes. Why?"

"Just trying to explain a few things to Lenth. Stay here. Both of you stop talking to each other."

Lenth was busy ogling Karen from behind his opaque mask and only gave a patronizing nod.

"You!" Gabe stuck a finger out at Karen. "You didn't see under a Provider's mask, am I clear?" His tone was less than menacing, only speaking out of procedure.

Karen nodded.

"You," Gabe turned to Lenth. "Come with me and keep quiet. I'm going to gas them, but keep quiet anyway."

As they passed the panel of buttons, Gabe pressed a few before pressing the ones to open the door to the grating.

"Gas them?" Karen asked. "I try to avoid that. But you're the Provider, whatever!"

Lenth silently followed behind Gabe. There was a quiet hiss, but it ended shortly. Gabe led Lenth in the direction that he knew as 'work', but there were no stations like he was used to.

Instead, there was a vast, vast area, much larger than the rest of Karen's domain combined. It was very bright, and very warm. The lights attached to the grating underfoot, shining down to the Subject's level, were different and large, with wide metal plates. Row after row of standing...'things' sat below. The tops were green and chaotic, held up by greyish, roughly-shaped...pipes? In the middle of each cluster of green, one big pipe, about forty centimetres wide, reached to the dark floor. At the top of the big pipe hung clusters of yellow roundish shapes.

Gabe pointed at them, and spoke quietly. "These are trees. Papaya trees. The yellow things are the papayas. They're one of the things used to make our food. Without these, no food. No food, we die. Everyone."

"It's so much!" Lenth said, looking out across the vast collection of these...'trees', as Gabe called them.

"This isn't the only room like this. They grow really slowly. We need more than this single room can make alone. There's also other rooms that grow other things that we need. The women here take care of these ones and collect the papayas."

Lenth was in awe. The air here smelled unlike anything he had smelled before. "Why didn't me and my Brothers do something like this?"

"You maintained filters. They help keep the air clean. That's a whole other story. We can't waste anything, which is why I brought you here. See the dirt?"

"Where?"

"The floor. You could grab a handful of it and toss it around if you were so inclined. It's also deep. The trees are about as big under the surface as they are on top, and they need that dirt to live. And we have to keep the dirt reasonably fresh. We have to make new dirt by adding compost. New dirt, sort of."

"The trees turn 'dirt' into food?"

"Yeah. That's a little simplified, but yeah."

Lenth nodded. "And we need to get them fresh dirt to eat. We feed them, they feed us."

"We do," Gabe said. "The compost we add is made out of a lot of things. Our crap, for one."

"Ew."

"Parts of trees and other plants that we don't use for food. Plants that die. Everything that can die..." Gabe stopped talking. He lifted his mask and looked to Lenth sorrowfully.

Lenth took off his own mask and knelt on the grating. He stared at the dirt and his eyes glazed over. "Slim..."

Gabe sighed. "Not quite yet, but eventually."

Lenth curled forward with a gasp.

"Oh, oh, no," Gabe said. "If you're going to throw up, do it into your mask or something."

Lent held a hand out, and stared at the size of the orchard. So many trees, so much dirt. "No...I'm. I'm okay. I just...it's all of us, right?"

Gabe helped Lenth to his feet. "We all help in this way after we die. And help those who come after us. It's how we all go on."

Lenth laid down, and curled up a little. "I..."

"I know," Gabe said. "That's how death works. It ends up being life again, but in a pretty roundabout way. Let's go, we can't stay here too long."

"Do the women know?" Lenth slowly got up. "Does Carin' know?"

"Maybe, Karen used to be a Provider, and many Providers know, but it's not really a level of knowledge that Rubbermen generally need."

By the time they got back to Karen's room, Gabe had put his helmet back on. He didn't pester Lenth to do the same, reconsidering enforcing the procedure in this matter against an ex-Provider. Karen was sitting in bed reading when they arrived. She stood up, stricken by the look on Lenth's face.

He was comforted to see Karen, until a moment later he realized that eventually, even she would die, and be made into fresh dirt. His distant gaze reinforced itself as Gabe went to Karen's button panel.

Karen put her hand on Lenth's arm. "Is everything all right?"

Lenth forced a meagre smile and put his hand over hers. "I guess it has to be."

"It's me. Let me out," Gabe said into the panel.

"Okay." came the response. The back door clicked, then pushed towards them by a few centimetres.

"Thanks." Gabe said. He walked by Lenth and Karen, opening the back door further. He looked back at them and muttered, "That's not good."

"What isn't?" asked Karen.

"Nothing, forget it," Gabe said. "Lenth, let's get going."

A moment passed and Lenth drew away from Karen, her fingers sliding off his arm slowly as he did so.

"Nice seeing you again, Lenth," Karen said softly.

As Lenth and Gabe left, Gabe frowned slightly as he ensured the door sealed behind them.

Gabe and Lenth didn't talk much on the way home. When Lenth went into his home, the door locked behind him. He thought that his new 'trusted a bit more' status would have won him more freedom. Maybe it was an oversight by Gabe. But right now, Lenth didn't care.

He sat at the learning chair and found it difficult to get motivated enough to turn it on. He went to the shower instead.

Under the warm water, he decided to get his mind off of the fates of the dead. His mind slipped back to Karen almost immediately. He wanted more of Karen. He wanted her to touch him again.

Feelings he didn't understand or bother to analyse seeped into his head slowly, pervasively. He imagined what it would be like holding her, and to be held in return. Tender thoughts turned into something alien to him. Something that made his heart pound.

He put his hands on the wall of the shower and pressed against it, as if trying to reach through the walls for her comfort. He hung his head and opened his eyes to see something else that wanted comfort.

It had never stood like that before! Startled, he looked at it, then poked it softly. Well, that didn't hurt at all. He grabbed it.

Woah, what? Hey, that's not normal!

He reached up to press the button that would blast him with warm air to dry off, then hastily put his clothes on. His abhorrent appendage was still sticking out firmly! It made his clothing look ridiculous! This wasn't good!

Walking carefully, he pressed the button by the door that would purportedly summon Gabe. It made a little buzz.

What to do now? He couldn't be standing there with this...thing protruding. He sat on one of the learning chairs and found he could position himself so that his malady wasn't so apparent. Every time his clothing rubbed against it, he was confused be the sensation.

Thankfully, by the time Gabe showed up, the swelling had gone down to normal.

"Hi Lenth."

"Uh, hi. It's better now, but I wonder if maybe I should go to the doctor."

Gabe leaned in, as if his brow was pulling down on him. "What's wrong? What happened?"

Lenth indicated the general area of his groin with both hands. "It swelled up, and felt really weird."

Biting his lower lip, Gabe tried to restrain a laugh. "Oh. Okay. Well, that's good!"

"Good? I don't think that's a good thing!"

Gabe put his fist against his mouth to repress himself. "No, no, it means your old meds are out of your system. That was faster than I expected."

Lenth's eyes widened. "I was taking medication that kept me from swelling up? Why would I want to stop that kind of medication? *What's going to swell up next? This is horrible!*"

"Calm down, calm down," Gabe said, putting his hands on Lenth's shoulder. "It's only that part that swells up like that. And for good reasons. The meds prevented it to keep you out of trouble. About half the male Subjects are on that med."

"Will it happen again?"

"Probably at least once a day, when you wake up."

"How can I prevent it?" Lenth asked, wide-eyed.

"Lenth, Lenth, it's *natural*, and you'll get to like it."

"How would you know? Wait...does *yours* do that?"

"Yup!"

Lenth eyed Gabe carefully. "Can I see?"

"*No!*" Gabe staggered back, guarding his groin area with his hands, as if Lenth could see through his clothes, or was liable to reach out and grab.

"Huh? Why not?" Lenth asked.

"Wow, some of you Subject types really have no concept of privacy, do you? It's not polite to... aw, I can't believe I'm explaining this to a full grown adult. That is a private area. You don't just go asking people randomly about them, and you don't go showing them to other people. Doctors can look for health reasons, but other than that, it's off limits."

Lenth absorbed for a second, then shrugged. "All right, so... why does it do that?"

Gabe shook his head. "Okay, *this*, I don't have to explain. There's a lesson for that on the learning chair. Ugh. Give me a second to find it." Gabe tinkered with the controls of the learning chair, searching through menus, and found the appropriate lesson. "Okay Lenth, have a seat, watch this, and if you have any other questions, ring the door button."

"Uh, all right." Lenth got seated and Gabe let himself out.

With a similar visual style as the exercise guides he used to watch, Lenth was presented with minimalistic figures of a male and a female, colour coded blue and red. As the calm, dispassionate voice explained, Lenth watched the figures engage in a strange activity. Then a close-up of the male part urinating white shapes that each looked like a ball with a wiggly bit out the back.

This wiggly thing and its peers went on a journey to another circle, and one of the wiggly things went into the circle.

"And thus, fertilization is accomplished." the voice proclaimed. The view cut to the female standing there. The voice told of time passing, and the woman became larger around the midsection. Very large. This swelling issue was apparently much more of a problem for women, and they caught it from men! Now, something called a baby was in her.

"And this concludes the basic educational lesson on fertilization and sexuality."

A menu popped up with several options, none of which Lenth could read very well. T...h...e...B...he managed to figure out "T'he burt-h-ee-nn-guh Pr-oh-kess", "Kohntrasehpt-eye-on", and a few others.

All right, he needed Gabe. He pressed the door button, and it was not long before Gabe arrived.

"So? What do you think?"

"I...if I put my...into a woman's...she gets swollen and something called a baby grows in her? That sounds unpleasant and dangerous!"

Gabe chuckled. "Uh, yeah, some of it is, but babies...they're young people! They come out and grow up to be...well, us!"

Lenth could barely remember being a lot smaller, but small enough to fit in another person? "Well, I'm not going to be doing *that!*"

With a smirk, Gabe fiddled with the controls more. "There, watch some of this. I'm gonna leave again. Just watch some of this, and see how you feel after."

Lenth peered at him with suspicion, but Gabe just smiled back as he left. "Oh, and don't feel bad if what you see makes you think of your buddy Karen! Ha, I wouldn't blame you at all."

Karen? But Karen's a woman, and she was nice. She was very nice! Lenth didn't want to think of her suffering as her body swelled and a human started living in her. Bracing himself for horror, Lenth put the visor helmet back on and played the new lesson.

He saw a room with a bed and little else. A woman and a man were there. Not simplified iconic images, but real people. And they started touching each other, and pulling each other's clothes off. *A woman! Without clothes! Startling and fascinating! The front swollen parts seemed to be ...well, what...? And now...*the man was suffering from the same swelling that Lenth had earlier!

The two people were talking to each other in low tones, with sounds that implied pleasure and strangely serious facial expressions. *What is he doing to her front bumps? She likes it at any rate. From the sounds of it, she likes it a whole lot!*

Lenth realized his swelling was returning. He shifted his clothes around a bit so that the waistband kept his swelling from protruding in such an undignified way.

The man in the lesson seemed quite proud. *What is he doing with it? What is she doing with it? That's not where the other video said it goes! He really likes it anyway!*

The duo went on and on, doing odd things to each other. Despite each activity being repetitive in their own ways, Lenth was entranced. He felt hot, his breathing was heavy, and that stupid swollen bit, well...stayed swollen.

When it was over, Lenth just stared into the screen. It was so...wrong. But fascinating. He thought about making it start again, but no. He decided not to. Not right away. He needed to talk to Gabe. He went over to the door button and pressed it in a mental daze.

"So?" Gabe asked when he arrived.

Lenth didn't make eye contact, just rubbed his chin. He then pointed abruptly at the learning chair. "Those people..." he said.

"Yes?" Gabe asked with a smirk, "What about them?"

Still avoiding eye contact, Lenth slowly shook his head. "Those people were having fun at that, weren't they?"

"Quite a lot of fun."

"I...wait a second," Lenth muttered. "Can *I* do that? Like, with Carin'? Or some other woman?"

"Wow, eager, are you?"

"No, no, no," Lenth went to sit down, waving his hands in the air. "No, I don't want to, that's a little too weird for me. I'm just trying to understand."

Gabe shrugged. "Well, yeah, you technically are capable of those things. But ideally, with a woman you love. And if you're not wanting to help create a baby, there's ways to prevent it, and of course she has to be consensual, and —"

"No!" Lenth yelled, "I would never do that to Carin'! With the big swelling body thing? That's horrible!"

Gabe sighed. This was going to take a while.

Chapter Twelve

Understand

Lenth's journey into literacy was going well. In a matter of days, he could instantly recognize hundreds of words and figure out nearly any other. Silent letters, and the ones that made several different sounds were still infuriating, though.

His access to lessons has been increased, and he was free to browse many lessons. Some he found interesting focused on farming and food production. It was still odd to think that his food was made of eight different things!

Even odder to think that the clothes he was wearing right now came from a plant, which came from dirt, which came from—among many other things—dead people. That thought led Lenth into an odd mix of sorrow, revulsion, and harmony.

He also learned more of the things that Providers did. Managing the water, air and heat, repairing things that broke, and making requests to someone called "the Messenger".

On a few rare occasions, the Messenger would bring things. Things that none of the Unit Subjects made. Things like learning chair screens and clothing. Even Rubberman suits, as well as the Providers' containment suits.

The Messenger has been different people over the years. There wasn't a lot of information about them, but they were highly, highly respected.

Every now and then, Lenth browsed through the... the other lessons, with the men and women doing things. They were getting less shocking and more interesting all the time. They still caused that swelling, though. And somehow thoughts of Karen intruded as well.

Despite this, studies in literacy continued to inch along.

Gabe came to Lenth, who was half way through a set of bench presses in the gym. "Do you want to see one of your Brothers?" Gabe asked in a subdued tone.

"What?" Lenth said, sitting up. "Really? Wait...one?"

Gabe grimaced. "It's the old one. Joints. He's had a stroke."

"What? What did he stroke, and why does it—"

"It's a medical problem. The Manager saw something was going wrong, gassed everyone, and called for help."

Lenth stood with alarm. "What? What's he...how is he?"

"He's stable," Gabe said, putting his hand on Lenth's shoulder. "He should be okay, but he's sleeping right now, up in the clinic. With one of the doctors."

"Let's go. I want to see him," Lenth said with resolve.

"You should know that you won't be able to speak with him. He has to stay unconscious—asleep—until he's returned."

Lenth sighed, already walking. "And the others?"

"The other three Brothers will be kept asleep also."

"You mean two other," Lenth said. "Blue and Spots."

"Lenth..." Gabe said as he pressed the elevator button.

Lenth lowered his head. "I've been replaced. I forgot that. Huh. So it's already happened."

Nothing was said until the elevator arrived. A Provider came out and passed them by as they went in.

"I mean, it makes sense. Look how fast Slim was replaced." They stared at the doors as they went up and said nothing until they got to the clinic. They came to Joints' bed. A cuff was on Joints' arm, and a nearby screen kept a record of his various statistics.

Lenth took his hand. "Hey old man," he said. Now with understanding of what came after 'old', the term offended Lenth a little. Old led to death, and compost. Nothing of Joints' personality, smile, or voice would remain. Just a final duty for the food supply and memories.

"He can't hear y—"

"*I know!*" Lenth scowled at Gabe. "I know. I... so, what, does he get replaced?"

"No. His recovery is going well. He might have to take a much easier exercise routine for a while, and he'll be on some other medications, but as long as he can function in the Unit, he'll go back. Besides, your Unit has had enough upheaval lately."

Lenth stared at Joints' face. "Why did this happen to him?"

"Age. Maybe triggered by stress, maybe."

"Did...did I cause this? By leaving?" Lenth leaned over to call down the hall to the doctor. "*Hey! Did I cause this?*"

"Can't think like that, Lenth," Gabe said.

"Why not? What else would be giving him stress? They have no idea if I'm even alive!" Lenth looked to Joints again. "I can't even send a note back with him, he can't read any better than I could." Lenth got up and paced about a little. "Put both of us in a small room, wake him up, and let me talk to him, then gas him again, and put him back."

"Lenth, no, we can't do that. He'd be compromised. He'd invalidate the work."

Lenth shot Gabe a fresh glower. "How would seeing me make it any harder for him to clean out filters?"

"Not that work. The tests."

"Tests?"

"Medication tests."

"One of these tests..." Lenth said, "one of them was what killed Slim, right?"

Gabe nodded. "Correct," he said meekly.

"Well did he at least die *right* for your test?" Lenth yelled. "*Are you happy with how that turned out?*"

"I don't know," Gabe said. "I really don't. Providers don't control the testing."

Looking first blankly at Gabe, then sliding his gaze to the ceiling, Lenth said under his breath, "There...there's more up? There's someone else?"

Gabe sighed and looked up as if he expected to see them. "Yeah. We keep our people fed, alive, and on the tests, and they give us the things we can't make ourselves."

"The Messenger..." Lenth said.

"You've been learning more than just porn, I see." Gabe smirked momentarily. "The Messenger just brings the things down. They don't talk about from where."

"Who are they?"

"There's a theory..." Gabe said.

"Go on...?"

"Some say that somewhere up there is another...world. Something older than this. A long time ago, according to the theory, anyway, there were thousands of thousands of thousands of people there. Millions of people. Do you know what a million is?" Lenth nodded, then Gabe continued. "They built incredible things. They invented everything we have here, and kept bigger better things for themselves. And worse things."

"Worse?" Lenth muttered. "Worse than turning your Brothers into dirt so that you can eat?"

"War."

"What's that?" Lenth asked.

"I've only read about it. It's when one huge group of people really hates another huge group, and they hurt each other. Kill each other."

Lenth smirked a little. "That doesn't make a lot of sense."

"I've read things," Gabe said with a look and a tone that wiped away Lenth's smirk. "Things that don't make much sense at all. A place without a ceiling, people ripped like cloth. People by the thousands. Torn, burnt. By tools that I don't understand."

Lenth scoffed lightly. "Whatever that was that you read...it must be written by someone as a joke. A dumb, mean joke." Lenth waited for Gabe to agree, or at least entertain the idea.

"No," Gabe said instead. "I figured that at first too, but there's just too many things that point to a huge war in the past. It just got worse and worse. The people before, up there; they must have been some kind of...I don't know."

"But wait," Lenth said. "If they're so awful, why do they send us things that we need?"

"Maybe they don't." Gabe shrugged. "Maybe they all finally killed each other off. Maybe it's just the Messenger, finding things and bringing them to us."

Lenth glanced at Joints lying there, breathing slow but steady. "So do you think that we... the Providers, the Subjects, the Managers... do you think we're what's left of those millions of people?"

Gabe sighed and looked around. "I don't know. I have no idea. It all seems pretty farfetched. A lot of it makes an odd kind of sense after a while, but... a place with no ceiling?"

Lenth's smirk returned. "Okay, but let's pretend that's true. What would be the point of us being in *this* place?"

"I don't know about you, but I don't see any wars in here. Maybe we're protected here. And if they did all kill each other, maybe it will be our job to go back there and... and put people there. Oh, which reminds me, have you gotten your head around this human reproduction thing?"

A little blonde girl's fist flew as hard as it could to the little face of a girl with black hair. No injury could be seen on the four-year-old, but she wailed. She wailed with a volume and pitch beyond Lenth's imagining. She wailed as if it were the greatest pain and indignity she'd suffered. And it was. At least today.

The assailant recoiled. Two innocent bystanders looked upward as a familiar figure plodded across the ceiling grating. "Rubberman," one of the girls mumbled. By this age, they had been taught that word by the learning machines.

The aggression in the blonde girl's face gave way to fear, and she stepped back from the dark-haired girl. "I'm sorry!" the blonde said. "I'm sorry!" Her voice squeaked as the pleaded, and the dark haired girl stepped forward. She hugged the blonde girl and said, "It's okay. It already barely hurts. But don't do that, okay? It's not good. You'll get shocked."

From the other side of a wall, unseen by the girls, Gabe and Lenth observed.

"Those young ones have a lot of hair," Lenth said.

"The girls don't have to shave their heads like the boys," Gabe said, "Kind of a weird rule, but there ya have it. It makes it easier to tell they're not boys, I guess."

"Girls?" Lenth looked at Gabe, then back towards the girls. "Girls? Like young women? They aren't lumpy like women."

"That happens when they get older. Like around the same age where you start growing hair in places," Gabe said.

"When I...oh! Huh. So, they came out of a women who did sex? Where are they?"

Gabe shrugged. "They did their job, and that's done. They're probably back at usual tasks. Doesn't matter. These girls have each other. They're Sisters, and their Manager takes care of the things they need. Their exercise machines also teach them stuff like basic language. You probably wouldn't remember being in a place like this."

"Of course I do! It hasn't been *that* long since I left home."

"I don't mean your old home. I meant your nursery. This isn't their Unit. This is where they learn the basics. Walk, talk, and follow what the Rubberman leads them to do. They'll get moved to their Unit, and if it's done right, they won't even notice."

"I..." Lenth tried to dig into his oldest memories. He learned a lot of words back then, and most of them, he didn't have a use for until he left his Unit. All but forgotten. The past was foggy, as the past tends to be, but he couldn't think of anything that suggested being somewhere other than his Unit when growing up.

This place was just looked like a Unit. This method of deception seemed like should be a big thing, but overall, it somehow didn't matter at all. "Was I really that small?"

"And before that, even smaller." Gabe mimicked holding a baby, but it wasn't really necessary. Lenth had seen those lessons on the learning chair.

Lenth squinted at the four girls, all roughly the same age. "I don't...wait...What about Joints? He was...no, there was another. Me, Slim, Blue, and...there was a fourth boy."

Leaning against the wall, Gabe shrugged. "Ideally, four grow up together and stay together, but things happen. Deaths, unexpected twins, all kinds of things can happen. It mostly works out, but there's almost always at least one Unit out there with less than four Subjects."

"Slim dying, Spots appearing, just the system adjusting itself, huh?"

"More or less. Spots was having a rough time in his old Unit. Timing just happened to be roughly right for him to join your Unit. Had to fudge his memory a little bit with meds. Doing that is kind of risky, but it was the best thing for Spots in the long run."

Lenth turned to leave. "Well, I guess that makes Slim getting killed all worth it," he mumbled.

"I didn't mean it like that." Gabe said. "Everyone's just trying to make the best of things."

"The *best*? *How many people*, sorry, '*Subjects*', work to support all this? None of them with any idea why? With no..."

"The Contact says 'Ignorance is needed in the Subjects'. Something to do with the Messenger," Gabe said, "and tests. I don't really understand, but it's about getting the things we need from the Messenger."

Lenth looked down and shook his head slowly. He sighed. "Contact?"

"He can talk to the Messenger. It's always a person selected from the Providers. Kind of the leader of Providers. I guess I'm a big enough fish to have a say in who the next one is." Gabe shrugged.

"Fine, fine, but *what is Contact?*" Lenth said.

"He controls the meds. Makes sure the right ones get to the right Subjects, looks at the results, and...and then somehow it has to do with keeping the Messenger coming, and bringing things we need."

"Then *he* killed—" Lenth stopped himself, and turned away to pace a few steps. "I have to talk with this Contact."

"It was an accident. I'm sure of it, Lenth."

"I'm not saying it wasn't. I just..." Lenth paced a little more. He'd already known that somewhere, someone put a med into the system that reacted fatally with Slim's body. But now he had a 'name'. Contact.

"He knows," Gabe said with a soft tone. "I'd wager he feels pretty darn bad about it. It's not like it's a regular thing, deaths like Slim's."

Lenth nodded slowly. "Yeah. But how many Subjects are there? When you're looking down on that many, one is sad, but you gotta realize...to me, with three Brothers. Three people I knew existed, not counting the Rubberman, one death was...one death was big. My world was..."

Gabe put his hand on Lenth's shoulder. "I get it. I do. Let's get out of here and grab a bite."

Chapter Thirteen

Fruits of Asking

"Want to try something other than the food disks? We might be able to get a slice of unprocessed papaya." Gabe held his finger in front of the elevator's buttons, roaming along them.

"You can *eat* them? I mean, just as...as they are?"

"I'll take that as a yes." Gabe chose a button, and the elevator started to move.

"Are we going to see Carin' again?" Lenth asked meekly.

Gabe gave a wry smirk. "I was thinking we'd go to where they turn the eight crops into the standard food...but I suppose we *could* go see Karen."

"Oh. Wait a second, *eight?* Right! I learned about that!" Lenth said, "Could we try them all?"

"Well, yes. But not if we went to see Karen. She only has papayas." Gabe let Lenth stew a little, and the elevator doors opened to the floor with the processing facilities. Lenth looked out the door, down another of those nondescript Provider hallways. He stood. He looked at Gabe. He looked down the hallway. He looked at the buttons.

"Would it be silly?" Lenth asked.

"A little," Gabe replied, pressing the button to go see Karen. "Going down."

Lenth tried to hide a smile.

"Karen's not like the Rubberman you had," Gabe said.

"Yeah, I know. He's...she's a woman."

"Yeah, yeah, but there's two ways to become a Rubberman. You can get promoted from being a Subject, like yours was, or a Provider can take the job. Depending on this and that."

"I think Carin' mentioned that she was a Provider once."

"Yup."

Lenth thought for a moment. "But she seemed to kind of be afraid of Providers being mad at her."

"Well, there's protocol. I was kind of...ehh, uneasy about us talking so casually to a Manager, but I let it slide because she used to be a Provider. She still has responsibilities. She still has to do her job. Dispensing food, directing Subjects to the next task, minor maintenance, cleaning, and dealing with trouble."

"And shocking us," Lenth added.

"If that's what it takes, but really...how often were you zapped?" Gabe asked.

"Enough to hate it."

"And enough to want to avoid it. Enough to get going, and doing the things you needed to do, to help us all continue on."

"And get medicated, and exercise," Lenth said.

Gabe gave half a shrug. "Pretty much."

They ended up in Karen's 'office'. She was presumably out over the grating somewhere, but they couldn't go out there and risk shattering the illusion of Karen's Subjects.

So they waited.

"So...Carin' knows like...what...everything you do?"

"More or less, I guess."

"Hm. Neat." Lenth looked over towards her bedroom, thinking of the books in her locker. "She can read, I guess, huh."

"I'd assume so."

"Huh. Hey, I still want to meet this Contact guy."

"You're not going to start any crap, are you?"

Lenth perked up with an indignant look. "Crap? Crap like what?"

"Crap like a fight, getting some kind of revenge."

Lenth held out his hand as if to push away the insulting notion. "I'm not an idiot. I understand that it wasn't on purpose. I just want to hear about how. Why. The reasoning behind it all."

"I already told you."

"But Contact can tell me more, can't he?"

"Like what?"

"I don't know. The name of the med that killed Slim. So I can hate that med by name. Maybe find out what it was supposed to do."

Gabe looked at Lenth with pity. "It won't make any difference. But I'll talk to some people maybe. Try to set something up."

Lenth nodded with a quiet smile. It was something, at least. They didn't talk after that, and they sat down to get comfortable. A few quiet minutes passed before the door to the grating area opened.

Karen, in her full Rubberman outfit, halted at the door. Lenth waved with a smile, and Karen came in and closed the door.

"Hi, Carin'," Lenth said.

Karen wiggled out of her hood and mask, and her hair fell around her face as before, and enchanted Lenth all the more. "What... what are you guys doing here again?"

"I thought Lenth deserved a treat." Gabe smirked.

"I'm going to try plain papaya!" Lenth said.

Karen raised an eyebrow. "You should both know that they're for processing. If you wanted to break rules, you could have gone to processing, you know."

"We," Gabe said, leaning his head towards Lenth, "chose to come here instead."

Karen blushed. "Well, I'm flattered," she said with a polite chuckle.

Lenth blushed more. "I...well...is being a Rubberman boring?" He wanted to ask 'lonely', but he thought better of it.

"I read. I listen in on what my girls are yapping about. I sometimes get into the exercise area and work out a little. It's a bit on the dull side at times, sure."

Lenth wanted to think of a smart question. Something that would require a long answer. Something that would cause her to talk at length. He wanted to hear her voice more. "So...do you go into the Provider areas much? I don't think my Rubberman did."

"Not a lot, but when I have business there, I tend to take my time. I'll try to trade a book if there's any available. If I get talking to people, I'll linger for a while, unless I expect to be needed here any time soon."

Lenth got hung up on how she said "linger". It sounded especially smooth. He resisted saying 'linger' out loud. *Another question, another. Think fast.*

Not fast enough. Gabe spoke up. "So, what do you say? Do you have a bit of papaya hanging around for our buddy Lenth here?"

Karen stood tall, almost at attention. "Skimming crops for personal use? That wouldn't be right!"

"I'm not trying to trap you." Gabe said with a leer. "If you'd been skimming any significant amount worth worrying about, you'd be a little plumper, wouldn't you? You've got to have a little here somewhere, huh?"

Karen rolled her eyes. "Not much." She headed towards her bedroom and Lenth stood up to follow. The act of standing revealed a minor problem, pushing the front of his suit out ungraciously. That damned swelling was back! He felt it right away, and Gabe saw it, stifling a laugh.

Lenth looked up at Karen. Thankfully she had her back turned. Overcoming panic, he wrangled his 'problem' to be held more or less under control using the waistband of his clothes. There was still a bulge if you were looking for it, but it wasn't nearly as obvious.

He looked over to Gabe, who gave him a thumbs up while biting his lips to keep a laugh at bay.

Karen leaned around the corner from her bedroom, already out of her Rubberman suit, and asked, "Are you coming, Lenth?" Gabe couldn't stop it this time. A loud but brief laugh escaped him before he clasped his hands over his face.

Lenth blushed even harder, and his eyes widened. He wasn't entirely sure what was suddenly so funny, but it was obviously something to do with the swollen problem.

Karen didn't seem to get the joke either, which was a relief. "What happened?" she asked, looking at Gabe.

"Papaya," Lenth blurted, desperate to steer the topic away from the...the problem.

"What? Oh, yes. Come on then, Lenth."

Lenth passed by Gabe, giving him a disapproving little glare. As he caught up with Karen, she was bent over in front of her closet with her posterior sticking towards him. A rear end was a rear end, but this was...was different somehow. Amazingly different! Hypnotized, Lenth's stare didn't flinch, even after Karen stood and turned to face him with a freshly cut chunk of papaya in her hand.

"Lenth. Are you all right?"

"Huh? Hmm? It's okay, the swelling goes down. So far, it always has."

Stunned, Karen took a cue from Lenth's eyes and looked down. "Ah." She smirked. "I see. Oh, I heard some of the males are medicated so...yeah, you're new to that, I take it?"

"Oh, you weren't talking about...the swelling?"

Karen bit her lip. "No, no I wasn't. I'm flattered, mind you, but...yeah."

Unsure what to do about it, Lenth glanced back at the bed. "You didn't want to—"

Karen closed her eyes with a faint laugh. "Nope. No, not to be rude or anything," Karen said.

"Oh, thank goodness."

Karen looked a little surprised by Lenth's reaction. "You—"

"Me? I don't know what I'm doing! Why, do you?" Lenth asked.

Karen shook her head slightly with a soft smile. "Just eat the stupid papaya."

For more than two decades, Lenth 'knew' what 'food' tasted like. The same thing, every day. The taste of standard food, water, a tiny bit of blood from cuts or gums, and in younger years, curiosity about inedible objects.

He was entirely unaware how much he didn't know about taste. Even before the moist, soft, yellow piece reached his mouth, the feel and the scent were reaching out, trying to prepare him.

Holding it in his mouth without chewing, his eyes widened in shock. This taste was tingling around his mouth, and seemed to be wrapping around his head from the inside. And it was incredible.

"Whuh vuh...?" As incredible as it was, it still didn't enable him to talk easily with his mouth full. He shoved the piece of papaya into his cheek, planning to talk, but not ready to swallow. Moving it released another wave of flavour, and he forgot that he wanted to speak. He merely whimpered and slumped to his knees.

"Lenth! Are you all right?" Karen asked with concern.

"Mmmmmmmhmm!" Lenth held his hands out to prevent any interference, chewing slowly with his eyes closed. He leaned over and steadied himself against the end of Karen's bed.

"Ah, I remember my first time," Gabe said from the doorway. "Messy, and wet, and..." Gabe stopped, seeing Karen's expression.

Better prepared, but still not swallowing, Lenth cried out, "*Why don't we all eat this all the time?*"

"A body needs more than what a papaya has, so we mix it with a bunch of other things," Gabe said.

Lenth mentally digested that, and his eyes lit up. "I...*I want to try them all!*"

Gabe chuckled. "Maybe we can work that in, but just to let you know, papaya's the best of the bunch, for sure. Rice? Beans? Lablab? *Wheat?* Those are boring as heck! Sweet potatoes and peanuts are okay, I guess."

Karen chimed in with a smirk, "And beets?"

"Gack! The only way I'm ever eating those is when they're hidden happily in the finished food disks," Gabe said.

"They're bad?" Lenth asked.

"Pretty horrible," Karen said, "at least most people think so."

"Then I *really* want to try beets some time!"

"Why, Lenth?" Gabe said with a puzzled look. "In case you're one of the few that love them?"

Lenth held his hands in front of his face, as if closely inspecting an invisible ball. "The experience! Knowing what it is! *Really knowing!*"

Gabe shrugged as Karen smiled, and Lenth went on. "All my life I lived in that little set of rooms, and what did I know? Lots of nothing! I knew how to eat, get clean, sleep, and do my little job. I didn't even know what my job was *for*. There's so much more out here! I want to meet Contact and the Messenger, and I want to see what other Subjects do. What they make, how it matters. I want to meet a lot more people, and I want to..."

Lenth stopped himself and crossed his arms.

Gabe sighed with a leer. "I *bet* you want to. But don't go rushing that."

Choosing to play dumb, Lenth turned to Gabe, very cautious not to look at Karen. "Rush? Rush what? Who said I was in a rush for what?"

Karen blushed and bit her lips to avoid smiling. She shook her head. "Are you two goofs going to get out of here? You know it's not allowed."

Looking Karen up and down, Lenth glanced to one door, and then the other. "I'm unclear about a lot of things. About what things are not allowed."

Karen took his hand gently, slowly, and put a small package in it. Papaya for later. She smiled softly. "This is also not allowed."

"How's your reading going?" Gabe asked while they rode the elevator.

"The machine says I'm almost done grade two." Lenth shrugged. "Is that good?"

"For the amount of time you've been at it? Seems really good to me. You know it goes a lot higher though, right?"

Lenth nodded. "I figured. There's still lots of words I see that I can't manage."

"Yeah. But that's still a ton more than your old Rubberman knew."

"Fill?"

Gabe smirked with a raised eyebrow and looked at Lenth. "So, you *did* talk to him."

Lenth's jaw dropped, and his eyes widened. "I...yeah. Don't give him trouble, all right? It turns out he's kind of nice, but he was pretty scared of Providers when—"

Gabe coughed. "Doubtlessly, you spoke to him when you were already in his ceiling, and he had no way of stopping you. Doubtlessly, helping you get out would have been be a bad thing for him to do."

"He..." Lenth nodded. "Doubtlessly."

The elevator stopped and opened. They started walking to Lenth's quarters. "Hey Lenth, if things end up going accordingly, how do you feel about becoming a Manager sometime in the future?"

Lenth slowed, forcing Gabe to turn back to face him, and they stopped in the hall in front of Lenth's door. "Me? A Rubberman?"

"It's not your only option, but think about it." With that, Gabe headed off. Lenth went into his quarters, where the learning chairs were the first things to meet him.

"Being a Rubberman," Lenth thought, *"Sounds lonely. Then again, Carin' said she can go to the Provider areas when she wants. And obviously, she can have visitors. Maybe it's not so bad."*

But whoever he was put in charge of... he'd have to shock them from time to time. That wasn't a pleasant thought. He had been shocked enough to not want to wield that ability. It often felt quite unfair when he was shocked.

He had hated the Rubberman. But somehow he didn't mind Phil. As if the suit itself were the bad guy. *Is that how Phil sees it?*

Heck, is that how Karen sees it? He hadn't even thought of the idea that Karen must shock the women beneath her from time to time.

Maybe it wasn't so bad. Maybe he could get used to it. Then again, would he want to be used to it? To be a person who didn't mind shocking people? He got used to being shocked. *Well...not really.*

Ugh. So much to think about. Could he change his mind later? What were his other options? All this effort being put into learning to read, and he had nothing to write with. It would be handy to jot down questions to ask Gabe later.

That was a pretty bold idea... that he could possibly write these ideas well enough to make sense in the morning. Right now he was only approaching the idea of reading simple sentences. He'd have to just memorize to basic concepts. Refine them as short as possible.

"Quit?" and "Other options?" He repeated them in his head until he was just annoying himself.

Lenth went to take a shower, and he found himself again thinking of Karen. She had been so close. Being that close, he could feel the... force of her presence. Thinking of it again made his blood pressure rise and his breathing deepen.

She had been close enough that he could have reached out and held her. What would she have thought?

What would she have done?

Lenth had no idea how she'd react, and it terrified him.

He wrapped his arms around himself while the shower continued to rain on him, and imagined squeezing her.

She might have pushed him away, or even hit him. But the drive towards fantasy painted a very different picture in his mind.

A confused picture, painted mainly by sterile education, but he knew better. A mystery, a fantasy, terrifying and invigorating. It was clear what his body thought of it all, and that only compounded the confusion.

He looked down at his 'condition' and decided he should go review some of those lessons on the learning machine. The ones that showed... what to do with it.

When Lenth woke up, the notions of becoming a Rubberman were far behind his immediate needs. He was hungry, but wanted to save his papaya treasure. All else aside, it was from *her*.

He got cleaned up and headed to the cafeteria. Lately, his door remained unlocked, and he didn't need to summon Gabe to let him out.

Food and water obtained, he glanced around to choose a seat. There were plenty available, but quickly he was people-watching more than anything.

Woman-watching, specifically.

Someone passing by caused him to snap out of it and go sit down. Then resume woman-watching.

They were each lovely in one way or another. He unconsciously compared them to Karen. What was supposed to be ideal? Karen was nice. Her smile and her laugh. The women here weren't smiling or laughing much, but then, there was no immediate reason to.

The idea of talking to a stranger, (a woman, even!) was intimidating. All the people he'd met and talked to weren't exactly his idea. Not exactly. Lenth used to have three people to talk to. They weren't strangers in the slightest.

They also weren't lumpy. Things were simple.

He finished his meal, regretting that he didn't eat his papaya piece. Then he sat there, leaning on the table, just watching people.

They were living a life so alien to how he had grown up, coming and going as they pleased with no threat of electrocution. No cuffs confining them to one place or another. Being able to read. Interacting with so many people like it was nothing.

This was normal to them. This was normal.

So focused on people, he failed to see a person. Gabe walked over and stood beside him.

"Found you," Gabe said.

"Wasn't hiding," Lenth replied.

"If you still want to go meet Contact, we can do it."

"What, right now?" Lent said, wide-eyed.

"Right now."

Lenth got up and followed Gabe to the nearest elevator. When they got off, it was another typical hallway, but one of the quieter ones. Gabe wasn't talking, and Lenth didn't feel like he should break this silence.

They came to a door, and through it sprawled a room larger than the cafeteria, but mostly empty. The walls curved in a wide arch to meet the ceiling, which was twice as high as most. On the other end of the room sat a desk, and around the desk stood four Providers in their contamination suits, headgear held under their arms.

"Well, isn't that fitting?" came a grim voice from an unseen man on the other side of the desk. "Get back at it, then. You know how important it is."

With that, the four tired-looking Providers turned towards Lenth and Gabe and headed past them for the door wordlessly.

Lenth and Gabe turned back towards the desk and the man seated behind it. "Yes?" he said flatly. The man was almost as wrinkly as Bones, but he had Provider amounts of hair, also on his chin and jaw. Grey and rough. He was wider than most people. A bit more than twice as wide, and it made him look soft, sort of. But not in any way that made him look any friendlier.

"Bad timing?" Gabe asked, taking a few hesitant strides forward.

The man shrugged, pinching his forehead. "No. Yes, but no. On top of everything, we brought out those shock sticks and found that the battery cells had bled out. Hopefully we can get...ah, never mind. Come on in."

Gabe gestured for Lenth to follow, and headed to the desk. "May I ask what that was all about?" Gabe asked with a tone of respect.

The man pointed at Lenth. "This guy's buddy just killed again." he said dispassionately. Lenth eyes widened.

"What's that, the fifth?" Gabe asked.

The man shook his head. "Sixth. Six killed six, isn't that cute." The man tapped a computer screen that was built into the top of his desk, and it turned off.

"Is that including his Rubberman?" Gabe asked.

"Ex...excuse me," Lenth interrupted, "Six isn't my buddy, I hope you under —"

"Yes, yes," the man said. "Lenth, right? You and I have something in common. Our names have meaning."

"You're..."

"Contact. I'm the contact with the Messenger. I used to have another name, but when I took this job, I got this name. And Lenth...well, it's a Unit Subject name, but that's not a word. What does it mean? Unit Subject names almost always mean things." The way he said *Unit Subject* made it sound almost like a slur.

"Length." Lenth spread out his arms to illustrate. "It's not a super long reach..."

"But bigger than your Brothers," Contact concluded.

"That's right." Lenth stared at Contact, but silence soon made him avert his eyes to the desk.

"Lenth, you had something to ask me? Gabe tells me you want to know more about why your Brother died."

Lenth sighed. If Contact knew that, why make Lenth ask? "Yes. The medication that killed him. What was it? What was it supposed to do? Did the rest of us get it?"

Contact seemed unaffected by Lenth's trembling tone and fidgeting. Contact seemed to find Lenth a bit...distasteful. "Air," he finally answered flatly.

"Air?" Lenth frowned. "Like, air?" he waved his hand in the air above his head.

"Yes, air. Very fine to breathe it, very bad to get bubbles of it in your blood."

Lenth looked at his wrist. "But the rest of us were okay?"

Contact frowned. "No, no, Slim was the only one to get air in his blood. The piping going to his cuff had a leak, and air got in with the mixture."

Lenth nodded with partial understanding. He'd felt the cuffs 'jab' him before, and he sometimes had found the mark of the tiny injections, but until recently, assumed they were... meaningless. Harmless. He gave a slow sigh, staring into the floor. "This leak... that put air in Slim... how did it happen?"

"Realistically? It could have been many things," Contact said. "Natural material deterioration, a pressure surge causing the lines to slip off the connector, the Manager might have bumped something, by accident of course, or possibly a combination of all those things."

"The Manager? My Rubberman? Fill."

Chapter Fourteen

Of Air and Ascending

Phil was resting as his Subjects slept, and no other tasks called him. He played cards with himself. He'd invented several games he could amuse himself with. Simple games of chance, building meaningless structures with them, or tossing them into his overturned mask from across the room.

The cards were a treasure he'd found under the desk, most likely left by the previous Manager of this Unit. Where they came from originally, he could not guess.

Phil didn't dare ask a Provider, for fear of having them taken away.

He had just started the third layer of a building when he heard his back door starting to open. In controlled panic, he scooped the cards into one tight pile and slipped them under his mattress.

Calm, relax, everything was all right. Quick look around for any wayward cards. *Nope.*

The door opened, and two Providers stepped through in the usual faceless suits.

"Hello? I wasn't expecting you, what's wrong?" Phil asked.

One of the Providers stayed near the door and the other came closer. "Fill," said a voice that seemed somehow familiar to him, "are you doing all right?"

"Yes, I am. No complaints," Phil replied.

"How is the Subject 'Joints'?" Lenth asked from the anonymity of the Provider suit.

"Joints? He...he seems to realize that he's being given lighter weights, but he hasn't taken advantage of the lower requirements for the work. He seems to be working as hard as he always has. He seems okay overall."

"Good. That's good. Spots and Blue?"

Phil nodded. "Same as always. The new one, Brow, he's doing well also."

Lenth paused, and Phil fidgeted nervously a little bit. The new one. Of course. Lenth knew that, and had heard it several times, but it still hadn't sunk in. Hearing the new one's name made it all the more real. He'd been replaced, just like Slim.

What must his Brothers be thinking of all this? They knew he left, Phil knew that they knew. No... wait, of course not. Joint, Blue, Spots...They were all gassed to sleep before Lenth went above Phil's ceiling. They probably think that Phil, their Rubberman, took him away, just like when Slim disappeared.

He wanted to go out there and tell them that at least, he was okay. He knew it wasn't possible.

Gabe, standing by the door, spoke from inside his mask. "Ask him what we came here for."

Lenth turned back towards Phil, who was now standing all the more rigidly.

"Right," Lenth said. "What happened to the one named 'Slim'?"

"He...he died," Phil said.

"I know. I meant why? There was a leak that got air into his blood. But how did the leak happen?"

Phil looked concerned. "I thought this was settled. I thought we all agreed it was an accident! I couldn't know the tube wasn't on tight enough; it's never been something I've had to check before! It's never been a problem before, but you can be sure I check them regularly now. I... I..."

Phil backed away and slumped against the wall. Lenth lowered his head and stepped closer to Phil, who began to tremble slightly.

"You *what*, Fill?" Lenth asked.

Phil tightened his body up, and mumbled for a bit. "It's not my place, not really, I know that..."

"*What* isn't your place?"

Phil shook his head slowly, still looking down. "They call each other 'Brother'. They care for each other, and... and," Phil looked up into Lenth's dark mask, seeking eyes to stare into. "—and I care for them too! I take care of them, I watch them grow, and talk, and have fun as much as they're allowed. It was the same four for a long, long time, then Slim dies, I have no idea where Lenth is, and the new boys are fine, but they're not Slim and Lenth, and as fine as they may be, they'll never be Slim and Lenth, and I sometimes feel like if they're all Brothers, then I..."

Lenth reached out gently grabbed Phil by the arms. "It's a shame you're not allowed talk to them. They might appreciate you if you could."

They stood there for a while, Lenth remaining masked as Gabe looked on. Finally, Lenth turned to leave.

"Are... are things all right then?" Phil asked.

Lenth paused before following Gabe through the door. "You... you don't have to worry. It was an accident."

After leaving Phil's Unit, Gabe and Lenth took their tinted hazmat headpieces off while riding the elevator. Gabe looked at Lenth with consideration. "For a moment there, I thought you were going to tell Phil who you were."

"You told me not to. So I didn't."

"It would have made things more complicated," Gabe consoled.

"I know, you told me. But you should let him know that I'm okay. He's stuck worrying more than he has to."

Gabe didn't reply, but perhaps he looked just a little thoughtful on the topic. "You care?" he finally asked Lenth.

"Sure. You were there, you heard him."

The door opened, and they started heading in the general direction of Lenth's quarters. "Lenth, I guess what I'm getting at... he was your Rubberman. He watched over you in a system specifically designed to keep him at arm's reach, with no emotional attachment. If anything, you should hate him."

"Not really." Lenth shrugged. "Feared him, I guess. He wasn't a person before, just a walking thing that stomped and zapped us."

Gabe nodded. "A thing, not a person. I get it. So once you saw his face—"

"And heard his voice. And talked to him. And found out he actually *likes* us."

They arrived at Lenth's door and stopped.

"So you forgive him for Slim's death?"

Lenth shrugged. "Kind of have to. I'm going to work on my reading, I guess, before I go to sleep."

"Right. I'll see you later." Gabe nodded and headed off.

Lenth lay down on the learning chair and stared idly at the headset. Would Gabe be far enough away now? Would Lenth be able to find Contact's office on his own? Maybe. He wasn't sure why he wanted to talk to Contact *without* Gabe around. He just did.

When Lenth finally got underway, he immediately got lost, but managed to put things together well enough to fumble his way along. The biggest error in his navigation was getting off the elevator on the wrong floor. The hallway looked so similar, it was a long ten minutes before he clued in why things weren't going as he expected.

Part fool, part noble explorer, he found his way again, and eventually reached Contact. The large curve-walled room was quiet, and uninhabited other than the sizable Contact himself, who looked up from his work as Lenth entered.

"Ah. Hello. Gabe isn't here," Contact said before looking back down at his in-desk monitor.

"I'm not looking for Gabe, I wanted to talk with you some more."

Contact sighed slowly. "Figures. All right, what did you want to talk about?" He tapped his monitor off, then leaned back into his chair, arms crossed casually.

"Well, quite a few things," Lenth said apologetically. Contact merely rolled his hand around, inviting the drivel to commence.

"Well, first, the meds. The stuff we were getting put in our blood all the time. What's in it? Normally, I mean."

"Right now? Nothing. Water. Oh, and you came from one of the units that were kept impotent, aren't you?"

Lenth didn't know the word, and shrugged.

"Your thingie never got hard, right?" Contact said. Lenth didn't react quickly enough, so Contact pointed at Lenth's groin.

"Oh! Yes, I mean, no, it didn't. I didn't know it—"

"Well there you go." Contact said. "Water, and no-hard-stuff. Now and then if you get sick or something, some antibiotics or whatever. Ask the medic if you care. All very routine. Next question?"

Lenth looked down, then back at Contact. "*It* was always supposed to get swollen? I don't understand. Why bother stopping it from...and you stopped that? Why?"

Contact shrugged dispassionately. "It was part of the Study. It is a step in preparation. Even units who aren't kept impotent get regular water injections. The water does nothing. The schedule of injections keeps the system ready for when we receive new orders, for testing new medications. We are currently in the 'control' phase of testing. Recording normal non-medicated conditions."

"You... record... keep track of how Subjects react to no medication? How long have we been in this 'control' phase?"

"Always."

"Always since when?" Lenth asked.

Contact frowned. "Always! Don't you know what 'always' means? And we will remain in 'control' until new orders and medications arrive!"

"When will that be?"

"What concern is it of yours? When it happens! Probably not in our lifetime, of course. But we *will* be ready."

Lenth ignored, or was oblivious to Contact's agitated tone, and asked another question. "Where will these medications come from? Messenger?"

The bitter expression that had been growing on Control's face while answering 'stupid' questions finally softened, into an almost-smile. He nodded and pointed casually at Lenth. "Ah, yes, he will bring it, but it will have come from Actual, and before that, it has been said, from Big Farm! Big Farm needs to test medications, as it was told."

Lenth leaned in with puzzled look. "I just learned about you and Messenger! Who's Big Farm? Let them test the medications on the farm! I don't care what happens to some stupid papayas! Who's Actual? Does he live on a farm? Why does any of that matter?"

Contact smiled broadly and stood. He walked peacefully away from his desk, gazing slightly upward. Now that he was standing, Lenth could see his size a little better. He'd have to ask about that. Some other time. Contact turned to Lenth.

"Young man, to know of Actual is to know of the highest of us. Even Messenger has not seen him, but Messenger has spoken to him, and will one day become him."

Lenth tilted his head. "But isn't Messenger picked from the Providers? So couldn't you, or Gabe, or any Provider eventually become this... Actual?"

Contact smirked and raised an eyebrow. "Ah. Simple, yes?" He patted his gut. "I would make a poor Messenger, I think, if you're implying I have such a goal. But it isn't that simple. The Messenger becomes almost entirely removed from us. From our world. Above us, different. He travels beyond our realm, out beyond the Citizenry, and beyond places with no names before reaching the halls of Actual. And as removed as Messenger is from us, Actual is removed that much more from him!"

Reaching up, Contact held his hand open, as if ready to receive from the great unseen Actual by providence of his Messenger.

After basking in Contact's own awe for a moment, Lenth asked, "So he's an Actual *what,* exactly?"

Contact looked momentary mortified by the question, but quickly decided to take the blasphemous ignorance with good humour.

"*Actual!* Actual. Is the one of us who has risen to be the truest of us. Actual is all of us! He *is,* and so by his being, we *are.* Almost as his children. Without him, we would live on for a time, but eventually ruin would overtake us all."

Contact gazed upward and fell silent again. Lenth spoke, but quietly, as to not disturb Contact's moment too much. "Actual makes sure Messenger can get us the things we need. Replacement parts, wall pieces, stuff that use glass, Gabe told me."

Contact turned to face Lenth. "Yes, yes, all that and so much more. We understand so little. I feel Messenger knows more. He has let slip the idea of places around us beyond what we know. We know much already, much we cannot understand, but we know also that there is much which we do *not* know."

"So why don't we ask him?" Lenth asked.

A sly smile crossed Contact's face. "I have tried. His answers say much, but tell me nothing. It is the path of the Messenger to learn as we ourselves would want."

"By becoming Actual," Lenth said.

Contact pointed at Lenth with a stubby finger. "Exactly. More or less. I think. I have to live with knowing that I will never know for sure. My place is only to try to keep things running smoothly here."

As mundane as Contact saw the everyday running of everything, it was still new and strange to Lenth. Even just the basic elements of the food he'd eaten all his life, and literacy. These were the frontiers of Lenth's reality. Lenth looked down at his clasped hands. "So this is it. Unless a Provider is chosen as Messenger, there's nowhere else to go."

With an incredulous glance, Contact said, "Where exactly would you want to go? We have food here, we have peace, and everything is fine here."

Lenth thought back a little. "Sitisrunny...? You mentioned a place Messenger goes through called—"

"Citizenry." Contact groaned a little and sat back down. "You don't want to go there." He shook his head a little. "Messenger doesn't even get off of the great central elevator there. Only to load off deliveries, and even then, he does not mingle with the... Citizens."

"Deliveries?" Lenth asked.

"Food mostly. From us. The Citizenry doesn't make their own food. They get air and water processed by us, too. If we were to feel the need, we could probably kill every Citizen in about as much time as it takes a person to die of thirst."

Lenth cocked his head and stared at Contact for a moment. "Are you serious? What do they do with their time?"

"Now and then, one of us goes up. They make you earn entry. I've heard of... let's see... five or so Providers going up? One came back down." Contact looked away and made a sound that mixed a scoff and a sigh. "She was not treated well there. Quite badly hurt."

Lenth leaned over, trying to catch Contact's averted eyes. "She was hurt? How? Can I talk to her?"

"I suppose it is possible," Contact said. "However, there isn't much point in doing so. She doesn't talk about her time in Citizenry, and says there's no point. That the Citizenry is worth forgetting about, but that we'd better keep supplying them with food and water. She was rather firm on that last part."

"Why?" Lenth asked. "I mean, it sounds like she didn't like the Citizenry at all. Why's she so worried that they're taken care of?"

Contact sighed and stared at his desk, spreading his hands across it slowly. "Perhaps merely a general sense of compassion." His tone was sarcastic. Almost spiteful.

"I don't under—"

"Forget it. Just know that we are safe here, even below on the Unit floors. Oh, and Gabe mentioned to me the idea of you becoming a Manager?"

"A Rubberman? Yeah, he mentioned it to me, too," Lenth said.

"You don't sound terribly attracted to the idea. It is not as if I'd assign you today. There *is* some training involved after all."

"Fill was a Subject like me, right? If I have the names of things right."

"Phil?" Contact searched his memory for moment, then the name clicked. "Yes. But not all Managers were previously Subjects."

"I know," Lenth said, thinking of Karen. "Fill seems like a good person, now that I've talked to him, but I...I don't want to be like him. He doesn't know things. Even how to read much. I already know more than him, and to be honest...I like knowing things. There's a lot out there."

Contact chuckled. "And you want to learn, hm? And once you know everything there is to know, what then?" Contact only really meant knowing everything below the Citizenry, but as the words left his mouth, he realized how it probably sounded to Lenth.

"I don't know!" Lenth said with a smile. "That's the exciting part! I don't know what I don't know, and until I know, how can I guess? I mean, I can guess a lot, but I don't know, you know?"

"No." Contact said, unable to resist. "Yes, yes, I understand you. Look, start with learning about what positions are available. If you find a few you're interested in, we can talk about them then. Your learning station should have access to everything you need."

Lenth replied only with a thoughtful nod.

"All right, then; if that's all, I do have other things to do today."

Lenth nodded again. "And I have learning to do."

Chapter Fifteen

Studying for Citizenship

Citizenry. Citizenry. It took a great deal of trial and error to get the system to understand him, due to Lenth's still-rudimentary spelling. Only scouring the listing displaying topics saved his sanity in the end.

Huh. No convenient videos. Lenth was forced to read, and it went slowly. Sounding out words, getting them wrong, then going back when he got the idea a little better, and maybe figuring those words out in context- or just skipping some, hoping they didn't matter too much. As far as he could tell, the Providers sort of feared the Citizenry, but at the same time, thought they were less. Less good. Less useful.

There was no obvious mention of how to go there. Either the topic was avoided, censored, or there just wasn't enough interest in going up to warrant mentioning—except for one link. Messenger.

Lenth's first impulse was to go ask Contact about meeting Messenger, but the idea of bugging him again seemed... it seemed like a good way to get Contact mad. Contact seemed to have a limited, or at least unpredictable amount of patience for things that he found stupid.

Gabe was the next best thing. Lenth found Gabe eating at the cafeteria.

"I want to meet Messenger," Lenth said bluntly, not bothering to sit across from Gabe. Gabe looked up, half a food unit in his hand, chewing.

"Mfy?" Gabe swallowed and tried again. "Why?"

"I want to go up. To see Citizenry."

Gabe stifled a chuckle. "Oh, Lenth. It's not a place you simply *go* to."

"Which is why I need to talk to Messenger. He brings the Citizenry food, right? So he can take me."

Gabe stood abruptly and pointed at Lenth. "You want to move there? You want to be one of them, that don't work for their food? They're consumers, nothing else. Parasites!"

Half of the other people in the cafeteria were looking at him. "No," Lenth said, "I just want to see. Have you seen it?"

"Who cares? Who wants to see a bunch of spoiled idiots lying around, eating our food and having sex everywhere like morons?"

"They... they do that? You've seen it?" Lenth asked, all the more curious.

Gabe rolled his eyes. "Well, no, I haven't seen it personally, but what else are they going to do with their time, if they don't work?"

Lenth looked at him and the faces now paying attention to Gabe and himself. "Anyone?" Lenth asked. "Have any of you been there?"

A man Lenth didn't know spoke up in an unconcerned tone, "They're a bunch of mooches. I always thought we should cut them off. Starve 'em, suffocate them, whatever. It's cruel to let them live like that."

Lenth stepped towards the man. "*You've* seen it?"

The man looked away, suddenly focusing on his food. "Nope, don't need to."

Holding out his arms to the room, Lenth called out, "*Anyone?*" He looked around in the silence. "No one here has seen Citizenry?" Lenth relaxed his arms and turned to Gabe. "*That's* why I want to go."

"People have gone before, and—"

"I know, Gabe. Contact mentioned them. The one that came back isn't talking, right?"

Diane squirmed through the crawlspace, doing a regular inspection of the various conduits that kept things running in the Provider areas. The darkness was cut by Diane's headlamp, a boxy little thing strapped to her head. The light, as much as it moved around, was enough for Lenth to follow her. Diane didn't show any interest in sitting for a chat, but begrudgingly allowed Lenth to follow her as she worked.

Piping, vents, and electrical cords. Diane inspected every inch, paying extra attention to joints and connectors. Lenth couldn't help but wonder if this kind of diligence would have saved Slim. Should Diane have caught that leak? If that particular little tube had been her duty, he couldn't bring himself to blame her. She seemed to be doing her job with fine attention to detail.

"How often do you do this?" Lenth asked.

"A lot. These things go everywhere. By the time we're done, it's time to start over."

"How far do you go?"

"Me? Provider levels only. Others go higher up or farther down." She sounded tired. Not in the way that a lot of work can make you tired, but in the way that a lot of life can make you tired. Before they had crawled into the darkness, Lenth had seen that her eyes matched that feeling.

"Have you ever been—"

"I know why you're here," she snapped. "I know what you want, and you're a *fool*."

"What was so bad about it?" Lenth asked.

Diane turned around to face Lenth, which was no simple task in the crawlspace. Her headlamp shone almost directly in Lenth's eyes, so she adjusted it a little. She took his hands in hers and squeezed hard enough that her knuckles cracked. "Don't go," she said quietly. Her eyes were a mix of anger and fear, and her breathing had become rougher.

Lenth stared into her eyes for a while, then asked what she'd likely been asked a hundred times. "What happened?"

Her eyes broke the stare and she looked away. For a moment, Lenth thought she was going to answer, but then abruptly, she turned back around and resumed working. Lenth followed silently for some time, hoping she'd have a change of heart.

Diane stopped. After a moment of shuffling, her light went out.

"What's wrong?" Lenth asked.

"Shh!" was the answer. As Lenth's eyes adjusted to the miniscule ambient light being supplied by an undefined source somewhere, he saw Diane reach to a pocket on her thigh and pull out a knife. Still facing away, she laid there silently. Lenth heard only her breathing, but Diane apparently heard something else. Her body shifted suddenly.

"Six, maybe," she whispered. "Go," she said, crawling backwards, forcing Lenth to do the same. Seconds later, Lenth heard what Diane had been hearing. Someone else was here, and they were now moving fast.

"*He's coming. Hustle!*" Diane said. There he was, a dark shape coming from the right, yanking on a pipe to help him move faster.

"*Monster!*" came a male voice, harsh and furious. Diane's body shifted to defend herself as the attacker reached them. Lenth tried to maneuver to go help, but Diane's foot slammed in his path as she tried to find leverage. She screamed as the attacker's voice came again, "*Die! Die! Get out of our way and die!*"

Diane yelped. Maybe as she attacked, maybe as she was cut. In the near darkness, and cramped space, Lenth couldn't make out much more than a struggle.

The sound of a fierce thrust came once, twice. Diane stopped moving after the second, but the sound came once more.

Stunned, Lenth froze. Quiet quickly returned, leaving only the attacker's heavy breathing, laced with hint of laughter with every exhale. Sounds of a little more movement, and then the voice came, now much calmer. "Ooh, handy!"

Diane's headlamp, now being held in a hand, was turned back on. It flickered past the attacker's face before being pointed right at Lenth.

"Hey! It's you!" The attacker said. "Were you after this one? Sorry if I spoiled your fun. How many have *you* gotten? I'm now up to six. If I want to kill any more, maybe I need to grow more toes! Get it?"

"Seven," Lenth said quietly.

"You're beating me, then! Knives sure make it easier than smashing their heads. Like this female, here? It would have been a real pain to find a good spot to bash her head against in this cramped space, or get a good angle."

"No. I mean you've killed seven, I think, not six." Lenth spoke quietly, but tried to not let his voice betray his fear. Or was it hate? Either way, his nerves were trying their best to make him tremble. "I heard someone say you'd killed six. I can't remember if that was before or after Eyes was found."

Six was quiet for a moment. "Oh yeah. Eyes. But he doesn't count; he wasn't a Provider." Six reached forward to smack Diane's rear end. "Well, her problems are just as over as Eyes'. I'm going to go grab a bite. I'd ask you to come with, but I've taken a liking to travelling alone, you understand." He took a moment to give Diane's rump a little squeeze before he turned to leave. "See ya, Lenth."

Lenth stared as Six crawled away, his looted light waving around in front of him. Six's movements were making enough sound that Lenth barely heard a soft gasp. He turned to look at Diane. In the dark, he couldn't make out a lot, but he saw movement, most importantly, breathing.

"Diane!" Lenth said, barely suppressing a shout.

"Shh," was her reply.

Six's light could still be seen, but he was a good distance away and still moving. Lenth got his mouth close to Diane's ear. He could smell the blood. "Stay quiet, I'm going to go get help," he said.

Diane just grabbed Lenth's wrist. "Wait," she whispered. "I can go with you, but wait." Her voice had a whimpering tone to it. Lenth obeyed and waited with her. Before long, he realized that she was trembling, and maybe crying.

"Shh," Lenth told her, putting his hand on her back. She flinched and tossed his hand off. She squirmed around, sniffling, getting herself under control.

"Let's go," she whispered, leading the way back out. When they climbed back down from the crawlspace, Lenth got his first look at her injury in the light. The deepest cut was across her left eye. Her eyeball and eyelids were intact, but the tissue above and below was badly cut and still bleeding. There were several other cuts on her face and a couple around her shoulder. Thankfully, bone had been in the way of any vital tissue. Either the struggle or her efforts to clean up before getting out into the light resulted in the blood being smeared across her face, onto her hands, and forearms.

"D... doctor, we need to go see the doctor," Lenth said, taking lead towards an elevator. Diane only gave a small nod.

"I thought you were dead!" Lenth said once they got into the elevator, and began moving up.

"I wasn't going to win that fight," Diane said. "Snagged my knife on my clothes before it really even got started. I decided to play dead." The tired expression Lenth had seen on her face before was now all the more defeated. She closed her eyes and leaned into the corner of the elevator.

"Diane! Wake up!"

Diane just huffed in response. Lenth stepped towards her, and grabbed her by the shoulders. "Diane, we'll be to the doctor's soon, don't worry."

Diane opened her eyes again, but just looked at the floor. A few sparse drops of blood marked her path from the door.

The elevator stopped before reaching the desired floor and another Provider came on. He stopped in the doorway in shock. "*What's going on here?*"

"We were attacked," Lenth said, "by a guy named Six."

"*Six?*" The Provider gave Lenth a suspicious glance and walked over to Diane. "Is this true?"

Diane nodded, but refused eye contact.

The Provider pressed buttons on the elevator control panel that had already been pressed. "We have to get her to a doc...oh that's where you're headed, isn't it?"

"Yeah. She...I mean, her injuries look bad, but it could have been much worse."

The Provider nodded. "And where's Six?"

"Still in the crawlspaces, he got away. I...I should have stopped him, but I..."

"No, you had to get her out of there; you did the right thing. You're Gabe's little pet project, aren't you?"

"Lenth," he corrected. 'Little pet project'. What an odd thing to call him, but maybe that's how he was seen by most Providers. The lowly Subject, up from the Units, being taught to learn a trade in the Provider's domain.

The elevator opened again and Lenth urged Diane forward, with the other Provider tagging along.

The doctor reacted with professionalism and hidden panic. Questions about the attack, the weapon used, how long ago it was, all came quickly. Diane wasn't talking, slipping further into a state of shock, so Lenth did his best to answer.

Meanwhile, the Provider that they met on the elevator had summoned Gabe and three other Providers. They spotted Diane's blood trail right away, and the extra three Providers left to follow it.

"Lenth, exactly where was Six?" Gabe asked Lenth.

"In the crawlspace!"

"Ugh, we need to be a little more specific." Gabe brought Lenth over to the clinic's computer and brought up a map. Lenth was paying more attention to Diane. She was still silent as the doctor cleaned her wounds and applied bandages. She was a mess of red.

"Lenth, look here. We need to know fast, if we're going to catch him."

Lenth had never seen a map before. "What am I looking at here?"

Gabe sighed, and explained the map, and after more time than Gabe was hoping, they decided on the location where the attack happened.

"I'm going to catch up with the others," Gabe said. "You're okay?"

Lenth nodded. "I want to help."

Gabe was already jogging off, and called back, "Let the doctor check you over, I'll talk to you later, don't worry."

Obediently, Lenth stood there. The doctor had just settled Diane into a bed. Diane was still silent, sitting up, staring into her lap. The largest bandages were across her eye and over her shoulder. A few smaller ones were placed in other spots on her forehead, cheek, and upper arm. Most of the blood had been cleaned off her skin, but she was still in her stained clothes. Lenth went to her.

"Diane?"

She didn't even blink. The doctor returned and motioned for Lenth to follow him. They ended up in the back of the clinic, where the doctor prepared two syringes.

"What are those?" Lenth asked.

"One will make her injuries hurt less; the other, I'm hoping, will help her snap out of it."

"Out of what?"

The doctor looked over in the direction of Diane. "How she's not talking. Catatonia. She had it before. Hopefully this is a relatively minor relapse from the stress of the attack."

"She was like this before? Was it after her trip to the Citizenry?" Lenth asked.

The doctor raised an eyebrow and nodded, picking up his tray of syringes. "Lenth, you're all right?"

"Yes, I think so. Gabe told me to let you 'check me over'."

The doctor looked down at Lenth's feet and up to his face. "Alright, done. Go home. Diane needs quiet."

Lenth nodded and headed out. As he passed by Diane's bed, he paused and looked at her. The urge to go talk to her was strong, but he resisted. He waved to the doctor and left.

He felt like he should go back to the crawlspaces and try to help, but the idea of going back into that darkness with a killer slowed his stride. The Providers know the terrain better anyway. He would just get in the way.

And these were perfectly good reasons not to go.

Excuses. But he accepted them.

Chapter Sixteen

Idiot

Karen had just supervised her Subjects' shower and sent them to bed. With their cuffs on, they talked to each other about the day's events, which were always the same overall. An in-joke that Karen didn't understand caused them all to laugh. Karen loved to hear them laugh.

She stood far enough away from the sleeping room that she wouldn't be seen. The visage of the black suit tended to make them silent, even if there was a smile under the mask.

When the Subjects settled down for sleep, Karen walked as quietly as she could towards her room. Once at the control panel, she closed the door, and dimmed the lights for the entire Unit. She took off the rubber suit and mask, piling it in the corner. When she got to her bedroom, she saw her closet open and a couple of feet sticking out.

Someone was sitting in her closet.

It had Provider pants and shoes, though not a containment suit. Was it this 'Six' she'd been warned about? Or a victim?

Lacking something to strike a foe with, she silently walked back to get her rubber suit. If she had to, she could use it to wrap Six, tackle him down with luck, and then...then what?

Would she win? Would she have to kill him? As she picked up the suit, she heard the invader getting up. She quickened herself, trying to remain quiet.

The footsteps were getting closer! Abandoning stealth, Karen pulled the suit up in front of her and charged around the corner. She saw empty hands around the suit as she tackled, glad there was no knife. They stumbled together against the corner of her bed, and after a moment on the very edge of it, they tipped over, with Karen on the bottom. She pushed up through the suit and found no resistance.

It flopped off of her, revealing her opponent.

"*What?* Lenth?" Karen wriggled to sit upright on the floor, with the suit mostly on her lap. "You scared the crap out of me! I thought you were Six!"

"Oh. Well, sorry. That's kind of why I came. I wanted to make sure you were all right, and to warn you, I guess." He put out his hand to help her up, and she accepted.

Lenth remembered touching her like this before. The moment he did, time seemed to slow down to allow him a chance to appreciate every detail. Her hand was much slimmer than his. Softer, too. His attention flowed from her hand, up her arm, and all over her body as she moved to stand.

She spoke, forcing Lenth back into real time as she reclaimed her hand. "I know about Six. Well, obviously. A Provider came to fill me in." She sat on the end of her bed and idly kicked the door of her closet shut. "What were you doing in here?"

Lenth cracked a little smile. "Reading!"

Karen looked to her closet, where she kept her little collection of books, then back to Lenth. "You...you can read now?"

Lenth beamed. "Yes! Well. A little. I remembered your books, and I hope you don't mind, but I started reading one. It's difficult."

Opening her closet back up, she saw a book of "Nursery Rhymes" on top. She picked it up to show Lenth. "This one?"

"Yes. There's a lot of words I don't know, though. I'm learning."

"There's a lot in here that I don't know too," Karen said.

"Really? I figured you were really *good* at reading, Carin'!"

"Yeah, well, a lot of books have...I have to say, mistakes. Or the person who wrote them was just being silly." She flipped open a random page. "'Baa, baa, black sheep, have you any wool?' What is that supposed to be? Baa? I have no idea about that. As far as I can figure, Sheep is a Subject name, taken from 'sleep', like your name is taken from 'length'. Okay, fine. So Sheep is black. Oh! I just realized. 'Baa' is the writer trying to write 'black', but making mistakes that just stayed in. Stupid. But 'wool'? *Wool?*"

"What's wool?" Lenth asked.

Karen blew a raspberry as she tossed the book back into her closet. "Your guess is as good as mine! There's a lot of crazy stuff in books that doesn't make any sense. I heard that there used to be a lot more books running around that made even less sense, and we got rid of most of those."

Lenth shrugged, then pointed at the ceiling. "This part doesn't look like it opens. No entrance through the crawlspace."

Karen nudged her little book stack into order at the bottom of her closet and closed it. "Yeah. I keep the door to the rest of the Unit locked when I can. He could get in the other way, and for that matter, I can't do my job camping out in here."

"It's got to be stressful."

"Yeah," Karen nodded, "but I don't think I have a lot to worry about. He's mostly going after Providers I hear. In your new clothes, you have more to worry about."

"Well...yes and no. I saw him, just a while ago."

Karen's eyes went wide. "What? Where?"

"There's Providers looking for him. I told them what I could. I was with a Provider named Diane in a crawlspace, and he came and tried to kill her. Then he talked to me as if I was like him. I..."

"Diane! What? How is she?"

"You know her, Carin'?"

"A little. But everyone knows *of* her."

"Because she went up to Citizenry?"

Karen nodded. "And how she was when she came back. Didn't talk for months, I heard."

Lenth exhaled a sigh. "She's kind of like that now. She got cut up some. Six thought he'd killed her. That's why he left. He knew I had been a Subject, I guess he figured I stole the Provider outfit. When I first met him, before I knew how he was...he was nice to me. Gave me a Rubberman suit to help me out. Now I know where he got it." Lenth picked up Karen's Rubberman suit, and held it close. "You be safe, Carin'. You have to stay safe. Is throwing your suit your only way to fight?"

Karen stepped closer and put her hands on the edge of her suit, looking Lenth in the eye. "There's a solid chunk of pipe I could keep with me."

"Strange. You can shock and gas people in the Subject areas, but up here, you're going to rely on a pipe?" Oh, but it was nice just staring into her eyes.

Karen shrugged with a meek smile. "A pipe is what I have."

"I might be able to get you something better. Have you heard of a knife?"

"*Yes*, I know what *knives* are." Karen smiled. "I'm a big girl. I could get myself a knife from a Provider if I wanted."

"Then why not do it, Carin'?"

"I already told you, I don't think Rubbermen are his main targets. You don't have to worry about me."

Lenth scrunched the side of his mouth up and stared for a moment. "Well, maybe I'll worry anyway. I'll try to get you something." Leaning against the wall, he looked up. "I'm planning on going there."

Karen reflexed to look at where Lenth was looking for a split moment before she clued in. "Citizenry? Why?"

"Ha, Gabe asked that too," Lenth smiled to himself. "No one in the cafeteria seemed to get it either, but none of *them* knew much about Citizenry at all. So, that's why. No one knows, and no one seems to care that they don't know. That seems stupid to me."

"But Diane—"

"Maybe Diane just got unlucky up there! Yes, I know there have been others who went up there and never came back. Maybe that's not a bad thing! Maybe they went to Citizenry and found an amazing new life!"

"Maybe they died," Karen said quietly.

Lenth shrugged. "Maybe. Maybe they did. I don't know. That would be something worth finding out, don't you think?"

"Don't," Karen said, staring at the floor.

"I'll bring a pipe," Lenth joked. "I'll tell you what. I'll bring back information. If I see danger, I'll run right back down and hide. If I see something perfect and amazing, I'll leave that alone too, and come back to tell you. To tell everyone."

Karen shook her head slowly. She took his hand and muttered, "Idiot." before letting out an exasperated sigh and pulling him close to hold him.

Lenth was stunned. Unmoving, he looked around as if someone would tell him what to do. Feeling her pressed against him was incredible...or it would have been if his brain would come out of shock and appreciate it. "Idiots get hugs?" He asked.

Backing up and taking both of Lenth's hands, Karen smiled with a bit of sadness in her eyes. "You missed out on a lot, living in a Unit."

Looking into her eyes, Lenth noticed his breathing was heavier. He had a lot of questions, but dared not speak the ones that he wanted to ask most. "You can tell me all about what I've missed when I get back, okay? Hey, I've been wondering... you came down to be a Manager. You were a Provider. Why not anymore?"

Karen forced a meagre smile from under sad eyes. "I was better for the job than the Manager who was going to do it. I was needed."

"What was wrong with the other Manager?"

Looking to the door towards her Subjects, Karen's expression grew a little bit angrier. "Subjects are vulnerable, you know? Some people are the kind to take advantage of that. I had to protect those girls."

Lenth put his hand on Karen's arm. "I'm not sure I totally understand."

She took his hand off her arm, and held it close to her chest. She squeezed it, and smiled into his eyes. "I don't suppose you would, Lenth." She broke eye contact and shook her head a little. "You really want to go see Citizenry, don't you?"

Lenth nodded.

She squeezed his hand a little harder. "I don't think you're ready. Be careful. Always. Careful. Don't get hurt, don't get killed, and don't end up like Diane."

"It goes all the way up, and all the way down," Gabe said. In front of them loomed a metal door, about five metres wide. It was closed, and a large handle bar was bolted to it so that it could be pulled sideways along tracks in the floor and ceiling.

Beside the handle was a little metal box with a little door, and a pipe running out of it and up to the top edge of the door. Just above that at eye level sat a small door that could be opened to peek through.

Except it was stuck. Lenth tried.

Standing behind them were stacks of containers, about a cubic metre, filled with food disks. Half a dozen other Providers stood around, also waiting for the elevator to arrive.

The large door behind them was open, leading into a lower floor of the Provider's realm. It was much like the closed door in front of them.

And so all they waited is this receiving room, staring at the closed door.
"Oops," Lenth said to himself quietly.
Gabe looked at Lenth, head to toe. "Oops what?"
"I meant to give Carin' a knife. For defending herself."
Gabe shrugged. "Then do it."
"I won't get a chance for a while; I'm leaving. Can you do it for me?"
"Leaving?" Gabe smirked and glanced up. "You're that confident he'll agree, are you?"
Lenth just nodded. "So can you, please?"
"I don't think she's in a lot of risk, Lenth."
"She said the same thing, but I'd still rather she be ready just in case, okay? If people could get a hold of him, I'd be even happier."
Gabe grimaced. "He's a slippery thing. Fine, yes, a knife. I might be able to scrounge up something better, but yes, I'll get her a knife at least."
Lenth nodded again, and resumed the silent wait. Eventually the distant sound of the elevator's motors could be heard. The sound got louder and closer. Lenth traced where he thought it was behind the wall, and heard it settle into place with a tremendous rattle and a deep, resonating clonk.
A mental clank sounded as the latch moved, then the whole door slid out of the way. The interior was almost the size of his Brothers' sleeping room. Several replacement panels stood inside, which Lenth recognized to be pieces of wall.
Before them stood Messenger. Somewhat older than Lenth, and leaner, his fine black hair laid flatly around his face, richly-dark with a hint of red. His eyes stared right through them all, and stood with a quiet confidence. Immediately Lenth understood what Contact had meant by Messenger being 'far removed' from others.
Gabe bowed respectfully towards Messenger, but Lenth seemed to be the only one to really notice. Messenger just stood aside as the Providers behind Lenth moved in, loading on the food and unloading the replacement wall panels using small wheeled trollies. Messenger turned his eyes to Lenth and Gabe, the only other ones not doing work.
"Messenger?" Lenth asked, stepping up.
"Mm," was Messenger's only reply. Lenth waited for more, but Messenger lost interest and turned his attention back to the cargo loading.
"Don't waste his time, Lenth," Gabe said.
"Uh, right. Messenger, I was hoping you'd take me to Citizenry. Please."
Messenger looked to Gabe.
"Contact approved it," Gabe said.
"Fine," Messenger said. His voice was quiet. He didn't sound irritated at all, but simply disinterested in general. He continued to stand there as Providers continued and finished loading food containers on. As the Providers disappeared down the hall, Messenger looked at Lenth, and at the thin gap on the floor where the elevator floor began. "Coming?"
Lenth nodded and stepped forward. Standing over the seam, he turned to Gabe. "I might not see you for a while. Thanks."

Gabe smiled with a wave. "Be safe and all that."

"Bring Carin' that knife," Lenth said.

"Yeah. Heh. Maybe you should have one," Gabe said.

Messenger shook his head softly. "Let's just go."

"Oh. Right." Lenth got on and gave a sheepish wave as Messenger dragged the wide door shut.

Lenth looked around the closed elevator. The cargo only took up a small portion of the floor space, leaving a lot of big, round emptiness. A few long light strips in the ceiling all but destroyed any shadows in the off-white metal space. There were seams here and there where the elevator had been put together, a nondescript panel flush with the ceiling, and one in the floor.

Lenth looked back to Messenger, who was facing away from Lenth to attend the control panel by the door. The elevator rumbled from all directions and lurched upwards, much like Lenth had felt in the other, smaller elevators. He wasn't near a wall to grab; nothing to stabilize himself against. He staggered, but caught himself before falling. The feeling was all the more disorienting in a large space like this. Only the fact that he had heard the elevator coming down earlier assured him that everything, everywhere wasn't being heaved around.

Messenger stood by the control panel, entirely unperturbed. The central elevator was the Messenger's domain. His throne, his second body. In fact, he didn't seem noticeably aware of Lenth. No more than any other cargo.

"So..," Lenth said, "get many passengers?"

Messenger looked over at Lenth and took a stoic moment to consider his reply.

"Nope."

Lenth waited for Messenger to continue, but his instead turned away to face the control panel. Lenth finally tried again.

"Do you spend a lot of time making deliveries?"

"Some."

"So. I heard you go as far up as Actual."

Messenger gave no reply.

"Is he nice?" Lenth asked.

"There are rules," Messenger said flatly.

"Rules about him being nice?"

Messenger sighed. "Providers can go from Subject level to the Citizenry."

"Okay. Oh, no, I wasn't trying to get you to take me any higher."

"Good. There are rules."

Well. Fine. Lenth sat down by a food container. He could feel the little vibrations from the floor more while sitting. It was disconcerting. "How much longer?"

With no rush to answer, Messenger lazily looked up as if he could see through the ceiling. "We're roughly half way now."

"How many floors is it?"

"No floors, just distance. Takes time. The central elevator isn't as fast as the smaller ones."

"We're not passing any floors?" Lenth asked.

Messenger shook his head.

Lenth got up and put his hand against the wall. "So...what's on the other side of this right now?"

"You ask a lot of questions." Messenger's voice was starting to leak signs of irritation

"Oh. Sorry. Rules? Am I not allowed to know, or do you not know? Is there empty nothing? Solid wall? Metal?"

"Will you just be *quiet?*" *Yeah. Irritation.* Lenth took the suggestion, and didn't speak again until he felt the elevator slowing.

"Are we there?"

Messenger's reply came only as a nod. When the elevator came to a full stop, he could hear exited voices. Messenger went over to the little eye-height hatch. He didn't open it, but yelled close to it.

"*You know how this works. Clear out.*"

The excited voices got louder, but affirmative replies could be made out from the rabble's noise. "*Okay.*" "*You heard him.*" "*Move it!*"

As the talking faded with distance, Lenth quietly asked Messenger, "Citizens?"

Messenger nodded. When silence resumed, a little buzz came from the control panel and a little green light turned on. Messenger opened the eye-level hatch and looked out for a few moments. He was finally satisfied, and went over to the control panel He did something Lenth couldn't see, then grabbed the handle, and heaved the door to the side.

The broad hall in front of them was almost identical to the one where he'd boarded the elevator. Messenger started carrying stacks of food crates, three at a time, using a trolley. There wasn't another trolley available, so Lenth tried to lift a single crate himself.

"Don't be a fool," Messenger said, wheeling off with his second load. "If you want to help, just load me up when I come back."

Lenth watched Messenger roll the trolley out about halfway down the hall, then unloaded the three crates over to the side. He came back to Lenth, who was ready to place a crate on. By the time he had grabbed another, Messenger had already loaded the second one on. With the third placed by Lenth, Messenger was off to add to the growing pile.

"The Citizens don't help?" Lenth asked as they continued on in a bit of a rhythm.

"There are rules," Messenger said as he loaded another crate. One was unusually heavy, so he just rammed the lip of the trolley underneath it.

"What, you can't be in the same room with them? And I can?"

"You're choosing to be around them," Messenger said. "I choose not to be. They need to follow some rules if they want to get fed. If you change your mind and want to go back, come back here and catch me when I bring them something else."

Lenth looked at Messenger, then the far door, then at the elevator, then Messenger again. "Right. How often do you come, usually?"

Messenger shrugged. "They usually need more food and call every thirty days or so, but they can call for other things in between." He began closing the door to the elevator.

"See you around, Messenger."

"Do better," Messenger replied.

Lenth cocked his head. "Better? Better than what?"

Messenger shrugged. "Better than Diane, at least."

Before the door could close entirely, Lenth asked, "You know Diane?"

"About as well as I know you," Messenger said. The door closed tight. Of course Messenger had met Diane when she made this trip. It suddenly struck Lenth with increased clarity that he was risking the same challenges that broke Diane.

The sound of the elevator moving started up, and behind him, Lenth heard the door to Citizenry opening.

Chapter Seventeen

Welcome, Lofu

The group of noisy strangers stopped cold when they saw Lenth. The leader, a lanky, bright-looking man held his arms out; less to embrace a new acquaintance than to hold his minions back. They were all wearing clothes like Lenth and his Brothers had, but different. A few of them were stained, and many of them had ripped their body suits in different ways. Scraps from clothing had been used to make things like headbands, armbands, belt decorations, and hair ties. Not being of Citizen culture, it all looked very garbagey to Lenth.

The leader had light blonde hair that stuck straight upwards a few centimetres, and was wearing a patchwork scarf that dangled down to his knees. He smiled and walked forward slowly, lilting a bit from side to side as if different angles would allow him to better understand this newcomer.

"Ah, hello? I'm Lenth."

"Right," said the stranger. "I'm... Mike. What sends one of your kind up here?" He tilted his head and plucked the air in front of him, as if lifting something to his level.

"My kind?"

"Providers," Mike said in a patronizing yet friendly tone.

"I guess I am. Recently anyway. I've come up to Citi—"

Mike frowned and held up a hand. "Wait, wait, recently?"

One of the people in the little mob at the door called out, "*What were ya before? A chair?*"

Lenth halfheartedly joined in the laughs over the chair comment. "No, no, I grew up below the Providers, I worked on filters every day."

The Citizens' expressions ranged from disgusted to intrigued. Mike was among the intrigued. "Oh my, young man, you certainly have come up in the way of things. Welcome to the top!" He put his arm around Lenth and smiled widely with a nod. "Oh yes, Oh yes, but of course, you know there is a fee to enter, correct?"

"A fee?" Lenth asked, standing in front of the month's worth of food he'd come with.

Mike chuckled. "Oh, no, we wouldn't expect you to have any material possession worth trading, but *entertainment,* on the other hand, would do nicely."

Lenth stood silent, at a loss.

"Well, my boy, there's two interesting things you can do, and we can provide a partner for either," Mike said, then turning to the others. "What do you think? Will we make the baby Provider fight, or fffffornicate?"

With a dozen of the Citizens already leaked past the imaginary line that Mike had set for them, and uncounted others beyond the door, the bulk of them began chanting, "*Fight, fight fight, fight*".

Lenth had scuffled with his Brothers before, but nothing serious. Certainly not much, since their Rubberman would shock the floor to settle them down before anyone got hurt.

He didn't know what to expect now. He backed away from Mike, in case he was the opponent, and kept his eyes on everyone. He spread his stance and clenched his fists. If Messenger was still here, Lenth would have been back on that elevator in a blink.

From the group at the door, a figure was seen pushing a way through. It was a woman, unlike any Lenth had ever seen.

Her wild, scraggly hair was held out of her face with a scrap of cloth tied above her forehead. The dark mess of hair shot in every other direction.

Her bodysuit was zipped open wide enough to see much more than Lenth had ever seen before, and the legs of the suit were cut off high. Any higher, and it would fall off of her.

"Yer not gonna let anyone bloody up this pretty, pretty boy, Mike. It's not like shiny Providers pop up every day! I want a turn with him!"

The Citizens by the door cheered and goaded the woman on. She revelled in it. She twirled and bounced with a wicked smile, exuding a type of joy that Lenth had never witnessed. It was mesmerizing but somehow horrifying. Her motions had a certain edge to them that implied experience. Maybe it wasn't simply joy.

Her dance ended with her body pressed up against Lenth, but when he clumsily recoiled, she deftly extended her dance to keep up. She stopped him by putting her arm around his waist. "Afraid of a little slippery fun, Provider?" she growled softly.

Not that this woman wasn't interesting. Not that she wasn't soft in the right places. Not that she was entirely unappealing.

If this woman was proposing what it seemed like...this was not how he imagined it. In front of so many people, so impersonal, and nothing at all like Karen. He looked at the other Citizens, who were leering and waiting with giant smiles.

The woman looked at them, then back and Lenth. She leaned closer and whispered in his ear, "Don't worry about them. You don't even have to take your clothes off. Just get it out and go for it, yeah? And our audience isn't into softie-style, so feel free to rush and get it over with."

She leaned back far, a thigh coming around him now, her head almost upside down, her cleavage struggling to escape the unzipped top. The 'audience' reacted to her showmanship with a wave of lewd cheers.

Coming back up, she found his other ear to whisper into. "I'm the show here, kid. Don't stress it. We all earn our place in our own way. Just enjoy it." As they came face to face again, her glossed over demeanour cracked a little. Her smile was gone, and she shrugged so slightly that only Lenth would notice. Just as quickly, her seductive facade was reasserted.

Lenth's gut was tight. Something wrong was going on, but he couldn't really identify it. He backed away, holding her with a soft push to her shoulder. She stared into his eyes as he did so. He couldn't read if this was a look of irritation or not.

Cries of protest rang out from the Citizens. "*Come on!*" "*Make her scream for it!*" "*Maybe he's into guys.*" "*Whip it out!*"

"Maybe you were more interested in the *fight* option?" Mike said in an accommodating tone.

Lenth shrunk away from everyone slowly, taking unconscious little steps backwards towards the elevator. "Maybe I should just wait for Messenger to come back," he mumbled. Moans and boos from the Citizens only pushed him back towards the elevator further.

One of the food boxes began to move. Grunts came from inside as it wiggled around a little. The top finally burst open. A fist holding Diane's knife shot up as smashed food units spilled in every direction.

Up rose Six with a knife in each hand. "Lenth! I thought these Citizens were supposed to be the best of us! They just seem like a different kind of awful than the Providers!"

Six spotted the woman and was quickly behind her with an arm around her throat, knife by her face. "Well! I've heard enough to know that *you* obviously work for your keep! Maybe you're the exception!" He pointed the other knife at Mike and the other Citizens. "Anyone want the soft one dead?"

"*Six!* Don't make this worse than it already is!" Lenth pleaded.

"Friend," Mike said, "you're clearly out of your depth here. I don't think you under—"

Six wrenched his arm against the woman to enforce his leverage. She struggled, but the daily workouts that Six had always done as a Subject made him more than strong enough to contain her.

"Out of my way, I'm leaving," Six said to the Citizens clogging up the hallway. He walked towards the Citizens with his free knife waving at them. Between a lack of organization and room to move, the group wasn't moving nearly as fast as Six was hoping for. "This is garbage," he seethed at them.

Six threw the woman at Mike as forcefully as he could in order to slow them both down. Before she even landed on Mike, Six had turned again. With two free arms and knives to wield, he charged at the Citizens, screaming.

Lenth looked at the woman and Mike. They were all right, just knocked down. He then moved closer to Six, intending to stop him, but Six was already slashing wildly. His third rabid slash sent an arc of red across the wall, as did the fifth.

Three Citizens were on the floor already. One scampering away backwards from Six as he held his bleeding upper arm. One Citizen was kneeling, guarding a third who lay motionless in a growing pool of blood.

"*Six! What are you doing? Stop!*" Lenth's cries went ignored, if Six heard them at all over the swarm of chaos he had created- and was still cutting his way through.

Lenth manoeuvred around the first few injured people, and tried to get closer to Six, but more wounded and panicked people made it impossible. "*Stop it, Six! You don't have to do this! They haven't done anything to you!*"

Ahead, then a turn in the hall, there was no fighting to be heard, only the yells and cries of Six's wake. Six was gone, swallowed into the chaos.

Lenth made his way back to the elevator's receiving room, where the woman was helping an injured man, tying her scrap-headband around his arm as a bandage. She had zipped her outfit back up to a somewhat more modest configuration. Lenth knelt down by and asked her, "Are you all right?"

Without taking her eyes away from her bandaging job, she drew breath to answer, but was cut off.

"I'm fine, thank you," Mike said, strolling leisurely towards them. "Oh, you meant Leena." He smirked smugly at his own joke.

"I'm fine," 'Leena' said quietly. "I've been through worse." She lifted her chin towards the two dead men visible from where they were, and a half dozen other Citizens tending to each others' wounds. "I guess I was lucky."

"I can't believe he...I knew he'd killed, but this..." Lenth looked at Leena. She was rough, and her beauty was somehow a little repulsive, but it was still beauty. "Maybe Six didn't want to hurt a pretty woman. If he's like me, he didn't grow up around any."

"You *know* that energetic young knife enthusiast?" Mike said, gazing down the hall. A few unhurt Citizens had begun getting into the food crates...carefully.

Lenth stood, fists forming as he looked at the casualties. "We've...run into each other a few times. Before this, he's killed seven? I lost track. A Rubberman and a bunch of Providers. I kind of understood his reasons for that, but Citizens? He's crazy. We have to stop him."

Mike shrugged. "Go ahead. As far as I'm concerned, that fellow's little show was more than enough entertainment for the day. Consider your entry...granted."

"*Entertainment?*" Lenth looked at Mike with a wrinkled brow.

Leena's patient was bandaged as well as she could manage, and as he stood, so did Leena. She put her hand on Lenth's shoulder and said in a tired tone, "Welcome to the Citizenry."

"Who's the leader around here?" Lenth asked.

Mike reached out with a theatrical shrug. "Leader? A lot of people do what I say, so maybe I am!"

Lenth silently pushed his repulsion down. He looked at Leena, who had no objection to Mike claiming to be leader. He turned back to Mike. "So, how long have you been kinda-leader?"

Mike counted on his fingers. "One, two...hmm, five years? The guy who figured himself to be leader before was a real prick. I caved his head in, people cheered. It was a big thing."

"He did a lot of things, that guy before," Leena said with a distant gaze. "His buddies, too. They..." She smiled, and pinched Lenth's cheek. "You're a damned virgin, aren't you? I shouldn't go trying to confuse a kid like you." She pulled out a bag made from a scrap of clothing and wandered over to the food crates. She filled her baggie up as much as she could, securing it to her hip through a couple of small holes in her suit. By now, Citizens had been coming and going to secure their own stash.

"He made a lot of use of spaces above the ceiling," Lenth said to no one in particular. He looked up. The ceiling here was solid, not like the panels that he'd seen in many places in the past. "Where could he go to hide, and maybe move around? You know, where he might not be seen."

Leena snickered a little. "So you want to go crawl into wherever that guy and his two knives went?"

"I can't believe how relaxed you all are!" Lenth said. "Look at how many people Six hurt and killed!"

"Someone will kill him," Leena said quietly, "or he'll end up being the leader or something." She paused to make eye contact with Lenth. "—And for the record, I highly doubt that will happen."

Lenth looked around to see if any of the Citizens around thought that what Leena said was crazy. "This...this is *normal?*" Lenth asked.

Leena shrugged. "It's not everyday or anything, and the fact that it's a Provider causing trouble is unique, but this kind of thing happens."

"Not where I come from," Lenth said. "Nothing like this at all! I didn't even know what death was most of my life, let alone *this!* Hey, where's Mike gotten off to?"

"He's probably gone to get his medical stuff. He keeps a bunch of it, and looks like a big hero when he comes along with a bandage and pain pills."

"But not heroic enough to go after Six, huh?" Lenth asked.

Leena shrugged. "He might. Mike's never been much of a brawler."

"But he caved in the head of the old leader? What, was he asleep?"

"That's not how the tale goes," Leena said, "but you're probably pretty close to the truth. What do I know? Someone needed to do it."

Leena began to wander down the hall, and Lenth followed. "Oh, Leena, Six isn't a Provider, by the way. He came from a couple of floors below that. Unit Subject. Like I was, but in a different Unit."

"I have no idea what you're talking about," Leena said.

"Units. We live below the Providers, and Rubbermen. Among other things, the Units grow what the food is made out of."

"Grow food?" Leena chuckled. "What are you talking about? Food doesn't grow, dummy."

"It does! I didn't know either. My Unit doesn't grow anything, but I've seen the 'trees' that they get the papayas from, and the papayas go into the food. And don't even ask what they feed the trees, not if you want to sleep tonight!"

Leena's incredulous expression stopped Lenth from explaining any more. It sounded ridiculous. *How do you explain that these tree-things are living, unmoving giants, twisted and hard, with weird green bits coming out of their many arms, who eat the rotting dead, and make food from it?*

Thinking about it made Lenth wish he'd taken the time to see the other trees. Like a rice tree, or a beet tree. Did they all look the same except the fruit? *So many types of trees. Strange to think they're alive. So life isn't just humans. It's humans and like...six kinds of trees! Who knew?*

"So, Provider guy, are you following me for a reason? Showtime is over. Are you thinking of some nekkid grunty fun? Because to be totally honest, I'm not in the mood after your buddy did his stabby thing."

"I...wasn't really thinking about that. I just...the only two people I know around here are you and Mike, and between the two choices..."

Leena scoffed in amusement. "Gotcha."

"And I'm not quite a Provider, I think. My name is Lenth."

"All right, not-quite-a-Provider-I-think-Lenth, what's your grand plan?"

The surrounding Citizens, some dealing with Six's attack, and some heading in for a resupply of food, were thinning out a bit as Lenth and Leena got further from the elevator. Lenth noticed how big the hallway was . Just as wide as the elevator, and a metre or so higher than most ceilings. The walls were marred with grime collected over time, and the occasional smudge which hinted at burns or blood. Pictures were on the walls as well. Some small, some grand, all crudely created, and all in dark, near-colourless tones.

"My plan?" Lenth said. "I *was* looking for answers about my Brother's death. Found 'em, too. But I guess while I was looking, I started finding things. Things I didn't know were out there." He chuckled and looked Leena up and down. "Like women! I never knew!"

"What? I was right? You've never..."

"Nope. I learned about it recently, though," Lenth said.

Leena couldn't help but laugh. "What, you learned about it? How, from a magazine?"

"What's a magazine?" Lenth said. "I learned it from a video."

That did it. Leena burst into hysterics, imagining Lenth perched in front of a little TV, taking notes in a studious trance—which hadn't been that far from the truth.

"How is that funny?" Lenth asked. "How is a person *supposed* to learn it?"

Leena forced her laughter down to a dark, rolling giggle. She pressed Lenth against the wall, unzipping her clothes half way down. "Have a peek," she said darkly. "Are you telling me you need instructions to get ideas?"

Lenth found himself staring, and being invited, he didn't feel a great need to look away in the name of manners. Mind you, he was stunned anyway.

"See, you get it," Leena said, zipping up and continuing down the hall. "It all figures itself out."

Lenth composed himself as well as he could and trailed along behind her. He was just thankful that he hadn't had to deal with any swelling. "I don't understand how you...and I guess I mean all Citizens I've met so far, can be so casual about sex and death. I mean, what Six did was horrible! I'm still expecting him to jump out and attack again! He could be anywhere! And you're teasing me and showing—"

They came to the end of the hall. The room it led to was the biggest thing Lenth had ever seen. His mind went immediately to what Gabe had once said about a place with no ceiling. There *was* a ceiling here. It was just very, very high, about eight floors up.

It curved slightly, like they were under some huge, wide bowl turned upside down. In the centre of the ceiling, the elevator shaft protruded, connecting the top of the dome to the structure Lenth and Leena had just exited. The elevator shaft ran right through the open centre of Citizenry.

Eight 'ribs' spread out from the top of the elevator shaft, reaching down along the curve, all the way to the edges of the grand room's floor. Each 'rib' was at least five people wide.

From place to place, the walls had arrays of windows into smaller rooms. Doors to them were joined by platforms railed off to help prevent falls, and once-graceful staircases joined them all to each other and the floor. The stairs had seen quite a bit of damage. Some were useless, and some had been repaired in obvious ways with metal plates. They were attached by many means. The only one he could make out from a distance were some kind of black rope. Some of the repairs left crude ramps where steps had once been.

As unsafe as it looked to Lenth, a few people were walking and even running on them.

The enormous sight stopped Lenth in his tracks, and his knees felt weak. A mild sense of vertigo swept over him, and for a moment, he didn't notice the activity in front of him.

"Lenth. Wake up," Leena said.

Lenth snapped out of his gawking. "Oh? Oh! What's going on?"

"Mike's feeling important and doing his thing."

Looking forward, Lenth saw the vast expanse of scrap and ruin. Structures made from anything and everything littered the area. They varied from from modest homes, to work areas, play fields, to things of unknowable intent.

Wide paths led out of the hall and through the scattered clutter, debris and 'structures' in the room. One brought Lenth and Leena to a crowd of about fifty Citizens around a raised platform, upon which Mike testified.

"Attention, people," Mike called out with tempered good will, "Many of you know what's happened, and some of you know bits and pieces. I was there, I saw it all, and I want to make sure truths are known before rumours get confused and muddied, as rumours tend to do.

"First, the good news. Yes, food has arrived as expected. I see many of you have already gotten yours. I don't have to remind anyone what happens if people get unreasonably greedy, so good is good.

"Second, I see some of you are bleeding. You've met one of our newest inhabitants, an angry fellow who likes knives. He's from really deep down, bottom rung Unit Lofu, so we can't expect much in civility. I saw four dead people on my way out, and a lot more hurt. I've sent runners to go fetch some medical necessities, and we'll get right on treating the injured as best we can.

"Thirdly, good news on that front. We also have another new inhabitant, at least for a while: a Provider!"

Mike held his hand out to point towards Lenth. The crowd turned to look at Lenth, and all he could do was shift uncomfortably. Mike quickly took the attention back.

"Our new friend Lenth here will take care of our little stabby-man problem, after which," and Mike paused for emphasis, "*after which*, I'll summon Messenger with the communication box, if Lenth wishes. Then he can go about whatever other adventures await such a hero! Ah, I see my runner coming back with medical supplies, so I'll just get to business. Oh, if you see that stabby Lofu, do tell Lenth here."

The gathering slowly started to dissipate as Mike stepped off the platform, stopping to talk to various people.

"Leena," Lenth asked quietly, "what's Lofu?"

Leena rolled her eyes with a smirk. "Lesser Outsider From Under."

"Lesser outsider?" Lenth asked. "Are there better outsiders?"

"You're a riot," Leena said mirthlessly. "Outside of the Citizenry. Lesser as in not as good as us."

"Ah." Lenth stuck out his chin and nodded slowly. "So I guess that counts for me, too."

"He didn't call you that," Leena said. "Maybe he counts you as a Citizen now. Or maybe you're just useful."

"Useful but lesser?" Lenth asked.

Leena smirked. "That attitude, minus the sarcasm, will get you far with Mike."

"And the people that make your food? Are they lesser, too?" Lenth wondered aloud.

"I guess!" Leena paused for a moment, only giving it real thought for a split second before her Citizenship reasserted itself. "They're not *as* lesser than other lessers, I guess."

"And Messenger? And Actual? Are they outsiders, or lesser?"

"You have odd thoughts, Lenth." Leena looked back at the elevator shaft that reached up to the lofty ceiling. "They're...outsiders for sure. But they're not like us. They're..." she stared at the ceiling, looking for the right words.

"Better outsiders?" Lenth offered.

Leena looked at him in all seriousness, and studied his face for a moment. "Yeah. Yeah, maybe that's a good way of putting it. We're..."

"Do you think they call you Citizens 'Lofu'?"

"Stop thinking so much, Lenth."

The group was nearly dissipated, and Mike wandered towards the two of them.

"Well, that went well!" Mike said, grinning. He accepted a large, worn medical bag from his runner and slung it over his shoulder.

"Subtle, Mike," Leena said, "how you spelled out that Lenth can't go until he's gotten rid of the other guy."

"Liked that, did ya?" Mike chuckled as he did a quick little inspection of his bag's contents. "I thought it sounded right leaderly of me!"

"His name is Six," added Lenth quietly.

"Who?" Mike closed his bag, apparently satisfied. "Oh, oh, Mister Stabby. Right. Six, whatever. Hey, do you have a knife, Lenth? I hope you have a knife, it might help."

Lenth shook his head.

"Ah. Pity. Leena, can you take our brave boy here up to our den and let him pick something out from the pokey-rack? Not my best ones, of course, but the main racks should have something that suits him."

"Sure," Leena said.

"You're a doctor, Mike?" Lenth asked.

Mike patted his medical bag. "Nope. No one here is, but I've figured out enough. I've read a couple of manuals. Lot of pictures."

"You can read!" Lenth said, partly as a question, eyebrows high.

"Yes," Mike said with a fairly smug look. "I've been able to read for a long time! I've mastered it! Well. Mostly."

"Don't tease the Lofu, Mike," Leena said. "Mike reads well enough to get by. As well as anyone."

"I bet 'anyone' is better than me at it," Lenth said. "I'm pretty new at it. The Providers, though, they all seem great at it. Probably better than any of us."

Mike coughed. "I highly doubt any Provider is better at anything than a Citizen is."

Lenth looked away and shrugged. Providers sure seemed to be better at doctoring, making food, or operating the central elevator, but it didn't seem worth bringing up.

"Come on," Leena nudged Lenth. "Let's go get your pokey poke."

Chapter Eighteen

Poking Around

Lenth followed along beside Leena as they crossed the huge common room towards one of the haphazard ramps. As they walked, they passed a group of three Citizens.

"Leena, food's here?" one of them asked.

"Yeah. Hey, you guys haven't seen a stranger in the last little while? Besides this guy here. Probably has bloody hands and stuff? Did a lot of damage, some dead people."

The trio looked surprised and didn't have any useful information. Leena gave them a brief warning before she and Lenth continued on their way.

"Who were those people?" Lenth asked.

"I don't know. I mean, I've seen them around, but I don't know their names."

Lenth looked back at them as he walked, then back at Leena. "They knew you."

"Yeah, most people know me. I'm kinda with Mike and stuff, and, well..."

"I only knew about four people all my life, and I know them all. Not knowing people that you live around..." Lenth glanced around, spotting others in the distance. "It's just really weird for me. I guess I'm weird to you and the other Citizens."

Leena shrugged. "Hadn't thought about it much. Four people all your life, huh? Does that have something to do with why you couldn't get a girl?"

"Pretty much. There were no girls." Lenth chuckled nervously.

Leena whistled a long, low note. "Boy. That sucks. Wait. Am I the first girl you've ever seen?"

"No, no, I met some Provider women. You're nothing like them, though."

"What, they got no...?" She swayed back and forth and ran her hands down along her body in an exaggerated way.

Lenth stared at her, shaking his head. "I'm not even sure what that was."

With a weathered gaze, Leena walked on. "Oh, you poor boy, you," she said sullenly. "Gonna have to get you an education."

They passed a few more Citizens as they approached the ramp, and asked them if they'd seen a stranger with bloody hands. No luck. They started up the ramp, and Lenth could now see that it was a mix of metal slabs built into the wall, fragments of the original staircase, and chunks of anything flat and big enough to be lashed on. Electrical cables, bungee cords, regular rope, and unidentified bits bound the whole mess together.

Lenth looked back across the huge commons. "Six was good at hiding in tight little spaces. I was hoping he wouldn't be as good in a wide open place."

If Lenth's stare across the commons was one of awe, Leena's was one of quiet disdain. "I think I know enough hiding places to get us a good start."

As she led in front of Lenth, he watched her stride and compared her to Karen. Karen walked with confidence and ease. Leena walked with confidence as well, but it was more determined motion. Maybe it was just that they were walking up an incline. Maybe it was the stress of the situation.

Lenth looked at the occasional drawings made by Citizens, like the ones by the elevator. This was one of the things that Citizens did instead of work. The pictures ranged from simple shapes, to crude portraits, to cruder sexual illustrations.

Leena turned her head from time to time, looking around the ramp and down in the commons.

"I should keep a better eye out for Six, too," Lenth said.

Leena looked surprised for a moment. "Huh? Oh. Yeah, Six. Him too."

"Him too?" Lenth asked. "Who else are you looking for?"

She shrugged. "No one special. Just habit. No one messes with me since Mike became leader, but then again, it might make me a target for anyone mad at Mike for whatever. But most people are pretty okay with him. Oh, look out; there's a loose chunk right here." She tapped her foot on a piece of the ramp as she kept walking.

Lenth took care to not step on the hazard, but his stride slowed. Then stopped. "Is that how it works up here? Really? People just...kill? What Six did doesn't seem to even have anyone that upset!"

Leena turned halfway around and looked at Lenth with a sad smile. "You're cute, kid. People mind if they get killed, but it's not like it's unheard of. Your buddy, though, he's made an impression, I'm sure. So much violence, and no real purpose? Yeah, that's going to unsettle folks."

"I don't get it," Lenth said, resuming the climb.

Leena shrugged. "Most people who get killed—they had it coming. Or at least there was a reason of some kind. People feel safer if they keep their heads down and don't piss others off. Some jerk like Six starts causing problems with no reason?"

A little surge of paranoia struck Lenth. He looked around and down off the ramp into the commons. "Do you mean...you're always in danger of getting attacked? Everyone is? By anyone?"

"Ha. No one lives forever," Leena said, continuing on.

"Yeah," Lenth said quietly as he followed, "and then they become plant food."

Leena stopped. "*What* food? Citizens don't eat dead people. We eat the food that Messenger brings."

Lenth shook his head. "So, Leena, what do you do with people when they die?"

Leena continued up. "We send them off with Messenger. He brings them to be with Actual."

"To be with?" Lenth asked.

"To live again, with Actual. Actual is not like us."

"He is separated from us," Lenth said, remembering Contact's words, "as separated and above Messenger, as Messenger is from us."

Leena smiled. "You know all about it, then."

What made Lenth think for a moment that a Citizen would be happy with the truth: that they were taken to be composted, to help produce food? If they felt that Providers were beneath them, it seemed like an obvious choice to believe that their dead went up to some singular unknown. To Actual. Did they even know what death was?

Lenth looked to the centre of the commons, where the great elevator shaft reached the ceiling. Actual was allegedly above that. How far? Was that ceiling Actual's floor? Or was Actual some unknown distance farther up? Lenth took a moment to take in the elevator shaft.

Where it met the floor, or specifically, the structure where he came out of the elevator earlier, there were remains of something. It looked like a collapsed attempt at making some kind of...ladder? Staircase? Either way, it was just mostly just a pile of debris around the elevator shaft. It looked like it had been there for some time and had been raided for materials.

At the top of the shaft, about a dozen lines of thick cabling dangled down. Some attached to the various ramps along the upper potions of the room. From the tiny bits of damage in the ceiling, Lenth wondered if the cabling had once been secured snug and flat along the top.

They reached the uppermost platform on the ramp. One of the dangling cables was attached on the outer edge of the flooring. Five huge windows wider than an arm-span stretched from the floor to just overhead.

At least, Lenth thought at first that they were windows. Once, they most certainly were, but the glass was gone. Only tiny bits of glass remained in the corners of the frames. By that token, it was maybe more remarkable that the frames themselves were mostly intact. They were a little dented here and there, and a few had rust creeping up from the floor. Leena stepped right through into this not-so-private environment and looked around.

"Welcome to my place! Well, Mike's place. Whatever."

She walked past a thing that she called a sofa, that had one end held up by a nondescript hunk of metal with nondescript vents on it. Trying to guess the ripped-up sofa's original colour was difficult.

Leena went over to a sink and filled up a metal cup from the faucet. Then she picked up a dull knife and took her water over a rusty bit of a window frame. She scraped some of the rust off into her cup and stirred it before taking a swing. "There's other cups over there if you want." She retrieved a new headband from under the sofa to replace the one that she'd used to bandage someone earlier.

"You drink rust?" Lenth asked.

Leena shrugged. "Didn't feel like water, didn't think the dizzy stuff was a good idea right now either." Lenth didn't feel like asking about dizzy stuff, but the term made him think of the 'sleep smell' he'd been subjected to from time to time over the years. He picked up a cup. It was, thankfully, pretty clean. He poured himself half a cup and downed it.

"We got a shower here and everything." Leena's tone edged on flirty, as did her hip swagger. Leena noticed his obliviousness, and it derailed her intent to educate him. "Ah, we came here for the hurty kind of pokey, didn't we?" Leena waved Lenth to follow her as she put down her cup. Lenth did the same.

The next room over was fairly large and badly lit. In one corner was a small doorway that led to another room. The middle of the room was a semi-organized pile of blankets, presumably with a mattress underneath. The far wall displayed a selection of items.

Tools, mostly. Lenth wasn't familiar with tools in general, but it seemed obvious that some were modified by Citizens, maybe by Mike.

A ball-peen hammer had a few nails attached to the head. A claw hammer had its claw battered down to be sharper than the original design. A heavy pair of gloves with barbed wire wrapped around them had a metal plate attached to shield the forearms. A set of crude spiked 'iron knuckles' hung near those. Some longer tool had lost its original working end, and the metal shaft had been hammered down into a blade, like a medium-sized sword.

Several more items filled out the display, but Lenth was drawn to the largest item, a sledge hammer. It stood on its head, handle sticking up. He knelt next to it and felt along the handle, picking it up with a bit of a grunt. He looked at Leena, who was looking at him with a raised eyebrow.

"Like it nice and big?" she purred with a sultry smirk.

Lenth heaved it up with both hands. "People fight with these? Seems kind of stupid. By the time you get it swinging, the person you're trying to hit would like...not be in that spot anymore."

"That was supposed to get a reaction out of you," Leena said.

"Huh? I answered."

Leena unzipped her top past the navel, and arched back to nudge out a bit of cleavage. It was a motion she'd done many times in the past, but this time she did it with no seductive smoothness. Just quick, blunt, and almost clinical. "Okay, a girl unzips in front of you, alone in a room with a bed. What does that make you think?"

"Oh. Oh! I'm sorry, I'll pick a better weapon and leave so you can get changed or whatever. Gabe taught me about privacy," Lenth said apologetically, turning back to the weapon display.

Leena clenched her fists and shrugged. "It's no fun telling you I'm not interested in actually fucking you when you don't even take the bait!"

Lenth dropped the sledge hammer where he'd gotten it from and turned back to Leena. "I'm confused."

Leena shook her head. "Yeah. Yeah, don't worry about it, I'm just wasting your time anyway." She flicked her hands dismissively at the weapons. "Go ahead, pick what you want. Don't rush on my account."

"Well, hold on, what's 'fucking', and why would I do it to you?" Lenth asked.

Covering her mouth and reaching out with her other hand to some imaginary audience, Leena turned about the room until she faced Lenth once again. "*Sex!*" she yelled. "*Fucking means sex! Have you heard of sex?*"

Lenth nodded and pointed at Leena. "Yes! I have. I leaned all about it, but I don't think creating children right now would help. Having more people helping me find Six would be good, but I also learned that children take a long time to grow inside—"

Leena screamed in exasperation, leaving a silent void.

After a moment, Lenth rallied his courage to speak again. "I'm pretty sure I remember being one, and it was a long time to—"

"Hush," Leena said flatly, shaking her head.

"And I've seen some children recently in the Provi—"

"Just. Just stop now, Lenth."

"Leena. Have you done sex?"

She put her hand on her forehead and nodded, biting her lip. "Yeah. Yeah, Lenth, I seem to remember doing sex a couple of times."

"Oh! So where are your children now?"

Leena squinted at Lenth. "When I first met you, I said I needed to educate you. I had no idea how bad it was. Just pick a weapon already."

Lenth waited for Leena to say something else, but she only answered his stare by pointing forcefully at the weapons. He turned and looked at them again.

"What should I take?"

"Something you won't hit yourself in the face with. Just...what looks easy."

Lenth walked up to the crude swords. He grabbed the contoured plastic handle. It felt nice in his hand, but when he waved the thing in the air, he grimaced.

"If I run into Six in a small space, I won't have room to swing something like this. I guess I'd be better off with a smaller knife."

"What does Six use?"

"Well, I've only seen him use knives."

"Wouldn't it be nice to be able to reach him before he gets close enough to use a knife on you?" Leena asked.

Pointing the sword forward, he tried to visualise using it in battle. He poked forward a couple of times, wiggled it, and slashed it sideways. "Okay. But it's still not good for crawlspaces."

"Then take two things from the wall."

"I can do that?"

Leena shrugged. "I don't think Mike'd mind. And if he does, fuck 'im."

Lenth's eyes widened. "*Fuck him?*"

"Not like that," Leena rolled her eyes. "The word is also used when you don't like something, or like, disrespect it."

"I'm starting to think you made that word up."

"No, no, everyone uses it, and I even read it in a book and everything. I thought people were stupid when they were using it for both things until someone showed me in a book. It's a pretty versatile word, but for some reason, you're not supposed to use it a lot."

"You seem to use it a lot, Leena. Do people get angry?"

Leena threw up her hands and laughed, "*Fuck 'em!*"

By the time Leena's amusement had faded, Lenth was already considering his second item. He'd grabbed one of the gloves with the barbed wire and the arm guard. He put it on his left hand. All of the wire's barbs were on the back of the hand, so he could still make a fist without serious problems.

"Huh, I thought you'd at least go for a knife," Leena said.

"Knives can get dropped."

"Well, those little spikes aren't going to do much damage, Lenth. I mean, it looks tough and stuff, but it's not too practical."

"I also like it for the arm guard part. Hey, maybe I could take both gloves, then have the sword in one hand, and a knife in the other!" Not hearing any protests from Leena, he did just that, grabbing a twenty centimetre serrated kitchen knife. It was the only item from the wall that he took which was not modified in any way. He stood in front of the weapons rack, facing Leena, and posed, holding both of his weapons out to the side.

Leena smiled quietly and took in the sight. "Hmm, Lofu, that's not a bad look on you," she said.

"All right then. I guess I'm as ready as it gets. You had an idea where Six might go?" Lenth found that the knife could sit snugly between the wires on the right glove, freeing his left hand for other things.

Leena went to the wall, and opened a box that Lenth had ignored. From it she took a belt, which carried a slender machete, and a flask. She put the belt on, as well as a pair of leather gloves. They were thick enough to provide some degree of protection, but were old and held together by duct tape. "Let's go."

"Oh, do you want to trade gloves? I have a lot of stuff, and..."

"Nope, I like these. Just don't get clumsy with your spikies, Lofu."

"Please stop calling me that, Leena."

Leena shrugged. "All right."

Leaving Mike's den, they headed back down the ramp for a bit, then took a lateral path that branched off about half way down to the ground. It looked to be headed to another window/opening like Mike's den, but Leena stopped at a metal grate that Lenth didn't notice until they were right beside it. Drawn around it were random-looking lines, some going up and down in a wiggly way, and some in various sizes of spirals.

"This isn't the most likely spot, but it's likely enough," Leena said as she picked at the edge of the grate. Where screws had once held it in place, there were now only thread-less rods, easily accessible.

"It's a small space," Lenth said. "Six might like it."

Leena put the grate aside. "Okay. Stupid things happen in here. If you smell shit, get away from it. Head back here if you need to. If I start talking stupid, get me back here. If you *see* anything stupid, get back here. Got it?"

"Sounds stupid," Lenth said with a smirk. "What do you mean 'smell shit'?"

"Some people save crap and let it sit in a sealed container. Then when it gets old enough, you can sniff it, and it messes with your head for a while."

Lenth looked down into the crawlspace and grimaced. "Please tell me you're kidding."

"Nope. And if anyone's in there sniffing, be careful. They might be seeing things that aren't there, and...they might get stupid." She crawled in first, and Lenth was suddenly faced with curves that made him momentarily forget that he was about to crawl into the realm of shit-sniffers.

It was dark inside, but not pitch black. His eyes adjusted to the minimal light. They were in a four-metre by eight-metre metal-walled room of sorts, only a metre or two high. "I think I smell it."

"That's nothing. Don't worry unless it's a bit more stomach turning."

In the left corner, a pile of blankets shifted and a face popped up. "Are you real?" asked the man.

"Yeah, man. Waiting to see stuff?" Leena asked.

"Yeah. I saw you guys carrying weapons and thought I might have started seeing stuff. I don't think I let this batch sit long enough. I'm not getting much out of it." He opened up an opaque jar and inhaled deeply from it before closing it again. "Yeah. Smell's not quite right either. I still have my old one. Maybe it still has a bit left to it." He started rummaging in the blankets for his back-up.

"Hey, before you break it out, answer me something, okay?" Leena said, holding her hand up in objection.

Container in-hand, the man stopped before opening it. "You guys aren't interested? I mean, I'll share—"

"No, no," Leena said, trying not to sound condescending, "me and the Lofu here are looking for another Lofu. A bad one who got all killy and stabby. He'd probably have blood on him still."

The man opened his eyes wide and stared at Lenth. "Killer Lofus...woah. No, I haven't seen anything like that. And I haven't gotten a good sniff yet today, so I'm pretty sure of that."

"Thanks. We'll leave you to your 'fun' then." She nodded to Lenth and they headed back the way they came, soon out on the commons scaffolding paths again.

"Is he going to spend all day in there?" Lenth asked in a hushed tone.

"Probably. Until he gets hungry or something."

"Sad. And gross."

"Gross, sure," Leena said, going ahead on the walkway again, "but why sad? I'm sure he'll get a good sniff eventually. Happy, happy," she said mirthlessly. "I've tried it a handful of times in the past. It's okay, but yeah, after a while it's not so amazing, and just gross."

Lenth couldn't put his finger on what made it sad, outside of the disgusting factor, but it certainly wasn't the kind of thing he'd grown up with under the direction of a Rubberman.

"You get everything from the Providers and Units," Lenth said, hoping to fight the idea of Lofus being 'lesser'. "Fresh air, clean water, food... I guess if you don't have to work for it, you have to fill the time somehow."

"Sniffing, art, games, fucking, dizzy water. Yeah, it's pretty good overall," Leena said. "Aside from violence, rapes, that kind of thing, being a Citizen is great!"

Lenth staggered and stopped. "Violence and what?"

Leena stopped, and still facing away from Lenth, lowered her head. She scoffed lightly. "I guess you *wouldn't* know," she said softly, "given your...lack of experience."

"But what is it?" Lenth asked cautiously.

"It's bad." She turned her head towards the middle of the commons. "It doesn't happen nearly as much as before Mike took over, though. No public exhibitions of it either. So that's...that's good."

"*What is it?*"

Leena turned to face Lenth with a sad smile on her face. She gently pinched his nose. "You're cute, Lofu. I'll explain it, but not now, okay?" Leena turned away and continued on. Lenth considered pressing the issue, but not now.

"Where are we headed?" Lenth asked.

"There's a space where a lot of the men play games." Leena leaned over the railing a little and pointed down. "Yeah, there it is. When we reach the floor, we'll be close to it."

Lenth looked over the side. An area about ten metres square was bound in by roughly three-metre-tall pieces of assorted scrap, with a ladders on one edge allowing access in and out. Either side had a tower of boxes like the ones the food had been sent in and an open box on top. Five men ran around shouting incoherent things and jostling around for a tightly-bound wad of cloth, about the size of a head. One of the men got it free from the others and ran towards one of the open boxes, only to be tackled before he could jump and place it in. The men fell onto the tower and it all fell over. The game was put on hold while the tower was reconstructed.

"Looks... fun?" Lenth said.

"Some people think so," Leena said. "Kind of a guy thing. It's more fun if the players are full of dizzy water."

"Okay, you mentioned dizzy water before. What's that?"

"Food, smashed up a bunch, soaked in water, and wait a long time. It starts to smell bad at first, then after a while the smell changes, and then it's really strong dizzy water. You usually add more water before you drink it."

"Sounds similar to sniffing," Lenth said grimly.

"Eh...not really. Dizzy water makes you relaxed, clumsy, and stupid. And happy. Or sometimes sad. Or angry. Or Horny. The more you have, the more you feel it, of course. Sniffing makes you super relaxed, usually happy, sometimes paranoid, and you often end up seeing and hearing things that aren't there. Sometimes those are cool, but a lot of the time, it's scary as heck."

"You make it all sound so *appealing!*" Lenth said with raised eyebrows.

Leena gave him a nudge in the ribs. "Oh, shut up. It's something to do. Some are really into it. A sniffer who goes too far? Those types are scary."

They got to the bottom and headed over to the game yard. A couple of younger women were hanging around chatting by the ladder. They looked at the well-armed Leena and Lenth, and said nothing...but watched them carefully.

"Hey girls," Leena said, "me and the Lofu here are looking for a trouble maker that stabbed a bunch of people. Seen any strangers with blood on their hands?"

"Nope. We just woke up a bit ago, though," one of the girls said. "Where's this stabber guy? I'd wanna *avoid* him!"

"I don't know," Leena said in a flat tone. "I was asking if you knew where he was. Whatever. Just stay safe." Leena looked at the ladder. "Hey Lenth, crawl up and ask the guys inside about it. It's your turn."

Lenth was fine with doing so, but wondered why Leena didn't do it, as she'd been doing so well taking initiative up to this point. A bit of that thought must have shown in his expression, so Leena felt the need to say something. "Just go up and get it over with," she said. "I hate it in there."

He handed his 'sword' to Leena and started up. The spiky gloves scraped against the metal ladder in ways that made Lenth's teeth itch. When he peeked his head up over the edge, the players inside were just hanging around, talking.

"Uh...hello?" Lenth called with a wave. The players all looked up at him.

"Hey. We're odd right now. You're welcome to play and even things out, but those spikes have to stay outside," one said.

Lenth looked at the metal protruding from his knuckles as if he'd only just noticed them. "Oh, I just wanted to ask you guys—although, if you've been here all day...well, I'm looking for a guy new to the Citizenry who stabbed a bunch of people when he arrived. Just a while ago. Probably still bloody, unless he found a place to clean up."

Another of the players piped up. "Huh! Does Mike know about this?"

"Yeah," Lenth said, "he was there. So was I. He sent me out to go look for him. The guy's name is Six, because he has six toes on each foot."

"So he's running around barefoot?" another player asked.

"Well, no," Lenth said, "but that's how he got his name."

"Then how does knowing how many toes he has help *anything*?"

"Never mind," Lenth said sullenly, "but if you see any bloody strangers with knives, just keep away and tell me or Mike or something." He started to head back down the ladder when one of the players spoke up.

"I saw a couple people looking bloody," he said, "but I knew them both. They said there was trouble at the elevator."

"That's where it started, yes," Lenth said. "Do you think *they* have any idea where the stabber went?"

The player shrugged. "I don't know. They were headed towards Edgar's place I think. I think they kind of live there."

Lenth heard a groan from Leena, behind him at the bottom of the ladder. He waved down to the players. "Well, that's something to go on. I think. Thanks."

"No problem," the player said, "and who are *you*, anyway?"

"Lenth. I'm from a Unit, originally."

"Lofu," another player explained to the first player quietly.

Lenth rolled his eyes, and headed down the ladder. "This Lofu stuff is starting to get old," he said to Leena. "So...who's Edgar?"

Chapter Nineteen

The Maybe Once, Maybe Future Kinda-Leader

A loose braid of three cables ran along the makeshift wall, and hung from it in bunting-like swoops. The wall was made from some of the finest scrap, with some of the largest pieces reaching more than five metres tall. The wall partitioned off about a sixth of the commons' floor space and backed against the edge. If seen from higher up, a person could make out a large tapered oval shape.

The only way into this area was through the open gate, with a sign at its apex reading "Edgar's Refuge". At the gate stood two guards, one on either side. They wore their clothing in similar ways, with extra padding around the shins and stiff armour plates strapped to their shoulders and forearms. They each held a spear; just metal banged into a long, pointy shape.

"Edgar's *refuse*," Leena huffed as they came within sight, still forty or so metres away. "Just try not to cause problems, Lenth."

"Me?"

"Yeah. Don't volunteer where you're from if you don't have to. Unless you're asked. Be honest if asked, but if you're not asked, play it cool. As if you were born here. In fact, let me do most of the talking, yeah?"

"I guess, Leena. Sure. So what's the deal with this Edgar guy?"

"A lot of people respect him, treat him like leader. A lot of people think that Mike's a jerk, which, face it, he is, and that the only reason more people like

Mike is that he mashed up the last leader, who was…a lot more than a jerk. All the rape clubs disappeared or were killed after that."

"Again, what's rape?" Lenth asked.

Leena sighed forcefully, and stared at a spot on the floor. "It's sex, all right? It's forced sex. At its best, it's terrible. It stays with you." Her voice became slowly weaker as she spoke. "It's humiliating; it's a wound in the brain. At its worst, it's…worse. And the clubs did that a lot. Bunches all at once. Holding down—often out where everyone could watch. Some girls didn't live."

Lenth stared in quiet shock. Leena had transformed, reminding him of Diane. "Leena. I…met a woman, a Provider, who had visited the Citizenry before. Her name's Diane. She had a really bad time, I think she was here when the old leader was still alive. Have you heard of her?"

Leena shook her head. "No. No, I can't say I have. But back then, I wasn't such a social person, you know?"

"Right."

"Right. So, anyway," Leena sighed again, recovering much of her confidence and poise, "Edgar was more or less on Mike's side and all, but now he's just…the second most popular leader."

"And that makes things hard?"

"It makes things uncomfortable at times. The Refuge people will be all right with us, but they're not all going to be our best buddies."

When the guards saw Lenth and Leena getting closer, and the fact that they were carrying weapons, everyone shifted their stance just a little. With Lenth half a step behind her, Leena stopped in front of the guards. "Hey boys."

"Leena," one of the guards said with a respectful nod, "you and your friend look ready for trouble. Are you bringing us trouble?"

"Nope. Lookin' to solve some. Have you heard about the stabbings?"

The guard nodded with a smarmy look on his face. "Sounds like Mike pissed off the wrong guy."

"Mike didn't do anything before Six had a knife to my throat."

"Sure," the guard answered.

"Think what you want, but the pile of people Six cut through on his way out sure didn't deserve it." Leena said.

That took some wind out of the guard's sails. "Ugh. How many people?"

"A dozen? Probably about four died. I didn't stay and count. We went to get some gear and get searching for Six before he hurts a pile of more people."

"—And before he came to the Citizenry, he killed at least seven people," Lenth added. He glanced at Leena, who gave him a little 'shut up Lenth' glare.

"Before he came to the Citizenry?" the guard asked. "So he's a Lofu? Been a while since we've had one of those around. Never a good sign. So, what, he killed seven Lofus, and four or more Citizens? Eleven?"

"Congratulations," Leena said, "you can add. Any idea where we can find him?"

"She should probably talk to Edgar," the first guard said to the other, "Kinda now. Okay, Leena. You and your buddy can go see Edgar. No trouble, all right?"

"Got it."

The interior of Edgar's Refuge was much like the rest of the commons. Scrap arranged into structures of varying quality, some of them decorated with drawings similar to those Lenth had seen elsewhere in Citizenry.

A woman walked out from behind one such structure and pointed at Lenth and Leena.

"You're keeping clean?" she said with wild eyes. "You look clean, but dust is sneaky. You have to be careful!"

"Dust?" Leena said. "For that matter, who are you?"

"It's me! Patricia! But that's not important! You have to keep dust away, or the things can come out of it and bite you! Go for their necks! You have weapons! If they try to bite you, you have to dodge their heads, then slash their necks! But that's only if they don't kill you with fire first!"

"What are you talking about? And what's fire?" Lenth said.

"She's nuts," Leena murmured to Lenth. "Ignore her."

Patricia collapsed to her knees, almost sobbing. "But no one wants to fight the dust-things! Mike didn't want to, Edgar doesn't want to, *no one wants to!* But someone has to, before they get in here! I read all about it! I've seen the pictures! Huge things, alive but not human! And terrible! Flying, with four sharp hands and breath for burning people!"

"People drew those pictures, lady," Leena said. "I've seen pictures like that for all kinds of things! You can't believe everything you see in books!"

"True," Patricia said, suddenly more calm. "Only the ones with the pictures are true. And it all makes sense. Only Actual keeps the dust-things away. They can't get past his power! I assume he's very clean."

Leena had begun to walk off, but Lenth lingered. "Really? How much do you know about Actual?"

Patricia shot her open hand upward to the top of the elevator. "Actual! He lives above us, and speaks to us through Messenger, and—"

"She doesn't know fuck all," Leena said. "Messenger's never said anything about things like that. This moron is just trying to make the books real."

"Terrible, huge, loud, full of fire," Patricia muttered, mostly to herself. "Only the brave and strong can hope to kill a dust-thing, and turn them back to dust. I've seen it in my dreams."

As she receded into her nook, Lenth picked up the pace to catch up with Leena.

"You said she's crazy?" Lenth asked.

Leena didn't break stride. "Hah. Huge things with four hands burning people with their breath?"

"I think I want to see the pictures," Lenth said.

"After we deal with your buddy, Six. I have a few books, but the one the lunatic is talking about is probably one sitting around Edgar's refuge. Or she keeps it somewhere safe for herself."

Lenth followed along listlessly, giving a glance back towards where Patricia had been. "My friend Gabe...he said that some people think that *above* Actual is a place where a war happened, and lots of people used something to kill each other." Lenth glanced up at the top of the elevator, "I don't know if he believed it, but he seemed...bugged by the idea a lot. What if it was a dust-thing?"

Leena halted and grabbed Lenth by the shoulders. "Lenth. Let that idea go. I know the truth," she whispered hoarsely. "The truth is that people with grey skin and big black eyes came and tried to fuck all of us, and take us away. The people here are those who escaped, and we're destined to fight back one day."

Lenth stared at her in a small moment of revelation until reason caught up with him. He started to smirk and Leena shook her head. "I heard that one from a shit-sniffer. So you know it's solid fact."

"Yeah, it's all silly," Lenth said. "The only things that are alive are humans and the six kinds of plants that make the food."

"You say the stupidest things sometimes," Leena said. "What the heck is a plant?"

"I saw some that are way taller than a person, and have big huge green hair. It doesn't have any arms and legs, though, and never move. I heard that others are small and flimsy, and also green, and they—"

"Stop sniffing, Lenth."

"*I wasn't sniffing!* I'd never even heard of sniffing before I met you."

"Ugh, whatever Lofus get stupid on."

"It's real. Food is made of plant chunks!"

"Whatever, Lenth."

They arrived at a huge doorway at the edge of the commons, a bit larger than the broken windows that led into Mike's place. One could see holes and grooves in the floor and ceiling where doors had once stood. Hanging there now was a wide curtain made from clothing shreds, a closed flap in the middle.

"Is there a lot of naked people running around somewhere?" Lenth asked, pointing at the clothing shreds.

"Messenger brings clothes, idiot," Leena said.

"From Actual, hm?"

"Yeah, I guess," Leena said, "and we take care of them. When they get too worn to use normally, we use 'em for all kinds of things." She tapped the scrap used to keep her hair out of her face.

"What does the Citizenry do for the Actual? Or the Providers?" Lenth asked.

"How should I know?" She pulled the curtain aside for Lenth to enter. A pair of guards stood just inside, watching but not interfering.

The interior was larger than Mike's place, but lit just as badly. The dim lighting at Mike's made things look run-down, but here, it had a noticeably different feel. Edgar's space was decorated like a casual throne room.

On the far wall, twenty metres or so away, banners hung from the ceiling, large enough to sleep under. They were made from thin sections cut from clothing, threaded through holes cut in blankets. One on the far right depicted the full body of a man; the far left, a woman. Next to those were heads, not detailed enough to look like any specific person. The ones farthest towards the middle depicted the elevator shaft and the top of the commons.

In the middle of all those sat a throne of large pillows, upon which lay, presumably, Edgar. Nearby on either side lay a naked woman, both of whom casually covered themselves when they realized they had company. One in particular was casting spiteful glares at Leena. Leena either didn't notice didn't care, or was happy to let the woman stew in her own bile, unacknowledged.

"Edgar," Leena called out.

"Yes, yes," Edgar grumbled. With a lot of grey in his untamed hair and a scraggly, short beard, he looked a good deal older than Mike. He took a sip from a cup of dizzy water, nodding as he did so. "You're looking for the Lofu, Six, yes?"

"Yup," Leena said. "Trying to catch up with him before he hurts anybody else. You know the whole story, I guess?"

"Whose version?" Edgar asked as she stood. His standard clothing was hidden under a robe made mostly from clothing scraps. It was hard to tell if the robe was supposed to inspire respect or if it was just warm and comfy.

"*Version?*" Lenth blurted out. "What do you mean, version?"

Edgar turned to the women lying around his pillow throne. "This might be boring for you ladies. Feel free to move into the next room." They stood. The one who was still glowering at Leena didn't bother to bring her covering with her, although the other didn't bother covering up very well, more interested in picking up her three books. Badly damaged, thin, floppy books filled with colourful pictures.

Lenth studied the women's forms closely, forcing himself to look forward before Edgar turned back around.

"I know the version that Mike would want known," Edgar said, taking his time, allowing his ladies to depart, "and it seems you support that position. Leena, your pet Lofu here, his name is...?"

"Lenth. So you can quit calling me Lofu. I've spent my life helping to make sure we all don't suffocate on our own breath. Others that you call Lofu have been feeding you, keeping your water pure, and keeping the lights on."

Edgar raised an eyebrow and turned to Leena. "Your Lofu has been sniffing?" He turned back to Lenth. "The things you speak of are gifts from Actual, brought to us all by Messenger. It is foolish to be ungrateful to Actual."

"Did Messenger say that?" Lenth asked with a furrowed brow. "Ugh. Not important right now. Do you know where Six is?"

Sipping once more from his dizzy water, Edgar paced in front of his pillow-throne slowly. "Hiding. He found Mike's welcome to be most unpleasant, holding him with his guards. It was only lucky that Six had weapons hidden on himself."

"Guards?" Leena spat. "There were no guards there! People were there to pick up food! No one tried to grab Six, they just couldn't get out of the way of him and his knives fast enough!"

"So you say," Edgar said, "and I'd expect nothing less from Mike's woman."

"I say so too!" Lenth said. "I was there. Six almost killed Leena, then he ran off slashing through a crowd!"

"Mike's woman and a Lofu!" Edgar chuckled. "Convincing indeed!"

"If the word of a 'Lofu' isn't any good to you, then why are you defending one?" Lenth asked.

Leena huffed and stared. "He doesn't care about Six one bit, he just sees a chance to make Mike look like a bad guy. That won't work, Edgar. There were too many people there who saw everything. Too many hurt. Six needs to be taken care of, or thrown back down the elevator at least!"

Edgar was silent, looking at his clasped hands.

"Edgar," Lenth said. "He's killed a lot of people for no good reason. In the Citizenry *and* below. I'm not looking for revenge's sake, I just can't sit by and let it go on."

"No good reason?" Edgar asked. "It sounded like he had some very compelling reasons. Did you know a man in a black rubber suit made him work for his whole life, and the man in the rubber suit was controlled by your precious Providers?"

Lenth lowered his head. "True. Actually, I came from a very similar situation as Six. I bet he got shocked by his Rubberman more than once, when he didn't do what he was supposed to. And he told me that his Rub—" Lenth paused, imagining Six's Rubberman crashing through the grating, killing one of his Brothers. An accident. And his own Rubberman, Phil, and the death of Slim. An accident.

If Phil had crashed onto Slim...if Phil had been right there to seek vengeance on right at that moment...

"No," Lenth said. "Even then. Then he went on killing Providers who had no connection to him."

Edgar peered at Lenth with quiet scepticism. "You do not hate that you were used by the Providers for their daily needs?"

"It's...difficult. I didn't take a lot of time to think about it before I met some. They're people. Most of them pretty nice. And don't forget, they're also making your daily needs. If they were using me, it was for your sake, too."

"Again with this blaspheme against Actual!" Edgar threw up his hands and faced the banners around him.

"Uh, Edgar," Leena spoke up, "you should worry less about where *Lenth* thinks food *comes from*, and more about where Six thinks it's *going*."

Edgar looked at Leena with a quizzical glare. "Explain."

"If Six feels like he's been used, and is out for blood, and he thinks like Lenth does—that Citizens are living off of his work...why do you think Six would stop at raging against Providers?"

"He said Mike's men were—"

"You talked to him?" Lenth asked.

"Oh lovely!" Leena said. "And how many of your own armed guards were standing around when this little chit-chat took place? Wanna know how many people were armed when Six cut into Mike's followers? Nobody but Six!"

"And why should I believe any of this?" Edgar bellowed.

Looking at the floor and shrugging, Lenth calmly replied, "—because every Citizen and Provider is a likely target to get stabbed to death next?"

"Yup," Leena said, nodding impishly at Lenth and Edgar, "that's a good motivator."

Edgar looked around as if spotting snippets of wisdom out of the air around him. He drank the last dribbles of his dizzy water and tossed the cup onto the pillow-throne.

"Edgar," Lenth implored, "I don't understand the conflict between you and Mike all that well, but this is more important than your...whatever it is."

Edgar stared at Lenth with one eye closed and pointed at him for a moment before letting his arm drop lazily back to his side. "Huh!" Edgar walked over his pillow-throne to get behind it and pulled out a long weapon. It was a length of pipe that stood a little taller than him. The blade, hammered flat from the top thirty centimetres of the pipe, was simple but dignified. Pipe fittings along the shaft served as grips, and the top one supported a modest flourish of fabric, stained dark from old blood.

He beat the shaft of his spear against his chest twice to punctuate himself. The sound it made told Lenth that his robe had more to it that just fabric. "We sort this out now," Edgar said.

"*What?*" Lenth gripped his sword a little tighter, wondering if he could counter Edgar's attack. Edgar undoubtedly had more experience in fighting than Lenth. The bloody rag on his spear spoke to that well enough. But Lenth was younger, and had been kept in optimal physical condition by his daily Unit workouts.

He remembered the weapons he had selected from, and how he had considered the weaknesses of a long weapon. Maybe if he could evade Edgar's first strike, even if it meant taking a hit from the blunt shaft rather than the blade, he could quickly counter with the sword. Better yet, the knife. In desperation, the spikes of his knuckles. He was well armed with options.

"Relax, Lofu," Edgar said, walking past him, "I don't leave home without Gungnir."

"Who?"

Not bothering to break stride, Edgar raised his spear over his head. "Gungnir! I got the name from a book!"

Leena prodded Lenth to get moving, and found that one of the two guards following behind. "I have to have a look at some of the books around here some time. Where did they come from?"

Edgar still didn't bother to turn back to face them as he answered, "They've been around for longer than anyone can say." He pointed his spear up to the top of the elevator shaft. "Likely from Actual originally. I'm not sure."

"Or Providers?" Lenth asked, catching up.

"Huh. I suppose that is possible, but it seems unlikely that a Lofu could make such things."

Lenth resisted lecturing Edgar again on all the things he owed to the Providers. It didn't feel like a good time to push his luck. "Aren't we going to go see Mike?" he said, noticing that Edgar wasn't leading them to the gate out of the Refuge.

"Yes. Yes," Edgar said, "but first we get Six. It just makes sense, no?"

"*What?*" Leena said. "You've been keeping him here?"

"Yes, I ran into him. After some difficulty with introductions, he explained that he was attacked outside of the elevator, and had to fight his way out. He climbed the wall of the Refuge, trying to hide. So I helped him clean up, and he offered to help with the next meal. Very nice fellow, really."

Lenth thought about it. Maybe all Six needed was some understanding and kindness. Maybe Edgar caught Six unprepared to start a fight, and that gave talking a chance. Maybe Six didn't feel the need to defend himself from things like Rubbermen and Providers any more. Six *did* get off on the wrong foot with them, after all.

"Oh," Edgar said as they came to a nook in the Refuge, where he expected to find Six. "Dead person." A man in pants and nothing else was lying in front of them, face down. A pool of blood seemed to come from the abdominal area, and a couple of smears of it were spread across the floor. Traces of the dead man's bloody hand-prints were around him here and there.

There was no way out, other than how they had come in. Lenth whirled to face behind them, and readied his sword. Getting the knife out of the glove's spikes was a little clumsier than he'd hoped, but he soon stood ready for combat with both blades ready. The guard who had come with them had the same idea, and had readied his spear.

"Boys, relax," Leena said. "From the look of the blood, this happened a while ago. Edgar, who's this guy?"

Edgar knelt down by the body and pulled him over by his shoulder. The wound left the floor with a wet sound, and no longer being held in with the pressure of the floor, more blood oozed out. "Eh, I know him. Is a good guy. Is...name starts with a 'D', I think. Eh, Daryl? Doug? Something like Doug. Dave?"

"You don't even know?" Lenth asked, still facing away, scanning around for signs of Six.

"I'm going to go with 'Dave'," Edgar said.

A woman ran in from around the corner. "Robert!" she cried, running to the body's side, collapsing to embrace him.

"I was close," Edgar said, standing back up.

This woman's reaction was more like what Lenth expected. Her display of grief at least told him that not all Citizens were so callous about death. Lenth knelt by her and spoke softly, "Excuse me. I'm trying to find the person who did this. Do you know—?"

She turned her head to Lenth, bleary-eyed with shock. "The Lofu?"

"Yes," Lenth sighed, "his name is Six—"

"I know. Damned Lofus! We should kill them as soon as they pop up!"

"Six is not like most of us," Lenth said quietly. "Do you have any idea which way he went?"

She shook and settled in to cry under Robert's chin.

"He said before that he didn't want to come here," Edgar said quietly. Everyone moved away from the body and the grieving woman except for Lenth.

"Is there...can I do something for you?" he asked. She only replied with a brisk hand motion, shooing him away. Edgar pulled him away. "I'll have the guards deal with the body and all," Edgar said. "Six saw that the elevator shaft went further up and said that he was trying to go up more. I told him all about Actual, and he said he had a lot to think about."

"Then we have to get to the elevator!" Lenth exclaimed. "Actual is in danger!"

"Six can't use the elevator, stupid," Leena said.

"No, the great Actual is beyond harm," Edgar rumbled, "but just maybe Messenger is in danger, if you believe such a thing is possible. Certainly Mike is in danger."

"Oh what the fuck do *you* care about Mike, Edgar?" Leena spat.

"I do not hate Mike, I simply know I would be a better leader. Mike is popular because it was he who overthrew a horrible leader. If—"

"Is anyone else coming?" Lenth asked as he walked off briskly.

"Where are you going?" Leena asked.

"To the elevator, of course."

"No," Edgar said, "I'll go, and I'll take send my guard to bring a few more guards to join me. You two go to Mike's."

Leena glared at Edgar for a moment. "You're right. Lenth, up we go again."

Lenth jogged to keep up with Leena. "Leena, why is going the wrong way such a good idea?"

"Elevator doesn't come unless it's a regular time to drop off supplies or Messenger is called. The machine to call him is at Mike's."

"How would Six know that?"

"Ask the dead guy. Doug, David, err..."

"Robert."

"Right. Robert might have told Six anything."

The trip to up the ramp was decidedly more strenuous jogging all the way. Lenth tripped a few times on the uneven surface, sacrificing caution for the sake of speed.

Short of breath, they arrived at Mike's place and heard a voice coming loud and clear from the other room.

"—And we could have him there in ten minutes."

"It's Six, it has to be," Lenth whispered.

Leena nodded and they readied their weapons, creeping as quietly as possible towards the bedroom. As they came in, they saw that the weapons rack had been ransacked. Half of the weapons were dumped on the floor, and most of the rest were hanging haphazardly.

They tensed up as they heard a crash from the darkened little doorway in the corner, followed by two more crashes.

"Fuuuuuuck, fuck, fuck, fuck..." Leena whispered to herself.

With bloody hands once more, and carrying Mike's longest blade, Six stepped into the light. Speckles and gobs of blood reached all the way up to his face, but his hands and forearms were nearly as red as the blade.

"What have you done, Six?" Lenth asked, weapons in hand.

Six smiled wide and tilted his head. "I just called for a ride, is all."

"*That's all?*" Leena growled, staring at Six with restrained rage. "Then what's the blood about? I've seen Mike use the machine a lot of times, and it never bled."

As if he hadn't expected anyone to notice the blood, he shrugged, holding his blade out to the side. "Oh. Oh yes, there were some problems," Six said, "A difference in opinion of what should be said to the machine. Did you know it doesn't talk back? At first I thought they were shy, but I think the talking back part might be broken."

Chapter Twenty

Deported

Leena brought her machete forward, holding it with both hands. She shifted her weight back and forth, looking for her chance to approach. Lenth followed her example, readying his 'sword'.

"Huh, I guess I should have expected this," Six said.

"Is Mike in there?" Lenth asked.

Six glanced back behind him. "Yeah. Well, someone is. I never got his name."

"Is he dead?" Leena almost choked on the word 'dead', only really considering the idea as it came out of her mouth. The blood seemed to bear an obvious answer, but foolish hope demanded that the question be asked.

Six smiled wide, looking around with mock incredulity. "What am I, a doctor? Do you want to rush in and see if you can help? Fine by me, I'll get out of *your* way, but *you* need to get out of *my* way first. A nice wide path."

Lenth looked over to Leena, who was standing with a wide stance, ready to fight. Her machete wiggled visibly from her trembling.

Six leaned his head towards the exit, raised his eyebrows, and asked, "Well?"

Leena yelled a guttural sound, and moved the machete to one hand, before moving back, out of the way. Lenth followed suit.

"Interesting company you're keeping, Lenth," Six said, dashing to the exit. Leena rushed into the small room where the communication device was kept.

Lenth stood there, looking in both directions. *Go try to help Mike, or chase after Six?* And if he caught Six, then what? Try to kill him?

Leena screamed. He dashed back to the communication room. In front of him, Leena was on her knees, staring at Mike's body. His neck was hacked so deeply that the ridges of several vertebrae could be seen easily. There were splatters of blood on the walls, and the floor was a vast pool of red.

Mike had other cuts and minor injuries, but his neck was such a mess, it was hard to focus on anything else. It looked as if Six was trying to chop his head right off.

Leena was still. Silent. Lenth didn't know what to do. He looked at the only other thing of note in the little room, a small table with something that was seemingly the communication device. It was smashed quite well, and much of Mike's blood was on it and in it. *Mike would have died what...ten minutes ago? Five? It depends on how long it took Six to figure out the device.*

"He's going to the elevator," Leena said in a squeak. "Go."

"Come with me."

"No," she whispered.

"I get it," Lenth said, "I do, but you can't stay here. At least come as far as another person. Don't be alone with this."

"With *this*? With Mike?" Leena finally turned away from Mike's body. As she turned, her knee came up from the blood, and she felt it trickle down her shin. She eyes widened as reality struck a little deeper into her mind. A desperate rasp, too rough to be a cry, came from her as Lenth helped her to her feet.

"We have to go," Lenth said, feeling more grief for Leena's loss than Mike's death itself. She was slow to leave the room, reliant on Lenth's arm around her shoulders. When they get out onto the ramp, Lenth saw Six running down it, already near the bottom. "There he is," Lenth said.

Leena looked up and her defeated posture snapped. She brought her machete up, adjusting her grip on it, then bolted forward with a grunt. Stunned for a moment, Lenth collected himself and gave chase. Leena was fast. Lenth had to struggle to keep up, already a handful of metres behind her. His gloves and weaponry were surprisingly cumbersome for running.

He tripped, handing hard on the ramp. It shook violently, threatening to break apart and drop him. He landed on his forearms and had the luck to keep his face away from the gloves' spikes. As he tumbled, he was unaware of letting go of the sword, but heard it clatter off the edge, fated to fall to the commons floor. When he stopped, he was sitting, facing forward. Leena was still running, having not noticed Lenth fall. Or maybe just not caring enough to stop.

He got up, checked the knife in his glove, and started running. Six was nowhere to be seen, but there was no question about which way he was going. Lenth was a lot farther behind Leena now.

"Wait for me!"

"No!"

"We have to stick together!" Lenth was suddenly reminded of being with Diane when she was attacked by Six. He didn't help much then, but he was determined to make a difference now. Even if he arrived too late to prevent an attack, he would at the very least avenge it. He pulled the knife out from his glove as he ran, and sacrificed caution for more speed.

A life of 'Lofu' exercise was winning out again, especially when they got off of the ramp. When Lenth caught up with Leena, she looked ragged.

"Gonna...get...him..." she said between breaths.

"Don't get caught alone with him," Lenth said. It was more likely that Six was headed right for the elevator, but an ambush from Six was far from out of the question. Lenth decided not to run ahead and leave Leena on her own.

The elevator shaft loomed closer and closer, but gave no clues about where Messenger and the elevator currently were. Ahead, a couple of Edgar's guards jogged into view, also headed for the elevator's building. Lenth glanced at Leena and she nodded at him. Lenth went ahead to talk to the guards.

"What's going on?" Lenth called out to them.

"Edgar's in there, and so's the Lof—" the guard said, while looking Lenth up and down as they ran, "that is, the other Lofu. The one with the kn—well, you have a knife too, but—"

"Yes, yes, Six. I get it. Has he hurt anyone in there?"

"At least one lady got slashed in the arm. Other than that, I don't know. Edgar just told me to go get more guys."

"Thanks." Lenth looked back to Leena. She was wiped out, limping, and holding her middle due to runner's cramp. He turned to the guard he'd been talking to. "Hey, I'm good to go ahead. Can one of you guys make sure Leena stays safe?"

The guard turned back without breaking stride. He tapped the other guard, and pointed back at Leena. "You, go look after her." The second guard nodded, and started jogging back towards Leena.

Leena dropped her pace to a walk, and looked to Lenth with arms spread. "Seriously?"

With no words coming to mind, Lenth just waved with a sheepishly apologetic smile. He turned back towards the elevator building and pushed himself to full speed. Fatigue was getting to him, but he was still doing notably better than the guards.

There were a few people leaving the building, chattering worriedly.

"What's going on in there?" Lenth hollered at them as he approached.

"Lofu...killed a guard!"

"And Edgar?" Lenth asked.

"He's in there, talking."

"Thanks," Lenth said as he passed them by, entering the corridor. He ran as quickly as he could, nearly knocking over a couple of Citizens along the way.

He came to the large loading room that had the door to the elevator. Six stood with his back against the elevator door, still a mess from Mike's blood. He held a guard as hostage, weapon against his throat. A dead guard lay nearby with an open throat. Near where Lenth came in, Edgar and another guard stood at the ready.

"*Ha!*" Six yelled when he saw Lenth. "Your pet baby Provider is here, Messenger! *Now* will you open the door?"

"He's here?" Lenth asked.

"Yes," came Messenger's voice from the little eye-slot in the door. "This man seems to think I owe him a ride."

"*Tell him, Lenth!*" Six seethed.

Lenth sighed. "Messenger, this guy is Six."

"He told me so. He also says he was in one of the food crates when you came here."

"Did he mention that the Providers want to catch him?" Lenth asked.

"Providers," Six spat. "I don't care about them. I want to go up! You want up too, don't you, Lenth? Maybe to see this *Actual*? To ask him about...to ask about everything!"

"Messenger!" Lenth called out, "He's killed about seven Providers, and I don't know how many Citizens, including an important leader."

"What? Mike?" Edgar said.

Lenth nodded. "It was...it was horrible. Leena was—"

"*Enough!*" Six screeched, giving his hostage a jerk. "Have we established I'm not a Citizen, Messenger? Let me on! I'm done with this place! Do you hear me? Messenger! Take me up to Actual!"

"*Blasphemer!*" Edgar took a step towards Six, still many metres away from him, and stood tall, with his spear planted firmly beside him. "Messenger cannot take you to Actual, you're mad! Messenger! Six must stay here and pay for his crimes with his life!"

Leena scrambled in beside Lenth at this time, squeezing the most out of her second wind. "Are we talking about killing Six? I stake claim! He killed Mike! I have the right!"

"Which Citizen did he kill first?" Edgar asked. "It would be the right of—"

The elevator slammed down about a centimetre, the weight of it shaking the room.

"Lenth," came Messenger's voice finally, "who was the first person that Six killed?"

"Why are you asking him?" Six snarled. "It was *my* Rubberman! Manager, whatever. He killed my Brother by smashing the grating down on him, so I killed him right back!"

"Six, you told me that story," Lenth said, "but are you sure it wasn't an accident? My Brother died because of a mistake that maybe my Rubberman made, but I don't—"

"*What do you know?*" Six jostled his hostage again in agitation, pressing the dull blade firmly on his neck. "Lenth, they turned you into one of them, a mindless Provider!"

"Augh, Six, you've gone way too far! Even if your Rubberman meant to kill your Brother, that might explain your killing him, but what about the rest? What about attacking Diane? She did nothing to you! Or your other Brother, Eyes?"

The elevator groaned loudly, rising by the lost centimetre. They shut up again, and Messenger spoke. "Lenth, Six. Give your weapons to a Citizen, and then all Citizens will leave the loading room."

"Then we can get on?" Six asked.

"Yes. Weapons and Citizens leave now."

Many Citizens were already obeying the voice of the Messenger. Among the handful who still lingered, Leena and Edgar stood forefront.

"What, you're just going to leave?" Leena said. "You can't just take off after all of that!"

"It's for the best," Edgar stepped up to say. "As long as Six never comes back here, it's good enough."

"The hell it is!" Leena readied her machete and stepped forward, unconcerned about the hostage. Before she got close to Six, he pushed his hostage away, with a firm, flat-footed kick to the backside. The hostage went sprawling forward, before scrambling away.

"I'm fine to settle this with you, little girl!" Six snarled.

"You worthless sack of blood," Leena snarled back, side-stepping to plan an attack. "You think you're the only killer in the room? Before Mike took over, do you have any idea how hard I had to fight every day? How many times my attackers ended up dead? How many had to die before I got any peace from the savages?"

"I'll give you peace!" Six screamed. He charged at Leena. Leena had not been ready for Six when they first met, but this time Leena's combat experience had her well prepared. She deftly sailed under Six's thrust, and she sprung back up with her machete sliding up.

Six dodged, but only well enough to avoid a fatal strike. A streak of red now decorated Leena's blade.

With a throaty bellow, Edgar threw himself shoulder first into Six. Six's hissing snarl ended with a pained grunt as they landed on the floor.

"Giant moron!" Six grunted. They struggled, Edgar's robe concealing their violence.

"Get off! I had him!" Leena yelled.

Just as Leena and Lenth were about to get into the fray, Edgar sat up, a fresh gash on one of his forearms. With one hand, he held Six down by his wrists.

Six still held his knife, wet with a streak of fresh blood. Six spat up at Edgar's face.

"You hold him still," Leena said, "and I'll gut him!"

"I want him alive," came Messenger's voice.

Edgar held his free hand out to Leena, signalling her to stop.

"Why?" Leena asked Edgar. "Why do we care what Messenger wants? This fucker slaughtered Mike, and I want the deserved justice!"

"Justice is for the one wronged first," Edgar said, "and you should care what Messenger wants. He is our link to Actual, and without him, we would quickly starve."

Leena reluctantly backed away and lowered her weapon. "Fine," she grumbled, "but I want a piece when others are done with him."

"I'm glad you see it that way, Citizens," Messenger said. "Now, as I said before, search Six and Lenth for weapons, remove them and yourselves, and we'll be going."

While Edgar roughly turned Six over, Lenth started handing over his arsenal to Leena.

"You're going?" Leena said, still regaining her composure. "I thought you were planning on staying. Isn't that why you came in the first place?"

Lenth made a tight-lipped face and looked away. "Well, not really. I came to explore. To find out what was up above where I was. Now I guess the only thing up is—"

"Actual!" Six scrambled away from Edgar, and got to his feet, up against the elevator door. "See, I knew you and I were on the same page! Going up!" Six banged on the elevator door twice. He winced, and put his hand against his arm where Leena had managed to cut him. It was hard to see his bleeding due to Mike's blood all over him.

Edgar, bloodied from holding down Six, was backing away from him, holding two confiscated knives. "Messenger, you will have to communicate with a new leader now if Mike is dead."

"And the asshole wrecked the device after calling for you," Leena said. "Can we get another?"

There was a moment of silence before Messenger's voice came from the door again. "It should be possible. It may take time. Next time I come, have the old one here so I can take it away."

"Many thanks to you and Actual, Messenger." Edgar said with a bow as he reached the doorway. "Coming, Leena?"

"Edgar, Leena," Lenth said, "work together, all right? I don't see any reason for the … uh…unfriendliness to continue."

Leena and Edgar eyed each other, both having expected to be the new leader. "Ehh, I guess he has experience," Leena said.

"And doubtless, Leena will retain Mike's followers," Edgar said. "An alliance of convenience would make some sense. We'll see."

"We'll see," Leena agreed. She smirked at Lenth.

"I might see you all again," Lenth said. "I'm sorry about Mike."

"Yeah, he was my favourite of my three men."

"Three?"

"*Can we just get on with it?*" Six wailed and winced in pain.

Lenth patted Leena on the shoulder. "Be safe."

She nodded. "You too. If you come back this way, I might have time and be in the mood to 'educate' you a little." She forced a smile, punctuated with a wink, then turned to exit with Edgar.

The door closed. A split moment later, a latch was heard from the elevator.

"'Bout time," Six murmured.

The elevator door slid open steadily as Messenger dragged at it. He peered at the bloody Six as he did so. "Get to the far end." Messenger gave Six a wide berth, and once Six was on the other end of the empty elevator and Lenth was inside, Messenger started closing the door. Without a second handle to help, Lenth just picked a spot on the door to press his hands against and push.

"Oh, who's the favourite?" Six teased.

Messenger ignored Six and closed the latch. "Thank you, but it wasn't necessary," Messenger said quietly to Lenth.

"Helpful Lenth! So helpful," Six hollered from across the elevator's big empty cargo space. "So helpful, helpful, helping Messenger, helping Citizens, helping Providers to help the Rubbermen make the little men work forever in ignorance! So helpful!"

Lenth scoffed. "Yes, because *killing* them is so much better, huh?"

"If it means freedom?" Six tossed his hands up, looking at the stains of blood on them. "If it means not getting shocked? Yes!" He pulled his injured arm back towards himself quickly.

"Six, the shocks weren't so bad, or that often. And I notice your freedom involves a lot of crawling around and hiding! The only thing I've had to hide from is *you*. And I haven't killed anyone."

"The shocks weren't so...Lenth, do you *hear* yourself? How did *you* get so much freedom anyway, huh? Why didn't the Providers toss you back in your hole, or kill you, or whatever?"

"I've been a little curious about that, too," Messenger said quietly.

Lenth gave them both a bewildered look. "Gabe said they didn't want to put me back down there and tell my Brothers a bunch of stuff, and they were lucky that could get another Br..." Lenth paused, seeing the problem. His freedom just meant that some other ignorant worker was needed.

"Lucky," Six mused. "And your Brothers? Are they free, or does your Rubberman still force them to work and support the Providers? And shock them when they don't?"

Lenth fell silent and stared at the floor. "How bad is that cut?" Lenth grumbled.

"Hurts. That revolting woman."

"Shut up. You more than deserved it."

"It doesn't look so deep," Messenger said, "I have a medical kit, if you want to bandage him, Lenth."

Lenth huffed, and after a moment, he nodded. "But I don't know how to do that kind of thing."

Messenger opened a little door below the control panel, and pulled out a cloth bag. He handed it to Lenth. "Dig out a white cloth, and dab off the excess blood around the wound. Pull his sleeve away from the cut first."

"All right," Lenth said, rummaging through the bag, "but why don't you do it? You know how."

"I'll talk you through it. It's easy," Messenger said without answering the question.

"What are you doing? Keep away from me," Six murmured.

"But you're bleeding," Lenth said.

"Just give me the rag, I'll deal with it. It's not that bad, my clothes protected me a little." Once he had the cloth, Six tried to use it as a bandage right on top of his clothes, but couldn't get it to stay on, much less tie it with one hand.

"I don't think that's how it's done," Lenth offered.

"It isn't," Messenger confirmed.

"Shut up, it doesn't matter." Six threw the now-bloodied cloth across the floor.

Messenger sighed, then turned to the elevator controls. "If it makes either of you feel any better," Messenger said, "the Units are the largest population section, so most of the work they do is to support themselves. It's not like

Providers get more food or something." He pressed a few buttons and the elevator groaned to life.

"Food? What about knowing things?" Six said. "What about reading, knowing who's out there, and women? I don't—wait a second!" Six bounced into a ready stance, hands out to the side. "We're going *down*, aren't we?"

Messenger nodded. "You need to go see Contact."

"*What?*" Six exploded, charging at the elevator's control panel. Messenger fluidly moved aside and watched Six fumble with the buttons. "*How do I make it go up?*"

"Sorry," Messenger said in feigned remorse.

Six slammed Messenger against the wall, his forearm under Messenger's chin. "*Make it happen, Messenger! Do it! Now!*"

"Can't," Messenger choked out, surprisingly dispassionate about it all.

Six grabbed Messenger by the back of the neck and arm, and forced him over to the controls. "Can. Or I strangle you."

Lenth had mustered the courage to tackle them, but Messenger spoke before it happened. "The controls are locked until the elevator reaches the destination floor."

Six backed off. "So...*can't* can't?"

"Can't."

Six stared at Messenger. He looked over to Lenth, who just raised his eyebrows and shrugged.

Six looked around, shaking his head in disgust. "All right, I'm getting out of this can." He ran over to the door latch and started yanking on it. "It's locked too, isn't it?"

"What would it matter, Six?" Lenth asked. "It would just open to a solid wall! And we're still moving!"

Six darted around the side of the elevator, looking for another way, finally giving up, and wandering to the middle.

"Are you done?" Messenger murmured.

Six stared blankly at Messenger, then looked down at a little recessed section of the floor. He reached down and pulled up at it.

"*Don't mess with that,*" Messenger yelled. Lenth stood ready to charge at Six.

Six pulled harder, and the nature of the floor-hatch became apparent. It was a square about a metre in size. "Oh look! A way out that isn't blocked by a wall!" He stepped off of the square and yanked it up hard. The hatch swung on its gritty, neglected hinges before slamming open with a deafening sound that rattled the floor.

"Idiot, you'll get yourself killed! Close that thing right now!" Messenger called out.

Six grinned, lay face down on the floor, and stuck his head down through the hatch to look around. "Oh! Nope!"

Messenger broke into a run and dove to grab Six's feet before Six could scramble down. Six kicked back, hitting Messenger in the face before Lenth could get his hands on to help. Six wailed in frustration and kicked harder. A foot got loose and jabbed a toe back down on Lenth's hand. Lenth recoiled in pain for a moment. It was enough of a chance for Six to slip down the hatch fluidly, leaving a wide but faint smear of blood on the floor. Mike's blood was drying on him.

"Six!" Lenth leaned closer to look. The dark, seemingly endless abyss below him hit Lenth. The dark concrete panels seemed to stretch the tube of the elevator shaft eternally, steadily coming at him as the elevator continued its journey.

"Did he fall?" Messenger asked. "Nope, wait, I hear him."

It sounded a little like footsteps, but when Lenth looked in the direction of the sound under the elevator, he saw Six swinging carefully from one grab-bar to the next, legs dangling below, moving to the edge of the elevator shaft.

"He's getting away," Lenth said, "hanging off the bottom! I'm...I guess I'm going after him!"

"No, don't be an idiot," Messenger said. "At best, you'll get into a fight under there and get you both knocked off."

Lenth obeyed. The gaping void below, and the dizziness it caused had dwindled his courage anyway. "Six, what are you trying to do?"

Six stopped at the last rung at the edge of the elevator car, right by the shaft. With the elevator still in motion, it looked like the shaft was creeping upwards at them continually. Directly in front of six was a ladder tucked in a vertical alcove that seemed to run the entirety of the shaft. He watched those rungs pass in front of him, one by one.

He cranked his neck to look over his shoulder at Lenth, still poking his head down from the elevator's interior. "I'm going up, Lenth!"

"You moron! You're going to—"

Six swung off of the elevator's last rung and flung himself towards the shaft's ladder. He hit a little harder than either of them expected and fumbled for a grip, falling about three rungs, and faster than the elevator's decent. He caught himself with a pained grunt, but was soon laughing to himself as the elevator passed him. "That was sloppy," he called out.

"Are you all right?" Lent yelled at Six—or rather, Six's feet, as the rest of him was already out of sight.

"Thanks for your concern," Six yelled back—and maybe even sincerely, "tell your Provider pals to...I don't know, die or something!"

"*Try to stop killing people!*" Lenth hollered back.

Six's reply was laced with laughter, but was muffled beyond comprehension. Lenth just watched the empty elevator shaft for a moment before pulling himself back up into the elevator and closing the hatch.

Messenger stood nearby, arms crossed. "Try to stop killing people?"

Lenth sat by the hatch, and shook his head slowly. "Yeah. Well," Lenth stammered as he stood, "I didn't know what else to say. I should have gone after him."

"And get stabbed, then flop dead down the shaft?" Messenger knelt down to fasten the hatch. "That would just make things worse."

"But he doesn't have a knife anymore." Lenth started pacing slowly. "So...so now what? Do we stop and—"

Messenger held up a finger to Lenth and went over to the control panel. He opened a little door and pulled out a slim headset attached to the panel with a tightly coiled cord. It had padded parts to go over the ears and a smaller part that positioned near the mouth. Putting it on, he turned a knob on the panel and pressed a button. He waited a moment before speaking.

"It's me. Things got a little crazy at the Citizenry. I'm fine, yes. I'll tell you the whole bit later, but right now you have to make sure the elevator access is locked. Lock off the service access too. Redundant? Yes, but...because the homicidal Subject is crawling around the shaft now. Yes. Six. I figured. Uh huh. That's kind of what I was thinking. Yeah. I'll ask Contact, he'll know better than me. Also this other Subject who's been...I don't know...exploring. He knows Six, and seems capable. Yeah. His name's 'Lenth'. I don't know, maybe it's about his dick."

"My what?" Lenth blurted.

Messenger turned to Lenth and asked, "Hey, Actual was curious what your name means."

"Actual? You're talking to Actual?"

"Yes, I'm talking to Actual. Where does your name come from?"

Lenth blinked and held out his arms. "My arms are a little bit longer than my Brothers' arms."

Messenger's shoulders sank. "Well. That's a little disappointing." He spoke into the headset's microphone again, "His arms. Yeah. That's what I said. Yeah. Okay, I'll call when I get there. Yeah. You too."

Messenger hit a button, twisted the knob, and hit the first button again.

"You're calling back now?" Lenth asked.

Messenger put his finger to his lips and shook his head. He waited, and waited some more. Finally he lifted his head, listening to the other end of the call. After a moment, he replied.

"Yes, Contact," Messenger said in a much more detached tone than he had used with Actual, "your Subject Six has been very busy. Yes, unfortunately. Citizens. It seems that Lenth put himself at considerable risk to be of assistance. Yes. I know he was, but he is not a Subject any more, is he? We can discuss this later. Right now I need to bring some people to the elevator. Whoever is available and capable. I will arrive very soon, we will discuss it then." He looked at the faint bloodstains left on the floor by Six. "He's not going to leave a useful trail. We're going for extra help."

Chapter Twenty-One

Almost

The elevator came to a stop. Messenger peeked out the slot to see Contact and a dozen or so Providers. He stepped back and opened the door. Messenger stood back to face them.

Contact bowed, face flush. "Messenger, my apologies. Six should have been caught long before he found a way onto y—"

"Quite," Messenger interrupted, "but right now we have to concern ourselves with where he is now. Obviously, he's not about to stay peacefully in the Citizenry."

Lenth stepped up alongside Messenger. "He wants to go to Actual!"

Contact's eyes widened. "...Insanity! *Blaspheme!*"

"He may even intend to *kill* Actual," Messenger said, "but of course, I've made that impossible."

Contact bowed again. "Of course, of course. And even if you hadn't, what could a *Subject* do to Actual?"

Lenth didn't have Contact's faith, and looked to Messenger. Messenger's face told nothing. Lenth made a mental note to ask Messenger some time when Contact wasn't around.

"Actual is safe, so worry about yourselves. Six has a dislike of Managers, and Providers by association. His activities cannot continue."

"He didn't seem to mind killing Citizens, either," Lenth said.

Contact huffed. "Citizens. I don't wish them any harm, but you'll excuse me if I don't lose any sleep over their safety."

"Then, you merely intended to get Lenth out of your way?" Messenger asked.

"What?" Lenth looked back and forth between Contact and Messenger. "Is that the reason I was allowed to go? I was being...thrown out?"

Contact was silent, but his face had gone rigid, not wanting to answer.

"That might be why *Contact* permitted it," Messenger replied, "but Actual and I had to give permission too. And 'throwing you out', was not our reasoning."

"Well, what did you expect?" Contact grumbled. "He couldn't go back to a Unit, knowing what he knows now, and he couldn't fit in as a Provider."

"Gabe seemed to think I could!" Lenth snapped. "Where is he?"

"Gabe's around here somewhere. He's a little soft, no head for the practical. You could have ended up turning out like Six; sending you to the Citizenry was the safest solution."

"And how's *that* working out with Six, huh?"

"Enough," Messenger boomed. "We need to focus. Contact, have one of your people bring a ladder to my elevator. Five or so armed volunteers are going into the elevator shaft to hunt down Six. His safety is not important. Do not give him the chance to attack again. Do not attempt to capture him."

Contact turned white. "In the...you mean in the ... where the elevator goes? Doesn't that go all the way up to Actual?"

"Almost," Messenger said, "and I know it is daunting. And yes, it is dangerous. Falling might become an issue, and of course, Six himself. However, when I last saw him, he had no weapon, and I don't see where he could get one now. For weapons, I recommend that your people have longer pole-type objects. Spears, I suppose. They would be harder for Six to take from you if Six attacks..."

"And me?" Lenth asked,

"You should be with them," Messenger said. "Do you have other plans?"

Lenth shook his head. "When people are safe, then I can make other plans."

Messenger nodded, then turned to Contact. "All right! Ladder! Five volunteers willing to go into the shaft with spears! Six is not standing around talking; we need to get on this!"

The task force came, in a sad little formation. Among the ranks came Gabe.

"So, how was the Citizenry?" Gabe asked, handing Lenth the ladder, and taking two spears from another Provider.

"Bloodier than I expected, thanks to Six. Other than that...interesting. I'll fill you in when there's time." Lenth took the ladder to Messenger, who pointed at the ceiling in the elevator. Directly in the middle, and aligned with the hatch

Six had used to go down, was a nearly identical hatch for going on top of the elevator.

"I'm going to run the elevator from the control panel," Messenger said, "and everyone else will stand on top, keeping an eye out for Six as we go up."

"And when we find him?" Lenth asked.

"Prep him for compost?" Gabe grimaced. "I'm guessing we kill him, right? Is that the only way?"

Messenger sighed. "I've been trying to think of another course of action, but with his violent disposition, almost anything else would be a risk to everyone."

Lenth wordlessly set up the ladder, then accepted a spear from Gabe. It was really just a length of pipe, with the end cut at an angle to make a point. "Looks like something a Citizen would use," Lenth said.

"Oh yeah? Well, the fancy ones aren't fixed yet. They hadn't been used in ages, and the batteries expired." Gabe started climbing. "I guess you're a Citizen expert now, huh. What's it like there?"

Lenth followed up while a couple of others were coming onto the elevator. "It's not quite as bad as it was when Diane went up, I think. Some of the worst people got killed. They do weird things in their spare time. It...it's best in the Provider layer though, for sure. Hey. Is it true? Contact was trying to get rid of me?"

The roof of the elevator was lit by a couple of small lights on the edges. Lenth looked at how the light coming from below made Gabe look eerie, even if he smiled. The light reached up around twenty metres into the shaft, but left a gaping darkness beyond that. Other dimmer lights were attached to the sides of the shaft, but the next set was high enough up as to not make much impact here.

Gabe helped Lenth up the last couple of steps, and waved to the others to hurry up. "I think maybe Contact *was* trying to get rid of you. Kind of. Well, you seemed so eager to go, you made it easy for Contact, I guess. I wouldn't paint his actions as malicious towards you, really. A Subject coming up from a Unit is unprecedented. To Contact, you threatened change. A lot of people are scared of change. Not you, I guess."

Standing with his spear at his side, Lenth looked up the shaft, vanishing into a dark point above. Massive metal fittings on either side of the hatch in the elevator's roof held onto a total of eight metal cables. Each cable was larger than a hand could wrap around. "Change? Change is interesting. Knowing more is interesting. I miss my Brothers, though." Lenth turned to Gabe. "Hey, any word on how Joints is doing? His health okay?"

Gabe smiled a bit. "Last I heard, yeah. He *is* old, though."

"He has to die?"

"Well, sooner or later. That's no Provider rule or anything, that's just how it goes."

Lenth huffed. "I'd like to talk to him some time soon, then."

"That would be hard to—"

Gabe was cut off by Messenger's voice below. "All right. The cables don't move relative to the elevator, so they're safe to hold on to when we get moving. In fact, I recommend it, at least until you all get used to riding up there. Is everyone ready?"

Lenth, Gabe, and the other four Providers all got a grip on their nearest cable. Lenth made a quick look at the team. "All set!"

"Right then." The elevator lurched, groaning as it slowly accelerated to cruising speed...which wasn't all that fast, but the vision of the surrounding walls sinking around them was imposing and unsettling.

"Woah," mumbled one of the Providers, "this is a first for me."

"I think riding the central elevator is a first for most of us," Gabe said.

"Well, yes, but I mean...ugh," another Provider said, gazing upwards.

"Everyone doing all right?" Messenger called up. "Is there going to be a problem?"

"No, Messenger."

"Good. See the access ladder running the length of the shaft?"

Lenth pointed at it with his spear to illustrate Messenger's words as the rungs continually passed down out of sight, one after another. "Six got on that," Messenger continued, "a few minutes up from here, and was headed up. He was probably heading for Actual, but that way is impossible for him."

Gabe, and some of the other Providers smirked. One does not simply climb to Actual. He is Actual.

"Obviously keep an eye out for Six himself, but watch the ladder also. Periodically, there is a panel that can be opened. When Six finds he can't go any further up, he's likely to try one of these panels. Holler when we're coming up on one so I can stop us to inspect the hatch. If he does manage to open one, it won't help him get to Actual, but it would be a place to hide from us, or just get lost in the walls again. Oh, also keep an eye out for traces of blood on the ladder. I'm not very hopeful of seeing any, but it would be helpful."

Gabe groaned. "What a pain. Let me take this moment to remind you all that this guy is a killer. Don't let him."

"Oh by the way, how's Diane?" Lenth asked quietly.

"A little better. Not super, but a little better."

Lenth nodded. "She might like to hear that the people who she had the problems with in the Citizenry are probably dead. Killed by a new leader, Mike."

"Ah. Thanks to Mike, then," Gabe said with a shrug.

"Well, Mike's dead."

"Oh?"

"Six killed him before calling for Messenger."

"Crap."

"It's not like Mike was a hugely nice guy. Just a lot better than the old guy."

"So who's leading them now?" Gabe asked.

"An old guy. I mean...a newer guy, but he's old. And a woman."

Gabe blinked. "The old guy is a new woman? How's *that* work?"

"No, no...two separate people. An old guy, maybe a little younger than Joints, and a woman. They're both well-liked in the Citizenry, but not quite buddies. I really hope they can get along."

"Why do you care, Lenth? Citizens are..."

"People. They've been through some bad stuff, and are in a weird situation, but they're people. Most of them seem mostly okay. I'd rather have a random one of *them* in the walls than Six."

Gabe sighed. "Well, I'd have a hard time arguing with that, I guess."

Lenth didn't bother complicating it further. *Many Citizens have probably killed, Leena and Edgar included. But they weren't like Six. That much was clear.*

Resigned to wandering thoughts on his Brothers, Citizens and Providers, his mind soon ended up on Leena, Karen, and...and women in general. Two of the Providers with him on top of the elevator were women. One was younger than Karen and Leena, the other, older.

Focus. Stop looking at curves and watch the ladder.

The quiet was accompanied by little mechanical grunts of the elevator. The motor was far above, but the elevator itself was not without its sounds. Unseen rollers kept the elevator from scraping metal along the walls, and the little sounds of people shifting their weight or a sigh here and there made the eeriness of the lighting all the more pronounced.

"There's a hatch!" a Provider called out. Sure enough, covered by a few rungs of the shaft's ladder, a hatch marked with faded yellow striping could be seen.

"Stopping!" Messenger warned. A second later, the elevator came to a standard stop. It still managed to stagger most of the passengers, especially those who had not kept their grip on a cable after setting out. Messenger poked his head up from the interior, and looked at the hatch. It was still well above everyone's heads.

"Ideally, we want it around knee-height, okay? I'm going back to the control panel, and holler down when it's at hip-height. Oh, and don't mess with it until I get a chance."

He went back down, and the elevator crept up slowly, bringing the hatch closer.

"Hip-height!" Gabe called down.

"Got it." Messenger slowed the elevator more, coming to rest with the hatch very much where Messenger had desired. He climbed up, and walked over to the hatch. He knelt down and peered between the ladder rungs at the hatch's release handle, and the edges of the hatch itself. "Nope. He hasn't been here. Well, at least he hasn't gone through this one. It's been untouched for a long time."

"How do you know?" Lenth asked.

Messenger stood and headed for the hatch to the interior of the elevator. "When you close them from the other side, the handle doesn't rest quite like when you close them from this side," Messenger said.

Lenth, Gabe, and several others leaned in to study the handle. "How so?" Gabe asked.

"It wouldn't lay as flat. The bottom edge sticks out a few millimetres. I always lay them flat when I close them from this side."

"So you can tell if someone went through? You planned for this kind of situation?" Lenth asked with mild awe.

Messenger snorted as he climbed back down into the elevator's interior. "No, it's just tidier looking."

They headed back up for a couple of minutes before encountering another hatch. When they stopped, Gabe called down that it looked the same, but Messenger felt the need to come up to see.

"You're right," Messenger said, "but I like to see for myself."

This pattern resumed for several more hatches, each one undisturbed. "That's different," Lenth said, pointing up to a huge hatch. "Hey Messenger, there's a big one on the other side of—"

"Yes," Messenger hollered up, "that would be the door to the Citizenry."

All of the Providers faced the approaching door. A couple walked to the opposite side of the elevator's roof. Lenth knew that the Citizenry had a bad reputation, but he had trouble not smirking at the Providers, nearly cowering from the large, approaching, yet closed door.

Then he spotted the look on the face of one of the Providers.

"It a messy place, but it's not *that* bad," Lenth said.

"No?" Gabe piped up, "and how many people did you see get killed while you were there, Lenth?"

"By people other than Six? None. I still can't get my head around the crap-sniffing, though."

"Crap sn—"

Interrupting from below, Messenger called up, "Okay, we're going to be making a stop at Citizenry, but I'm just going to talk to them through the closed door."

Lenth scurried down the ladder into the elevator while the others watched the Citizenry door creep down past their feet. The elevator came to a stop.

"Messenger," Lenth called out, joining him by the little peeking-hatch, "I want to check in on them, too."

Messenger nodded and took a look through. A couple of Citizens were standing nearby, awaiting to be addressed.

"Citizens," Messenger said in his authority-voice, "has the one called Six returned here?"

"No," the taller one said, "and we'd just as soon not have him. If he was a test from Actual, like some people are saying, I sure hope we passed, and well enough that we don't need more testing!"

"Actual did not send him, and nor did I. Six came for his own reasons. If he does show up again..."

"We'll call you!" the Citizen said.

"We can't. The caller things is broken," said the other.

"I will get you a new one as soon as I can," Messenger said, "but know that if a Citizen has to kill Six to prevent Six from killing again, that would be acceptable. Do not put yourselves at undue risk either way."

"Yes, Messenger."

"We understand, Messenger."

Messenger looked to Lenth and said quietly to him, "You had other questions?"

Lenth nodded and stepped closer to the peek-hatch. "Hey, you two. This is Lenth, remember me?"

"Who?" said one.

"I do!" said the other.

"Good. How's Leena? What's going on?"

"Leena's fine, as best I know. She and Edgar went off to talk somewhere about stuff."

"Talking friendly, or talking fighty?"

The Citizen shrugged and thought about it for a moment. "Talking worried about stuff, I guess. They seemed to be worried about the same things."

Lenth wanted to go talk to them, but Six was the priority. It really hadn't been that long since he'd left Citizenry, so 'worried talk' was probably the best he could hope for right now. "Tell Leena...well, tell them both that I said hi." He headed back to the ladder to go to the roof of the elevator, and Messenger closed the peek-hatch.

"Leena?" Gabe asked when Lenth got up. "Who's Leena?"

"A woman I met there," Lenth said as the elevator started heading up again, "she was confusing, but nice, I guess."

Gabe smiled a sly sort of smile. "You met a woman? Met her, or *met* her?"

Naïve Lenth clued in after a moment. "Her 'favourite man' was killed by Six. I just hope she's..."

"Ah." Gabe's smile faded. "Well, at least Karen doesn't have to worry about competition from *her*."

"Carin'? What did she say?" Lenth felt himself blushing.

"Relax, lover-boy, I'm just teasing you. I'm not saying she *doesn't* like you, I just don't know. Forget I said anything."

"Forgotten," Lenth said, "and focusing on finding Six."

"Right."

Eyes scanning the walls of the ever-sinking elevator shaft and the maintenance ladder, his mind wandered to the opposite sex frequently. Well, mainly Leena and Karen.

Leena implied she was willing to do sex with him. That was mostly before Mike died, though. Her feelings could have likely changed. Lenth didn't understand her, or her relationship with Mike, but...well, at the very least, the last time Lenth had seen her, she had other things on her mind than educating some naïve Lofu.

"Well, at least we're away from the Citizenry," one of the Providers mumbled. A few others nodded or hummed in agreement.

"Well, away from the door, anyway." Lenth pointed at the wall. "It's a big space; it's probably right through the walls all around us. I saw the elevator shaft from the outside; it goes up right through the middle of Citizenry."

"As long as it's through walls, that's good enough," another Provider said.

"Maybe more Providers should visit Citizenry. They don't seem to understand *you*, either," Lenth said.

"Do they understand that they would starve to death in the dark without us?"

Lenth smiled halfheartedly. "Well, yeah. I think so, but they don't seem to really...well..."

"They don't appreciate us," Gabe said.

"They appreciate Actual." Lenth looked up, and was surprised to see that the light had found an end to the shaft. A large door, like the one to Citizenry awaited.

The elevator came to a stop before reaching it, and Messenger climbed up. He looked around. "Nowhere else to go. All right, everyone get back in the elevator."

Messenger went first and went to the control panel. He took out the headset again, checked the knob, and pressed the button. "Hi. Yeah. Have you heard anything? Yes, that's us. No. Well, it narrows things down a little at least. He might. Did you find the communications set for the Citizenry? Of course. I can come back—well, that's your call. Good point." Messenger looked over at Lenth, then continued his conversation. "Really? Is that a good choice, all things...oh, yes. The timing would have been awful too, with Six running around. Okay. Sounds good. I'll call him now."

Messenger pressed the button, then turned the knob. He looked to Lenth and the Providers. "I'm calling Contact next."

"Was that Actual?" Lenth asked, voicing what the others wondered.

"Yes."

"And that door up there—"

Messenger stared at Lenth for a moment and said quietly, "Providers are not prepared for what is behind that door."

"Forgive Lenth," Gabe said solemnly. "He's been a Subject all his life, and doesn't appreciate how monumental it is to be this high."

Lenth felt like he'd been lectured, like maybe he had offended Gabe.

"Actual feels that everyone's lives are important enough to warrant you all up here," Messenger said. "I convinced him that I needed to come up to make sure Six wasn't tampering with things he had no business dealing with, but since he's not here, we take the next step in finding him."

"What now?" Lenth asked.

"I call Contact." He adjusted his headset and hit the button. "Yes." Messenger's tone for Contact was back to his authoritative mode. "Six is still missing, it is possible that he may be back in your levels. I'll be bringing your people home to assist in keeping people safe. Yes."

Messenger pressed the button one last time, jammed the headset in its compartment, and started the elevator down.

The grand elevator door finally slid open onto the Provider level. Most of the Providers filed out, and made a sloppy little formation beside Contact, who was waiting for their return.

"Messenger," Contact said with a bow.

Messenger stood stiffly, holding one of the spears at his side. "Six is still unaccounted for," Messenger said. "I'm going to continue looking, but your people belong here. You need them more than I do. It is possible that Six may have found his way back into your areas."

"Messenger, that's quite imp—" Contact stopped himself and lowered his gaze. "He's sneaky. We'll have to be very careful."

"Keep your people safe," Messenger said. "Make no mistake, it would be good for everyone if Six died, but don't risk people trying to make it happen. Providers, Managers, Subjects. They all deserve to be treated with respect."

At that, Contact eyed Lenth. Just for a moment, but it was enough to redirect Messenger's attention. Gabe's, too.

"What are you thinking, Lenth?" Messenger asked in a calmer, slightly less official tone.

"I kind of want to check in on people. My Brothers, Carin', Fill, I guess. But I think it can wait. I think finding Six is more important. Gabe, can I help look? Is there some kind of organized... I don't know—"

"Or you could come with me." Messenger had reasserted his authoritative tone, and in the wake of his words, an uncomfortable silence pressed against everyone.

Lenth looked around at everyone and fiddled with his hands. "Where would we go?"

"Looking for Six. Just because he might be in the Provider area doesn't by any means exclude other places."

Gabe looked to Contact. "May I go too? You have enough people now, that—"

"Just Lenth," Messenger said, resulting in another bout of silence.

Contact stared at Messenger while Gabe and Lenth exchanged sheepish glances. Gabe got off of the elevator and grabbed the edge of the door, pulling it partly closed until Messenger stepped close enough to take over. Lenth waved to everyone outside the elevator while he still had the chance, and called out to Gabe, "Say hi to Carin' for me!"

Gabe and Contact watched the door shut. A few moments later, the elevator hummed and creaked to life.

"Fine," Contact said grumpily, "that's just fine."

"Are you worried for Lenth, Contact?"

Contact gave Gabe a critical glance. "Lenth. Ha. Listen to that elevator."

Gabe looked upwards, listening to the elevator's sounds fading. "It sounds...it sounds okay to me."

"Yes, but you're looking the wrong direction, Gabe. It's going down."

Chapter Twenty-Two

Heart

"Are we going to the Subject Unit areas?"

"It's possible to access them from the shaft, but no, the Providers have those areas covered. At least, they should."

Lenth nearly asked about the Manager/Rubberman layer, but that was silly. *It's practically the same place as the Subjects, and just as well covered by the Providers.* He wanted to ask dumb questions, but didn't want to sound dumb in front of the Messenger.

After a while, Messenger broke the silence. "Do you ever wonder how this all got here?"

"Yes, but hang on, slow down," Lenth babbled, holding out his hands. "Are we going down further *below* the Subject levels? I just learned that there was an *up* all this time; now you're telling me there's a *down?*"

Messenger smiled wide, nodding, and holding back a chuckle. "There is always more down, always more up, always more left, right, forward, and back. It's just that there's usually a huge amount of rock in the way."

"Yes! Fine! But right now—We. Are. Going. Down. And not through solid rock!"

"Correct, Lenth."

"How far does the rock go? Why is it here?"

"Arg! Big questions! And I don't think I have the answers you want! Actual might, but I don't. Let's focus a little closer to the moment than the nature of all existence, all right, Lenth? I meant this place, your old home, the Provider's space, the Citizenry, all of it...how do you think it got here?"

Lenth looked around. "It's been here...always?"

"Someone made it all," Messenger huffed. "Everywhere you've ever been used to be solid rock. Someone used some kind of tool to make the empty spaces we live in. How, I don't know. Where the rock went that was here, I don't know. I assume that wherever they put it had to have empty space already."

Lenth tapped at the elevator wall with his spear, staring beyond it into the rocky unknown. "So why aren't we in a space that was already there?" he asked, feeling stupid as he said it.

"Exactly! Why? They built the elevators, the rooms...I know, because I spend a lot of time fixing things. I've been in the Unit you used to live in, as a matter of fact. Many times. Fixing this or that, replacing a screen on the exercise machines, the work stations, the showers, all kinds of things. I have to ask Actual for supplies, and they show up days later. Actual knows more than me. Much more."

Lenth held a hand out to interrupt Messenger. "Do you fix tubes that give us the medicines through the tether cuffs?"

Messenger stared at Lenth with a hint of remorse for a few moments. He stopped the elevator. "We're here."

"Do you?" Lenth asked.

Messenger peeked out the little hatch, then headed to the handle to open the door. "Yes, sometimes I do. Often a Manager or Provider does. I *am* sorry about your Brother. Now and then, no one finds out about a malfunction until too late." He dragged the door open.

The room was much like any of the other rooms connected to the central elevator. Another big door on the opposite side, and lots of room for cargo. It was very clean. Cleaner than the room connecting to the Citizenry, easily, but even cleaner than the one connecting to the Provider area.

On one side, a dozen Rubberman suits hung on the wall, the masks hanging at the top, overlapping the coat, boots sitting neatly below the pants, and gloves in the boots. The row continued with eight sets of hooks for suits that had been taken.

"Where is this?"

"Have you ever been in the dark, Lenth? I mean, total dark, not the 'dimmed' sleep-time in your Unit?"

"Yes," Lenth said, idly looking to the ceiling. "As soon as I got out of my Unit, I was between ceilings and floors. There were bits of light sometimes. It was..."

"I'm sure it was. If it wasn't for *this* place, everywhere would be dark. Even those 'bits of light'. Air and water would stop being circulated, heat wouldn't get generated, the elevators wouldn't work, and so on."

"You mean we'd all... die of thirst in the dark, freezing?"

"Something like that. So we keep this place running well. Grab a suit."

Lenth walked up to the nearest suit, and reached under the mask on the top hook, to grab the coat. "It...it's heavier than the last one I wore."

"The Managers just wear a bio-hazard version," Messenger explained, "and most of those aren't even up to original specs anymore. Eroded seals and dead filters, at the very least. These ones here are well-maintained, also have protection from radiation, and—" Messenger paused, looked at Lenth's blank expression, "—and you have no idea what I'm talking about, I'm guessing."

"Protection from radi-what?" Lenth asked as he put the suit on.

Messenger started on a suit for himself. "Radiation. It's...kind of like heat, but not. You can be in it, and not even feel it, and still soak enough into your body to kill you."

"That doesn't make any sense," Lenth said as he pulled the last piece, the mask, off of the hook.

"Hey, don't wear the mask, just have it handy. The mask strap can hook onto the bit on the hip of the coat. And stick the gloves in the mask."

Lenth looked at Messenger incredulously but followed directions. "What, this radiation stuff doesn't hurt your head or hands?"

"Sure does, but we're not headed into a dangerous area, at least not yet. Best to be prepared." Messenger headed for the door further into the reactor section. "Oh, Lenth, before I forget, don't mention this place to anyone in the floors above, except Contact. Some Providers might know, but that's Contact's business. We wouldn't want to mess up anything he's set up."

Lenth picked up his spear, ready to go. "Can I tell Actual?"

Messenger smirked. "If you happen to talk to him, yes. He knows all about it."

"Oh. Well, yeah. I guess I should have known."

Messenger, spear in hand, opened the door. On the other side was a round room, ten or so metres wide, with three evenly spaced doors. The door ahead was a double-door that looked to slide open into either side of the walls, and it was bulkier than the others. It had a circular design on it with six alternating wedges of black and yellow.

Messenger pointed at it. "That thing means radiation danger. The little room through that door is sometimes dangerous, and the places after *that* room are *always* dangerous. To make things simple, before you go through that door, put the mask and gloves on."

Lenth eyed the door as if it were looking back at him. "Are we going in now?"

"Nah, we'll talk to some of the Engineers first." Messenger led to the left door, and headed in. A short hallway later, and they were in a larger room with desks and computers everywhere. These computers were larger, and most were built into the walls, or the bulkier desks. Bright geometric designs were on most of them. Some fluctuated very slightly, and most had small words next to them. Many looked difficult to read, but Lenth's attention was soon drawn to the people here.

"Messy!" called out a woman who rose from her seat by a computer desk. "How are things?" She wasn't in a Rubberman suit, but one sat folded nearby. She was an older woman, maybe a little older than Messenger. Her once-black hair showed prominent streaks of grey, and her smile for Messenger was a bit wrinkled.

"Messy?" Lenth quietly asked Messenger.

"Looks okay to me," Messenger said gesturing to the largest technical-looking display on the wall. There were dozens of technical screens, and as many screens showing other locations, including the radioactive door. "We're actually looking for a rogue Subject,"

"Six?" the woman asked. "We heard from Contact, some time ago now. He's still on the run?"

"Yeah. Actual and I thought it would be smart to check in here, since—"

"Well, understandable," the woman said. "So Six is crawling around the shaft, hm?"

"Messy?" Lenth asked a little louder.

"Messy. Short for Messenger," Messenger explained. "Huh, I should introduce you two. Tara, this is Lenth. He was a Subject, and, well...got loose. He's a good fella, though. Made friends with the Providers, took a trip through Citizenry, and is being generally helpful. Lenth, Tara here used to be a Provider, but was selected by Contact to come down here and join the reactor crew. We call the Providers that get moved down here 'Engineers'."

"And you brought this fellow down here," Tara said. "Does it mean this one's joining the crew?"

"Maybe," Messenger said, looking Lenth up and down. "His education is pretty wanting, being a Subject and all, but he could learn, I think. He has a lot of potential, and doesn't have a...a 'Contact' attitude."

Tara forced back a smile and nodded in understanding.

"Were you part of the crew here?" Lenth asked Messenger.

"Yeah. I worked with Tara for a long time before becoming Messenger. Most Messengers are drawn from the crew here."

Lenth absorbed it for a bit, and imagined doing Messenger's job one day. He knew some of the tasks already, but he also knew there was a lot more that he'd only heard hints of. "Wait. Wait you have a *name*."

"Excuse me?" Messenger said with a smirk.

"*Messenger* is just what you do! A job name! You had another name before that! And maybe Actual had one too! Messengers become Actuals, right? That's what Contact said! Oh! And Contact! Does he have a regular name? I should have known! My Rubberman has an actual name!"

"Slow down, Lenth, your head's gonna pop. Yeah, I had another name."

"Neil," Tara chirped.

Lenth looked at her. "Kneel? Why?" he asked. Tara chuckled.

"It's not the kind you're thinking!" Messenger snapped. "I wasn't a Subject, Neil is a regular name. It's spelt differently, and has nothing to do with kneeling."

"That doesn't make any sense!"

"Just forget it. I'm not supposed to use it anymore anyway. Tara, we were going to head over to the residential section and ask around. I mean, if you haven't heard anything about Six being down here, odds are no one else knows either, but it's worth a shot." Messenger signalled for Lenth to follow him to the door.

"All right, Messy, good seeing ya," Tara said.

"Messy..." Lenth mumbled with a suppressed smile.

"And you're not calling me *that* either!"

They passed through the round room, passing by the large door with the radioactivity symbol on it, and entered the residential section. The first room was a lot like the cafeteria in the Provider area, and as they wandered about, fruitlessly asking Engineers about Six, the similarities to the Provider area seemed to continue. A small office, like an ode to Contact's office, a smaller clinic, and so on.

Most of the Engineers seemed to know Messenger, and some had worked with him before he was the Messenger. He spoke with them as equals. As friends.

When Messenger spoke to most others—Providers, Citizens, Contact—he spoke with words and timbre of authority. A representative of the great Actual, far above, but here in this lowest of places, Messenger found people closer to being peers.

"Do you come here in your free time?" Lenth asked Messenger when he had a moment.

"Not really. I am not one of them anymore."

"Seems like you kind of are."

Messenger smiled a little. Sadly, a little. "It's complicated."

They stopped to talk to another Engineer who had no information, then nabbed a disk of food each as they passed by the small cafeteria.

"Is it because you'll be Actual some day?"

Messenger paused, and leaned against a wall as he idly pecked at his food. "He teaches me things. Trains me to do what he does now. I know my path, and see *my* future happening to him *right now*. I've known my future since becoming Messenger, maybe better than anyone. And I learn more of it every day."

Lenth took a small bite so he could speak sooner. "I don't know much about my future. You don't sound happy about yours."

Messenger crossed his arms. "I will be Actual when he can no longer perform his duties. It is the greatest honour. I...I will live the same life that I am now watching him live. And then another after me, the same, always."

Lenth scratched his head and smirked. "Reminds me of being a Subject. Every day, the same. No other choices."

"*You* chose," Messenger said.

"Well, yeah, but I wasn't supposed to."

A voice, Tara's voice, interrupted Lenth from a fixture in the ceiling. "Available people, suit up. Someone's gone into the reactor unprotected. Move, people!"

"What does—?"

"Move, Lenth. We're already suited up."

Messenger led, and Lenth tried to keep up. Several un-suited Engineers were coming with them to the round room. Once there, the panicked Engineers rushed to the hall with the radiation-protected Rubberman suits.

Messenger put his mask on and sealed it, watching to make sure Lenth was doing it right. He corrected a one of the seals between Lenth's hood and the mask, then reached for the large horizontal handle to the radioactive door.

"It's locked!" he called out to the ceiling. He had to yell a little. The mask was built to let sound through around the mouth, but it couldn't do so terribly well.

"Inner door was left open," Tara's voice came, "I'll do an emergency unlock. Get in there and shut the outer door, fast." There was a *clunk*. Messenger heaved the door open, and shoved Lenth in before following. He yanked the heavy door shut behind them, and it locked immediately.

The room they found themselves in had a grating for a floor, with darkness below. Overhead and on the walls, an array of spray nozzles.

The inner door was wide open. "Crap," Messenger called out. "Tara, when I get in, just start purging the decontamination cham—"

Tara's voice cut in from above. "Yeah, yeah, go!"

Lenth and Messenger went in and started pushing the inner door shut behind them. "Do you think it's Six?"

"Who else?" Messenger replied. "He has no idea what he's doing to himself right now."

"Radiation? Here?" Lenth looked around, spear ready instinctively, as if he could stab the radiation away.

"A fair amount. More of it further in. Lots more. Pick a direction, 'Subject'," Messenger said to Lenth, hoping that Lenth's hunch would be enough luck to find Six, another Subject. They had three options. Each with spartan industrial walls and ceilings, with piping and conduits bolted on, or cabling draped from place to place. All three paths looked cold and desolate, despite the omnipresent hum of unseen machines.

Six would want to be sneaky, so straight ahead was no good. The way the door hinged, he would have seen the left passage first. It made the right passage feel more...hidden, in some small way. Lenth took the passage, and Messenger was right behind him. Lenth was feeling cautious, wanting to listen carefully as they went, but Messenger pushed for a quicker pace.

After a corner, the hallway came across a four-metre-wide door, with a smaller, person-sized door built into it. A sign on it had two words. Lenth tried to read it. Did it say *Picker Garbage*? What was that?

"Stay out here, Lenth," Messenger said, peeking into the smaller door. "I'll just have a quick look in the Garage. Not really any good hiding spots in there. Holler if you see anyone coming."

Picker *Garage. That makes even less sense, what's a garage?* Lenth watched Messenger for a moment as he rushed in. *Ah. So a picker garage is a big barren room with a few...shelves on four wheels with handles and...whatever. Watch the hall.* Lenth heard Messenger poking about, when two Rubbermen came rushing around the corner; Engineers who had come through the decontamination room after Lenth and Messenger had.

They stopped when they spotted Lenth and his spear, and spoke to each other. Several metres away, and with the masks, Lenth couldn't hear anything other than muffled mumbling.

Lenth waved at them with his free hand. "Hi!" Lenth called out, hoping that he was heard clearly enough. "Messenger is in the Picker Garbage, looking for Six."

The two Engineers looked at each other, and one said something unintelligible before lightly smacking the others' arm. They jogged over to Lenth, one keeping a close eye on Lenth's spear. "You're not Six, are you?" one said. When they were closer, and making a point to be heard by Lenth, it was easier to understand.

"Nope, I told you, Messenger is in the Picker Garb...ack. *Garage*, looking for him. Hey, is there any way that Six might get into the ceiling? Or the floor?"

The Engineer that had been hesitant about Lenth's spear was now looking at the ceiling as if Six were going to leap on them at any second. The other one spoke up. "No, the reactor wing is designed to seal stuff in, not—"

Messenger stepped out from the garage. "Yeah, seal in radioactive particles, inside sections of this wing. There's still lots of places for a person to hide."

"Stupid question, here," Lenth turned to Messenger. "Is there any way Six can survive in here for a long time? Is there another way out?"

Messenger shook his head. "Even if he was in a suit, it's not like there's food or water in here. Not water you'd want to drink, anyway. But no, going outside and waiting for him to come out or die isn't really a good option, if that's what you're thinking."

"Because he could turn everything off?"

The nervous Engineer laughed. "Off? Off? That would be a best case scenario! Off can be turned back on! It's hard, but doable. I'm more worried about him screwing the coolant system up, setting us critical, or whatever *boom*! These suits won't mean anything if—"

"Enough." Messenger said. " We just have to find him before he manages anything stupid. Let's just keep looking."

An Engineer spoke up, "others are taking other directions out of-"

"Good, good, let's move," Messenger interrupted.

After twenty or so metres down the hall, the other Engineers split off to go check 'the cask room', whatever that was. It wasn't long after that yelling was heard ahead.

Messenger and Lenth broke into a full run, navigating turns as the sounds of commotion directed. A pair of Engineers in Rubberman suits joined them from another hall, and they were soon at a large room.

"The pool," Messenger said. "He *had* to go to the cooling pool. Moron."

In the middle of the giant room sat a circular hole, about fifteen metres wide. In the hole, filled nearly to the top, water almost seemed to glow a mesmerizing, pale blue. From this far, Lenth could not see the bottom.

Around the room were eight Engineers in Rubberman suits, all keeping their distance from Six.

Six stood at the edge of the pool, still red with Mike's dried blood. He was smiling nervously, sweating, and trembling. "Rubbermen! Rubbermen everywhere! Is this where you come from? And here I am without a knife!"

Messenger stepped closer, but still several metres away from Six and the pool. "Six. You're in...you're in so much danger right now. We have to get you out of here."

Six howled a sharp, delirious laugh. "Out of here? And into where? Into a 'Unit', with nice cozy tethers? Getting shocked by one of you whenever I work too slow, get up too slow, or drop my food? Every day wondering if I'll be able to feel my hands when I go to sleep? *And then?*"

This was not how Lenth remembered living in his Unit. Shocks? Yes, but rarely. Feel his hands? What was going on in Six's Unit?

"I'm not going with you freaks!" Six looked down into the pool. It went down for over twenty metres, although the refraction in the water made it difficult to judge. Near the bottom sat a circle of shelves that obscured what might be under them. On the shelves stood grey cylinders, which looked to be about a metre in height.

"Think I can make it through? The bottom's got to go somewhere..."

"There's no way out the bottom, it's the cooling pool! It's just a big tank of water!" Messenger pleaded, "and those are spent fuel rods down there! That water will kill you, if you haven't *already* taken in enough radiation to do it! If you touch one of those rods, you'll be dead before you can float to the top again!"

Six looked down into the pool, and then around to all the Engineer Rubbermen watching him. He clenched his fists, pushed out a hard breath before taking in as much air as he could and jumping in. The water washed off some of the blood, and the blue hue began to turn a gentle violet.

Every Engineer recoiled in horror.

Having never seen more than a cup of water concentrated in one place, Six found that he did not know anything about swimming, much less diving twenty metres. He tried, pushing down in futile grasps at the water, trying to yank himself down through it, clawing at the wall to gain traction. Needing air, instinct forced him back up. A frustrated yelp came with a gasp before he tried again.

Lenth dropped his spear, ran along the side of the pool to where Six had jumped in, and held out a gloved hand. "Grab on, Six!"

"Never!"

"Grab on! You're getting nowhere like that, idiot!"

"Rubber can go—get away—not again—kill you—" his repeated attempts to dive were only getting weaker and more pathetic. Lenth grabbed at his arm when he got a chance, but Six yanked free with a scream. "*Don't touch me! You can't touch me! I'm not—don't!*"

Lenth yanked his mask up above his face. "Six. It's me! You need to get out of there."

"*Lenth!*" Messenger hollered, "*Get that mask back on! Now!*"

Lenth held his hand out, waiting for Six to look at him. Six floundered to stay afloat, finally submitting that he needed to grab the edge of the pool at least.

Despite the opportunity, Lenth did not take advantage to grab at Six's wrist. He just held out his hand. "Come on."

Six stared up at Lenth and all the Engineers stared at them both. The hum of the machines, the occasional ripple of water, the shifting or squeak of a rubber suit. And a silence.

Finally, Six reached up and let Lenth help him out. He was dripping, less bloody, and shivering.

"How do you feel?" Messenger asked. "Headache? Sick to your stomach?"

"N...no..." Six said, not used to conversing with a Rubberman.

Messenger nodded. "Might be a while before it sets in. Let's get you out of here."

Six reluctantly followed directions from the Engineers, despite being Rubbermen. He stayed well out of reach from them though, including Lenth, who had put his mask back on before collecting his spear again. Most of the Engineers were happy to give Six a wide berth.

"Why?" Six mumbled as the loose procession headed down the halls. "Why any of this?"

"This place keeps the lights on and stuff working," Lenth offered, following behind Six.

"Fine, whatever. Why the Units? Why Subjects? Why Citizens?"

They continued on for a few moments more, before Lenth replied. "How else should it be?"

Six replied immediately, nearly screaming. "*I didn't need to be treated like that, in the Unit.* I didn't need to think there was only a handful of people in existence. I didn't need to be forced to work every day on things when I had no idea what they were!"

Lenth couldn't argue, and added meekly, "I didn't need my Brother to die, and disappear with no explanation."

"And now you're one of them," Six said spitefully.

"It's not..." It wasn't worth trying to reason it out to Six if he couldn't quite reason it out to himself. It was time to visit people. Karen. Gabe. Leena. His Brothers. Phil. Joints. How was Joints feeling? A bitter taste washed over Lenth, thinking that Joints might die soon, without knowing so much of what's out here. Slim had died in even more ignorance.

Why.

Why indeed.

When they got to the decontamination room, about half of the Engineers came in with Lenth, Six and Messenger. The rest would have to wait. The inner door sealed behind them, and the outer door to the central round room remained shut.

"Six," Messenger said, "strip down. Even if they weren't so stained with blood, your clothes are garbage now. We'll have a fresh set when we get out the other side."

Six looked around with disgust at the Engineers standing around, all suited up with masks on.

"Lenth," Messenger continued, "you too. You had your mask off in there. You'll need to scrub down to the skin to be safest."

"What's going on?" Six seethed. "As you may have noticed, I just had a nice little wash-down."

Lenth threw his gloves and mask onto the floor. "You were in some bad, bad stuff, I think."

"What do you mean? What bad stuff?" Six was on the edge of yelling.

"You've been shocked? As a Subject?" Messenger asked.

"Ha! *Yes*, one or twice," Six rasped with barbed tones, "maybe, now that I think really hard on it! *Yeah*, I might have been shocked!"

Messenger tried to look Six sternly in the eye; a futile attempt with the mask on. "To vastly over-simplify things, what you swam in is linked to the source of all the shocks, all the lights, the power that makes the elevators move, that pumps the water and the air around. The human body isn't made for that kind of thing."

"I feel fine!"

"So far. The onset of the radiation sickness is usually delayed. You could start feeling it in a few minutes more, or maybe a day..."

"Radiation sickness? What is that?"

"The cleaner you get, the better. Wash off any additional particles before they can infest your body."

By this time, Lenth had removed his Rubberman suit entirely. "I don't totally get it either, Six, but these guys work with this stuff all the time, I think they know how it goes."

"Obedient little Lenth!" Six wailed, backing into a corner. Still soaking wet from the coolant pool, he seemed to shrivel back, doing his best to hide in plain sight. He touched one of the spray nozzles on the wall. "Shower time? Get your clothes off, it'll be fine? Where's my cuff, Rubberman? Why aren't I cuffed, Rubberman? If I don't do what you say, do I get the sleepy-gas, Rubberman?"

"Six, this is already uncomfortable," Lenth said, trying to calm Six down. Lenth was already half way out of his clothes. "Let's get this over with, scrub down, and get out of here."

"All right, Tara, you may as well start it up," Messenger called up to the ceiling.

"Okay," came the reply.

Every nozzle in the walls and across the ceiling sputtered to life, spraying warm water. Most of the Engineers began rubbing themselves down in their suits. In the sound of the spraying, you could barely hear Six whimper. Lenth just let the spray his body from every direction, and watched the still-clothed Six cower in the corner. The pressure and warmth of the spray washed away much more of the red that the pool didn't clean. But not all.

"Six. It's all right."

Messenger began walking towards Six, but Lenth put a hand out to stop him. "Messy. Give him space. He's terrified."

Messenger looked at Six, and looked at Lenth. "He's got to strip down," Messenger said, backing away. He said something else, too quiet to be clearly understood through the mask, but Lenth guessed it was something about the nickname 'Messy'.

Lenth turned his attention back to Six. "Look, I stripped down, and I'm fine. Gotta get the radiation off."

Engineers continued cleaning themselves and each other, often using the sprayer hoses from the walls to spray the nooks and crannies of their suits. Six just stood in the corner holding himself and glowering at everyone.

Finally the water stopped. A few of the Engineers hopped up and down, or shook off excess water. The sounds of the trickling drainage below became the quiet, but dominant ambiance.

"I didn't get naked," Six said flatly, with quiet, defiant pride.

Messenger pushed back his hood and pulled off his mask. His face was grim and resigned. "Honestly... I don't think it'd make much difference overall." The outer door cracked open, and some of the Engineers walked out towards the hall where the suits were stored.

"What do you mean, it won't make a difference?" Lenth asked.

Messenger looked at Six. "He swam with the spent fuel rods. They're no good for making power anymore, but they've got more than enough to kill. He's dead. His body just hasn't processed it yet."

"I feel fine!" Six stood up straight. "I feel fine!"

"And you," Messenger turned to Lenth, "how long were you sitting there with your mask off? I'm not sure how bad it might be for *you*."

Lenth echoed Six's statement in a whisper. "I...feel fine..."

Messenger looked at them both and sighed. "All these years, nothing quite like that has ever happened. Let's clear the chamber, others want through."

Lenth picked up his clothes, and Messenger helped carry his Rubberman suit. With the decontamination chamber clear, Messenger closed the door. An Engineer came with towels and fresh clothes for Lenth and Six.

"Thank you," Lenth said. It was only now that he realized that three Engineers standing around were here in case Six got violent.

Six took his bundle and hastily changed, not spending much time to dry off before putting the clothes on. As such, they didn't go on so easily, and looked to be ill-fitting, clinging in uncomfortable ways.

"Six, back when you were in your Unit..." Messenger said quietly, "your Rubberman...what kinds of things did he do?"

The tone of Messenger's voice made the hair on the back of Lenth's neck stand up. Six seemed mildly irritated. "The usual, you know."

"For argument's sake, pretend I don't know."

Chapter Twenty-Three

Flee

Lenth was told to go make himself comfortable. Grab a bite to eat, find a place to get some sleep, whatever. Messenger took Six elsewhere, with a couple of Engineer escorts for safety.

What were they going to do to Six? Likely nothing that he doesn't deserve. How many people had he killed, or just injured? How can someone do those things?

Despite being offered a bed when requested, Lenth realized almost immediately upon putting his head down that sleep wasn't about to happen. Maybe this was a chance to go visiting people—except that he'd have to use the central elevator. That would strand Messenger, and it wasn't as if he knew how to use it.

Not knowing where exactly Messenger went, Lenth headed over to Tara's computer-filled office space. There were also a few more Engineers in there now.

"Hi. Len...Length, was it?" Tara greeted.

"Lenth, yeah. Hey, does all this stuff keep track of everything that...does stuff?"

Tara chuckled. "Electrical stuff, a lot of it, yeah."

"Does it zap Subjects?"

Tara's smile faded. "It doesn't control the zaps, but it does supply the power to do it."

"Right," Lenth said. "Rubbermen...I mean Managers control it. Does this thing remember?"

Tara gave a sad smile and tapped a bunch of keys on a nearby keyboard. "It logs, ah...'remembers' overall usage. To monitor need. What was your Unit number?"

"I have no idea. My Manager's name is Fill, though, it that helps."

"Yeah, Phil, Phil...okay, yeah, here's your Unit's power consumption over the last year. A little below typical for a Unit."

Lenth stared at the mess of numbers on the screen, and the colourful graph above it. "And...how about Six's Unit?" Lenth didn't know the Manager's name, or the Unit number, but Six's breakout was notorious, and Tara was able to find it easily enough.

The numbers didn't tell Lenth much, but the graph did.

"Woah." Tara pressed a few keys to examine more detail. "This isn't some power bleed somewhere. He just shocked them a lot. I mean...a lot. Oh my..."

"How much is a lot?" Lenth asked.

"Looks like...looks like he almost always shocked them all at once. In a twenty-four hour span, like...looks like maybe fifty or more times. And this stopped right when that Manager was killed. The new one has been more reasonable."

Lenth backed away from the computer slowly. "We have to tell Messenger! And Contact! Fifty times a day?"

Tara nodded. "Yes, Contact should be told. That would be Messenger's job to tell him. I mean, that Manager is dead, but the fact that it happened at all..."

"I'll go find Messenger," Lenth said.

"He's probably in a storage space with Six, once you're in the residential wing, keep to your left."

Lenth had only begun wandering the left section of the residential wing, when Messenger came along.

"Messenger! We found out from Tara's computer that Six's Manager shocked him a lot! I mean a ton!"

Messenger seemed unmoved, and put a hand on Lenth's shoulder. "I know. Six told me. His Manager did a lot more than that, too."

Lenth's eyes widened. "What? Like...like what?"

"Quite often, he would incapacitate them. Gas, often, and when they were helpless he'd go to their floor and...and do things to them." Messenger was pale, and staring into the floor.

"What kinds of things?"

Messenger swallowed hard. "I certainly can't blame Six for killing him when he got the chance."

They stood there in the hall for a moment before Lenth took a guess. "Stuff like the Citizens used to do to each other?"

Messenger looked into Lenth's eyes. "Yeah. Yeah, something like that."

"So what happens to Six now?" Lenth asked.

"Well, I can forgive him killing his Manager, but the others...Six is...I highly doubt that he could be corrected. Even a risk as part of a Unit. I don't know. I just don't know what to do with him."

"Ask Actual?"

Messenger nodded. "Yes. Yes, that makes sense. The ridiculous thing of it is, it's not as big of a dilemma as I've let myself think. His radiation poisoning will kill him, and I don't think it will be all that long. A month at most? I don't know. Either way, the decision of what to do with him has been made for us."

Lenth cleared his throat. "And me? How long do I have?"

Messenger sighed. "Sorry, I forgot about your exposure. It wasn't full-body, and not for nearly as long. And you certainly didn't dunk your head in the cooling pool. On the other hand…"

"On the other hand, it's still my *head*, and those things are kind of important."

Messenger sighed again. "Yes. But if you're lucky, you'll recover completely. Maybe some time with some bad headaches? Or a fever?" Messenger put his hand on Lenth's forehead. "Well, not right now anyway, but like I said, it can take a while to show effects."

"How about the clinic in the Provider area?"

"They know less about radiation poisoning than the doctor here…or even anyone who's worked in the reactor area."

"Well then," Lenth said faintly, "I guess I'll just have to wait and see."

"Let's go to the control room. I want to check in with Tara before we head out."

"Back so soon?" Tara asked when Lenth and Messenger walked in.

"We're going to head to the elevator pretty quick here. I need to talk to Actual," Messenger said, "about what he thinks we should do with Six."

"What's his condition?" Tara asked.

"He says he feels fine. At least so far, but he was flailing around in the coolant pool, no suit. The longer it takes to manifest, the longer his death is going to take. It's not going to be nice."

"I feel fine right now, too," Lenth said.

"And you probably *are* fine," Messenger replied hastily.

Lenth grimaced. "You're awfully quick to assume he's going to die, and I'm fine."

"There used to be a tool for reading radioactivity in a person," Tara said. "It broke long before I started here. It sure would be handy right about now."

"Lenth's fine," Messenger said. "We can't run around waiting for him to drop or something."

"Thanks," Lenth mumbled.

Messenger grunted. "I didn't mean it like…Ugh. I need to talk to Actual. Come on."

The pair went to the central round room when three Engineers came out from the residential wing. They were wide-eyed and jittery. "*Did he come this way?*" one asked.

Messenger cocked his head. "Did *who* come this way?"

"No, no, no…" Lenth groaned. "Is anyone hurt?"

"A couple of people, but they'll be fine, I think."

The hum and groan of the great central elevator was heard from the other end of the entrance hall. Messenger broke into a sprint, with Lenth following close behind with the three Engineers. They arrived at the elevator shaft far too late. Messenger opened the outer door to see the elevator shaft. Leaning in, he looked up and saw the elevator growing smaller by the second. "*That's MY elevator, you murderous waste of air!*"

Messenger turned to the others. "Lenth. Climb. I'll catch up, I have to get the power cut off from the elevator." He started talking hastily to the Engineers as they rushed off, leaving Lenth facing the elevator shaft.

Dropping his spear to free both hands, He found a miniscule ledge to slide along and reach the ladder that ran the height of the shaft. A couple of metres below was the definite, absolute bottom. It was staggeringly plain compared to the view up. Up was breathtaking. The elevator was already far enough up that the distance looked a little bit like forever. He clutched the ladder anyway and started heading up. He hurried, feeling stupid for it, since the elevator was already so far up, and going faster than he could climb. *Pace it out. Just like the exercise machine. It's going to take a while.*

The quiet was broken only by his own sounds for what felt like a long time. That elevator was still a long way off. Hopefully Messenger had managed to get it stopped by now. It was hard to tell if it was still moving from this distance. No...he was getting closer. Probably. The monotony of the climb began to overtake the focus of why he was climbing, and was becoming almost as bad as the strain on his muscles.

Grab, pull, other hand, grab, pull, step, step, step, up, up, up.

"*Lenth!*" came Messenger's yell from below. When Lenth looked down, he was a little startled at how far he'd come.

"*You stopped it?*" Lenth yelled back.

"*Yeah! Keep going!*"

Lenth continued. Back to grab, pull, grab, pull, step, step, step. The fatigue had passed beyond feeling. This was a lot longer than his exercise had ever been.

Despite this, he found that he was a bit faster than Messenger. He had no desire to get to the elevator before Messenger. After all, even if Six wasn't in there, he'd need Messenger to operate the elevator's controls.

"Hey Messy! We...we *are* going to take the elevator when we get to it, right? We're not climbing all the way to the Provider level, are we?"

A sharp single laugh echoed up the shaft. "Oh yeah! Sure, for fun, let's race to Actual with just the ladder, why don't we?"

All right, then. Sarcasm and climbing it was, until the elevator. And then maybe a nice little lie-down. Lenth knew that the climbing had to be getting tiring for Messenger too. Lenth worried for Messenger, but a quick check made him think that Messenger had been doing a better job of pacing himself all along. He probably had several climbs in the shaft over the years. Experience counts.

He finally got up to the bottom of the elevator. The rungs that went across the bottom of the elevator to the hatch in the middle looked like torture in his tired state, and a fine way to slip to his death. The bottom hatch was probably closed from the interior anyway.

Lenth kept going up on the shaft's ladder, up beside the elevator, and onto the top of it. Once there, he collapsed on top and spread out on his back. He stared up the elevator shaft. Six was nowhere to be seen, but the Provider level was. Lenth had climbed well over half way to it. Six could have easily made it to the Provider's level by now if he'd started climbing right after the power was cut...

...but the hatch on top of the elevator was still closed.

Had they left the ladder in there? Without it, Lenth didn't see how Six could have gotten out the top. Six could be in there.

Then what? A yelling match? A fight to the death?

Lenth, still on his back, struck the top of the elevator with his fist twice. "Six! You in there? It's me, Lenth!" It dawned on him that Six might have a spear or something. Lenth had to give up his spear to climb; Six didn't.

Then it dawned on him that maybe Six had collapsed. That maybe his radiation poisoning had asserted itself.

"Anything?" Messenger said as he pulled himself onto the elevator.

Lenth shook his head. "Haven't heard anything."

Messenger crawled over to the hatch and opened it, looking in. "Gone." He looked up. "Well, I can guess where. Get in, Lenth, we can rest while the elevator's moving." Messenger climbed backwards into the hatch, and climbed down the ladder which had never been taken back out. He ambled over to the control panel.

Lenth was soon behind, and sat on the floor, back against a wall. "How long until we're there?"

Messenger was already making a call. "Yeah, we made it. Nope, probably went to Provider level. Light us up. Yeah. Thanks." He put the headset away, and turned to Lenth. "We'll have main power any second, and then, like...less than five minutes." 'Any second' arrived with a mechanical *clunk* and a momentary soft hum. "Here we go."

The elevator heaved to life and Messenger slumped against the control panel. "When we find Six, I say we just lock him in a little room while everyone has a nap."

"Yay!" Lenth weakly cheered.

Messenger tried to use the communication set again and gave up. "Contact isn't in his office." With a sigh that threatened to be a yawn, Messenger looked over to the control panel, then to Lenth. "Might be a good idea to show you how to use this, some time."

"What? What does that mean, I—"

"We're here." The elevator halted, and Messenger walked over to the door.

"That wasn't five minutes," Lenth bemoaned as pulled himself to his feet.

Messenger worked on opening the door. It was tougher than usual, and he had to yank on it harder, producing deep metal clangs. "Jerk didn't close the outer door behind himself properly. I should have gotten out and checked it before ...eh, whatever." It made a more satisfactory clang and opened to the Provider entrance hallway. A couple of Providers were waiting.

"He's here somewhere!" one said.

"We figured," Messenger said, "Got anything more helpful? He hasn't gone to the clinic? He's dying and he knows it. Might be aiming to get fixed up."

"Dying? How?" the Provider asked.

"It's complicated. Contact has people searching?"

"Yes, but—"

"But he's proven he's good at hiding. All right, fine, we continue the hard way, I guess."

"I want to check on some people," Lenth said. "Just to check on them as I look, you know?"

Messenger nodded. "It's not a bad idea, search-wise. About as good as any idea, really."

"Who's closer from here, my Unit, or Carin's?" Lenth asked.

"Not really my department," Messenger said.

Lenth turned to a Provider. "Do you know? Units managed by Fill and Carin'?"

The Provider shrugged. "There's like... three hundred Units."

Lenth looked down the hallway to see if memory stirred up directions. "Ugh. How about Gabe? Where's he?"

"Let's just head to Contact's office," Messenger said. "We might get lucky. If nothing else, I can use his computer to look up Phil and Karen."

Lenth agreed, and the two of them headed towards one of the smaller elevators. As they passed an intersection, Lenth got his bearings. "Oh! I know how to get to Carin's from here." He took a couple of steps in the right direction, urging Messenger to follow, but Messenger hesitated.

"Maybe I should be heading for Contact's office still."

"Well, if you want," Lenth said. "I can make it on my own; I'm sure of it."

Messenger shook his head slightly. "I don't know, Lenth. I don't like the idea of you running around the tight little spaces while Six is running around...probably in the same tight little spaces."

Lenth looked at the floor, and thought about their time at the coolant pool. About when Six accepted his help, even if very reluctantly. "I don't think he'd try to kill me," Lenth said. "I'm a Subject like him. It's Rubbermen that he has problems with."

"Are you sure he doesn't see you as one now?"

"Well, I don't look like one right now," Lenth said, holding out his arms. "Besides, it's a pretty slim chance that I'll run into him, anyway."

Messenger shook his head again. "Fine. But be careful anyway."

Chapter Twenty-Four

Roots

When she was distant, the idea of Karen was fairly abstract. Someone he liked, and was concerned for. As he got closer to her Unit, he began to remember her with a smoother, warmer clarity. Her voice, the way she moved, her curves.

When he arrived in her rooms, she wasn't there, likely out on the grating, managing her Subjects. The adrenaline of anticipation twisted into paranoia. Yes, she was probably safe, out over the main Unit, but there was a chance that Six had come. Had killed her. The odds were in Carin's favour. If Six was in the mood to kill some random Manager, he had … what was it? Three hundred to choose from?

Still, Paranoia is paranoia. He went to the door in her control room which went to the main Unit. He opened it, but didn't step out. He knew he wasn't supposed to be seen by the Subjects.

The idiocy struck him.

Why? He used to be a Subject. He had gotten out, and was glad for it overall. Why did he now hide to protect the ignorance of the Subjects here? Why didn't he go tell his own Brothers everything?

His thoughts tied knots in his head. The Providers and Managers weren't bad. They were nice people. Keeping Subjects ignorant was normal. It was expected. Normal.

When a Rubberman appeared from around a corner out on the Unit, his paranoia returned. Who was behind the mask?

It waved at him. Meaning what?

Lenth forced a smile and backed into the control room to await the Rubberman. *Oh...yeah, Six does not walk like that. Hello, Karen.* His smile softened with sincerity, and she waited until she closed the door before he spoke.

"Hi Carin'. How are you doing?"

She pulled off the hood and mask. Her hair tumbled down around her jaw. "Hey, Lenth. What brings you to my little corner? Are you after my papayas?"

Lenth forgot to reply for a moment as Karen was getting out of the rest of the Rubberman suit. She suppressed a smile when she noticed him watching. Unable to resist teasing a little, she took her time, and maybe stretched a little longer at a few key moments.

"Ah, no. I mean, I wouldn't refuse papaya, but it's been a while, and I wanted to check on you."

"Gabe said a while ago that you've been busy."

Lenth nodded. "Met Messenger, went to the Citizenry...went to a lot of places."

"And Six?"

"We had him, and he got away. We think he's somewhere in the Provider's levels. I came right here to make sure you're okay."

Karen shrugged with a grimace-like smile. "So far."

"He's dying," Lenth said. Best not to mention Radiation to Karen; she might not be allowed to know. Another step of ignorance that Lenth was complicit to. "I don't know how much longer he has, though."

Karen's eyebrow perked. "Huh. So what do you think he's planning with his time? Is he going to do as much damage as he can while he can still do it?"

"Possible, but he gave up a chance to do some huge damage. I don't know." *Certainly, he could have found a way to cause a bigger mess down at the reactor.*

"He's scared, you think?"

"Sure, probably. I guess I should be too. The thing that is killing him got me a little bit too. I'm probably fine. Messenger says so."

Karen took Lenth's hand. "What...what happened?"

Lenth fixated on the feel of her skin. The warmth. He desperately wanted to touch her hand with both of his, but resisted. He just stared at her hand. "Carin'...how do you feel about your Subjects?"

Karen flinched. "My Subjects?"

"Yeah. Do you like them? Do you hate them? Do you think they're worth less than a Provider?"

"Lenth, they're an important part of making the food that we all rely on!"

"That's not what I asked," Lenth said. "I know they're...they're *useful*, but how do you *feel* about them?"

Karen looked towards the door, and the hint of a caring smile warmed her face. "They're my reason to smile each day. They're wonderful," she said softly.

"Would you ever tell *them* that?" Lenth quickly asked, almost snapping.

"I...that would be nice, but of course you know I can't."

"Why?" Lenth asked.

"Because I can't! It's not the way things are done!"

"Why? If they knew that their Rubberman was definitely a person, and even one that liked them, would they just decide to stop working?"

"Maybe that's a risk. I...I don't know. They'd have questions. So many questions, and I don't think I could ever answer them all. What if—"

"Yeah. What if, Carin'? If they knew how many people need them? And how many other people who are out there that they need just as badly?" Lenth's rant was sliding slowly in wistful wonder. "Other Subjects, growing other foods, maintaining filters to keep the water and air clean? Providers fixing things, organizing things? Keeping everything together?"

"Would you go back, Lenth?"

Lenth stared Karen in the eyes, questioning himself for a moment. "If I didn't *have* to? If I could talk with my Brothers, *my Brothers!* About things, about the truths, and if they could go out as well to meet people like you, other Subjects, Providers, if they had freedom to work because it was a good thing to do, and not because they just didn't want to get shocked. I don't know, that sounds like it could be a pretty good way to live."

Karen leaned against the wall, studied Lenth's face, and thought. "What if it didn't work?" she said. "What if one of them turned out like Six. What if it all ends up like the Citizenry?"

"The *Citizenry* isn't even like the Citizenry. I think good people are getting more control." Lenth went over to the door and opened it. The metal grate of the Unit ceiling stretched out before him. The sounds of the four Sisters working out and chatting reached them through the silence, from the other side of the Unit. "Say something to them," Lenth whispered.

Karen dashed over to the door, shoving Lenth out of the way. She was ready to close the door, but hesitated. She looked out across the Unit and heard them.

She leaned ever so slightly out of the control room.

"Hello." she said affectionately. She quickly closed the door, sealing the control room up.

"Do you think they heard you?" Lenth asked.

Karen was melting against the door. "I love them!" she said weakly. "I love them, I know them so well, and I'm just somet*hing* in a suit. I want them to *know me.*"

Lenth knelt by her, and put his hand on her shoulder. "I think it's more or less the same with my Manager, Fill. I got to speak with him a tiny bit. He didn't know it was me, though." Lenth regretted that part.

"Do you forgive him?" Karen asked, leaning over to look Lenth in the eye.

"Forgive him?" For Slim's death? Did he talk to Karen about that before?

"Shocks. How many times in your life were you shocked? Shocked when words might have been more than enough."

Lenth smiled softly. The shocks he received were always after plenty of warnings, usually in the form of stomps on the grating. Apparently Six's experience with *his* Manager was not nearly the same. "Yeah. I forgive him. He really seems like a kind person."

"Thank you, Lenth." Karen wrapped her arms around Lenth, sobbing. Not knowing what else to do, he held her. He was quite pleased to have been somehow...beneficial? But he was mostly stunned. His pulse was racing, and he dared not move and risk ending the moment. They sat there on the control room floor for a while, just holding each other.

"I'm sorry, Lenth. I'm not generally such a...whatever."

"No. No, don't be sorry. I'm happy to...uh...spend time with such a whatever."

Karen giggled softly, and began to stand. "You're sweet, ya know that?"

"Am I? I thought I was mostly just confused." Lenth got up as well.

"And that's sweet too. You've been exposed to so much new stuff since you came out of your Unit, and you're just...sorting it out. You're doing your best."

Lenth swallowed hard. "I—well, thanks. Thanks for noticing. I don't always know what the best way is."

"I think I trust you to pick the right kinds of ways."

Lenth tapped on the door to the rest of the Unit. "Maybe trust them, too."

"I don't think that's my decision." Karen gave Lenth a soft, slow little kiss on the cheek.

Well. He knew he had something to say about decisions, but the kiss on the cheek pretty much scrambled his brain. He desperately wanted to hold her again, but was terrified that it would be presumptuous. Unwelcome.

"I...I should keep looking for Six."

"Alone? Is Gabe around to help, or..."

"No. I've been doing a lot with Messenger lately, but I don't think Six is likely to attack me."

"Because you're not a Rubberman? That's kind of a big risk, there."

Lenth gave a single little solemn nod. "Yeah. Well, it's complicated."

"Hey, Lenth, did you say Messenger?"

"Yeah. I met him when I went up to Citizenry, and after I left, we've been together a lot. I even found out his name. And his nickname."

"The Messenger... so few get to even see him, and you... wow." Karen nervously laughed a little. "Next you'll be telling me you're having lunch tomorrow with Actual."

Lenth realized she was trying to make a ridiculously unrealistic joke—but it didn't feel all that unrealistic. "I'll tell him that you said hi," Lenth smugly said with a dismissive smile.

"Jerk," Karen said with a laugh. "Just be careful, okay? I mean it. Be careful. And don't wait so long before you visit, okay, big shot Messenger-buddy?"

"I will. I mean, I won't. I mean I want to see you again soon."

"Go, dork. And be careful."

"You said that."

"Right. So you'd better do it."

Wow. He was almost to his old Unit, and his chest still felt...wow. It was difficult to ignore the urge to scramble back to Karen and just...just be there. But no, people's safety was more important right now.

He found the back door to Phil's space. Huh. Lenth didn't have a Rubberman suit or anything. He couldn't wander in without revealing himself. How much was Phil supposed to know? Lenth knew he wasn't the same as Karen, exactly. Karen came from the Providers. Phil was a Subject, once upon a time.

Again, the imposed, idiotic layers of ignorance slapped Lenth in the face. This was stupid. He opened the door, and went in. Almost immediately, Phil came in from the front control room. "Provider, I didn't expect..." Phil stopped cold. "Lenth? Lenth, is that you?"

"Hi, Fill. Yup. I'm checking in to see how you're doing."

"Lenth! You're alive!" Phil hurried over and grabbed Lenth by the shoulders. "And you ... you're okay? The Providers didn't catch you?"

"They did! And we got along! Fill, there's so, so much I'd like to tell you, so much has happened, and I've seen so much. Even things that most Providers don't know exist! There's so much. I wish I had time. There's so much. Oh! How are my Brothers? And the new one? Are things all right? Is Joints all right?"

"Yes! Yes!" Phil was smiling wide, eyes wide with awe. "Yes, Lenth, they miss you, they think you're dead! I figured you were dead, too!"

"Well, that's not right!" Lenth knew he was feeling overconfident. He knew he was about to act rashly, but he felt like pushing his luck. Just a little more. He ran to the door that went to the main Unit, and opened it up. "Brothers! It's me, Lenth! I'm alive, I'm fine, don't worry about me, but I have to go right now! Don't cause Rubberman too much stress, he's actually nice!"

Phil was behind him, trying desperately to hush him without being heard by the Brothers. Lenth closed the door and smiled at Phil.

"It's okay! It is! Really!"

"How is *that* okay?" Phil squealed. "You just...you can't! That just isn't done!"

"Why?" Lenth asked with a huge smile. "Why, why, why?"

"It just isn't done!" Poor Phil was trembling. He went over to get his 'decontamination cloth', since Lenth had leaned out into the Unit, but Lenth turned away Phil's attempts to clean him.

"Fill, while I'm here, I should let you know what's going on. That killer Subject is running around again, so be careful. Mind the door, maybe push your bed against it or something. But be careful."

Phil was bewildered. "Lenth, what have you been doing all this time? You've changed! And..."

"There's so much, Fill. So much. Be safe, right? Be safe, I'm going to keep looking for him. When it's settled, I'll come back and visit, okay? There's so much to tell."

"You're scaring me a little Lenth, I don't know what's going on!"

"And that's awful," Lenth said. "You deserve to know more. Be safe. Oh, and another Rubberman asked me if I forgave you for the shocks. The answer is yes, I know you didn't like to."

"Lenth..."

"I have to go! Be safe, be safe!"

Chapter Twenty-Five

Come Undone

Lenth assumed that places like the clinic and the cafeteria were well enough travelled that they had either been searched, or just too visible of a place for Six to consider hiding in.

And so he tried to think like Six. Finding the cramped little spaces, service access, places hard to find one's way in. Several times, he found himself wishing for just a little light. Was this where Diane was stabbed? No, but it was similar. It was cramped. Lenth kept going. He wondered if Messenger was worried. Sometimes when he found a recognizable place, he'd consider heading towards Contact's office, just to check in.

The crawlspace he eventually found himself in overlooked a large room. He opened a panel, and leaned over it to look around. It was a big drop, so he wasn't about to go down, but he could see a lot from here.

The room was darker than most provider areas, walls of darker metal than even the Units. To make things even less welcoming, the lights were set pretty low.

The vast room was filled with huge vats, with piping and machinery attached to them. Each of the thirty or more vats stood at least twice as tall as a man, and possibly deep into the floor. Each was around ten metres wide, and from here, he could see at least nine of them. He crawled along, peeking down every few ceiling panels, and looked around.

Then he saw Six.

Six was sitting with his back against one of the vats, knees pulled close. "You're not as sneaky as you think you are, Lenth," he called out without looking up.

"What? And how did you know it was me?"

"You're pretty noisy when you crawl, and I figure a Provider would march in through the door. Maybe carrying a ladder to get up there or something."

"I don't think a ladder could get this high," Lenth said.

"Fine. So stay up there. You don't need to come down here to talk."

"Okay. So...what do you want to talk about, Six?"

"Do you know what's in these vats?"

"Water?"

"Nope."

"I don't know, Six, what?"

Six reached out and banged the vat with the base of his fist. "Death!"

"Death?"

"Dead things! Dead people! Leftover food, dirt and crap, and everything awful! This is where we all end up!" Six stood and started yelling at the vat. "*This is where the Providers stuff us when we're done working ourselves to death!*"

Compost. Where fresh dirt was made for the farms. Slim was probably in there somewhere. Somehow being turned into dirt. Lenth didn't really understand decay very well, but he knew enough.

"Providers end up in there too, Six. And Managers, and Citizens."

Six stood, and listlessly paced about, dragging his fingertips along the side of the vat. "Yeah," he said, barely loud enough for Lenth to hear from above. "Yeah, you, me, the Providers, all so...all so, so *equal!* So equal in there. But *before* we die?"

Six looked up at Lenth and pointed at him, then waved his hand around, pointing every random direction. "Out *there*? How equal are we *out there*, huh? Tell me Lenth, how much did *you* know, growing up? Did you know you were going to end up in one of these one day? Did you know there were other people? Did you know they didn't care about you any more than a..." Six took off a shoe and threw it up at Lenth, trying to hit the ceiling near him, but fell short. "They care about us about as much as a *shoe! We're useful!*"

Lenth stared down at Six. Was Six crying? It was hard to tell from this far, and in this lighting. "What now, then, Six?"

Six spread his arms wide. "I don't know! How should I know? Do you expect me to keep running from them? I'm running out of places! I've stopped killing, does it matter?"

"You've stopped killing?"

"I could have killed those Providers down with the nuclear thing area! But does it matter?" He kicked the vat. "They'll end up in a vat anyway! I'm dying right now! I don't know when, but Messenger made it sound like it was soon! If I knew how to open these, I may as well crawl in now!"

Six paced a little more. "Lenth, did you know, growing up, what death was? I sure didn't! When I..." He stood still, shaking his head slowly.

"When what, Six?"

Six leaned back with a deep breath and screamed, "*When I killed my Brother, I didn't know he'd STAY dead!*" He staggered forward, gasping for air, fighting sobs.

Of course. Why would he know that? "His name was Eyes, right? The one I met?" Lenth asked. "And your Rubberman, he—"

"No," Six said sharply, "he can stay dead. I'd kill him again if I could." Six chuckled through his crying. "That would kind of ruin the point though, wouldn't it?"

Lenth remembered about the huge amount of shocks that Six's Manager had used, and the things Messenger implied. "He was really bad, huh?"

Six scoffed. "He's being useful *now*," he said, tapping the vat with his foot.

"You know, most Managers aren't like that," Lenth said, "not nearly that bad. For that matter, did you know what some of them used to be Subjects?"

Six gave one breathy laugh. "What? Why would they? How can...would you be able to be a Manager, Lenth? Could you *stand* it?"

Lenth shook his head. "I don't think I could. My Manager was a Subject once. I don't think the Providers tell him everything. He's pretty scared of Providers, but I've met other Managers who used to be Providers. I don't know how they pick who they do...maybe it's up to Contact. Or Actual."

"Actual." Six resumed pacing. "I...I've heard that word before."

"He tells Messenger what to do," Lenth said.

"And Messenger tells Contact, Contact tells the Providers, the Providers tell the Managers, and the Managers tell us lowly useful people when to eat, work, sleep, die,"

"They don't tell us when to die!" Lenth hollered down.

"You're right..." Six continued pacing for a bit, then put both his hands on the vat, and spread his feet apart. "They tell us to do other things!"

Lenth didn't understand, but he understood how Six felt about it. "They're not all like that."

Six started pacing again, flailing his arms in the air. "Lucky Lenth! Lucky, Lucky Lenth! I guess that makes it all okay then!"

Lenth watched in silence, and Six eventually settled down, sitting against the vat, just as Lenth had found him. "Think there's anyone we know in this one?" Six said quietly as he patted the vat. "Your Brother, my Brothers? My Manager?"

"How about the other Managers you've killed?" Lenth asked, without spite in his voice, "or how about those Citizens? Did you understand about death when you killed *them?*"

Six looked up at Lenth with weariness showing in his eyes. "They... they were just in the way."

"*And does that make it all okay?*" Lenth yelled, echoing Six.

"I was bad. Managers and their kind are bad, okay; we're all bad, bad bad. So what now, huh? What are the Providers going to do with me when they get me? Kill me outright? Toss me into the Citizenry? That's what it's for, right? People they don't want get tossed in there and... and whatever."

Lenth felt it was likely. Contact had planned to throw *him* out just for escaping his Unit. "How do you feel, Six?"

"*Oh right! How could I forget! I'm dying!* No, I don't feel sick yet, thanks for asking!"

Lenth sighed. "Yeah, I still feel okay too."

"Right." Six turned his head. "Right, I forgot. How long does Messenger think *you* have?"

"He says because I didn't get as much radiation as you that I might be safe. I think he was lying to be nice. It was my head, y'know?"

Six grunted, and they sat in silence for a while; Six below by his vat, Lenth above in the ceiling. "If I fell asleep, do you think they'd find me here? Or would you just turn me in?"

"I probably should have turned you in as soon as I saw you."

Six grunted again. "So why didn't you?"

"I don't know. It's been a rough day. Don't we both need a break?"

Six laughed. "Some nice quiet time before dying! Super!" Six laughed some more, and louder, but the laughter was riddled with sobbing, and shards of screams. "*I've seen and caused enough death to know I don't want it!* I know it's coming, and I can't do *anything* about it! Is it going to hurt, Lenth? *How much is it going to hurt, Lenth?*" Six curled up into a ball, sobbing and ranting to himself, once or twice reaching out to strike the nearby vat.

Sooner or later, Lenth would have to find a safe way down to Six, and then...then what, hope he'll come along to Contact's office? First thing's first. Getting down. For that matter, would Six just run off as soon as he heard Lenth crawling away? He looked around below for hints of a nearby elevator, or even something to climb down on. Nothing was immediately apparent. Looking around himself in the ceiling was even less fruitful, as it was fairly dark, and littered with structural obstructions.

Lenth's thinking was disturbed when he heard Six get to his feet in a hurry. Six was looking off to his right, and his stance suggested that he was ready to run.

"They're here, Lenth." The lights flickered to a regular level of illumination, showing the aged streaks in the dark metal dominating the room.

"Please don't start a fight, Six."

"Nope!" Six said loudly enough that the gradually approaching Providers could hear him, "I'm not gonna fight. Even ignoring that they probably have big sticks and I have nothing but fists."

Lenth could now see the Providers. Four of them surrounded Six, and yes, they had sticks. About the size of the spear that Lenth had been carrying before.

Six was holding up his hands. "No knives, no nothing. It's okay. I'm...I'm going to behave."

One of the Providers struck Six with his stick. Not with a lot of force, but Six screamed anyway, falling to his knees.

"Shocks?" Six gasped as he tried to stand. "Really? You don't have to use those, I'm giving up, let's just—"

Two other Providers touched Six with their sticks. He shrieked and collapsed, gasping and whimpering. Lenth could now see some kind of box attached to the sticks, and a bit of small machinery attached to those. These were the 'fancy' sticks Gabe had mentioned needing repairs. They were rather operational now.

"*He was giving up!*" Lenth yelled down. "*You didn't need to do that!*"

The Providers looked up, finally noticing Lenth.

"I'm not taking that risk. Who are you?" one of the Providers asked.

"He's the other escapey-guy. The one that's been hanging out with the Messenger."

"Lenth! My name is Lenth! You don't need to hurt Six, he—"

"He's a killer!" One of the Providers said, giving Six another shock. Six was moving, but not a lot, spread out and defeated. A Provider walked up with some kind of strap and bound Six's wrists behind his back.

"Let's get him out of here. Lenth, people are probably waiting for you in Contact's office." They dragged Six to his feet, staggering, and started guiding him away.

"Yeah..," Lenth said, "yeah, I'll find my way there."

In the ensuring silence, Lenth was left looking down at the compost facility.

Was Slim in there somewhere? He stared at the tanks. As disgusting as the reality might be, Lenth knew the facts of it all. It was...natural. In was his final role in life. Complete. Not glamourous. Just complete.

"Slim," Lenth called out quietly to the vats, knowing the foolishness of it. "I miss you, Slim." He tried to comfort himself with the idea that Slim wasn't able to suffer any more. He'd never be shocked again, never lie awake with a pulled muscle from work, never get jabbed by the cuff again.

He'd never have to do a lot of things. But it felt hollow.

He'd never taste a papaya. He'd never meet Fill, or Gabe, or Messenger, or know what a woman was.

He'd never do a lot of things.

It had taken Lenth quite a while to find his way back, although not nearly as much time to randomly stumble across the compost facility in the first place. It had been just a matter of getting to a normal hallway and asking for directions from the first Provider he saw.

Contact's office had a few Providers milling about, looking moderately busy, and Contact was behind his desk. He perked up a little when he saw Lenth come through the doorway.

"Lenth! Do you have news from Messenger?"

"No. I just got back from the compost, where I saw Six get caught."

Contact nodded in a knowing fashion. It was a nod that reminded Lenth a little of how Contact bowed to Messenger. "I understand what you did," Contact said.

"Oh yeah?"

"Of course. And so wise. It was not Messenger's job to catch Six, and it was not yours, but you provided a distraction so that Providers could catch up to him! With gentle assistance, you helped us do what should fall to us; minding the Subjects."

Well. It was daunting how Contact spoke to him now. As if he were as revered as the great and enigmatic Messenger. Greatness by association? And was that really how Contact saw the situation? A representative of Messenger, slowing down the most hated Subject so that he could be caught?

"So where's Six now?" Lenth asked.

"We hold him for you and Messenger, he is secure. I put Gabe in charge of it; I hope this is satisfactory. As for what's next—that's what I was hoping you might know."

Lenth lowered his head in thought and could feel Contact staring at him expectantly. He had to say something. Something that reflected the wisdom that Contact now assumed from him.

"Keep holding Six secure until you hear from Messenger or me."

"Of course, Lenth."

"And don't treat him too rough."

Contact cocked his head in surprise. "W...why?"

"His Manager was already rough enough on him. It seems to have a lot to do with why he killed him, and why he came out angry."

"Are you blaming—?"

"No," Lenth said, "not totally, but it's not as simple as some Subject just feeling like killing people."

Contact strained to understand, but merely gave a nod. "If you say so, Lenth."

Lenth gave Contact a nod in return, and left. He should have asked where Messenger was, even got Contact to call him in the central elevator or something, but he needed to get away from Contact. It was unsettling to be spoken to as some sort of superior. He headed to the central elevator, and lucked out. The elevator was still on the Provider level. The door was closed, so he knocked on it. "Messenger! Are you in there?"

The little peeking-hatch opened, and Messenger looked out. "Hang on, Lenth." A few clanks of metal later, Messenger was sliding the door open. "I heard you led the Providers in capturing Six."

Lenth laughed. "Is that what Contact told you?"

Messenger chuckled. "Well, he made you sound wise, and..."

"Yeah, yeah, that's me; wise, wise me."

"Step into my office, Lenth."

Lenth got aboard the elevator, then helped Messenger close the door. He went to the control panel, and sent the elevator up a few dozen metres. "Just so Providers don't listen in. Not that I expect them to, but still."

"Top secret Messenger time?"

Messenger smirked. "I guess so."

"So...what were you thinking should be done with Six?"

Messenger gave a calm smile. "Maybe we need to talk to someone about this."

Lenth didn't dare speak his guess, but he couldn't think of anyone other than Actual that Messenger would consult with. Lenth just glanced upwards.

"Do you want to go?" Messenger asked quietly.

"To go talk about Six?"

Messenger just nodded.

Lenth swallowed hard. "I don't know if I'm ready. There's so much I want to do. Some I can't, some I can. I want to talk with my Brothers, I want to spend time with Carin', I want to see—"

"Lenth! I didn't ask you if you wanted to *die*."

Lenth took a deep breath and exhaled. "All right. Okay. I'm ready. To see him. Not die." Lenth remembered the threat of his radiation positioning, and Six's terrified rant was still fresh in Lenth's mind.

"Good. We have a stop to make first."

The elevator stopped at the Citizenry. Messenger looked out the peeking-hatch. "Citizen," he called out.

"M—Messenger!" came a voice from the other side, "What...what do you want? Wish? Uh...how can I do for you?"

Lenth snickered, and whispered, "He's going to hurt himself if he keeps that up."

Messenger smirked, and put a finger to his lips, then turned back to the Citizen. "I require the broken communication device, so I may take it to be repaired."

"Okay! I'll hurry!" the Citizen said before running off.

"I was talking to Actual earlier," Messenger said to Lenth, "he has the replacement already, but he wants the parts of the old one."

Lenth leaned against the wall while they waited, and glanced up. "So...who gets to go see him, usually?"

Messenger blushed a little. "Ehh, one kind of person. People like me."

"You...what are you saying?"

"I'm not saying now, I'm not saying soon, but eventually time forces change. When Actual is done, I'll be Actual; then who's Messenger?"

"I...I'm not ready for that!"

"No, you're not. You might never be, but you can learn."

"What happened to a Messenger being taken from the Providers, or the Engineers, or whatever?"

Messenger shrugged. "I could see you in the Engineer crew. For now, live down there, learning about it, and maybe eventually spending some time up top learning about my job. For that matter, you might find reasons to stay on with the Engineers or something."

Lenth gave a nervous little smile. "So, you're serious about thinking that I'm not dying."

"I'm almost positive. I'm Messenger, after all! Hasn't Contact told you? I know almost everything!"

"Ha. Then I'd have a lot to learn, then."

"Yup."

A voice came from outside.

"I knew it. You're here, you're back, aren't you?" It was Leena. "Lenth? You *are* in there, aren't you? It sounded like your voice!"

"Leena!" Lenth called back.

"Lenth, I brought the communication thing. I...I cleaned it. You remember how it was. A couple of the tinier bits might be missing. Can you come out? I locked the other door. Messenger? I'm not armed or anything, I won't try to get on the elevator, just let me see Lenth, please?"

Messenger looked to Lenth, and thought about it for a bit before calling out to Leena. "Go stand on the other end of the hall."

She obeyed, dashing over and then standing at attention. Messenger unlocked the elevator door. He opened it wide enough for Lenth to get out. "Stay on that end, Citizen. Lenth, proceed as you wish."

Lenth smiled a bit and jogged out towards Leena. He heard Messenger collect the communicator behind him, fumbling with a few of the loose pieces.

"You've been okay?" Lenth asked as he neared Leena, "With Edgar, and everything? I mean...there's peace at least?"

Leena nodded. "Yeah, yeah. He thinks he's the greatest and whatever, but I think I can keep him in check at least. And you? And Six?"

"Six is caught. Haven't decided what to do with him yet."

Leena flushed crimson. "Bring him here and let me mash his head in!"

Lenth smiled and held her. "Oh, it's messy complicated. And he's dying anyway, if that makes you feel better."

She backed away, less angry, but still tense. "Not a lot better. What's killing him? Some kind of giant metre-long spike being slowly driven into his face?"

"Leena!" Lenth held back a laugh, but not his smile.

"I'm not kidding! Much. What is it then?"

"To keep it simple, he's poisoned. The kind of thing they can't fix."

"Well, good," she said, "will he suffer?"

"Actually, yeah, it sounds like it, quite a bit. I'm not sure what it'll end up like, but it could easily take weeks."

"Well, good. He deserves it."

Lenth's first reaction was to criticize her nasty attitude to Six suffering, but she had good enough reasons. "Overall...how are you doing?"

"It's...it's all right. Lots of people are happy enough to be all right at this time, y'know? He did a lot of damage."

Lenth held her again, and this time, she held him back.

"I have a stupid question, Leena. If you could change something about what Citizenry is like...well, what would you change?"

Leena looked over Lenth's shoulder to the open gap in the elevator door. "A lot, I guess. Nothing I can wrap up in a little package. I don't know. It just feels like things are wrong. Like they've always been wrong."

Lenth let go and gently backed away. "They are, and they have been, and not just in Citizenry."

"You're going?"

Lenth nodded. "I have a pile of junk to deliver, I guess."

Leena's face melted to a hollow stunned look. "Deliver? You..."

Lenth glanced up.

"What are you now?" she asked in nearly a whisper, "Are you a..."

"No. I'm not sure what I am right now, or what I'll become."

Lenth could see her attitude change. Fear? No...Reverence? Maybe a little. "Don't look at me like that."

Leena pointed a finger towards the elevator. "If you're going to be a...then one day you'll be..." Her now-timid finger pointed up.

It hit him now. Actual. He could end up on the path to being Actual. The unseen revered source of the things that no one can grow, or make, or fix.

The vital thing which he grew up ignorant of, and could have died having no idea it even existed. From knowing nothing, to knowing everything.

He put his hands on Leena's shoulders. "When you put it like that…it's a little scary." He looked into her eyes. They were wide and ready to overflow.

"Don't forget all of us down here, okay? When you're everything."

"It's not going to happen for a long time. If it even ever does."

"Don't forget."

"Never."

Chapter Twenty-Six

The Big Room of the Enemy

"Girlfriend?" Messenger asked after the elevator got underway.

"Huh?"

"Girlfriend. Female you have a romantic relationship with. Generally exclusively."

"Leena?"

"If that was Leena, sure, yes, Leena."

"No, I...she's very nice."

"You're new at this females thing, I forgot."

Lenth just stood and thought about it for a bit. Yes, Leena was very nice. "I think I have a different favourite."

Messenger laughed. "Oh! Then I got the wrong idea! You're a real ladies' man!"

"You confuse me sometimes."

The elevator finally came to rest at the top. The peak of everything. Messenger got on the elevator's communication device. "We're here. Yeah. Oh, good idea. Hang on." he hung up and put the device away.

"What's wrong?"

"Actual wants us to check out the exterior of the elevator and make sure Six didn't somehow hitch a ride before he unlocks the door."

"It that really—"

"Six did practically the same thing to get to the reactor level. Yes, he's locked up. As far as we know, but…"

"All right. Better safe than sorry."

Messenger headed up the ladder, followed by Lenth. They walked around the top of the elevator, peeking over the edge, finding nothing unexpected.

"Stay up here, Lenth, I'm going to look underneath." Messenger went down the shaft's ladder and was back in a few moments. "Okay we're clear." They went back into the elevator, where Messenger called Actual again and repeated himself. "We're all clear. Yeah."

Some metal clunked around on the other side of the door; then Messenger started pulling it open. Lenth was surprised that the little hall looked much like the ones that attached to the Citizenry, Providers, and the Reactor level.

Messenger picked up the remains of the Citizenry's communication device and led Lenth off of the elevator. "Welcome," he said as he closed and locked the door behind them.

"Thanks." Was it just in Lenth's head, or was this hall quieter than the others? Not that he could think of any particular sounds in the other ones. The silence here was its own entity, a thing unto its own, surrounding everything, and Lenth felt like a tolerated guest of it.

The door on the other side was closed, but Messenger was able to open it easily enough.

It opened up into a wide space which looked…it looked a lot like a much smaller version of the huge commons area of Citizenry, except tidy and clean. No, more than that. Phil's Unit was tidy and clean, even if a little rough. The Provider's area and the reactor areas were tidy and clean.

This was smooth. It was soothing to behold. The white walls weren't flat utilitarian panels; they were smooth and curved slightly. A blue, almost fluid-looking rim about two fingers thick ran along the upper edge of the walls, which were twice as tall as the typical Provider room. The floor was shinier, and tiny flecks of metal under the smooth surface reflected light in ways that changed as the viewer moved. The ceiling was smooth, and abstract shapes built into it seemed to embrace the wide, diffused light fixtures.

Did the Citizenry used to be like this? Was it this overwhelming before the Citizens wrecked it? It must have been incredible.

Messenger put the wreckage of the communication device by a seven metre wide closed door to the left. They walked by the middle passage, which led to another large area. "This way," Messenger said, leading them to a third passage to the right. Voices and footsteps echoed very slightly, but the silence was quick to swallow the echoes.

The right passage continued the clean beauty, if in a slightly more restrictive size. The passage was 'only' four or so metres across. Doors with little words on them were on either side. The first two they passed had pictures above them also. One was of a simply portrayed outline of a person standing. It reminded Lenth of the figures he'd seen during exercise times back in the Unit. Next to that was a person sitting on a half circle that curved from the back of his knees, around to the lower back. The other sign was similar, except that the person standing had a triangle shape for legs.

They passed another that had a picture of some kind of container with a couple of sticks poking up from it. Half a dozen doors after that just had words, or a blank spot, where it looks like words should be put.

They came to a stop in front of the last one. Lenth tried to quickly read the word...*A...d...m...i...*and then Messenger opened the door.

"Actual?" he called out.

The room was about the size of Contact's office. While it wasn't as smooth looking as the last rooms, it was still smoother than any other room he'd seen before today.

On one side sat three white desks with four computers sitting on them. On the right side of the room sat a bed, that had...no...this big thing wasn't a bed. It was for sitting on. It was wide enough that half a dozen people could easily be accommodated. Like an extremely wide, slightly lower chair. Mike had a smaller one of these. Leena had called that a sofa, so maybe this was a sofa, too. This one was in far better condition.

In the middle of it sat Actual.

Just a man.

Lenth was surprised by this, but didn't know what he was expecting. He knew it was just a person, once a Messenger, once probably a Provider, but the corners of Lenth's imagination had mused that he would be far more grandiose, perhaps floating on the ceiling, or wearing some exaggerated Rubberman suit, with pipes and hoses going in every direction...

But, no. It was just a man. Predictably, a fairly old man. He was even wearing the same thing Lenth was wearing, a standard set of Provider clothing.

"You're Lenth!" Actual said. His voice reminded Lenth so much of Joints, it almost hurt. He was so familiar, so normal. This being that lived above everyone, and supplied so much, was normal. Welcoming, even.

"Y...yes, I'm Lenth. It's...nice to meet you!" *What else does one say?*

"What do you think of things outside of your Unit, Lenth?"

Lenth looked at his hands and shook his head slowly. "There's so much. So much, and it's all so confusing."

Actual nodded. "That's understandable. This place *is* so much, and also so much that it almost was. There's pieces of many things, half of which are doing their jobs. And you know what?"

Lenth shrugged.

"Most Providers don't notice that it doesn't make sense. They grew up with it."

Lenth nodded. "Uh...that makes sense, I guess. I used to think that my Unit was normal."

Actual stood up, a feat which looked to be a little difficult. He pointed at Lenth, smiling. "Ah, you get it! Normal is...normal is entirely dependent on where you've been. What do you think of your Unit now?"

"My Brothers are there, but we don't get to know things." Lenth looked at Actual who looked ready to speak, but Lenth spoke first. "What is normal for you, Actual? From here, and everywhere you've been, what is normal?"

"You've seen most of the Provider's home? And Citizens?" Actual asked.

Lenth nodded.

"And the reactor, I know you've been around the nuclear reactor."

Lenth nodded again.

"Well, I think you have a pretty good idea of what my normal is, then. They all get along, and when they need something, they ask Messenger, and I get what's needed for him from Division."

"You do a bit more than *that*," Messenger said.

Actual shrugged. "Ah, not really. Not much. I'm what happens when a Messenger gets too old to crawl around and fix things."

"Excuse me," Lenth said, "I think you mentioned something important there...you get stuff from Division? Who...who is that?"

Actual smirked and looked to Messenger. "He's going to need the whole tour, isn't he?"

Messenger shrugged with a smile. "May as well!"

Actual went over to one of the desks, got seated in the one of the chairs there, and tapped at a computer a few times. "Well...it's nearly an ideal time for it; the Enemy should be retreating. We can wait a little bit longer."

"Enemy?"

Actual made himself comfortable and smiled. "Have you heard the story about how there was a war?"

"Gabe told me a bit. He didn't have all the details, and he figured it was a story. Something about lots and lots of people burning."

Actual turned to Messenger with a quizzical look.

"Gabe," Messenger explained. "He's a Provider. Taught Lenth a lot of basics after he got out of his Unit. Got him started with reading, for one thing."

Actual nodded and turned back to Lenth. "Well, the old ones all saw it coming, but they couldn't prevent it. That nuclear reactor we have? They used to be able to *throw* those at groups of people, far, far away. It would grow into a ball of fire and force that would turn millions of people and things to ash, and those further away would get sick and die anyway, depending on how close they were."

Lenth laughed nervously. "What? Why would people use those?"

"Because they were afraid of the other guys throwing one at them first."

"That's insane!"

"Indeed!" Actual laughed. "And they made themselves ready for it, even knowing it was insane, because they were all worried that everyone else was *more* insane."

"How do you get ready for having someone throw something like that at you?"

Actual spread his arms and looked around. "You hide. You hide where the fire can't reach. They first built this place to hide. The fear faded with time, and before the threat came back, they wanted to use this space for other things. Citizenry? It was once was a place where a kind of people called 'tourists' could stay and visit. They'd come right through my level, from outside, like it was nothing. This place has been given many tasks, most of which have been ended and forgotten. At some point, the Units were a place for bad people, and then a big person called Farm...big Farm...wanted to test medicines on the bad people, and—"

"The medicines!" Lenth burst out. "The medicine is pointless! Subjects are forced to take not-medicine! For what? To keep us soft? It killed my Brother, Slim!"

Actual's face grew morose. "I'm so sorry, Lenth."

"*Why?* Why do the not-medicines at all?"

"Farm may need us, if anything of him survived the war. The system has worked for a long time. Deaths like your Brother's are almost non-existent."

"It's stupid!"

"We can't just change the way things work without knowing how it would affect everything else, Lenth. You know the Rubberman suits that the Managers wear? They were originally worn because Subjects were going to get experimented on with dangerous stuff. Most of those experiments never happened, certainly not the hazardous ones, but we kept the suits to help maintain a healthy, professional distance between Managers and Subjects."

"Healthy..." Lenth whispered in disbelief. Lenth paced about slowly, wanting to understand. There were so many questions. "There's a lot of things I think would change."

"Well, as you learn, you might gain some perspective on things."

Fine. A worry that could wait for now. "You were saying about the war's nuclear things, and the sickness...that's radiation sickness that you're talking about, isn't it?"

Messenger stepped in. "Actual, Lenth had his mask off by the coolant pool for a while, and Six was in the pool without a suit for several minutes."

Actual nodded with a concerned look. "You didn't mention this before. How deep did he go?"

"A couple of metres. He had to have air, of course."

Actual chuckled. "A couple of metres? He wasn't anywhere near the spent fuel?"

"No..."

"Well then they're both fine!" Actual yelped. "Didn't a Geiger counter tell you that much?"

"Aside from the ones that are part of the reactor, there hasn't been an operational Geiger counter for some time."

"What?" Actual stood up, shaking his hand in disbelief. "We have a *nuclear reactor* without any Geiger counters?"

"It hasn't seemed important in the past," Messenger said in an apologetic tone.

"No Geiger counters!" Actual said to Lenth. "In the nuclear facility! No Geiger counters!"

"Did...did you lose count of your...Geigers?" Lenth asked.

Actual smiled at Lenth. "It...I don't know why it's called that. It measures radiation. And I guess I have to ask Division for a couple of those, too."

"So...I'm not going to get sick?" Lenth asked.

"No, no, and that other fella's going to be fine, too. Until you get a lot closer to the bottom of the pool, you're as safe as you are in this room. Well, other than drowning, Actual chuckled.

"What?" Messenger said quietly, "Then...then why the radiation-proof suits?"

"Around the pool? Usually not needed at all! They're very important for other things down there though, and until we get some counters down there, you may as well keep wearing them anywhere you think it might be a problem. I'll dig you out some procedural manuals later. Better paranoid than dead."

"Well. Six will be glad to hear that," Lenth said, almost to himself. "Which complicates things."

"Ah," Actual roamed over to the computer desks. "You both thought he was going to die all on his own, and you wouldn't have to figure out what to do with the murderer. Yup, that would have been handy."

"So what now?" Messenger asked. "Put him alone in a Unit? Kill him?"

"I wouldn't be first in line to do the killing," Actual said grimly.

"I sure know someone who would," Lenth said, thinking of Leena.

Actual grimaced. "I suppose there's a handful of people who'd like to, hm?" He poked at the computer again. "Good time for a walk. We can safely see the Enemy, if we suit up."

Lenth's eyes widened, and he glanced up. Perhaps more like gawked, because Messenger noticed.

"Wrong way," Messenger said, pointing out the door.

"Hang on. I may as well call Division before I forget," Actual said. He went over to the computer on the end and tapped a pile of keys, read the screen for a bit, nodded, tapped, and read. This went on for a couple of minutes before he reached to a box beside the computer, and pulled out a headset just like the one Messenger had on the elevator. He put it on and fiddled with the controls.

"Division? Come in, Division. This is station four Actual. Come in, Division." Actual covered up the microphone and looked at Lenth. "He's not actually going to come in, it's just something I have to say. I don't understand the way he uses half these words, so get ready to be confused." He perked up and then replied to the voice on the other end.

"Yes, Division, I'm requisitioning a few items to be transferred to station four?" He peered at the computer screen, reading off the letters and numbers and...things. "An RH stroke 5-7-3-0 bee. Oh? Well what is...RH stroke 5-7-3-0 see. Ah. It functions the same? Fine, then. And we also need three...no, make it *four* GRM stroke 300s. Yes. No, that's all for now. Thank you, Division. Roger. Over and out." And with that, Actual put away the headset, and closed the box.

"Who's—"

"There is no 'Roger'. As I said...just something I have to say. I don't understand why; it's been passed down from one Actual to the next."

"...Oh."

The three of them headed back to the first large, smooth room. Actual went over to the wide closed door, taking a moment to kneel down and poke at the wrecked communication device. "Yeah. I have a spare you can take down. I just ordered a new spare. He said he doesn't have this kind any more, and he's sending a new type that works the same. Seems like a waste of effort on his part. Whatever. Anyway, It's not like Division is always super fast, and you never know. Always good to have spares."

Actual led them back out, down the hall, to the large round room. He went over to the seven-metre wide door Lenth had seen on his way in.

Actual grabbed a handle on the door, and Messenger grabbed another. They both pushed up, and the door rolled into the ceiling with a startling rumble. Actual grimaced, and rubbed his shoulder. Another thing that reminded Lenth of Joints.

Inside the door was a huge, boxy room, quite unlike the smooth, attractive rooms behind them. This was utilitarian. Boxes and boxes of things laid about, as well as one of the 'shelves with wheels and a motor' like Lenth had seen in the "picker garage".

Several large, heavy pieces of wall stood lined up in one corner. A few dozen metal gratings, like the kind he grew up under. Several computer things, beds, a pile of neatly stacked cups: beyond counting. The longer Lenth looked, the more it looked like his life had been neatly taken apart and stacked up.

"Division brought all this?" Lenth asked.

"That's right. And he takes away the broken stuff that we can't fix. Like that." Actual used his foot to shove the broken communication device through the doorway. "I may as well fish out the spare while we're here." He hummed and clicked his tongue while walking along several piles. "Aha!" He pulled out a fresh one, and handed it to Messenger, who put it out into the central room for the time being.

Actual was opening another huge door on the other end. Since Messenger was still on the other end, Lenth stepped up to help with the other handle.

The room was comparatively empty and about half the length. Two Rubberman suits sat slumped in the corner.

"Messenger!" Actual yelled over, "We need a third suit! You know where the—"

"Yeah, got it."

With all three of them in the new room, Messenger and Actual closed the door behind them.

"Okay, Lenth, like at the reactor, okay?"

All three put on radiation-proof Rubberman suits. Messenger checked a few details in how Lenth put his on, and gave him the thumbs up.

"You're going to want to be looking at the floor at first," Actual said, going over to a panel much like the one on the big elevator. Lenth took the suggestion and kept his head down as the door was pulled up by a motor.

He saw bright amber light reaching in from under the door. As the door raised, he watched the light creep onto his feet, up his legs, over his hips. He held his hand out to catch it as it rose, almost expecting to be able to grab it. He knew it was going to reach his head soon and could not resist looking. He lifted his head and saw it. A light unlike any he'd ever seen, so distant, across a room he could never have imagined.

The floor ahead of him was very light brown and cracked apart into pieces not much bigger than a spread hand, as far as the eye could see. Walls? There was some kind of skimpy metal grating, a couple of metres high, many metres away, but a wall?

There was none. And no ceiling. None he could see. This wasn't like the giant commons room in Citizenry. In Citizenry, you could see the ceiling, it was just ridiculously high.

This was... this was different...and the light. The light was master of it all. Coming from an incredibly bright spot, the light seemed to be spread wherever it pleased, weakening directly overhead into a slight darkness.

The light, especially its middle, was terrifying but beautiful. His eyes began to hurt from looking at it, and he had to look away.

"The Enemy," Actual said in a sombre tone. "I don't know what it looked like up here before the war, but you can see what's left now."

Lenth pointed to the lack of walls and ceiling. "It...it's all gone? The Enemy destroyed it all?"

"And it comes back, every day. I can only assume that it means we...or the people before, anyway, lost. And now we live where we do. It's difficult to mourn something we didn't know we had, but when I see the Enemy...well, it's never easy."

"Are we being hit by radiation right now?"

Actual nodded. "Funny thing is, it's a different kind. A Geiger counter doesn't detect it, but I've felt it. I've taken my mask off in this before. Stupid, I know. I could feel the heat from it almost immediately. Low levels of radiation don't feel warm, but...well, it was scary."

Lenth gasped. "Did you get sick?"

"No. It was only a second or so. I'm just fortunate that the Enemy wasn't closer. It flies along its patrol route, very slowly, every day. In the middle of the day, it's so bright. At night, it's somewhere else, maybe keeping other people in hiding, like it does to us."

"Like this Division guy? Where does he come from? Does he come while the Enemy isn't looking?"

"No. Somehow he comes when the Enemy is close. I don't know how he survives."

"Have you asked him?"

Actual laughed. "I don't go anywhere near him! I'm safely inside when he brings things to the front room. I bring it further in later, after the Enemy has left."

"How does he survive?" Lenth asked, agape.

"For as long as he must be out here? I'm not sure, but look at the ground."

Streaks of the floor were smeared out across in curves and lines. Always at least two streaks about fifteen centimetres wide, and two or so metres apart. "Tracks from some kind of picker? Bigger, though. I can only assume he has something like our suits. See, there's footprints, too. Maybe it's something better. But no, I only talk to him through the communication devices. Even with our suits, I don't want to press my luck when the Enemy is close."

"Well, have you asked Division about these kinds of things over the communication device?" Lenth asked.

"I tried a few times. It didn't go well. He only wants to hear specific things, like things we want him to bring. Outside of that, it's like he gets confused. One time I made him angry, I think. The last thing any of us need is for Division to be angry."

"He might stop bringing things?"

"Exactly. I may have come very close that time, too...just imagine. No new light bulbs. No new parts of any kind, no new supplies for the clinic. I can't believe how I endangered us all. It would have been a gruellingly slow end to us. Never again."

"Change is dangerous," Lenth murmured in a tone on the edge of patronizing Actual. When Lenth came up from his Unit, Phil was frightened by change. Did Contact want to get rid of Lenth in Citizenry because he represented change? Messenger wasn't afraid of whatever change that Lenth might represent. Neither was Gabe, Karen, or Leena. Actual? Maybe a little.

"Can we get inside now?" Messenger asked. "It's creepy as heck out here."

The blistered, raw skin of a place ravaged by war. There wasn't even any signs of wreckage. For that matter, even the blackness of burning had faded away. How long had it been? In any event, Lenth agreed with Messenger.

No walls? Creepy.

Chapter Twenty-Seven

Necessary

The delivery to Citizenry was uneventful, and Leena wasn't there, so they continued down to see Contact.

"We're ready to remove Six," Messenger said.

Contact nodded solemnly. "Come with me."

After a small walk and a single floors' trip on one of the smaller elevators, they came to a door with two Providers guarding it. They each held one of those shock-sticks. They saw Contact and Messenger coming, and stiffened their stance to make a good impression.

"Messenger is here for him," Contact grunted.

"Go ahead, Sirs," one of the Providers said.

Contact reached forward and opened the door.

"*Just like that?*" Lenth blurted. "It wasn't even locked? Not very sec—"

"I'm here, I'm here, relax," Six said as he came to the doorway. His hands were still bound behind his back. "I only went out to go to the bathroom, and the zap boys escorted me all the way."

Messenger raised his eyebrows, looking at Six but speaking to Contact. "Remind me at some point to discuss ideas about security. Not that I expect the need to come again anytime soon, but an unlocked door is less than comforting."

"It was comforting enough to me!" Six smiled. "So! What now? You stuff me face first into the bottom of a compost vat? Or will you just cut me up and eat me directly?" His smile was wide, but his eyes spoke of panic, darting about as if he was expecting to fend off an attack.

"I had another idea, Six. I think you might actually like it," Lenth said.

Six gave Lenth a sideways look, glanced at Messenger, then shrugged a tiny bit. With a few gestures from Contact, the two Providers with the shock-sticks took position to follow behind Lenth, who was behind Six, which was behind Messenger and Contact.

When they made their way to the central elevator. Messenger opened it up, while Contact moved back to stand with his two subordinates. "I can go no further."

"Of course," Messenger said, finally taking the ladder out and handing it to Contact. Messenger called out, "Six? Lenth?" Six looked back, checking with Lenth. Lenth nodded, and they filed in, followed by Messenger.

"What will you do with him?" Contact asked, having heard about his apparent radiation poisoning. "How long do you think he has?"

Messenger paused halfway through dragging the door shut. "Honestly, I don't know." He closed the door the rest of the way and started towards the control panel. He pointed at the wall farthest from the door. "Six, stand over there for the duration, if you please? Lenth, keep an eye on him."

Six looked around and finally started to go where he was supposed to. "I'm surprised you guys didn't bring the zappy sticks along."

"There's two of us," Lenth said plainly as the elevator bumped and groaned to life, "and with your hands like that..."

"I can still kick!" Six said. "I could even lie on my back and kick all over the place! Or I could just come at you face-first and bite! Oh, how I could bite." He spat on the floor. "Oh! Or that! I could moisten you both, and you'd be *helpless* to stop me!"

With a wretched twist of his expression and an inward collapse of his poise, his protective jovial membrane broke. He leaned face first against the wall. "*Why don't you just kill me already? Where are we going? Are you going to let the radiation get me? Is that it? Are you taking me somewhere to watch it do...whatever it's going to do to me? Is that my punishment? I get it! I get it already!*"

"Hey, Six," Lenth called out loud enough to break Six's rant, "how are you feeling right now?"

Six turned and gave Lenth a dark, spiteful look, but didn't speak.

Lenth stared back. "You're not dying."

Six continued glowering, but his expression softened. A little. "What, you're taking me to get cured? What for, to throw me into Citizenry and get killed?"

"The pool wasn't a risk, we found out," Messenger said. "Actual set us straight. Much the suit usage in that area, it turns out, is a little on the paranoid side."

"Same with the Manager suits," Lenth mumbled, "there was going to be some dangerous experiments once, and they kept the suits out of...all paranoia."

"*What?*" Six yelled, "*Those freaky rubber suits are for nothing?*"

"No, no," Messenger said, "In some parts of the reactor, and for some jobs, they're entirely vital."

Six, with his hand still bound, could only kick the air to vent his frustration, then started walking around. He caught a warning-glace from Messenger and skipped back from some imaginary line, continuing his pacing closer to the far wall. "So! It's all about experiments that never happened?"

"It was, at some point," Messenger said. "But before that, it was about hiding from war, from a killing of impossible scale. Between the time it was first built and the war itself, there was a peace, where people tried to make other uses for this place. Then the war came. Now it's about plain living. We live here. Some of us make food, some of us work on filters to help keep the air and water clean, some of us keep things organized, some of us fix things…"

Six burst out laughing. "*Well! That's just super!* And why are you telling me all this?"

"If everyone knew, it would be chaos. The Enemy is still out there, and it doesn't drop off food and water; it drops off buckets of radiation."

"Then I ask again! Why tell me?"

Messenger was silent for a moment, and Six clued in. "You're putting me out there, aren't you? Out with this Enemy who doesn't drop food or water. Wha…from the sounds of it, I'd be better off in Citizenry!"

"The Citizens wouldn't feel that way," Lenth said.

"We're not just tossing you out," Messenger explained, "and you'll be prepared, and we'll send you when the Enemy isn't looking. It just left a while ago."

"Lucky me." Six stared into nothingness, and slid down against the wall. He started mumbling, mainly to himself. "I got out. I got out, and things were supposed to be good. Things were supposed to be good because the Rubberman was dead, and he couldn't do those things to me any more. To me, or my Brothers. But ooh, no, there's more Rubberman! And rubbery-er men, and the grand and mighty *Messenger!*" Six broke from mumbling, and quickly slid towards yelling, now limp on the floor, face half-pressed against it.

"*Where were you, grand and mighty Messenger?* When I was living under that grate, dreading the next time that Rubberman showed up next to us? Where were you? Where was anybody? When he fell, and the Brothers weren't tethered in, what was supposed to happen? I had… I had…" Six took a deep breath, and squirmed to right himself to at least be sitting up. He looked at Lenth and Messenger, who were both at a loss.

Six nodded small, abrupt nods. "He's gone now. He's gone. A lot has happened, but he's gone. Let's just…. okay. Let's just get there."

The elevator arrived on Actual's level and Lenth dragged the door open. "Here we are." He watched Six's face as he absorbed the surreal, smooth room. Six's expression was one of wonder, but wonder caged behind bars of anger and fear.

"Well," Six said, still looking about the immediate surroundings, "Where's this Actual guy?"

"You won't be meeting him." Messenger said. "On account of your violent history, we figured that would be unwise."

Six turned away from Messenger so that his bound hands were pointed in Messenger's general direction. He wiggled his fingers out in the most menacing way possible. "I'm going to pluck your eyes out and pick your nose! Flee! Flee!" Six spat on Actual's beautiful floor.

Messenger sighed. "Yes, and we don't need Actual's nose picked for him."

"Really? Are you sure? I mean, did you ask?" Six laughed his nervous laugh once more, eyes wide.

Messenger pointed down the hall that Lenth hadn't been to before, the middle hall, leading to the other 'smooth' room. It was wide, and had seating for dozens of people around the sides. A large, smooth, glossy desk sat in the middle, facing a sealed five-metre wide door on the other side. The front of the desk had large letters on it. *W...e...l...c...oh forget it.* There were dozens of letters. There wasn't time for this.

Narrow metal racks standing up to the hip were positioned in a few spots, holding nothing. Whatever they were made to hold weren't much bigger than a hand, and each rack had four or more spots where these objects might be held. On the top edge of some of these racks, there were strange images, almost entirely faded away. Smiling people in strange clothes. One had a picture of the cooling pool that Six had jumped into. One showed...Citizenry? From when it was new. Undamaged. Lenth gazed at it, wishing the image were clearer.

"This way out doesn't pass through all the supplies and stuff," Messenger said quietly to Lenth, drawing him away from the racks. *Focus.*

Near the desk sat a pile of supplies meant for Six. A Rubberman suit (the radiation-proof kind), a khaki backpack filled mostly with food, and a long belt with half a dozen opaque bottles of water, about a litre each.

Six looked at the pile and looked at the large door. "Gonna be hard to put on the suit with my hands like this," he finally said grimly.

"Hold on, right there," Messenger said. "Lenth, can you lift that door on your own? It hasn't been used in a long time."

Lenth want over to it and grabbed one of the handles. It was tough. He knelt down to position his shoulder below the handle and pushed up with his legs. Once it got moving, it was a little easier, but it complained about the ordeal, rattling and scraping as it went.

As it rose, it revealed a second identical door, only three metres beyond the first. "This one too?" Lenth asked.

"Actual said he'd leave it unlocked. Should be safe. If you see any of the Enemy's light coming through as you open it, slam it shut right away—but I'm pretty sure it's gone."

Lenth looked at the bottom of the door with a wary eye and positioned himself by a handle for another tough lift. He pushed up with all the effort the first door took, and then he pushed with more. The rubber rim on the bottom edge moved a tiny bit, but it wasn't going to go much further. Lenth slid down the door to sit, and rest his arm. "Ow. Ow, ow, and hello, ow. Let me have a little rest, and I'll try again."

"Let me know when you're ready," Messenger said, "and you're going to get help this time, from Six."

"He is?" Six asked.

"He is. I'll undo your restraints when it's time."

"And why do you think I'm motivated to help you two kick me out?"

"Because now you're curious," Lenth said, rubbing his shoulder. "And to make it better, it's far from any Rubbermen that you hate so much."

Six laughed. "And I'll be dressed as one when I go!"

"You don't need to wear it when the Enemy isn't there," Messenger said, "but it might be easier than carrying it. I recommend you wear most of the suit most of the time, and only put the mask and hood up when you see the Enemy creeping into the sky."

"What...what's it look like?"

"You'll know it when you see it," Messenger said. "I've seen things out there that you can hide behind. The suit will do the trick, but hiding behind something is better. Try to travel only when the Enemy is gone."

"Travel...travel where?"

"My advice is to turn right once you're out the doors," Messenger said, "and then keep going forward. That's the way Division comes from. The ground is different in a wide stripe that direction. I think it's like a hallway without walls that he uses. Some distance further to the right are a few huge pipes that are partly under the floor out there. I don't know where either goes. Maybe to other survivors of the war, maybe even someone still fighting. Division can't be alone. I'm not sure where the hall or the pipes go, but—"

"But they probably go somewhere. Fine. Lenth? You were out there, yeah? What's it like?"

"The Enemy is amazing, and hurts your eyes if you look right at it for very long. It's—"

"Oh, not the Enemy, I'm avoiding it, remember? What's the rest of it like?"

Lenth turned his head as if looking through the door. "Amazing. Can't see any wall, can't see any ceiling."

"Actual said that a couple of times, he's seen big puffs of white smoke that look like they're really high up, but they don't seem to come from anything," Messenger said.

Six exhaled. "Messing with my head. You're messing with my head, both of you."

Lenth smiled. "I'm a little envious, you know. I'd love to explore it, but there's things I need to do here. And people I'd miss."

"I never caught up with my last surviving Brother," Six said.

"He's fine now," Messenger said. "He got assigned to another Unit."

"Pah. Lucky him."

"It's Spots, isn't it?" Lenth said. "He has freckles, and showed up after Slim died!"

"Spots..." Six said grimly, staring into Lenth's eyes, "he's okay?"

"Yeah, he was kind of hazy when he first arrived, but he's doing fine, last I saw. We had no idea then..."

"Sounds like he was given some zepam," Messenger said. "It gets rid of memories. The more recent the memories, the better they're erased."

Six squinted at the floor. "Would he remember me? And what happened?"

Messenger shrugged. "If he's lucky, he forgot the killings. Probably would recognize you, since you'd be a long-term memory for him."

"All right, guys," Lenth said, "let's get this thing open."

Messenger walked up to Six, who'd turned his back to make his hands accessible. "No acting up now, Six." He released the restraint and tossed the strap into the hall.

Six looked back at Messenger with a resigned, if not sad expression. He mumbled something about playing with people's heads, then took a deep breath, and righted his posture. "Yeah. Yeah, it's okay. No acting up. You guys have pretty much convinced me. It sounds interesting at least. Hiding from the Enemy, though...sounds tricky."

"The Enemy is very predictable. It never changes direction; you just have to avoid the radiation that it's always flooding out."

"Super." Six went over to the other handle on the door and copied Lenth's stance. "All right, let's go!"

Lenth and Six heaved upwards on their handles, and with even more complaints than the last door, it began to give way. They all kept a close eye as it lifted, and no light from the Enemy spilled through. Behind the door stood four metal frames—like doors, but with no middle section, as if the middle had been cut out. No...a few bits of the glass stuck in the inner edge of the frames told them that these doors had once also been windows for some reason. Without the glass in place, they didn't even serve any real function as doors.

With the second large door all the way up, Six wandered through the nearest frame, onto the fractured, dirty floor outside, and into the dark expanse. Whereas earlier the... ceiling area... had been flooded with light from the Enemy's radioactivity, there was now blackness. So much blackness. His eyes, and Lenth's adjusted to looking into the darkness.

Random tiny dots of white light littered the darkness above. They seemed to have no pattern, and didn't move from their positions, but many changed how bright they were—subtle changes, continually.

Lenth pointed at them, and looked in at Messenger. "Those! Are they the Enemy? Uh...Enemies?"

"No," Messenger said as he walked closer. "I don't know what they are. Sometimes I think they're pieces left over from the war. They remind me of bits of glass, like they're slowly spinning or something. I'm not really basing that on anything, but they don't give off any sort of radiation that Actual or I have been able to detect."

Six backed away from the darkness, bumping into Messenger as he stepped back in through the metal frame.

"And sometimes, when the Enemy is gone," Messenger said, "there's something else up there. Big and white. It looks damaged, scarred almost. And it doesn't... well, sometimes it's kind of bright, other times, entire chunks of it are dark. My theory on that is that it's something like the Enemy. Something that doesn't work well anymore, maybe after losing the war. I don't know. It's not nearly as bright as the Enemy, and has no radiation."

Six silently stared out into the darkness. It was a little chilly. No walls, no ceiling, strange lights. An Enemy that wants to douse him in radiation? There was so much *nothing* out there! Was the nothing hiding something? Even Messenger didn't seem to know much about this great room where the Enemy lives. What else was waiting out here? In the vast dark, the emptiness wrapped itself around Six, squeezing a strange form of terror into his lungs, and sending a quiet tremor throughout his body.

"Do you think those tiny lights are part of the other thing?" Lenth asked.

Messenger shrugged. "Maybe, maybe."

"No," Six said quietly.

"No?" Messenger asked, "What do you figure they are then?"

"No, *I'm not going out there! Into that nothing! You can't make me!*" Six bolted for the passage to head deeper inside, but Messenger was too quick for Six to escape. He tripped Six, who went sprawling forward.

Lenth was stunned. Six scrambled away from Messenger, conflicted between getting away, and getting to his feet. Messenger got his hand around Six's arm. Six yanked free, tossing Messenger to the floor in the process, and started running.

By now, Lenth had rallied himself, and blew past Messenger, who was still getting up.

Six ran right for the elevator door, and threw himself at the door handle, yanking on it as hard as he could. "*It's not—*"

"*Six, calm down!*" Lenth yelled as he drew close.

"Open this thing! I don't need the elevator, just get me into the shaft!" Six leaned over to yell at Messenger. "*Open this thing!*"

"Not happening," Messenger called back, matter-of-factly.

Six was nearly hyperventilating. "I can't, I can't just go out there! Out there and what?" He lunged at Lenth, wrestling his way behind him. His hand lacked a knife, but he improvised, pushing his forearm under Lenth's chin. "Sorry, Brother," he rasped.

"*I'm not your Brother!*" Lenth grabbed at Six's arm, only trying to loosen the choking, but he realized that he had some leverage. He heaved forward and sent Six sprawling onto the floor in front of him.

Lenth backed off, but Messenger had caught up, and wasn't inclined to give Six any unnecessary leeway. He was on top of Six, and with Six stunned from being tossed over, it was simple enough for Messenger to turn him face-down and pin one of Six's arms behind his back.

"*Let me go!*" Six cried out.

"I will. That's the point," Messenger said. "Lenth, get me the strap for his wrists, I tossed it in the…yeah, it's over there."

As Lenth ran over to the restraint, Six squirmed to look towards the outside door. Towards the waiting darkness. "No, *no!* Not out there, let me go to…to Citizenry! Or throw me in a Unit! *Just don't put me out there!*"

"No one's safe around you, Six," Lenth said as he picked up the restraint. "I understand why you are the way you are, and your Manager was horrible, but…but Six, you kill! It's like it's a part of you now. You've killed so many innocent people!"

"*Innocent?*" Six shrieked. He wrenched himself away from Messenger, tossing him on his side. Six fired down the hardest punch he could to Messenger's face before leaping off and coming after Lenth.

"Innocent! Innocent!" He swung at Lenth, missing. "Who's innocent here? The Subjects, maybe! You?" He swung again, clipping Lenth's shoulder.

Lenth punched back at Six's ribs. Six landed a small jab to Lenth's jaw before wrapping his hands around his throat. "*Innocent Lenth! Innocent Lenth!*"

Messenger was on his feet again, ready to pull Six off Lenth, when the air split.

The sound of a 'crack' resonated against the walls, and was followed by silence.

Six released Lenth, and slid clumsily to the floor, eyes wide. Blood was coming from his side, soaking into his clothing. He took a breath, gasping through pain.

Actual stood at the entrance to the hall of offices. In Actual's hand was a convoluted little thing made of metal. He walked over to the three of them.

"What happened?" Lenth asked. Could the metal thing in Actual's hand have caused Six's wound?

"Get back, Lenth," Actual said. Six grabbed at his midsection and writhed in agony, leaving a curved smear across the floor. It was difficult for Lenth to abandon him, but trusted that Actual knew what to do. He backed away and Actual stepped closer.

He held the metal thing with his finger through an odd little loop, the longer end pointed at Six's head.

The sound happened again.

Lenth didn't see it happening; it was just suddenly done. It happened. A piece of Six's head was smashed open. Blood and soft red tissue were exposed, much of it spread out across the floor in a chaotic fan pattern, littered with pieces of Six.

Actual dropped the metal thing, the shard of war, and sunk to the floor. "I...I'd only ever used it outside on rocks and things. I knew it would work...but..."

"He's dead?" Lenth asked, knowing the stupidity of the question. Six wasn't moving, he wasn't breathing, and he wasn't in pain. The blood from his head continued to spread slowly on the floor and his eyes stared into infinity.

"You're all right?" Actual asked, looking at Lenth and then to Messenger.

"Yeah."

"Yeah, thanks," Lenth said softly. "I just hoped he...he could have been...I don't know."

"If he hadn't hidden so well when he killed his Manager, we might have been able to prevent him from becoming this," Actual said.

"What? How? Oh, by explaining that his Manager wasn't normal for most Managers, and—"

"No," Actual said, staring at Six's body. "One of the medicines we *do* have can erase very recent memories. We could have erased the killing of his Manager from his head, erased his Brother's death. Then he'd...he'd be innocent." Actual picked up the metal thing, stood, and faced away.

Lenth tried to grasp it. "The same that got used on Spots..."

"Six was still victimized by his Manager," Messenger said. "The abuse would still be there, but he wouldn't have become a killer. Maybe. Ideally, we would have known about his Manager a long time before it all."

"Then Spots probably still remembers the way his old Manager treated them," Lenth said. "He didn't say anything about it, at least not while I was still in the Unit." Lenth realized tears were dribbling down his right cheek. He gestured out to the red mess that used to be Six. "Ha. I'm crying for this jerk. This killer."

A heavy sigh came from Actual as he walked off to his office. "That can be forgiven easily enough."

Messenger looked at Lenth, then to the darkness and the survival care-package meant for Six. "I've been kind of assuming that you'd want to work in the reactor... maybe work towards being Messenger in the future, after some more education, but..."

Lenth glanced to the darkness. "It's very interesting." Lenth sighed and looked at the elevator door for a while. "Do you know Gabe? Gabe could make a good Messenger, I think."

Epilogue

"You look better in that horrible suit than anyone," Lenth said after Karen closed the door.

She took the hood down and wriggled out of the mask. "Oh yeah?" she asked slyly. "Do tell."

"Well, you move smoother than I normally see from people wearing a Rubberman suit, and you have—"

"Yes...?"

Lenth could feel himself blushing. This was not helped by the fact that Karen was shedding the suit as he spoke—or rather tried to speak. Her curves were all the more visible through her normal clothes as she slipped out of the suit's layers.

"You have nice hair," Lenth blurted out.

Karen laughed, tousling her hair, which was a mess from the mask's straps. "Smooth. Hey, you're in a lot better mood than the last time I saw you. Six...?"

Lenth shrugged, and let out a heavy sigh. "Dead. Killed by Actual. It was really surreal."

Karen balked a bit. Her grip on the suit loosened, and she stared at Lenth."You weren't...you weren't kidding about having lunch with Actual."

"Kind of. Anyway, I think I'm going to be around a lot more. Here and there. I have plans, and some ideas. I talked to Actual about them. Actual's not too fond of some of them, but he's going to let me try a few...see how it goes."

Karen was speechless. She leaned against the wall, looking Lenth up and down. "What...are you Messenger now? What do I call you? Are you even supposed to be down here?"

"Call me Lenth." He smiled and stepped a little closer. "I'm still Lenth. And if someday I *am* Messenger, you can always call me Lenth, okay?"

Karen looked like she was struggling for words, or deeper understanding, but for the moment she settled for a small smile and a nod. She took his hands, and looked into his eyes. "Okay."

Phil came back from checking on his sleeping Subjects. They almost never needed anything at this hour, he just liked to check. Over the years, he had become very good at walking very quietly on the grate in those boots when he wanted to.

Lenth, the Subject who left, was waiting for him. Still in his Rubberman suit, Phil went over to his old rag to 'sterilize' before taking off the hood and mask.

"Back for another visit?" Phil asked with a cautious smile.

"Yeah. How are my Brothers?"

Phil chuckled softly. "Troublesome! They ask me questions all the time about you after your little stunt. I can't answer, of course."

Lenth smiled a crooked smile. "Why?"

"Oh, you know it's not done! I asked a Provider about you talking to them, and he told me to not worry about it. He sounded kind of worried, though."

"Heh. I wonder it that was Gabe," Lenth said.

"Gabe?" When Phil was done sterilizing the Rubberman suit, he hung the rag back up to take the rest of the suit off.

Lenth snatched the rag off of the hook. "You don't need this, you know."

Phil's eyes went wide. "I most certainly do! To sterilize!"

"Fill, this rag is so old, it probably has more dirt on it than...well, you don't need it. I spent some time learning about things. Do you even know what you're trying to sterilize yourself *from*?"

Phil looked slightly confused and slightly annoyed. "It's...it's sterilization!"

"You don't need to," Lenth tucked the rag under his sleeve, "and you don't need the rag. You don't need the suit, either, but...little steps, hm?"

"What do you think you're doing, Lenth?"

Lenth smiled. "I have so much to tell you, Fill. I'm...to keep it simple right now, I'm kind of like a Provider now."

"That's...that's impossible."

"Why is that impossible, Fill? I heard that you used to be a Subject. Did you used to think it was possible to be a Rubberman?"

"How did you know that I—"

"Told you, I've been learning things. There's a lot *more* to learn, too. There's so much that I don't know. So much. But I might be ready to start teaching, just a little." Lenth looked up at the ceiling, through the Provider's levels, through Citizenry, through Actual's home, and to the open place of no walls.

"There is so much more."

The Rubberman Series
will continue with:

RUBBERMAN'S CITIZENS

Leena grew up in the Citizenry.

Her story begins long before Lenth came along,
and continues long after he leaves.
Without labour or duty, the Citizens have always been able to
spend their time as they please.
Without a just leader, cruelty has become the daily expectation.
Entertainment, exploitation, and public exhibitions of the worst side of
humanity shatters Citizen after Citizen, as the leader smiles on in approval.

—until Leena learns of a thing called 'revolution'.

Also check out the Lifehack series:
Starting with *Lifehack*, continuing in *Watching Yute,* and concluding in
Echoes of Erebus. Love, loss, nanotech-driven evils, and a madman who
refuses to accept death as the end.

LIFEHACK

Regan has her ups and downs.
—Dumping her girlfriend: Down.
—Moving in with her loving brother: Up.
—Waking up to a plague of undead: REALLY down.

After the undead began roaming the neighbourhood, Regan lost track of her brother. She's spent the last two years searching for him. In the meantime, she's fallen in love, only to be told, "Sorry, I'm straight. And you're a lunatic." There's a psycho out there somewhere who caused the outbreak using nanotechnology, just for the fun of it, and Regan intends to hunt him down.

Oh, and the crush she still has on the straight gal? Dangerously distracting, when there's a zombie around every corner.

WATCHING YUTE

An ideal post opened up for Lieutenant Cassidy Stanton when she wanted a fresh start. She expected a measure of peace, guarding a historic temple in the middle of the desert.

She didn't expect to find a new girlfriend; maybe even a soul mate.

She didn't expect to be in the crossfire of a terrorist, a cowardly scientist, and a fleet of microscopic invaders.

She didn't expect to lose.

ECHOES OF EREBUS

Sarah's got daddy issues.

He lives in her head, built her out of fish, and killed millions of people.
But he's really sorry.
Honest.

A father that lives in your head wouldn't be so bad if he wasn't the killer of millions. At least it's comforting to know that he didn't murder the fishes used to create your body.
Or the seagull.
Sarah hides her illegal nanite origins in an effort to build an ordinary life, but the legacy of dad's horrors makes it difficult. Especially when new but familiar zombie-like abominations begin to appear in the city.

Find Joseph Picard's books in multiple formats at:

OZERO.CA

Amazon.com, Smashwords.com, and other outlets.

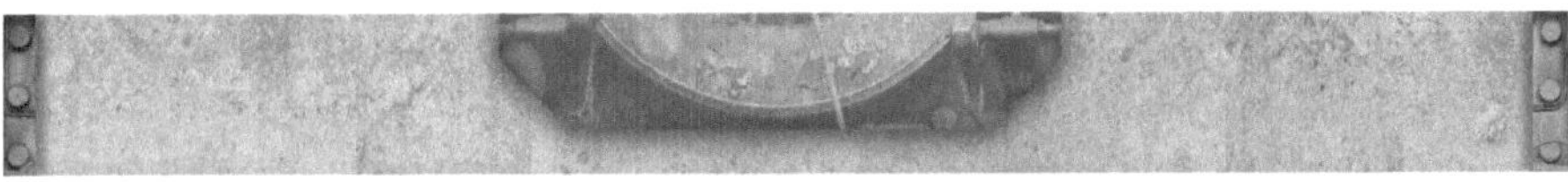

About The Author

B.C. Lower mainlander since 1992, Joseph has always tinkered with art, music, and writing.

He chose to focus primarily on writing in the early 2000s, and his short stories have since evolved into character-driven novels of science-fiction and broader speculative fiction.

In 2001, he found out that cars are harder than mountain bikes, and has been a paraplegic ever since.

Miraculously, this has not altered his career arc as a quarterback, basketball star, pole-dancer, or kung-fu movie stunt double.

Thankfully he has that whole 'life-long-nerd' thing to fall back on.

With a daughter, Caitlin, born in 2007, and a son, Lachlan, in 2011, free time has become a very valuable asset, and most of it gets poured into writing.

Email feedback to Joseph: joe@ozero.ca
Facebook: www.facebook.com/ozerobook

www.ozero.ca